SOPHIE VON LA ROCHE
THE HISTORY OF LADY SOPHIA STERNHEIM

SOPHIE VON LA ROCHE

THE HISTORY OF
LADY SOPHIA STERNHEIM

Edited by

JAMES LYNN

PICKERING & CHATTO

1991

Published by Pickering & Chatto (Publishers) Limited
17 Pall Mall, London SW1Y 5NB

British Library Cataloguing in Publication Data
von La Roche, Sophie
    The history of Lady Sophia Sternheim. –
(Pickering Women's Classics)
    I. Title   II. Lynn, James   III. Series
833[F]

ISBN 1–85196–021–X

Printed and bound in Great Britain by
Billing & Sons Limited
Worcester

CONTENTS

INTRODUCTION

The History of Lady Sophia Sternheim (1771) is a landmark work in the history of German fiction: Sophie von La Roche's epistolary tale of the ordeals of a virtuous woman is the first published novel in the German language by a German woman writer. Its enormous popular and critical success gave La Roche a kind of status and prestige in the world of German letters to which no French or English woman novelist of the eighteenth century would have dreamed of aspiring in her own culture. For the brief period of three or four years the forty-one-year-old mother of five children and wife of a senior minister in the government of the spiritual electorate of Trier was maternal friend, counsellor and source of literary inspiration to a group of young writers which included future literary giants such as Goethe, Schiller and Herder, along with important minor luminaries such as the dramatist J.M.R. Lenz, the Jacobi and Stolberg brothers and Goethe's friend and collaborator, Johann Heinrich Merck. On the threshold of the 'Storm and Stress' epoch, Germany's belated and breathless contribution to the culture of sensibility, Sophie von La Roche became the focus of a cult in which author and fictional heroine were merged in a single arresting image of literary femininity.

Under La Roche's pen the German language seemed to Goethe and Herder to have discovered nothing less than the secret vocabulary of the soul. For the first time in German literature a writer had succeeded in developing an emotionally and psychologically expressive prose to rival, and even excel the nuanced intensity and subjective immediacy of Richardson and Rousseau, the two great foreign masters and models of the sentimental idiom. In the still rather thin literary atmosphere of late eighteenth-century Germany Sophie von La Roche was a débutante novelist who challenged emulation and perhaps the most famous literary response to that challenge was Goethe's *The Sorrows of Young Werther* whose indebtedness to *Sophia Sternheim* has been the subject of several studies.[1]

Such was Sophie von La Roche's standing after the appearance of her first novel that even her most perceptive modern critics have been unable to suppress feelings of disappointment or bafflement when contemplating her subsequent development as a writer. By the time of her death in 1807 her fiction had been for decades simply outside the purview of a national 'high culture' in which it had once seemed set to play a vital role. Much of the discussion of her career as Germany's first independent professional woman writer involves the search for reasons for the decline in literary ambition which began almost immediately after the initial resounding success of *The History of Lady Sophia Sternheim*. Certainly this judgment of decline assumes that La Roche's ambition needs to be defined in relation to initial expectations, but, since these were held by writers and critics whose later criteria of 'literary art' are still part of the pre-history of modern criticism, they have some validity, and Sophie von La Roche's development of the novel simply into a vehicle of female pedagogy remains problematic for later as well as for contemporary readers.

EARLY LIFE

Marie Sophie von Gutermann was the daughter of the physician and medical scholar George Friedrich von Gutermann and his first wife Regina Barbara von Unold. She was born on 6 December, 1730[2] in the small imperial town of Kaufbeuren in the border area between Swabia and Bavaria, the eldest of thirteen children of whom only four survived infancy. Her early years were spent at Lindau on Lake Constance and she then lived for three years with her grandparents at Biberach in Swabia, before rejoining her parents in 1743 at Augsburg where her ambitious father had become the chief health officer of his native city and Dean of its medical faculty.

Although one of his ancestors had been ennobled by the Emperor Ferdinand for services in the wars against the Turks, Gutermann's style of living and outlook were essentially those of the self-assured, if rather provincial bourgeois patriciate. Widely travelled in his early years, he had studied under the famous Dutch naturalist Hermann Boerhaave at Leiden where he became acquainted with Gabriel Harvey's revolutionary discovery of blood circulation and immersed himself in the new science of physiology. His intellectual drive and proselytizing enthusiasm for the fledgling science of medicine earned him the respect of his professional colleagues and his home was a locally renowned meeting place for Augsburg's enlightened men of learning.

Domestically Gutermann was an irascible and hot-headed tyrant. Glimpses of his paternal methods and practices can be obtained from the 'Autobiographical Sketch' which Sophie wrote in her old age at Wieland's request as a preface to her last novel *Melusina's Summer Evenings* (1806). A precocious child by her own account, she claims to have been able to distinguish the titles of her father's books at the age of two, to have been reading at three, and to have read the Bible through by the time she reached five. Her quick grasp of facts and her intellectual curiosity led Gutermann to arrange private tuition for her in the rudiments of the natural sciences, astronomy and history. At twelve she was considered competent enough to act as 'librarian' to his circle of friends, her good memory enabling her quickly to locate and fetch books required in the course of their 'Tuesday colloquium'. Gutermann's programme for her was academically piecemeal and unsystematic and, since formal higher education was closed to her as a woman, somewhat self-gratifying. But this does not alter the fact that by the prevailing standards for middle-class German women her education was unusually broadly based. Gutermann's 'enlightenment' in matters of learning and scientific enquiry, as well as that of her carefully chosen tutors, inevitably rubbed off onto his clever daughter.

As the daughter of a fairly well-to-do, if not wealthy, household Sophie also applied herself under her mother's instruction to the more narrowly gendered skills of cookery, sewing and domestic management, and took lessons in dancing, painting and French. Her mother was responsible for her religious and moral upbringing which was strictly pietistic and consisted of daily readings from J. Arndt's *True Christianity* (1606-1609) and Sunday meditations on the sermons of August Hermann Francke (1663-1727). Although it is difficult to reconstruct the content of her instruction in secular subjects, it is possible to see in *Sophia Sternheim* the pervasive presence of pietistical principles, notably the privileging of living faith over dogma and good works over theological refinement.

Sophie was sixteen when she fell in love with the Italian doctor Giovanni Lodovico Bianconi, who entered the Gutermann house as her tutor in singing, Italian, art history and mathematics. Initially her father's professional acquaintance, Bianconi was personal physician to the Prince Bishop of Augsburg and fifteen years her senior. He was cultivated, widely travelled and very much the polished courtier, a combination which Sophie, who was perhaps already rather too highly educated for the comfort of the eligible sons of the local Augsburg bourgeoisie, found irresistibly congenial. Gutermann at first opposed the match on religious grounds – Bianconi was a strict Catholic – but seems to have given into the persuasions of mother and daughter, and the couple became officially engaged. Preparations for the marriage were well advanced when Mrs Gutermann died suddenly in 1748. The marriage plans were shelved during the year of mourning, after which Gutermann proceeded to renege on his agreement with Bianconi that any children of the marriage should be brought up in their father's faith. Sophie's views do not appear to have been canvassed at any point in the confrontation between the two men. Bianconi insisted on his rights and was forbidden the Gutermann house. He tried to persude Sophie to elope with him but, ever the dutiful daughter, she was unwilling to 'cause her father distress' and opted to dissolve the relationship. Gutermann celebrated his victory with a display of parental vindictiveness that Sophie was still able to recall in all its savage detail in her old age:

> My father made me bring to his study all his [Bianconi's] letters, verses and fine alto arias; all my neatly written exercises in goemetry and mathematics, and ordered me to tear them up and burn them in a small stove. I was forced to cut Nilson's portrait of Bianconi [...] into a thousand pieces with a pair of scissors. With two rods of iron inserted at opposite sides I had to break apart

a ring with his initials set in diamonds and bearing the inscription 'without you nothing' (sans vous rien). I watched the diamonds scatter across the red tiles of the floor. My father's language during all this was indescribable. This then was his way of erasing the memory of a man who had brought so much intellectual beauty into my life and from whom I anticipated so much happiness, who had never chided me and always loved and praised me.[3]

The Bianconi affair seems to have devastated Sophie and certainly damaged her affection for her father who is seldom mentioned in her later private correspondence, despite commemoration in one of her *Letters on Mannheim* (1791) as the original of the equable Colonel Sternheim.

In 1750 she went to Biberach to stay at the home of Pastor Matthäus Wieland whose wife was Gutermann's cousin. The 'Autobiographical Sketch' recalls this period as essentially a time of recovery from the pains of the break with Bianconi – 'Quiet reading [probably Richardson and Klopstock] and quiet living became my lot' – and deals quite perfunctorily with the rather messy relationship with the pastor's talented young son, Christoph Martin Wieland (1733-1813) that was to be the central event of a desultory personal life during the next three years.

Wieland, who was later, with Lessing, the foremost writer of the pre-Romantic German Enlightenment, had already exchanged letters with his older 'cousin' but did not become properly acquainted with her until his return from the university of Erfurt in the spring of 1750. By the time of his departure for Tübingen the following autumn the couple were engaged. Thereafter their strangely undefined relationship seems to have been conducted largely by post apart from a brief meeting in 1752. Although clearly bursting with undisciplined talent, Wieland was inexperienced, immature and very probably sexually daunted by this young woman with her interesting recent past. In a letter to Sophie in 1805 he wrote: 'Nothing is more certain than that if fate had not brought us together in 1750 I would never have become a writer' and this is probably true – just as without him Sophie herself might never have published a line. Young Wieland was looking for a muse rather than a wife and this receptive, handsome, poised and impeccably sentimental young woman was perfect for the role. The 'angelic' Sophie features in the 'seraphic' Klopstockian odes of his Tübingen period as the personification of virtuous femininity.

Whatever his shortcomings as a lover, Wieland did help Sophie to recover the self-esteem that had been so badly damaged by her father. This he did mainly by encouraging her to express herself in writing. The specimens she sent to him have not survived but appear to have consisted first of verse and later of prose. 'How delighted I am, my angel', he writes in the spring of 1751, 'to know that the noble tenderness and virtuous feelings of your heart exceed those of all the world's poets and poetesses and that you are possessed of all the attributes of mind required by divine poetry. In brief, you have the potential to become a perfect poetess.' This is lavish and no doubt exaggerated praise, though the equation of good writing with virtuous sentiments was one of the key signatures of the sentimental idiom to which Wieland was currently attached.

Wieland also stimulated Sophie to practice writing in 'the German language, which is so much more beautiful than French'. Like many children of well-to-do German middle class families in the first half of the eighteenth century Sophie had been educated largely in French – Bianconi for example spoke no German – and a good deal of her correspondence with Wieland and her literary friends and acquaintances was in that still culturally more prestigious language. Her written German of this early time was probably a version of the Swabian dialect spoken in Augsburg, and interspersed with Wieland's encouraging 'reviews' of her work are hints on correct High German grammar and usage. Wieland was serious about writing if nothing else and under his critical supervision she absolved a technical and linquistic apprenticeship that was to stand her in good stead twenty years later when she wrote *Sophia Sternheim*. A fair indication of her progress was the fact that Wieland's new literary patron the respected Swiss poet and critic J.J. Bodmer (1698-1783) was sufficiently impressed by her unpublished literary efforts to ask her to judge the likely reaction of young female readers to the figure of Assenat, the wife of Joseph, in his verse epic *Jacob and Joseph* (1751).

Neither Gutermann nor Wieland's parents were at any time enthusiastic about a match between Sophia and Wieland, though both were initially prepared to await developments. It is perhaps small wonder that in her old age Sophie recalls these years as an essentially uneventful period, for, despite protestations in letters to his parents of undying love for Sophie and his confident anticipation of being unable to survive her loss, Wieland saw remarkably little of his inspirational 'Doris' and did next to nothing to prepare for their future as a married couple. By 1753 when he accepted Bodmer's invitation to visit him in Zürich it seemed that he was prepared to allow her to languish indefinitely, preferably at his parents' house in Biberach but if necessary at her father's where after the latter's remarriage in 1752 she was treated more and more as a guest and a drain on the family resources. Piqued by Wieland's neglect and worn down by the tensions of which she was the centre, Sophie hesitated little before complying with her father's instructions, issued towards the end of 1753, to dissolve the engagement and prepare herself for marriage to the eligible courtier Georg Michael Frank de La Roche. La Roche was a Catholic but this no longer troubled Gutermann and the marriage of convenience, which turned out to be remarkably successful, was duly solemnised at the end of December, 1753. From Zürich Wieland expressed dismay but was happy enough to remain on a footing of friendship with Sophie and certainly quick to recommend himself to La Roche who was to prove a very useful source of patronage. With her marriage to La Roche Sophie crossed the rigid social line separating bourgeoisie from aristocracy and entered a world of which she had no previous knowledge or experience. Her social rise was in many ways the enabling act of her literary creativity.

Georg Michael Frank de La Roche (1720-88), apparently[4] the late-born son of an elderly surgeon named Johannes Adamus Franck, had been adopted as a four-year-old child by Count Friedrich von Stadion (1691-1768), First Minister at the court of the Spiritual Elector of Mainz, and given the name 'La Roche'. Stadion, who at the height of his influence was regarded by many as the effective ruler of the small German state, tutored him from an early age in the arts of statecraft and diplomacy and his tractable pupil assiduously cultivated his adopted father's artistic tastes, worldly scepticism, and political personality. For much of his professional life he was the count's right hand man, functioning as secretary, companion and administrator of the extensive Stadion properties in Würtemberg, Bohemia and Swabia. In mid-career at the time of his marriage to Sophie, La Roche had proved himself on the stage of diplomacy and learned effortlessly to negotiate the slippery surfaces of court society. Sophie moved to his apartment in Stadion's palace at Mainz where the glittering, highly politicised society of the court could hardly have presented a greater contrast to the secluded bourgeois academic milieu in which she had grown up. In the 'Autobiographical Sketch' of 1806, ignoring the revolutionary dramas by which she had been surrounded for the past decade, Sophie von la Roche looks back on this period as a sort of disinterested expansion of her socio-political horizons:

> I had been born into and educated in academic circles ... I was thus acquainted with the intellectual world and with all manner of scholarly writings. Through my marriage to La Roche and life in the house of Count Stadion I learned to appreciate the glorious achievements and merits of the *aristocracy* by which I was daily surrounded. In addition to his involvement in the business of the Mainz Cabinet, my husband was also responsible for all the great Stadion properties in Swabia, Bohemia and Würtemberg, so that I also came to recognize the virtues and abilities of the so-called *common man* of these various countries ... and to judge the inner and external value of the concerns of both the small world and the great world.[5]

The world that Sophie came to know is essentially the world she was to reproduce in her first novel; knowledge of the small and the great worlds appeared to her to be a necessary qualification for writing.

Under Stadion's guidance Sophie quickly familiarized herself with the complex hierarchy of a small catholic princely court and adapted with her customary diligence and energy to her new role of court lady and society hostess. The La Roche household at Mainz existed largely to ensure the efficient conduct of Stadion's affairs of state and to organize his social life. Sophie's part in this was significant: in addition to numerous social duties she had the responsibility of providing the count with interesting topics of conversation during his hours of relaxation or at the dinner table. It was a

task calling for careful preparation and invisible orchestration. La Roche
would begin his day by leafing through newspapers, pamphlets or recently
published books in search of likely material which Sophie would then edit
into a form suitable for apparently casual insertion into the evening's table-
talk. Sophie also supervised her husband's excellent library, learned English
and was eventually entrusted with the conduct of much of Stadion's foreign
correspondence. She was soon as indispensable to Stadion as La Roche
himself.

Sophie's life in Stadion's house was arranged so as to leave her unencum-
bered by domestic cares and responsibilities, which meant in practice that
her social obligations always had precedence over her family life. She had
little time to devote to her children and was even prevented from breast-
feeding them lest this adversely affected the unruffable composure and
'equable temper' that the house of Stadion regarded as her most important
assets. In later years she was to reproach herself with having been a poor
mother to her older children and was inclined to blame their marital
dissatisfactions and unsettled lives on her lack of intimate maternal contact
with them in their early years. She gave birth to eight children of whom five
survived infancy. The oldest daughter Maxiliane (Maxe) was admired by the
young Goethe before her arranged marriage with the much older Frankfurt
merchant and widower Peter Brentano.

In 1762 Stadion used the excuse of a minor political defeat to step down
from his high office and retired to his estate at Warthausen near Biberach,
where he set up as a very active *éminence grise* and surrounded himself with
men of learning, artists and intellectuals. The La Roches followed him there
and for the next six years Sophie's life remained very much as it had been in
Mainz: privileged, agreeable and stimulating – Sophie described it retrospec-
tively as the most blissful period of her life – but never really her own. She
had resumed friendly contact with Wieland after her marriage and now
prevailed upon La Roche to introduce him to Stadion with whom he
developed a firm friendship. She also began a lively and intimate correspondence with the Swiss woman of letters Julie Bondeli (1731-1778), a
friend of Rousseau and until recently Wieland's second 'intended', and
seems to have begun to write again in her spare time.

Stadion died in 1768, leaving La Roche nothing more than an administra-
tive sinecure in the small town of Bönnigheim. He had no doubt expected
his heir to find him suitable new employment, but La Roche did not feature
in the plans of the new Count and he was therefore compelled to move to
Bönnigheim and a position that hardly stretched his abilities. Although in
the event short lived, the Bönnigheim interlude was a difficult period for the
La Roches. Both were keenly aware that they had stepped down the social
ladder and La Roche, who was approaching fifty felt that fate had man-
oeuvred him into an obscurity from which he was unlikely to emerge.
Sophie's relief to be at last out of the treadmill of her social duties was
tempered by regret at having to send her two girls to a Catholic convent

school in Strasbourg when she would have preferred to take over their education herself. Her younger son Fritz had gone to Erfurt with Wieland who had been appointed to a professorship shortly before Stadion's death. Without the enforced peace, quiet and leisure of the Bönnigheim period, however, she would probably never have found time to write.

Sophie had begun to write again during the 1760s. Wieland read and praised her work - novellas, fables, small anecdotal pieces and a longish autobiographical piece – and encouraged her to continue. As with the earlier work, none of this has survived. Her earliest surviving work was a story originally written in French entitled *Les Caprices de l'amour* and published in her own German translation in 1772. But this was after the extraordinary success of her first long novel. The work which achieved its final shape as *The History of Lady Sophia Sternheim* was begun in 1766 and published in two volumes under Wieland's name as editor in May and September, 1771. It was reprinted three times in that year, again in 1772, and four times over the next fifteen years. French, Dutch, Russian and English translations were published in the period immediately following its first appearance.

THE NOVEL

Sophie von La Roche's correspondence with Wieland suggests that *The History of Lady Sophia Sternheim* originated in a series of 'lettres à C.' composed during 1766 and 1767. Wieland wrote in admiration of her 'manière de moraliser', and from his words 'Je souhaite que le jeune Demoiselle se rende digne de ce que Vous faites pur elle', it seems that at this stage Sophie may have intended them as a sort of informal moral conduct book for one of her own daughters, possibly Maximiliane. In 1767 the 'lettres à C.' or 'lettres à ***' are gradually re-fashioned into the 'moral letters' of a certain 'gouvernante', whose author is finally identified as Sternheim in March, 1768. By this time Wieland was also confident that the work in progress could be placed with a publisher 'who will pay us enough to enable you to satisfy the generous impulses of your heart'. Its publication would, he assured the still rather diffident author, be a 'service to your sex ... it should and must be printed, and I shall be its foster-father.'

In the *Letters on Mannheim* of 1791, twenty years after the first publication of *Sophia Sternheim*, Sophie von La Roche credited an acquaintance of her Bönnigheim years, a certain Pastor Brechter – the 'original model for all the many clergymen of my stories' – with having first inspired her to write a long novel. There she recalls how, observing her fretting over the absence of her two daughters at boarding school, he suggested that she try to clear her head by making a precise written record of the random thoughts and ideas with which she was trying to calm her worries:

I thought this an excellent suggestion [. . .] but I then wondered: what would my good husband, what would J. say were they to see me writing so much or were they to come upon my pieces of paper? – Be that as it may, I simply wanted to devote myself to bringing up a paper girl, since I no longer had my own girls with me, and my imagination came to my aid by giving me the idea of Sophia's story.[6]

Sophie von La Roche's description of her authorship as a substitute for motherhood chimed in well with the image of 'educator of Germany's daughters' which she had assiduously cultivated since *Sophia Sternheim*, but it is also an accurate enough recapitulation of the spirit in which both she and Wieland had wished it to be received and understood as a work of the imagination.

Wieland's part in the publication of *Sophia Sternheim* was considerable. With little previous experience of professional authorship, Sophie von La Roche relied considerably on his managerial know-how. He arranged for the work's publication by his own publisher, the prestigious Reich, personally supervised its passage from manuscript to printed text, and negotiated her author's fee. She also frequently called on his services as her 'literary adviser' during the period of composition: completed chapters were dispatched to him for comment and his advice sought on plotting, characterization and structure. Yet the Wieland of the late 1760s, the celebrated author of *The History of Agathon* (1766-67), preferred Fielding to Richardson and the Augustan Pope to Klopstock or the English 'graveyard' poets, and despite a writerly appreciation of Sophie's skill as a portrayer of refined feelings his own now basic lack of sympathy for the sentimental mode in which *Sophia Sternheim* is cast surfaces in the correspondence where he urges her to curb a tendency to excessive flights of sentiment and sensibility – what he refers to in the preface as 'Enthusiasm'. He exhorts her to rely upon her own voice and to avoid borrowing from the now debased sentimental vocabularies of Young and Klopstock. On linguistic matters, her German grammar was still a little too regional for his tastes, and her syntax and phrasing rather obviously French and he pleads with her to practise correct usage by writing to him exclusively in German. How much of this advice bore fruit is difficult to ascertain as Wieland himself corrected what he regarded as the more striking grammatical and linguistic flaws of her manuscript.

Some of Wieland's reservations concerning the style and form of his friend's novel reappear in a transfigured form in his letter preface to *The History of Lady Sophia Sternheim*. Initially regarded as his own editorial fiction, this diplomatically worded introduction to the world of letters of a woman addressed merely as 'dear friend' is at once an act of deference to the cultural–historical context of her authorship and an attempt to reconcile her deviant product to its norms and ideals. His editorial pretence of having published the manuscript without her knowledge and authority, the purported citation of a letter in which she describes her writing as the modest issue of the odd hours of leisure left to her after the performance of her essential female duties and the assiduous denial, on her behalf, of any unbecoming public literary ambitions are components of a tactic familiar, and probably copied, from the often elaborate disclaimers that accompanied contemporary English and French women's fiction. Both Sophie von La Roche and Wieland were anxious to appear to acknowledge a construction of femininity – firmly in place, in Germany, as elsewhere in western Europe, since the mid-eighteenth century – that stigmatized the woman with professional literary ambitions as the betrayer of her 'naturally' ordained role of wife, mother and domestic manager. The text is therefore carefully projected as the continuation of that role by other means: What makes it worthy of publication is 'the truth and beauty ... of [the] moral descriptions', its use value as a vehicle of moral instruction for young women. Although the work is described as partly a 'satire of court life and the great world', its heroine Sophia Sternheim is less the figure of a novel than an image of exemplary femininity. The exalted language and the careless German expression which Wieland had earlier criticized are excused on the ground of La Roche's concern with the direct representation of nature rather than the smooth rhetorical refinements of 'authorial art'.

Despite its emphasis of pedagogy at the expense of fiction, Wieland's preface is a generally well-meaning and in the circumstances finely calculated and judicious attempt to direct the way in which La Roche's novel should be understood and received by a mixed readership. His critical footnotes to the text itself, however, seem at times almost deliberately to undermine the good work of that intervention by challenging or offering to clarify presumed opacities of meaning, or by unerringly alerting the reader to weaker passages of writing. Some, such as his wrist-slapping retort at the beginning of letter XLI (p. 163) to Sophia's desire to know why a woman must never be the first to declare her affection for a man, are openly corrective; some are leadenly pedantic; others appear simply ungracious and even snide. If anything they display precisely the kind of male denigration of female writing and female intellectual ambition that the preface was designed to prevent. Perhaps he was oblivious of their effects, perhaps merely attempting to cover himself in the event of his anonymous protegée's possible, if not expected, critical failure. If the latter, he certainly paid for his faint-heartedness: the work's huge success left them looking tactless and insensitive, and exposed him to the sarcasm of the reviewers, once the name of the real author had emerged. Madame de la Fite[7] silently omitted the notes she found most offensive from her French translation of the book, and inspired by her precedent, Joseph Collyer reduced them to a token presence of one. They have been included in all German editions of *Sophia Sternheim* since the first, however, and are effectively treated as part of the novel itself; they have accordingly been restored in this new edition of Collyer's translation.

The association of *Sophia Sternheim* with Wieland – indeed it was at first thought that it was actually his book – certainly helped to bring Sophie von La Roche immediately to the notice of Germany's leading male literati. But to explain the universally positive response to her first novel it is necessary to bear in mind its appearance at a point of transition in German literary culture. Sophie La Roche was welcomed on both sides of an intellectual division between an older, though still dominant, rational enlightenment and the new non-rational hypersensibility of the so-called 'Storm and Stress' movement. It was a division that was to widen considerably in the years following the publication of *Sophia Sternheim*.

The strongly didactic aspect of *Sophia Sternheim* appealed to mainstream enlightened critics with their typical and comfortable attachment of aesthetic to moral and educational values and ideals. Although he wished that it might have been demonstrated by means of a plot with fewer 'extraordinary incidents' the aesthetician Sulzer praised the heroine's 'moral heroism' and recommended the book for its sensible and 'healthy morality'[8]. Sophie La Roche's most enthusiastic admirers, however, and certainly those most responsive to her literary form, were the young and still unproven writers of the Storm and Stress generation of the 1770s and it was principally through them that she enjoyed a fame that extended well beyond the exclusively female readership at which the work was initially aimed. In his review in the *Frankfurter gelehrten Anzeigen* (4 February, 1772) Goethe described *Sophia Sternheim* as less a 'book' than a portrait of 'a human soul'. Herder too fastened upon Sophie von La Roche's ability to fashion 'glimpses of the inner workings of the soul' and wrote of author and heroine – the two were henceforth to be fused into one – in terms bordering on religious veneration. The episode of Sophia's imprisonment by Lord Derby in the Scottish 'leadhills' struck him as 'more moving than the Book of Job'[9], and he was not alone in regarding La Roche's 'paper girl' as a morally more creditable figure than the eponymous heroine of Richardson's *Clarissa*, which was the work with which it was most often compared. Herder's fiancée, Caroline Flachsland, felt positively shamed by Sternheim: 'This is my complete ideal of a woman! soft, tender, beneficent, proud, virtuous and deceived [. . .] Oh, how far I still am from my ideal of myself!'[10].

Both Goethe and Herder show a tendency to reduce the 'history' of *Sophia Sternheim* to the status of a vehicle for emotions, feelings and psychological intensities. Severely reductive though this type of emphasis may appear to the modern reader, it does not of itself amount to a tacit male depreciation of La Roche's abilities as a novelist, as has sometimes been suggested. Indeed it was an essentially appreciative response to her handling of one of the central techniques of sentimental fiction, a form of writing towards which Goethe and Herder were far more sympathetically inclined than the sceptical Wieland. Like the English and French novels of sensibility by which it is inspired, *Sophia Sternheim* abounds in set-piece situations of heightened pathos: moments or sequences in which the flow of the narrative is arrested in a gesture or scene of singular poignancy and the reader openly invited to be affected to the point of tears by the heroine's exquisite refinement of feeling or by the indescribable, and hence only silently 'performable' exemplariness of her predicament. Tableau-like scenes such as the death of Sophia's father, with its careful grouping of weeping tenants and retainers around the central, soft-focus figure of their beloved and now orphaned young mistress, or the affecting helplessness of her situation at the court of D. can hardly have failed to impress the young Goethe, whose later *Sorrows of Young Werther* is a virtuoso exploitation of precisely this type of sentimental technique.

Sophie von La Roche's concern to create a female figure of inner depth and refined moral sensibility struck a new note in German fiction. Her *Sternheim* was judged an altogether more credible, psychologically differentiated figure than the heroines of male novelists in the sentimental mode such as C.F. Gellert, whose *Life of the Swedish Countess of G.* (1747-48) was still enormously popular, and J.T. Hermes, successful author of stiffly Richardsonian novels such as *The History of Miss Fanny Wilkes* (1766) and *Sophy's Journey from Memel to Saxony* (1769-73). The convincing quality of Sophia Sternheim was attributed to Sophie von La Roche's insider status as a woman, although again it would be simplistic to construe this as merely another form of male 'put-down'. For when considering the impact of her novel on younger male German writers it is necessary to remember the feminine and feminizing dimension of European sensibility as a whole cultural and literary mode. Sophie von La Roche's command of the idiom of sentiment and sensibility was in a sense simply the outer expression of her already perfected womanhood. The heroine is a fully-fledged ideal, without need of further definition. The man, or perhaps men, who win Sophia Sternheim in the end are those who recognize her for what she is and then seek to render themselves more like her.

Indeed it might be said that in the age of sensibility the feminine becomes a moral, spiritual and psychological ideal for men: a mode of being incomparably richer, kinder and more authentically 'human' than the marketplace mentality of the increasing majority of men. At its most radical, as in *Werther* or in J.H. Mackenzie's *Man of Feeling* (1771), this involved the creation of heroes endowed with qualities of character and mind regarded as essentially feminine. The hero of Storm and Stress prose and drama is typically and proudly unable to control his feelings or impulses, generous with his tears, frank in his affections, natural or naively unguarded in his dealings with the world. The possession of these qualities distinguishes Werther from the other male characters of a novel which pits his transcendent statutes of the heart against the bourgeois male world of work, duty and responsibility. Goethe was later to try to reverse or at least assume control of the meaning of his early novel in the 1787 edition of the work by including a posthumous admonition to the assumed male reader, to 'be a man' and not attempt to 'follow the path I took'. By this time, La Roche's formerly filial friend – he addresses her, apparently without irony, as 'Mama' – had also parted intellectually from La Roche. As a novel *Werther* had pointed to the cul-de-sac of feminizing sensibility for the male; since its writing there had been another cultural shift and, with the waning of sensibility in the 1780s and the advent of the romantic epoch, the male construction of the feminine assumed its more familiar modern shape of a self-consciously male projection of an ideal 'other' of the opposite sex.

The portrayal of exemplary womanhood is the overriding concern of *The History of Lady Sophia Sternheim* and Sophie von La Roche repeatedly underlines this priority in her statements about the work:

> You know that I took away from the sensitive Sophia everything she and the world valued most highly: good name, reputation, the means of doing good to others, the hope of regaining the affection of her husband, books and finally even the sight of beautiful nature which was always so refreshing to her spirits. But the patient suffering of unhappiness and injustice, the forgiveness of insults, the conquest of the desire for revenge, the calm acceptance of the dispensations of heaven and the exercise of kindness along with devotion to work and small accomplishments were supports with the aid of which she was able to sustain herself until the period of her trial was over.[11]

Like Samuel Richardson, whose novels she probably read in English, and who, with Rousseau, is arguably the greatest single influence on the work, La Roche had little interest in fiction not subordinated to the higher purpose of moral instruction. Certainly, 'Virtue Rewarded', the programmatic subtitle of *Pamela* (1740-41), would hardly have appeared out of place on the title page of *Sophia Sternheim*.

La Roche's indebtedness to the great English writer is evident at every level in *Sophia Sternheim*, from her adoption and adaptation of his revolutionary epistolary form to details of character and plot. The villainous Lord Derby is plainly modelled on Lovelace in *Clarissa* (1748) and, although undoubtedly a more original creation than Derby, Sophia Sternheim herself is a virtuous young woman in the mould and predicament of Pamela and Clarissa. Her degradation at court by her aunt and uncle, the Count and Countess of Löbau, to the status of a commodity to be offered to the prince in exchange for legal favours, recalls Clarissa Harlowe's reduction to the object of a property transaction by her unscrupulous siblings, James and Arabella, and like Clarissa she is torn between the wishes of her family and the opposing imperatives of her own moral insights. Twists and turns of plot such as Sophia's abduction and imprisonment, her contemplated suicide and the villain's death in a state of anguished remorse are again familiar Richardsonian motifs.

The fictional pretext of Sophia's story is a request from an unnamed 'friend' of the framing narrator for details of her former mistress's life. This narrator is Rosina, sister of the Emilia addressed by Sophia's letters, and companion-cum-lady's maid to her during the period of her extraordinary early life. As she begins the work of sorting and imposing editorial coherence on letters and various other writing exchanged by the protagonists over two dramatic years, Rosina is stirred by the prospect of creating a monument to the memory of a woman who was, while she lived, 'an honour to our sex'. As with Pamela and Clarissa, and with the heroines of the sentimental novel in general, this honour is located in her unstained 'virtue'. Sophie von La Roche's understanding of the term is less narrow than Richardson's, however, particularly as defined in *Pamela*, where it is more or less synonymous with virginity. Sophia Sternheim's virtue is if anything enhanced by her capacity to survive the deception that costs her her 'reputation'. Physically battered, abused and betrayed by the all-male 'great world', and for a time degraded in her own eyes, her almost superhuman capacity for endurance and her unbroken faith in a benign Providence enable her to convert even the prospect of an early and ignominious death into a somehow merited punishment for her self-regarding obsession with precisely that more narrowly defined virtue.

Despite a more generous and inclusive interpretation of virtue, *The History of Lady Sophia Sternheim* is closer to the spirit of *Pamela*, with its visible scale of rewards for the woman who passes all the tests, than to the more problematic and pessimistic text of *Clarissa*. Certainly Sophia's high-minded preoccupation with her virtue renders her naive in her dealings with the world and is itself the means by which she is tricked into a sham marriage by Derby: as in *Clarissa*, virtue fails to protect, let alone secure the worldly happiness of the woman who embodies it most completely. Yet where Richardson allows us to question the value and credibility of the code by which Clarissa's actions are governed, the almost magical *dénouement* of La Roche's novel, the eleventh-hour rescue of her heroine and her happy marriage to Seymour, operate to dispel any reservations as to the model character of Sophia's life that may have accumulated in the minds of her female readers. Sophie von La Roche does not allow her writing to become a means of testing and probing the code itself rather than those subject to it. There are occasional undertones of resigned melancholy in *Sophia Sternheim*, but the bleak disillusionment of a work such as Frances Sheridan's powerful post-Richardsonian *Memoirs of Miss Sidney Biddulph* (1761), whose heroine watches her life slowly being destroyed by the inner tyranny of her virtue, is quite alien to her basically optimistic and affirmative temperament and would hardly have met with her approval.

Often criticized as facile and simplistic, Sophie von La Roche's moral and social optimism is rooted in a belief, dating back to the pietistic religious education of her early years, in the regenerative and redemptive effects of living for others rather than oneself. The secular narrative of Sophia's life mirrors the spiritual drama of the soul's temptation, humiliation and final elevation described in the writings of August Hermann Francke. The precondition of grace is a period of active despair during which the soul, abandoning its own selfish obsessions, opens itself to a community of others and repossesses itself in and through a practical commitment to their welfare. Sophia Sternheim's penitential devotion to 'practical virtue' is, in effect, Sophie von La Roche's trump·card against Richardson's masculinist virtue-in-itself.

Time and again in the novel, Sophia returns to the austere disciplines of her childhood which taught her to regard all uncontrolled emotion and all non-purposive activity as moral health hazards. Although emotionally devastated by the Derby affair, she quickly begins to blame her misfortunes on her own 'excessive sensibility' and 'self-love'. Where Clarissa enters a terminal decline after her rape by Lovelace Sophia sets about picking herself up, and it is this capacity for self-renewal that caused Herder and Bondeli to regard her as morally the more creditable of the two figures. In changing her name and moving to a distant town Sophia symbolically divests herself of her former tainted identity; with the financial support of a group of older single or widowed women she devotes herself to socially useful projects such as the instruction of young children, the establishment of a training school for domestics, and the rehabilitation of families ruined by financial frivolity, rather in the manner of the good women of Sarah Scott's utopian *Millenium Hall* (1762). Gradually she recovers control of her life and a sense of the purpose of her existence. La Roche's message is clear: the healthy, happy, fulfilled life is the life of work, service to others and ceaseless goal-directed activity, and it was precisely his failure to subject his own 'excessive sensibility' to a similar régime of self-denial that underlay La Roche's later disapproval of Goethe's Werther.

The social setting of Sophia Sternheim's almost mythically transfigured life at the end of the novel is a version of the milieu of her childhood. The reward of her virtue is a return to country life, the world of her parents. Some of the best of La Roche's writing in *Sophia Sternheim* is concentrated in her highly critical sketches of life at a duodecimo German court; indeed this 'satire' as Wieland called it is in many ways the most radical aspect of the whole work. The sudden changes of perspective on the same event or sequences of events achieved by the rapidly alternating letters of Derby, Seymour and Sophia enable La Roche – who was by now intimate with the textures as well as the more notorious real-life narratives of eighteenth-century German feudal absolutism – to register something of the frenzied social momentum of the court itself.

Sophia Sternheim begins her reluctant sojourn at the court of D with a blunt critique of the Prince. His dissipation and lack of regard for the welfare of his subjects disqualify him for her respect before she is even presented to him, and his reputation is further damaged by a comparison with her late father's benign patriarchal rule as the lord of Sternheim. Yet the thrust of La Roche's critique of courtly aristocratic society is moral and cultural rather than political. Sophia struggles to find merit in the court as the cutting edge of civilized refinement, but the Rousseauian country-girl in her is unable to adapt to its useless and time-wasting rituals and compulsive craving for novelty and distraction which she sees as a form of 'disease'.

Sophia's failure to settle at the court is not an unqualified rejection of the aristocracy as a class, for she is herself of aristocratic birth, the sole surviving child of an exotic marriage between the ennobled son of a professor and the daughter of an English baroness and a German nobleman. Her values, however, are essentially those of her bourgeois father. Colonel Sternheim's patent of nobility is the reward of his exemplary qualities as an army officer, qualities which in fact conflict with the moral cynicism, venality and 'unnatural' life of the aristocracy as it appears in the scenes of the court at D. To the court aristocracy Sophie von La Roche opposes a bourgeois aristocracy of merit whose place is the country rather than the court or city. The materialistic court aristocracy of the residential cities of eighteenth-century Germany too closely resembles the mercantile bourgeoisie to be acceptable to the idealistic La Roche – herself an accidental mixture of bourgeois and aristocrat – as a model of cultural aspiration. The pronounced anglophilia of her novel puzzled her German contemporaries, yet in the idealized form in which it appears in the English sentimental novel – typically in the second part of *Pamela* – the life-style of the English country gentry is a felicitous blend of bourgeois ethics and quasi-feudal social relations. This was a combination that was inevitably appealing to Sophie von La Roche as the optimal setting of Sophia Sternheim's canonized life as wife and mother. Her marriage to the penitent and pliant Lord Seymour provides her with all the opportunities she will ever need for the exercise of the 'practical' bourgeois virtues and all the wealth and patronage necessary to implement and enjoy them.

The contemplation of oneself performing acts conducive to the happiness and welfare of one's fellow human beings is one of the deepest, and least questioned, sources of pleasure and gratification to the heroes and heroines of the sentimental novel. Sophia Sternheim delights in the reported joy of a poor family at the coins she has tossed at them from her passing coach, and we probably lose count of the number of times we are offered the sight of her hands bathed in the tears of grateful recipients of her kindness and instruction. There is none of Mary Wollstonecraft's questioning of the psychological effects of benevolence on the unfortunate. Like her father Sophia regards the possession of wealth largely as the ownership of the means of doing good, while remaining oblivious of the complicity of this projection in the maintenance of social and economic inequalities. Objectively her academy for domestics will enable the lower orders to cater more efficiently for the needs of the higher, just as Colonel Sternheim's plan to improve the moral and economic situation of his tenants is the expression of his need to increase his profits from his estates. The quite literally 'self-regarding' or ideological aspect of sentimental virtue is masked here, as in countless other novels of this and later periods, by its very definition of the moral act as the laudable gratification of a spontaneous, and hence strictly individual moral impulse.

The influence of Rousseau, like that of Richardson, is pervasive in *The History of Lady Sophia Sternheim*, from the emotional style of *Julie or the New Eloisa* (1761) to the sexual philosophy of *Emile* (1762) and the criticism of court and city culture in the *Social Contract* (1762). *The History of Lady Sophia*

Sternheim is the first fictional rehearsal for German women by a German woman of Rousseau's influential ideas on sexual difference in *The New Eloisa* and above all in *Emile*. In conversation with Herr**, a distinguished German man of letters, Sophia is warned of the dangers for a woman of literary ambitions of adopting a 'masculine tone'. The woman who mistakes her voice mistakes her 'natural determination' and poses a threat to the 'natural order'. Sophia is instructed to match her mind to her natural feminine existence which makes her the exact complementary opposite of a man: where it is his business to be sexually conquering, she is tender and passive; her mental agility and grace offset his intellectual depth and singleness of mind; where man goes out heroically to meet his fate head-on she is patient and yielding, and where he resorts to anger she places her confidence in 'moving tears'. Rousseau's gendering of the mind and psyche was one of the most powerful philosophical rationalizations of early modern biological theories of sexual difference and contributed much to the cultural sealing of women into the roles of wife, mother, spiritual help-meet and muse that is one of the notable features of European society in the second half of the eighteenth century.

Overwhelmed by the honour of his notice, Sophia listens without comment to Rousseau's German interpreter and indeed her pietistic belief in fulfilment and redemption through self-sacrificing service to others is fundamentally compatible with Rousseau's scenario. Sophia bows to Mr.**'s superior wisdom as a clear-thinking man, allowing herself merely to develop his thoughts a little further in reflecting that woman's superior capacity for distraction, or for looking at an object from several different viewpoints, ought surely be useful to men of science and learning whose many contributions to the general advancement of mankind so often originated in a serendipitous change of angle of vision.

Not surprisingly perhaps, Sophie von La Roche's authorial consciousness is only spasmodically 'gendered' in the modern critical sense. Where her mother had in her time earnestly reminded her brother Baron P that a 'girl may not declare her love until she has been asked for it' Sophia, observing the disadvantages of such an injunction to the party obliged to be silent, finds herself wondering why women should not be free to declare themselves to men. Sophia's acquaintance at Vaels, the beautiful and wealthy widow Madam C. is also momentarily disconcerting with her description of marriage as a yoke and her bitter reflection that doing good for others has generally involved her in grave disservices to herself. Such subliminal moments of rebellion are memorable for their extreme rarity, however, and cannot support a reading 'against the grain' of the sort provided for nineteenth-century texts in Sandra Gilbert and Susan Gubar's *The Madwoman in the Attic* (1979). There is no 'madwoman' in Sophie von La Roche's text, no daemonic narratorial *alter ego* calling to Sophia from between the lines to ditch her unprofitable virtue and take the silly prince and his simpering minions for all she can get.[12] Her absence may be problematic to the contemporary feminist critic in search of historical harbingers of her own form of awareness, but it is not so to Sophie von La Roche whose text remains locked into a pre-critical discourse of womanhood that she was either unable or unwilling to exchange.

The Richardsonian and Rousseauian instructional novel of sentiment is firmly non-ironic. As one recent critic has noted, it is a form of fiction that deliberately seeks to 'buttonhole'[13] the emotions; to engage the reader's sensibilities directly, soliciting sympathy, identification, tears and emulation. *The History of Lady Sophia Sternheim* differs not so much from itself as from the narrative practices of later women writers – Jane Austen is an obvious example – whose liberal cultivation of the demons of irony cannot be read into it without falsifying its specific character as work with its heart worn unashamedly on its sleeve. In her first and most famous novel Sophie von La Roche emerges as an author untroubled by doubts about her place.

LATER LIFE

Sophie's overnight fame coincided with the revival of her husband's political fortunes. In 1770 La Roche was appointed to the post of Privy Councillor at the court of Clemens Wenzeslaus, the Electoral Archbishop of Trier. Here Stadion's old pupil advanced rapdily through the ranks of senior government, received the patent of nobility in 1776 and became, as Minister for War and later Chancellor, one of the most powerful men in the state. In the circumstances he was hardly likely to grudge Sophie her success and the La Roche house at Ehrenbreitstein, opposite Koblenz on the Rhine, became the intellectual centre of the Middle Rhine. Himself the anonymous author of a series of *Letters on the Monastic Life* La Roche was a tolerant and enlightened, if somewhat dull figure, who was happy enough to concede to Sophie the mental space necessary to her writing.

Parts of Sophie's next work *Rosalia's Letters to her Friend Mariane von St*** *(1780-81)* first appeared in *Iris* (1775-76) a magazine for women launched by J.G. Jacobi. Like almost all her work published after *Sophia Sternheim*, this epistolary novel has only very recently been retrieved from oblivion and has never been translated into English. In a rather uneventful narrative describing the inner development and worldy fortunes of a young girl from her engagement through to marriage and the birth of her first child, Sophie von La Roche hangs out the sign of her future authorship. The self-assertive, passionate, undomesticated and Werther-like figure of Madam van Gudens in the first part of the novel appears fleetingly as a new narrative possibility for the author only to be jettisoned in the second part in favour of an ideal of bourgeois feminine subordination, passivity and stoic self-control. Henceforth Sophie von La Roche was to use the novel mainly as a vehicle of female pedagogy. A sequel to *Rosalia's Letters* appeared in 1791 under the title *The Country Life of Rosalia and Cleberg*. It was preceded by the *Moral Tales* in the Style of Marmontel (1782-84), New Moral Tales (1786), Letters to Lina (1785-87), a work on the education of young girls with no apparent fictional ambitions, and the novel *Miss Lony and the Bond of Beauty* (1789).

Sophie von La Roche did not become a professional writer until the 1780s. The royalties for her first novel had been donated to the family of her late friend, Pastor Brechter, and it was not until her husband's dismissal from his post as Chancellor of Trier in 1780 that she felt the need to write for gain. La Roche's fall, which was indirectly connected with the anti-clerical stance of his *Letters on the Monastic Life*, hardly reduced him to penury; he had no pension but had earlier been granted the customs franchise of the small Rheinland town of Boppard, and his senior colleague Christoph von Hohenfeld who resigned in protest at his dismissal offered him his house in the small Palatinate town of Speyer. Sophie had developed expensive, not to say extravagant habits, however, and saw writing as a means of maintaining her standards. After some years in Speyer the family moved to Offenbach, to the east of Frankfurt on the river Main, and at the time of La Roche's death in 1788, Sophie, who was now fifty eight years old, was an experienced literary entrepreneur. With her two daughters now married and only her youngest son still at home, she had plenty of time to devote to writing. With the appearance in May, 1783 of the first of 24 numbers of her woman's journal *Pomona for Germany's Daughters* ('she is the goddess of autumn. I am in the autumn of my life', *Pomona*, Preface, to Vol I, 1) she became the first German woman editor of a periodical. Her reputation at this time can be judged from the fact that the Empress Catherine of Russia was happy to subscribe to and pay for 500 copies of this journal.

Although far from combative in its aspirations, *Pomona* was pointedly positioned in an expanding market of male-edited magazines for middle class women as the mouthpiece of woman's views on female education. Sophie had hoped for contributions from Wieland but along with other German writers who had admired her *Sternheim* he had begun to distance himself from his friend's didacticism and she wrote most of the contributions herself. These consisted of reflections in letter form on topics such as women's education, literature, music and the arts. Special numbers were devoted to descriptions of other countries or individual German territories. The series of 'Letters to Lina', which originated in *Pomona* contain sentimental and sympathetic words of advice for a young girl, along with simple practical household hints. A popular letter section replied to readers' enquiries and provides an insight into the kind of matters that occupied the minds of a large female readership without intellectual pretensions.

The letters and articles often reveal the appallingly narrow lives and the primitive cultural horizons of middle class German women even in the late eighteenth century compared with the lives of men from the same class. Sophie von La Roche occasionally comments on male indifference to female education – 'We and our abilities were always only ever regarded as household servants' – but always refrains from challenging the right of men to decide the lives of women. Her abiding concern is to teach women to find fulfilment in domestic duties and motherhood. Having herself invaded and secured for herself a position in the hitherto exclusively male terrain of authorship and editorship La Roche made no attempt to argue for the rights of other women to do the same and was for most of her life concerned to adapt herself to the demands of the men around her and to retain the good opinion of male authors.

Although *Pomona* was a success Sophie gave it up after just 24 numbers. It is not entirely clear why, but running the project single-handedly was an onerous business, and it seems likely that she wanted to free herself in order to indulge her desire to travel and to switch to the more lucrative business of travel books which enjoyed an unprecedented boom in the 1780s, in Germany as in France and England. Her visit to Switzerland in 1784 (recollected in *Diary of a Journey through Switzerland*, 1787) was followed in 1785 by a trip to Paris (recorded in *Journal of Travels through France*, 1787) and in 1786 she passed through Holland on her way to England, the country she had so often praised indiscriminately in novels peopled by sirs, lords, ladies and misses, but never actually seen. The *Diary of a Journey through England and Holland* appeared in 1788; the section dealing with England appeared under the title *Sophie in England* in 1933 and is so far the only one of her travelogues to be translated.

The ailing La Roche was unable to travel with Sophie and her unaccompanied journeys were quite unusual for a woman of her class in the eighteenth century. The ramified connections of thirty-five years as the wife of La Roche and close friend of Wieland, together with her reputation as the author of *Sophia Sternheim* opened numerous doors to her. In Switzerland, where she was widely feted she became, at fifty-three, the first woman to complete the strenuous Mont Blanc tour, met the poet Gessner, the physician Tissot, and Edward Gibbon whose *Decline and Fall of the Roman Empire* was nearing completion. In Paris she was introduced to the court at Versailles, met Buffon and Madame de Genlis and shed tears on Rousseau's grave. In England she met Warren Hastings, the astronomer Herschel and the Genevan natural historian de Luc. Through Madame la Fite, her French translator and reader to Queen Charlotte she was presented at court where her exalted sentimental style came under the coolly satiric eye of the novelist Fanny Burney, then second keeper of the robes to the queen.[14]

Much of Sophie von La Roche's late work consists of reminiscences of earlier periods and personalities and includes *Letters on Mannheim* (1791); *From my Writing Desk* (1799) *A Journey from Offenbach to Weimar and Schönbeck* (1799), *Autumnal Days (Herbsttage)*, (1805). Her last novel, *Melusine's Summer Evenings* (1806), edited like the first by Wieland, was completed shortly before her death in relative obscurity in 1807.

With the exception of Lenz, all the male writers whom Sophie von La Roche had known in the early days of their literary careers, are today primarily associated with the German cultural and literary phenomenon known as 'Weimar Classicism'. In the male-dominated aesthetic enclaves of Weimar and Jena, Goethe and Schiller and their Romantic successors developed theories of the 'autonomy' of literature and the special character and calling of the writer which, via their reception and elaboration by other cultures – most notably English Romanticism – continue to influence the way literature is read and its purpose or project defined. One of the main historical casualties of these new definitions was the literature of sentiment and sensibility, whose supposed subordination of 'literary art' to the pedagogy of moral sentiment or, as in the young Goethe's case, to a propaganda of the emotions, conflicted with the 'new' Romantic formulation of the quintessential difference between art and our immediate human interests.

Sophie von La Roche's failure to develop away from the sentimental mode, her obstinate refusal to become a female Goethe or Schiller, caused her to be consigned by Weimar to the scornful category of mere writer of trivial books of instruction for women. It is of course necessary to be clear about who is adjudicating 'failure' here but, in view of our current ambivalences about what is 'literary', it is worth emphasising that what makes the case of Sophie von La Roche particularly teasing was the contemporary notion that she had refused the option of joining the men on her own terms to help in the great late-eighteenth century project of establishing a serious national German literature. It may of course be asked whether La Roche herself was ever conscious of needing to choose between 'literature' and pedagogy; the evidence suggests that she was not. Although she seems to have rated herself fairly low as a writer, she appears genuinely baffled at the silence that greeted her second novel. In a letter to Wieland she wrote:

> I am only a woman, so tell me why Klopstock – and the Stolbergs – and Goethe who were all so warm and enthusiastic have suddenly grown so cool? And the Jacobi brothers too, oh Wieland explain it to me – in men of such accomplishment and refinement of soul, tell me the reason for it [...] *You* must read my Rosalia – Wieland must read my Rosalia, and do me the kindness, the *old* and the *new* kindness of writing something about it, please, please [...][15]

But perhaps the more important question posed for the modern reader by La Roche's neglected work after *Sophia Sternheim* concerns precisely the viability of the distinction first comprehensively theorised in Weimar between the literary and the non-literary. On the one hand critics loyal to the possibly idealistic idea of literature as an heroic and Romantic activity requiring total dedication to an original personal vision, and even critics only slightly touched by this paradigm, have regretted La Roche's 'decline' into pedagogy after *Sophia Sternheim* and blamed it on an ideology inherent in that work which inhibited her development of the novel form into more critical attitudes. On the other hand, feminist cultural historians and sociologists have found in La Roche's later work a rich feminine historical resource; to them it may well record an achievement as the educator of Germany's daughters rather than the failure of an artist.

NOTE ON THE TRANSLATION

Joseph Collyer (d.1776) who died shortly after completing his translation of Sophie von La Roche's *History of Lady Sophia Sternheim* was a modestly successful London publisher and bookseller with a shop in Plough Court off Fetter Lane and a house in Islington. His wife was Mary Mitchell Collyer (1716–62), a minor author associated with the Bluestocking Circle and a well known and prolific translator of contemporary French and German literature which Collyer published. Joseph Collyer was also a compiler of scientific and historical works, his most ambitious project being *A History of England from the Invasion of Julius Caesar to the Calling of the Parliament in 1774*, published in 14 volumes in 1774–5. He does not appear to have taken up literary translation until after his wife's death after 'a lingering illness, occasioned by the agitations of mind' she suffered in translating *The Death of Abel* (1758), a now forgotten epic by the Swiss poet and illustrator Salomon Gessner (1730–88). He completed and published her translation of the first two volumes of Klopstock's religious epic, *The Messiah* (1763). This was followed by J.J. Bodmer's Klopstock-inspired *Noah* (1767) and the third volume of *The Messiah* (cantos 11–15, 1772).

The *History of Lady Sophia Sternheim* shows a firm, confident and sympathetic handling of Sophie von La Roche's affect-laden idiom and it seems likely that he was influenced by the style of his wife's own epistolary novel *Letters from Felicia to Charlotte* (1744) and her 1742 translation of Marivaux's *La Vie de Marianne (The Virtuous Orphan, Or The Life of Marianne Countess of* *****), greatly influenced by Richardson. The translation of Sophie von La Roche was something of a re-importation of Richardson for there can be no doubt that the Collyer household breathed his literary atmosphere.

By twentieth century standards, eighteenth-century translators were remarkably cavalier in their treatment of their original texts and most seemed to have subscribed to Dryden's famous dictum that 'a translator that would write with any force or spirit of an original, must never dwell on the words of his author'. Poetic and dramatic form set certain intrinsic limits upon a translator's discretion, but novelists in particular were vulnerable to travesty, paraphrase, cutting and carelessness. *Sophia Sternheim* is relatively free from this kind of interference. Where Mary Mitchell Collyer provided Marivaux's unfinished novel with a conclusion and set about transforming his psychological comedy into an edifying didactic novel along the lines of *Pamela*, Joseph Collyer mainly confines himself to occasional prunings of the text.

His most important omissions are Wieland's (unsigned) letter to

D.F.G.R.V****** (alias Sophie von La Roche) which appeared as a preface to the original German edition, and a letter from Sophia to Emilia describing her encounter with a certain Mr.** during a visit to the country home of Count T. The letter preface has been translated for the present edition and the missing letter is included as an appendix. Other omissions include passages of a reflective or moral-philosophical character. Thus Colonel Sternheim's wedding-night account of his philosophy of life described by his wife in a letter to her step-mother is shorn of a passage on the shortcomings of the German clergy (p. 25) and Sophia is prevented from developing her thoughts on nature and artifice (p. 91) and the discrepancies between the moral and the natural world and the perils of affluence (p. 165). These and other significant passages have been restored to the present edition in footnote form.

On May 21, 1773 Wieland wrote to Sophie von La Roche telling her that 'your Sternheim is being translated in London – but as my work. I have given orders for the correction of this mistake.' It seems fairly certain that he was referring to Collyer's translation rather than the slightly later rival – and rather chaotic – version of Edward Harwood[16], but it is not clear whether Collyer simply never received the order or whether the preamble to his edition was supposed to represent his compliance with it. The title page to *History of Lady Sophia Sternheim* described the work as 'attempted from the German of Mr. Wieland', but in the 'translator's preface' which he substitutes for Wieland's letter preface he reports his apparently last minute discovery that the work was actually the work of a certain Madam von La Roche, 'wife of a senior minister of the Elector of Trèves'. Since Collyer's stop-press item was now over two years old, he might have been trying to sensationalize his 'correction'.

Many of Collyer's minor cuts fall in exactly the same place as those of Madame de la Fite in her French version of *Sternheim* of 1774 and it is clear from a comparison of the two translations that he simply copied many of her editorial decisions. The most important of these was the suppression of Wieland's notorious footnotes, though here Collyer went to work more ruthlessly than la Fite, discarding sixteen of the seventeen, where she removes only three. Rather carelessly, and indeed possibly translating directly from the French, he repeats la Fite's strange practice of removing the footnotes and then silently conceding their points by omitting or scrambling the passages of Sophie von La Roche's text to which they refer. In restoring the footnotes to the present edition it has sometimes been necessary to include a full translation of the original passage. Collyer also follows la Fite in having Sophia close all, rather than just some, of her letters to Emilia with 'adieus' and fond farewells etc. These passages have been removed from the present edition.

With two exceptions mentioned in the notes, Collyer's renderings of German proper names and titles have been left undisturbed. Obvious mistranslations and misprints have been silently corrected and spellings modernized. Collyer's punctuation has been left intact, except that on the rare occasions on which they occur – usually in quotation of letters or documents – running quotations marks have been eliminated.

Wrocław, 1991   JAMES LYNN

NOTES

[1] The most recent is Sally Winkle's *Woman as Bourgeois Ideal: A Study of Sophie von La Roche's 'Geschichte des Fräuleins von Sternheim' and Goethe's 'Die Leiden des Jungen Werthers'* (Peter Lang, New York, Bern, 1988). See also Wilhelm Spickernagel, *Die 'Geschichte des Fraüleins von Sternheim' von Sophie von La Roche und Goethes 'Werther'* (Greifswald, 1911).

[2] Most studies of Sophia von La Roche cite 1731 as the year of her birth, but 1730 is the date entered in the baptismal register at Kaufbeuren. See Michael Maurer, 'Das Gute und das Schöne: Sophie von La Roche (1730-1807) wiederentdecken', *Euphorion* 79 (1985), pp. 111-38.

[3] Sophie von La Roche, *Melusinens Sommer-Abende*, ed. C. M. Wieland (Societäts Buch und Kunsthandlung, Halle, 1806), p. XVII. (All translations in the following pages are mine – Ed.)

[4] It has never been established beyond resonable doubt that La Roche was not Stadion's illegitimate son. Compare Rudolf Asmus, *Georg Michael de La Roche* (J. Lang, Karlsruhe, 1899), p. 2 and Werner Milch, *Sophie La Roche* (Societäts-Verlag, Frankfurt am Main, 1935) pp. 35-42.

[5] *Melusinens Sommer-Abende*, p. XX.

[6] *Melusinens Sommer-Abende*, p. XXV.

[7] *Mémoires de Mademoiselle de Sternheim*, publiés par M. Wieland, et traduits de l'Allemand par Madame *** [de la Fite], I, II, (A La Haye, Chez Pierre Fréderic Gosse, 1774).

[8] His review appeared in Friedrich Nicolai's *Allgemeine Deutsche Bibliothek* (Vol 16, 1772, pp. 469-79), a prominent journal of the German Enlightenment.

[9] *Briefe an J.H. Merck von Goethe, Herder, Wieland und anderen bedeutenden Zeitgenossen*, ed. (?) Wagner, (Darmstadt, 1835), p. 29.

[10] *Herders Briefwechsel mit Caroline Flachsland*, ed. Hans Schauer (Verlag der Goethe-Gesellschaft, Weimar, 1926), p. 238f.

[11] *Melusinens Sommer-Abende*, p. XXVII.

[12] For a contrary view see Helen Kastinger Riley's lively 'alternative' reading in her 'Tugend im Umbruch: Sophie Laroches *Geschichte des Fräuleins von Sternheim* einmal anders', in *Die Weibliche Muse* (Camden House, Columbia, S.C., 1986) 27-52.

[13] See Janet Todd, *Sensibility, An Introduction*, (Methuen, London), p. 2.

[14] 'Madame la Fîte called the next morning, to tell me she must take no denial to forming me a new acquaintance – Madame de la Roche, a German by birth . . . an authoress, a woman of talents and distinction, a character highly celebrated, and unjustly suffering from an adherence to the Protestant religion . . . Madame la Fîte received me in transport; and I soon witnessed another transport, at least equal, to

Madame la Roche, which happily was returned withthe same warmth; and it was not till after a thousand embraces, and the most ardent professions – "Ma digne amie! est-il possible? – te vois-je?" etc. – that I discovered they had never before met in their lives! – they had corresponded but no more!

This somewhat lessened my surprise, however, when my turn arrived! for no sooner was I named than all the *embrassades* were transferred to me – "La digne Miss Borni! – l' auteur de Cécile? – d'Evelina? – non, ce n'est pas possible! – suis-je si heureuse! – oui, je le vois à ses yeux! – Ah! que de bonheur!" etc.' *Diary and Letters of Madame D'Arblay* [Fanny Burney] edited by her niece Charlotte Barrett, vol. II, 1785–1788 (London, undated), pp. 170–171.

[15] *Lettres de Sophie La Roche à C.M. Wieland*, ed. Victor Michel (Berger-Levrault, Nancy, 1938); quoted by Barbara Becker Cantarino in the postscript to her edition of *Die Geschichte des Fräuleins von Sternheim*, (Reclams Universal-Bibliothek Nr. 7934[5], Stuttgart, 1983), p. 392.

[16] *Memoirs of Miss Sophie Sternheim, translated*, 2 vols. London 1776.

CHRONOLOGY

6 December 1730 Sophie Marie von Gutermann born in Kaufbeuren; oldest of 13 children.

1731–43 Childhood in Lindau and with her grandparents in Biberach, Swabia. 1740–41 publication of *Pamela*.

1743 Joins her parents at Augsburg, where her father had become Dean of the city's medical school.

1746 Tutored in mathematics, Italian and art history by Bianconi to whom she becomes engaged.

1747–48 Publication of C.F. Gellert's *Life of the Swedish Countess of G...*

1748–49 Death of mother in 1748 precipitates dissolution of engagement in 1749.

1750 Stays at the home of her relative Pastor Matthäus Wieland where she becomes engaged to Christoph Martin Wieland.

1750–52 Lives with father at Augsburg. Sends her first literary efforts to Wieland.

1753 Engagement to Wieland broken off; enters an arranged marriage to G.M. La Roche.

1753–61 Residence at Mainz in Stadion household. Birth of eight children of whom five survive infancy. 1761 publication of Rousseau's *New Eloisa* and Frances Sheridan's *The Memoirs of Miss Sidney Biddulph*. 1762 publication of Rousseau's *Emile*.

1762–68 Residence at Stadion's estate at Warthausen after the latter's retirement from politics. Encouraged by Wieland begins to write in 1766.

1764 Publication of Wieland's *Triumph of Nature over Enthusiasm, or The Adventures of Don Sylvio of Rosalva*. 1767 publication of Wieland's *Agathon* and Sterne's *A Sentimental Journey*.

1768 G.M. La Roche forced to accept a minor post at Bönnigheim.

1768–71 Writes *Sophia Sternheim*; Wieland arranges for its publication.

1771 G.M. La Roche appointed to a senior post in the Electorate of Trier. *Sophia Sternheim* published.

1771–80 The La Roche home at Ehrenbreitstein visited by leading German writers including Goethe. 1774 publication of Goethe's *Werther*, Wieland's *History of the Abderites* and Lenz's *Tutor*. Contributes stories to periodicals. Marries (against their wills) her daughters Maximiliane (to

Brentano 1774) and Louise (Hofrat Möhn, 1779). 1778 publication of Fanny Burney's *Evelina*. 1779 first performance of Goethe's *Iphigenia at Tauris* (prosè version).

1780–81 Lives at Speyer following G.M. La Roche's dismissal from his post.

1780 Goethe writes *The Triumph of Sensibility*. 1781 attends first performance of Schiller's *Robbers* at Mannheim. Publishes *Rosalia's Letters*. Writes to support her family. 1782–84 Publication of *Moral tales in the Style of Marmontel*.

1783–84. Launches *Pomona*, a periodical for 'Germany's Daughters'. 1784 first of several journeys to Switzerland.

1785 Travels to Paris. 1786 Moves to Offenbach. Travels to Holland, and then to England, where she is presented at court and meets Fanny Burney.

1785–87 Publication of *Letters to Lina* (begun in *Pomona*); *New Moral Tales*; *Journal of a Tour of Switzerland*.

1788 Publication of *Diary of a Journey Through Holland and England*. Death following a long illness of G.M. von La Roche.

1789 Publication of *The History of Miss Lony*.

1791 Publication of *Letters on Mannheim*. Death of her favourite son Franz.

1792 Publication of Mary Wollstonecraft's *A Vindication of the Rights of Woman*.

1793 Death of her daughter Maxe Brentano.

1794 Loses customs franchise of Boppard during the French revolutionary wars and becomes increasingly dependent upon the income from her writing.

1795–99 Publication of *Beautiful Portrait of Resignation* (1796), *Events on Lake Oneida* (1799).

1799–1806 Lives in relative seclusion at Offenbach. Publication of reminiscences and novels. Wieland edits her last work *Melusina's Sommer Evenings*.

18 February, 1807 Dies at Offenbach.

Works by Sophie von La Roche:
Memoirs of Miss Sophie Sternheim, trans. Edward Harwood, 2 vols., (London, 1976).
Two Sisters, in *Bitter Healing: German Women Writers, 1770–1830*, ed. Jeannine Blackwell and Susanne Zantop (Nebraska, 1991).
Sophie in England, a translation of the passages on England in the *Journal of a Journey through to Holland and England* (1788), trans. Clare Williams (Jonathan Cape, London, 1933).

Further reading:

Sally Winkle, *Woman as Bourgeois Ideal: A Study of Sophie von La Roche's 'Geschichte des Fraüleins von Sternheim' and Goethe's 'Die Leiden des Jungen Werthers'* (Peter Land, New York, Bern 1988).

   'Innovation and Convention in Sophie La Roche's: *The Story of Miss von Sternheim* and *Rosalia's Letters*', in *Writing the Female Voice: Essays on the Epistolary Novel* (Pinter, London, 1989) pp. 77–91.

Ruther-Ellen Joeres, ' "That girl is an entirely different character!" Yes, but is she a feminist? Observations on Sophia von La Roche's *Geschichte des Fräuleins von Sternheim*', in *German Women in the Eighteenth and Nineteenth Centuries*, ed. Ruth-Ellen B. Joeres and Mary Jo Maynes (Indiana University Press, Bloomington, 1986), 137–56.

Peter Petschauer, 'Sophie von La Roche, Novelist Between Reason and Emotion,' *Germanic Review* 61 (Spring, 1982), pp. 70–7.

Janet Todd, *Sensibility: An Introduction*, (Methuen, London, 1986).

Jane Spencer, *The Rise of the Woman Novelist*, (Basil Blackwell, Oxford, 1986).

Robert Markley, 'Sentimentality as Performance: Shaftesbury, Sterne, and the Theatrics of Virtue', in *The New Eighteenth Century: Theory, Politics, English Literature*, ed. Felicity Nussbaum and Laura Brown (Methuen, London and New York, 1987), pp. 210–30.

CONTENTS

The History of
Lady Sophia Sternheim

Volume I

To D.F.G.R.V.[1]

Do not be dismayed, my dear friend, to receive a printed copy of your Sternheim, instead of the manuscript you were expecting. The full extent of my betrayal of your confidence is thus instantly revealed, and your initial feeling must be that I have acted quite irresponsibly. Under the sacred seal of friendship, you entrusted to me a work of your imagination and sentiments, written solely for your own diversion and entertainment. 'I am sending it to you', you wrote, 'in order to obtain your opinion of my sentiments; of the aspect in which I am disposed to judge the affairs of human life and of the reflections prompted by the vivid impressions of my heart. I ask you to correct me where you think I am in error. You are acquainted with the circumstances that have led me to devote to this restful diversion some of the few hours remaining to me after the performance of my essential duties. You know too that the ideas which I have sought to express in my descriptions of the character and actions of Sophia Sternheim and her parents have always been close to my heart; and what better occupation for the heart than the objects of its profoundest affections! There have been moment when this occupation became an inner need for me. Imperceptibly, the little work came into being, although I began and continued it without knowing whether I would ever be able to conclude it. You will perceive its imperfections as clearly as I feel them. But then, I tell myself, it is intended only for you and me and – if, as I hope, the principles governing the thoughts and actions of this daughter of my musings meet with your approval – for our children. Your friend can imagine no greater satisfaction and joy than that they, in reading it, might be strengthened in virtuous sentiment and in true, general and active goodness and honesty.'

These were the words with which you committed your Sternheim into my care. But now, my dear friend, let us see whether I have abused your confidence. Let us see whether I am truly guilty of a crime in having failed to resist my desire to present to all the virtuous mothers and all the charming young daughters of our nation a work which seemed destined to promote the cause of wisdom and virtue – the sole true mark of humanity, the one source of true happiness – among the members of your sex and even mine.

There is no need to apprise you of the general benefits that meritorious writings of the type of your Sternheim are capable of disseminating. All reasonable people are of one mind on this point and, after all that has been said by Richardson, Fielding and so many others, there could be little merit in pleading the cause of a truth that no one doubts. But it is equally certain that our nation is still by no means lavishily endowed with natives works of this kind, which are at once diverting and capable of promoting the love of virtue. Are these two considerations not enough to justify my undertaking? You will, I hope, be more disposed to share my opinion, or at least to forgive me more readily, when I have revealed to you how the idea of making an author of you first arose.

With the dispassion with which has become familiar to you over the years, I sat down to read your manuscript. I must say that the unusual character which you give to your heroine's mother at the very beginning of the work tended rather to prepossess me against the work than for it. But I read on, and all my dry philosophy, the late issue of a long study of humanity and its boundless follies, began to crumble before the truth and beauty of your moral descriptions. My heart warmed to your story, and I began to love your Sternheim, his wife, his daughter and even his vicar – one of the worthiest clergymen I have ever encountered. Numerous little dissonances occasioned by the differences between my own convictions and your Sternheim's strange, at times almost enthusiastic, mode of thought were resolved in the most agreeable unison of her principles, feelings and actions with my soul's liveliest convictions and most elevated sentiments. In a hundred places I found myself exclaiming: may my daughters learn to think and act like Sophia Sternheim! May Heaven grant me the supreme joy of seeing imprinted on their souls this unadorned candour; this invariable goodness; this melting susceptibility to truth and beauty; this inner disposition to practical virtue; this undissembled piety which, far from tainting with gloom the beauty and nobility of the soul, is its best and loveliest virtue; this tender, sympathetic and charitable heart; this art of considering in a healthy and genuine manner all the objects of life, and of setting a just value on happiness, reputation and pleasure – in a word: may all the qualities of heart and mind which I admire in this beautiful moral portrait be united in these delightful beings who, though still in their infancy, are the sweetest joy of my present and the dearest hope of my days to come!

My first thought now was to commission a copy of your manuscript which I intended to present to our little Sophia (for you are so kind as to regard her as yours too) when she is older. Picture to yourself my enchantment at the idea that this might also be the means of propagating in our children all the sentiments of a friendship refined to purity by the trials and tests of long acquaintance! From the contemplation of this pleasant prospect it was but a short step to the reflection that, at this very moment, through the length and breadth of our German provinces, there must be countless mothers and fathers harbouring similar wishes for the future well-being of children just as promising and just as tenderly loved as ours! Would I not be doing them a most agreeable service in permitting them to share in a benefit that could lose nothing in being communicated to others? Would not the good effects of the virtuous example of the Sternheim family thereby become available to all? And is it not our duty to strive, as far as it lies within our powers, to extend the scope of our beneficence? And consider how many noble-minded persons would, by this means, become acquainted with the inestimable mind and heart of my friend, and bless her memory long after she and I have ceased to be! – Tell me, my friend, you who for so long have known a heart that has remained true to itself through all the inner and outer transformations wrought by the passage of years – how could I have resisted such a prospect? I immediately resolved to have copies printed for all our male and female friends, and for all those who would be our friends, were they to enjoy our acqaintance. I held our contemporaries in such high esteem that I assumed that many copies would be required, and I therefore dispatched my fair copy to my friend Reich,[2] requesting him to print as many as he considered appropriate.

But no! The matter was not concluded quite as swiftly as this. Amidst all the ardour of my heart, my mind retained a coolness sufficient to enable me to consider everything apt to deter me from executing my plan. Never, so far as I am aware, have I allowed my prepossession for those whom I love to blind me to their shortcomings. You know this aspect of my character and are as little capable of expecting or even wishing for flattery as I of arguing against my true convictions. Considered as a work of the imagination, as a literary composition, or simply as a piece of German writing, your Sternheim, for all its charm, contains faults which will not escape the notice of the *petty fault-finders*. However, these are not the people whom I fear most on your behalf. The professional critics, on the other hand, and the odious *connoiseurs* from the ranks of the great world – let me confess, my friend, that I am not entirely unconcerned at the thought of being guilty of exposing your Sternheim to the judgement of people of such divergent ways of thinking. But let me tell you how I contrived to put my mind at ease.

Touching such faults or infelicities of *form* and *style* as may be censured in your work, the critics will be dealing only with me. You, my friend, had no intention either of writing for the world at large or of creating a work of art. You are, I know, thoroughly acquainted with such writings of the most distinguished authors of the various languages as can be read without the possession of formal learning. You were, however, ever wont to attend, less to the formal beauties and perfections of a work, than to the moral values of its content; and this consideration alone would always have made you dismiss the thought of writing for the public at large. It therefore fell to me, the unauthorized publisher of your manuscript, to remedy such faults as I might expect, if not to offend the critic, then at least to cause him to desire their absence. But when I speak of critics of art I have in mind persons of refined taste and mature judgement; men unlikely to be offended by the small blemishes adhering to a beautiful work, and withal too fair-minded to demand of the spontaneous fruit of pure nature the same perfections as the laboriously tended product of the cultivator's art (though, in point of taste, the former not infrequently excels the latter). Discerning critics of this kind will, unless I am much deceived, be inclined to share my opinion that the moral narrative, with its concern to execute an interesting and instructive character study, as opposed to a tale of elaborate intrigues and complicated developments, and in which the diversion and entertainment of the reader is subordinated to the primary purpose of moral instruction, may all the more readily dispense with artistic form where the work possesses special inner beauties of mind and heart, which compensate us for the absence of a plot elaborated in accordance with established rules, and indeed for the lack of everything that might pass under the heading of *authorial art*.

Unless I am very much mistaken, these same critics will also discover in the style of Sophia Sternheim a certain originality of image and expression; and in the latter a felicitous energy and aptness – often enough in passages with which a strict grammarian would be least satisfied – which they will readily accept as the just reward of their forbearance in the face of moments of stylistic carelessness, and the use of uncommon turns of phrase and figures of speech. Their tolerance will doubtless extend to the lack of perfectly rounded and polished phrases – a shortcoming I could hardly have remedied without detriment to what I consider to be the essential beauty of my friend's style. They will also perceive that although it is everywhere evident that our heroine has enjoyed a most careful education, her particular tastes, as well as her manner of thinking, speaking and acting, owe more to nature, personal experience and individual observation than to formal instruction and the emulation of established models. It is for precisely this reason that she so often feels and acts differently from other persons of her class; that the unusual and extraordinary quality of her character and, above all, the unique cast of her imagination will necessarily influence the manner in which she expresses her feelings and articulates her thoughts; that for each original thought she immediately invents a singular expression, whose vigorous strength and truth are perfectly adequate to the intuitive ideas which are the well-spring of her reflections. And will our critics not agree with me that precisely this completely achieved individualization of our heroine's character is one of the rare merits of this work; and moreover one that is far more indebted to nature than to art? In short, my regard for the finer sensibilities of our critics is such that I am confident that they will judge the faults of which I have spoken to be interwoven with so many features of outstanding beauty and merit that they would certainly take it amiss, were I to try to exempt my friend from criticism on the grounds that women are not professional writers.

Have we then perhaps more to fear from the refined and exacting tastes of sophisticated society than from the professional critics? Here I must own that our heroine's singularity, her enthusiasm for moral beauty, her strange ideas and moods, her rather wilful predilection for English lords and everything originating in their country and, to make matters worse, the permanent conflict between her feelings, actions and opinions and the tastes, morals and customs of the great world seem unlikely to win her many friends there. All the same, I am reluctant to abandon my hope that her very originality as a phenomenon might enable her to make substantial conquests as a *charming eccentric*. Indeed, for all that the peculiarities of her disposition appear at times to border on excess, or on what some would call pedantry, she is and will remain a charming creature. If her story may be regarded as a satire on court life and the great world in general, it is abundantly clear that our heroine's perception of the virtues and weaknesses of those who move in these glittering circles could hardly be more tolerant or fair. The reader can see that she speaks of matters with which she is intimately acquainted, and that neither her heart nor her understanding is to blame if she fails to comprehend, and is herself incomprehensible to, a world in which art has entirely supplanted nature.

Forgive me, my friend, for prattling for so long on a point on which your mind should be at ease. There are persons whose capacity to please is never in doubt, and I should be most grievously mistaken, were your heroine not of that class. Her many talents and gifts – the naive beauty of her mind, her purity and boundless goodness of heart, the fine discrimination of her taste, the truth of her judgement, the perspicacity of her observations, the vividness of her imagination and the harmony of her discourse with her thoughts and feelings – are surety that, for all her little shortcomings, she will not fail to delight all whom Heaven has blessed with a healthy reason and a sensible heart. And whom else do we strive to please? – However, our heroine's fondest desire is free from all self-regard: she wishes to do good and to render herself useful. And indeed she *shall* do good and, in doing good, justify my boldness in sending her into the world without the knowledge and permission of her dear creator. I am etc.

The Editor[3]

The

History

of

Lady Sophia Sternheim

My complying with your desire in committing to paper the events of Lady Sternheim's life, scarce entitles me to your thanks. You know I had the happiness of being brought up with that excellent lady, and believe me, it gives me a very sensible pleasure, that I have an opportunity of employing myself in a task that will recall to my mind the sacred remembrance of the virtues and endowments of a person who is an honour to our sex, and even to human nature.

The father of my dear Lady Sidney was Colonel Sternheim, the only son of a professor at W. who had given him an excellent education. He was early distinguished by his noble sentiments and goodness of heart. At the university he contracted an intimacy with the young Baron P. whom he afterwards accompanied in his travels, and for whom he had such an affection, that he entered with him into the army. By his conversation and example the baron, whose mind was naturally haughty and impetuous, was humanized, and he became of so mild and engaging a disposition, that his parents almost idolized the young gentleman who had thus reclaimed their darling son. An unforeseen event separated them: the decease of the baron's elder brother obliged him to quit the service, and apply himself to the management of his estate. Meanwhile Sternheim who enjoyed the highest esteem of the officers and soldiers, continuing in the service, rose to the rank of colonel and the prince ennobled him. Merit and not fortune has preferred you, said the general, in the presence of many persons of distinction when he delivered him, in the name of his sovereign, his commission and patent of nobility. He afterwards worthily maintained the reputation he had acquired, and all his following campaigns served to give him opportunities of exerting his valour, his greatness of soul and his humanity.

On the return of peace, his first wish was to see his intimate friend with whom he had constantly corresponded. His heart knew of no other connexion; for his father, whom he had lost long before, being a foreigner at W. had left there no relations of his son. Colonel Sternheim accordingly went to P. there to enjoy the tranquil delights of friendship. Baron P. his friend had espoused a very amiable lady, and lived with his mother and two sisters at a very agreeable seat left him by his father, where he was frequently visited by the most distinguished families in the neighbourhood, and where he dedicated his more retired hours to reading and rural improvements. Sometimes they had little concerts, the younger sister playing on the spinnet, and the elder on the lute, which the baron and some of his retinue accompanied with their voices.

The elder sister's disposition, however, threw a damp on their happiness. She was the only child of Baron P. by Lady Watson, his first wife, whom he married while he was envoy in England. This young lady, with all the endearing gentleness of an English woman, seemed likewise to have inherited from her mother an air of melancholy. A settled gravity had spread itself over her countenance. She delighted in retirement, and she employed herself in reading the choicest books; yet did not neglect conversing with the family, when they were free from company.

Her brother, the baron, being in fear of her health, neglected nothing that could divert her, or enable him to discover the cause of her settled dejection. Sometimes he conjured her to open her heart to him, her affectionate brother; this she would return with a serious look, thank him for his concern and with tears entreat him to let her secret remain in her own bosom, and only continue to love her. This increased his uneasiness; he apprehended that some false step might be the source from whence this melancholy sprang; but though he kept a most watchful eye over all her actions, he could not discover the least trace that could countenance any such apprehension. She was always under his or her mother's eye; conversed only with the family, and avoided all kind of mixed intercourse. Once she so far prevailed with herself as to come into company, and from her cheerfulness on this occasion, the family had hopes that her gloom would be dispersed.

This pleasing expectation was farther confirmed by the unexpected arrival of Colonel Sternheim, whom the whole family had heard highly praised, and whose letters had made them often admire the excellence of his heart and his many extraordinary perfections. He surprised them one evening as they were all walking together in the garden. The baron's joy and exultation on this occasion were as incapable of description as the eager inquisitive attention of the others, and the colonel's noble and engaging behaviour soon diffused a like joy through the whole family.

The colonel was soon introduced to the nobility in the neighbourhood as a friend for whom they had a particular esteem, and he made one in all their visits and assemblies. To the baron's family he occasionally related the most interesting incidents of his life; particularly the memorable actions at which he had been present, and in a manner which increased the family's opinion both of his intellects and his heart. On the other hand, they represented to him in the strongest colours the pleasures of a country life. The baron enumerated the advantages accruing to the vassals[4] from their lord's personal residence; the old lady dwelt on the endearing offices of the mother of a family, while the young ladies represented the various entertainments and recreations to which every season of the year invited them. These discourses gave rise to the following question.

Would my worthy friend be willing to pass the remainder of his life in the country?

Yes, my dear baron, provided it were on my own estate, and in the neighbourhood of yours.

That may be easily brought to pass; for there is a pretty estate to be sold within a mile from hence, and as I have free access to the house, we will go and take a view of it tomorrow.

Accordingly the baron and the colonel went thither accompanied by the minister of the parish, a very worthy man, who afterwards entertained the ladies with the description of an affecting scene that passed between the two friends. The baron, after leading the colonel over the grounds, took him into the house, which besides its elegant garden, had a delightful situation, and here they breakfasted.

The colonel expressed his entire satisfaction, admired every object, and with some earnestness asked the baron whether so charming a property was to be sold.

It is: and do you like it?

Entirely; and the rather as it will not draw me to any great distance from what I most love.

Oh my friend! said the baron, how happy do you make me! this estate I myself secured three years ago, merely with a view of offering it to you. I have repaired and improved the house, and here in this parlour where we now are, I have often prayed for the preservation of your life, and eagerly longed for your presence. What joy does the thought give me, that the guide of my youth will now be a witness of my life!

The colonel was so warmly affected at his friend's noble behaviour that he was unable to express his joy and acknowledgments. He assured him that he would there spend his days; but at the same time desired to know what the estate cost. The baron explained himself on that subject, and showed him the deed of purchase. The revenues it produced appeared to be greater than could be expected from the sum given to purchase it; but the baron protested that he would accept of no more than what he had advanced.

My worthy friend, said the baron, for these three years past, I have laid out the whole income of the estate in repairs and improvements, and the satisfaction, the delight of thinking that I was providing for the repose of the best of men, in whose engaging company I should renew the delights of my youth; that his advice and example will secure and add to my felicity, and may contribute to the welfare of my family – These thoughts have been my recompense.

On their return, the baron introduced the colonel to his mother and sisters as a new neighbour, and all expressed themselves highly delighted at the certainty of frequently enjoying his company.

Having taken possession of the manor, which consisted only of two villages, he repaired to the mansion house, and after giving an entertainment to the neighbours, he amused himself with building and planting, added two elegant wings to his house, and formed a delightful grove with walks in the English taste. But amidst the assiduity with which he carried on these improvements, a thoughtful gloom was now and then observed to overspread his countenance. The baron himself perceived it; but at first seemed to take no notice of it; till in the following autumn he observed some striking indications of a very great change in his disposition, which filled him with apprehensions that rendered him very uneasy. Sternheim was now less frequent in his visits, less communicative and cheerful in his discourse, and sooner returned home. The change was visible to everyone, and even his own domestics laid to heart their master's unusual melancholy.

The baron, whose uneasiness was now increased by his eldest sister's having relapsed into her former lowness of spirits, went to the colonel's, and finding him alone and pensive, embraced him with affectionate sympathy. O my friend! said he, how frail, how unsubstantial are even the most noble, the most pure and refined joys of the human heart! For a long time I wanted nothing but your company; I now see you – I even hold you in my arms – yet I see you dejected, and you appear reserved and displeased. I have lost your affection, your confidence. But speak freely, have you made too great a sacrifice to friendship in fixing your residence here? If you have, cease to torment yourself; your happiness is dearer to me than my own. – I'll take the estate again – its value is, in my esteem, now increased, since every part of it will renew the pleasing remembrance of such a valuable friend.

Here he was silent, tears stood in his eyes, which being fixed on the face of his friend, he perceived him agitated with strong emotions. The colonel instantly rising ardently embraced him, crying, Let not my incomparable friend harbour the thought that there is any abatement in my friendship and confidence; and oh forbear thinking that I repent the resolution I have taken of passing my remaining days near you. – No, no, I value the blessing of having you for my neighbour more than you can conceive – but I am forced to struggle with a passion from which my heart has been hitherto free. I flattered myself with possessing a tolerable share of sense and disinterestedness; but alas! much do I yet want of that strength and firmness which the state of my mind requires. But it is impossible for me to enter into this subject with you. Solitude is all that I want, and my own heart must be my only confidant.

I know your steady virtue, said the baron, pressing his hand, and do not question the assurances you are pleased to give me of the continuance of your friendship: but tell me, pray, how comes it that I see you so seldom, that your visits are so short and constrained, and that you leave us with an air so cold?

Cold, my friend! what I, leave you in a manner so cold? my visits to you short and cold! Ah did my friend but know the eagerness with which I post thither, and the affection which makes me stand hours together at my window viewing the dear house, the centre of all my desires and of all my happiness! O my dear friend ! —

This put the worthy baron for some moments on the rack, from the apprehension that his friend had conceived a passion for his lady, and had avoided the house the more effectually to extinguish the guilty flame. He therefore resolved to appear more reserved, and more closely to watch the colonel's behaviour. Sternheim remained immoveable, and the baron was under a tumult of jarring passions, and not without even alarming fears. At length, breaking silence, he cried, I venerate my friend's secret: I respect it too much to wrest it from him. Yet you have given me room to think that a part of this secret concerns my family. May I not at least be informed, who amongst us. —

No; no. I entreat you to ask me no questions. Leave me to myself. The baron ceased his enquiries, and went away dejected and buried in thought.

The next day the colonel waited upon him, to ask his pardon for letting him depart with so little cordiality, which he said had not allowed him to close his eyes during the whole night. My dear baron, added he, honour lays a restraint on my tongue. But question not my heart, and continue to love me.

Being prevailed on to stay the whole day at P. Lady Sophia and Lady Charlotte were earnestly pressed by their brother, to strive to divert his friend; but the colonel mostly conversed with the old lady, and the baroness. In the evening Lady Charlotte touched the lute, in which she was accompanied by the baron and two officers of his household, and Lady Sophia, after many entreaties sang.

The colonel stood at a window, where behind the curtain, which was partly drawn, he listened to the little family concert, with which he was so taken up as not to observe, that the baroness was so near him, as to hear him utter the following ejaculation. Lovely Sophia! Dearer than my life! Why art thou the sister of my friend! Why does the superiority of thy birth oppose this warm, this honourable affection!

The lady was struck at this discovery; but to save him the confusion into which he would naturally have fallen, had he imagined she had overheard him, instantly withdrew, overjoyed that she could now remove the baron's solicitude concerning the colonel's melancholy, and on the family's retiring to rest communicated her discovery to him. The baron now saw the meaning of the colonel's justification of himself from the charge of coldness. Tell me, said he to his lady, should you like the colonel as a brother-in-law, as well as you do now, as my friend?

Most certainly, my dear. His eminent merit fully counterbalances any disadvantages of descent.

Excellent creature! cried the baron. I now depend on your assistance to overcome any prejudices in my mother and Sophy. –

I am less afraid of their prejudices than of a prior inclination which has taken possession of Sophy's heart. I don't know the object: but I am sure she is in love, and has been so for some time. Of this I am persuaded from some passages of her writing which I found in her escrutore,[5] wherein she complains of her destiny, and laments a separation: but though I have ever since kept a watchful eye over her, my discoveries have reached no farther. I'll talk with her, said the baron, and see whether some insight into her heart is not to be obtained.

The next morning the baron went to Lady Sophia, and after some affectionate enquiries after her health and spirits, took her by the hand. My dear Sophy, said he, you say you are perfectly well; why then have you that uneasiness in your looks, that languid faintness in your voice? Why are you so fond of being alone? and why those frequent sighs? – Did you but know the concern your melancholy has long given me, you would not conceal it. It shall be my care to promote your marriage with the man you love.

Affected by these words, she was so far from drawing away her hand, that she pressed his to her breast, and with her head reclined on his bosom, O brother, said she, you break my heart. I love you as my own life and can't bear the thought of giving you pain. Believe that I am happy. Let me beg of you to bear with me, and never more mention a word about marriage.

Why so child? it will be making some worthy man superlatively happy.

And a worthy man would likewise make me happy: but I know —— Here bursting into tears she could say no more.

O Sophy! no longer check that emotion of confidence: but deposit your sensations in a brother's trusty bosom – I am persuaded there is a man with whom your heart is linked. –

No brother! I am a stranger to any such connection.

Do you say so in earnest Sophy?

Yes, brother I do! –

Here the baron embraced her – Oh that you had the firm virtue of your mother! What do you mean, brother? answered she with some amazement: In what have I transgressed the rules of the strictest virtue?

In nothing yet, my dear; but you may if you suffer yourself to be governed more by prejudices than by reason and virtue.

You quite alarm me brother; in what am I in danger of departing from reason and virtue?

Do not mistake me, my dear, I have no such harsh meaning; your case, in my opinion, contradicts neither virtue nor reason, yet may weaken in your mind the just claims of both.

Speak plainly, brother; for I am now determined to conceal nothing from you; but to answer agreeably to my most hidden sentiments.

As you assure me, Sophy, of your being a stranger to any particular connection, give me leave to ask you, what you would do, should a person of distinguished sense and virtue; but not of the ancient nobility, profess himself your humble servant, and apply for your hand?

At these words she was seized with a visible discomposure; when the baron thinking to put a speedy end to it continued, and should this person be the very friend to whom your brother is indebted for the reformation of his morals, and consequently for the principal happiness of his life; tell me, Sophy, what would you do?

Here she made no answer; but sank into a deep pensiveness, and her colour went and came. Forgive me Sophia, for throwing you into this disorder; but the colonel is in love with you, and this passion is the only cause of his melancholy, from his fear of success. For my part, I freely declare, that I could gladly reward, by your marriage to him, the many good offices which I have received from him; yet, if your heart does not agree to it, forget all I have said.

The young lady endeavoured to recover her fluttering spirits, and after a silent effort of some continuance, asked the baron, Are you certain, brother, that the colonel loves me? – The baron now related his conversation with the colonel, and the heart-felt wish which his lady had overheard. – Brother, said Sophia, I am sincere, and you so well deserve my entire confidence, that I make no scruple of declaring, that the colonel is the only man living to whom I could give my hand.

The disparity of birth, then, is no objection with you.

No; not in the least. His abilities, his accomplishments and virtues, together with his friendship for you, amply compensate for any deficiency with respect to his ancestors.

Generous girl! that observation, dearest Sophy seals my felicity – But why did you so earnestly conjure me not to talk to you of marriage?

Because I had not the least prospect of its ever being accomplished, answered she in a low voice, and reclined blushing on her delighted brother; who, embracing her and kissing her hand, said, with transport; What a blessing will this hand be to my friend! and I shall be the happy instrument of his obtaining it! But, child, you must expect a severe opposition from the old lady and from Charlotte. Do you think you shall be able to stand your ground?

Yes, yes, brother. You shall see that I have an English heart – but having now answered all your questions, I must now put one to you: What were your thoughts of my melancholy on the cause of which you have so long importuned me?

I really attributed it to a secret passion, and from your reserve had not the best opinion of its object.

So my brother little thought that his friend's letters, which he used to read to us, and the particulars he related concerning that excellent man, could make any impression on my heart.

Then, dearest Sophia, it was my friend's conspicuous merit that rendered you so reserved and thoughtful – Happy man to be beloved by a deserving woman who had never seen him, merely on account of his virtue! Heavens bless my sister for her frankness! Now can I relieve my friend from the anguish of his heart.

Go, brother, and kindly endeavour to set the colonel's heart at rest; but don't overlook a proper regard for your sister. A young woman; you know, is not to make the first advances.

You may be very easy, my dear, on that article. Your honour is mine.

Here leaving her, he went to his lady with the joyful account of his discovery; and his next business was to ride to the colonel, whom he found wrapped in gloom and pensiveness. Many subjects were suddenly started and dropped, and an extreme disorder betrayed itself in his whole behaviour – Dear colonel, have I disturbed you, said the baron, in the accent of the respectful friendship of a youth for his governor.

Yes, my dear baron, you have disturbed me in a resolution I was forming to make an excursion for some time.

An excursion? and without company? –

Worthy baron, I am sensible that the present state of my mind gives a disagreeable cast to my behaviour and conversation. I'll try whether travelling and a little distraction will not amend it.

May I not probe your heart a little farther? Can't I contribute to its repose?

You have done enough for me! you are the joy of my life. What is amiss, time and prudence must set right.

The last time, Sternheim, we were together you intimated that you had a passion which you must by all means suppress. A criminal passion, I know, your heart could never cherish: it must then be love which thus embitters your days.

Excuse me, baron, but what it is you shall never know.

My worthy friend, no longer dissemble. The object of your love is no secret to me. Your fondness has involuntarily transpired, and I am happy that you love my sister Sophia. – Here the baron, embraced the colonel, who being filled with confusion, strove to disengage himself.

How, is that, baron, what would you have me tell you?

Tell me whether my sister's hand would be welcome to you.

That must not be thought of: it would be a misfortune to all concerned.

You own it then: but pray how would it be a misfortune?

Yes, you know the object of my tenderness. Lady Sophia is the first of her sex who has become the mistress of my affections: but I will overcome them. Never shall you be reproached on my account, with having forfeited the just regard due to your ancestors. Far be it from me to stand in the way of Lady Sophia's claim to superior splendour and distinction. I must insist that you will pledge your honour, never to say a word more about it, or you shall see me no more.

Your sentiments, colonel, are always noble: but God forbid that they should betray you into such a step. Your leaving us, not to mention the anguish it would give me, would exceedingly trouble both Sophy and my wife. No, no, you shall be my brother.

Your giving me your consent, baron, distresses me more than the impossibility which obstructs my wishes.

My friend has my sister's voluntary and cordial consent, with which my good wishes, and those of my spouse most heartily concur. We have already closely canvassed every circumstance – Would you have me formally request you to marry Sophy?

Heavens! What a heart does this suppose me to have! So you impute my steadiness to caprice and obstinacy.

To this, I have no reply. Embrace me, and call me brother. Tomorrow, I promise myself, you will be so. Sophy is yours, and now, instead of considering her as my sister, look on her as a lovely and valuable young woman, who is to constitute the happiness of your life, and accept with joy a present of the hand of the most tender friend.

Sophia mine! and by her own voluntary consent! What superabundant goodness! This, my friend, is giving me everything, and the only return I can make, is to decline so inestimable a gift.

Decline! How! after an assurance of being beloved! O sister, how cruelly have I injured thine excellent heart!

O baron, forbear such cruel reproaches. As you are so generous, should not I be so too? ought I to be blind to the consequences, and to expose us to public censure, to the contempt of the nobility?

They, my friend, are beneath your notice, where the repose and happiness of your life are at stake.

Well, then, what would you have me do?

With your leave, I'll return home, and open the proposal to my mother. You will come to us, if I send you a line.

The colonel ardently renewed his embraces, after which the baron repaired directly to his mother, with whom he found his lady and sisters, and desiring the eldest to step into her apartment, he followed her thither, and after having given her an account of what had passed in his visit to the colonel, desired her to stay there, while he went to make the proposal to the old lady and Charlotte. On his return, he made a formal proposal in behalf of his friend, at which the old lady reddened not a little, which the baron observing, continued, Madam, your scruples are not entirely groundless. The rank of ancient nobility should be kept up by suitable alliances: but it should be considered that such virtues and merit as Sternheim's have been the foundation of the most noble·families. I confess that people are not to blame in believing that great mental qualities may be transmitted to children; and consequently, that a noble father ought to choose for his son the daughter of a nobleman: I am not therefore for marrying beneath a person's rank: but this is a singular case, such as indeed very seldom occurs. Sternheim's personal merit, together with his post of colonel, and his being already raised to the rank of nobility, justify the hopes which I have given him.

Indeed, son, I am not without any objections; for this match, in the eye of the world, will have its dark side; but the gentleman has entirely gained my esteem, and it will be a pleasure to me to concur in his happiness.

And what says my dear spouse?

That such a gentleman as he is affords very just grounds for an exception, and I shall with pleasure call him brother.

Indeed but I shan't, cried Lady Charlotte.

Why so, my dear?

Because this fine match is to be made at the expense of my honour and happiness.

How so Charlotte?

Who will look out for a match in our house, after the eldest daughter has been so wretchedly degraded?

Degraded! what by a person of such distinguished merit and virtue! Degraded by your brother's most intimate friend!

There may possibly be some other very deserving college friend of yours who may seek my hand to prop his rising dignity, and you will always have the same reasons ready to obtain consent.

Charlotte, can such language come from you?

I am forced to it, as nobody else shows the least regard either for me, or for their ancestors.

How, Charlotte, said the young baroness, can't we show a proper regard for our forefathers, without injuring a most deserving person, and through him wounding an affectionate brother?

I have heard your exceptions in favour of this mighty man of merit: but families will also have theirs when their sons would choose to marry me.

Charlotte, he who renounces you on account of the colonel, will be neither worthy of receiving your hand, nor of contracting an alliance with me. You see that I am not without pride for my younger sister, however malapert she may be, though I degrade the eldest, by marrying her to a college acquaintance.

Very malapert, indeed, because she is not willing to be dishonoured and degraded.

Sister, your spite is very ill founded. You need not be apprehensive of any proposals from me. Sternheim is the only person for whom I would open my mouth on such a subject; and a character like his carries with it nobility enough, even were you a princess.

You hear, mother, how I am abused about that upstart fellow.

It is you, Charlotte, who have abused your brother's patience. Can't you propose your objections with more temper?

She was going to reply; but her brother stopped her by adding, Not a word more Charlotte, that expression *upstart fellow* has lost you your brother. You have no longer any concern with my family. Your heart disgraces those ancestors on whom you so highly value yourself. Oh how would the number of the nobility be reduced, were only they allowed to assume that title who could make good their claim to it, by the possession of the distinguished endowments which raised the founder of the family!

My dear child, moderate your resentment; indeed it would not be at all commendable for our daughters to be easily led to close with a marriage beneath them.

O there is no fear of that. Such young women as Sophy are very thin sown, who love a man purely on account of his sense and his virtues.

Here Lady Charlotte retired.

But have not I heard you yourself say, that the English, whom you so much admire, will hardly forgive a daughter who marries below her rank, while in a son it is not so much minded; because a daughter parts with her name, for that of her husband; and thus, of course degrades herself.[6]

True: but in England, my friend would be a general and universal exception, and the young lady would be honoured for placing her affections on a man of such conspicuous merit.

I see very plainly, my son, that this marriage has been preconcerted; but did you ever reflect on the reproaches to which it will expose us, that you will be said to sacrifice your sister to an excess of friendship, and that I shall be esteemed a true stepmother for consenting to it.

Dear Mama, let it take its course; our motive precludes every cause of uneasiness, and my sister's manifest happiness, together with my friend's deserts, will silence all unfavourable remarks.

Here the baron left the room; but soon returned with the Lady Sophia. She instantly kneeled to her mother, who with a tender embrace, raised her, saying, Your brother, my dear, has assured me, that this connection is perfectly agreeable to your own wishes, otherwise I should not have given my consent. Indeed the deficiency in point of family is the only circumstance against the gentleman. However, I pray to God to bless you both.

The baron stepped out again, and returned leading in the colonel, who almost overpowered with the sense of his felicity, immediately made up to the old lady, and respectfully kissing her hand, with a manly gracefulness, said, Madam, I beg you will be assured that I look on your consent as the kindest, the most condescending act of goodness; and that I shall never prove unworthy of the honour.

To this he kindly answered: It gives me pleasure colonel, that your eminent merit has found a recompence in my family.

He then kissed the hand of his friend's lady, saying, What thanks and acknowledgements are due to her who has so generously exerted her persuasive eloquence in my behalf?

None at all, noble colonel, I am rather proud of contributing to your happiness, and your brotherly affection will be an ample recompence.

He was now going to speak to his friend, when the latter prevented him by showing him Sophia, when kneeling, after a short silence, he said, Most excellent lady, it was impossible for me while I had the least regard for virtue, to observe a mind so richly fraught as yours, and to see your endowments accompanied with every external charm, without a wish – a wish I was endeavouring to suppress, when your brother's unbounded friendship encouraged me to beg your approbation, which you have condescended to grant: for which may Heaven reward your bountiful heart, and never suffer me to depart from that virtue to which I owe your esteem! Sophia answered only by a gentle inclination of her head, and reaching out her hand to him as a token to rise.

Here the baron coming up, and taking them both by the hand, led them up to his mother: Madam, said he, nature in me has given you a son, who, I hope, has never been wanting in any proof of filial duty, and now in my friend, Providence gives you a second son, deserving of your esteem and goodness. You have often poured forth prayers for Sophia's happiness, and I promise myself that your fondest wishes will be answered in her connection with so sensible and worthy a gentleman. Be so kind as to lay your hands on your children's heads, for I am sure the blessing of a mother will rejoice such hearts as theirs.

They both instantly kneeled, and the old lady affectionately laying her hands as desired, said, Should God grant you all the good which I shall never cease to beg of him, nothing will be wanting to complete your happiness.

Here the baron embraced the colonel as his brother, and thanked his happy sister for her regard for his friend. The colonel stayed and dined with them; but Lady Charlotte did not appear at table. Afterwards the marriage was celebrated privately.

Some days after this happy event Lady Sternheim wrote the following letter to her mother:

Letter from Lady Sternheim to her Mother[7]

The foul weather and a trifling indisposition hinder me from paying you my personal respects; but I cannot deny myself the pleasure of conversing with you by letter.

The company of my dear spouse, and the consideration of the duties incumbent on me in this new circle of life, compensate for the loss of all other amusements and diversions; but at the same time revive every praiseworthy sentiment and disposition that ever had a place in my heart. Among these is the grateful affection which your goodness, your vigilant and tender care, have for many years demanded from me, and which could not be exceeded by the parental affection of my own mother. Yet I must own that I esteem your so generously consenting to my union with Colonel Sternheim, as the greatest kindness I ever received at your hands. This has fixed the happiness of my life. My sole wish has been to live agreeably to my personal character and station, and this wish indulgent Providence has gratified, by uniting me to a man who deserves my highest esteem; with a moderate independent fortune, yet sufficient to enable us to live agreeably to our rank, and at the same time to allow us the noble pleasure of relieving the distressed.

Permit me to lay before you a conversation which passed between the gentleman whose name I bear and me, which arose on the following occasion.

When you, Madam, my brother, and sister-in-law were gone, I at once became sensible of the vast importance of my new connection. The change of my name instantly represented to me the entire change of my duties. This consideration, which employed all my powers, was, I believe, rendered the more lively, by every external object: a new place of abode; the absence of those with whom I had lived from my childhood; these thoughts with the emotions I felt at your going away, imprinted on my looks a seriousness which my husband instantly perceived.

I had seated myself in my closet: he came to look for me with a countenance expressive of a placid joy, he stopped in the middle of the room, and after viewing me with a tender solicitude, began:

You seem very pensive, my dear, perhaps I disturb you.

Being unable to speak, I only held out my hand to him, which he kissed, and reaching a chair, sat down by me.

I, said he, have a most sincere respect for your whole family; but shall particularly ever prize the day when all the inclinations of this impressible heart became devoted to my dearest bride. Having honoured me with your esteem, add to it your confidence, and rest assured that you will never be unhappy with the man whom you have so generously preferred. Your family seat is but at a small distance, and in this, a heart so well disposed as yours, will take delight in making both me, your tenants, and servants happy. I know, that for some years, your valuable mother, has entrusted to you the œconomy[8] of her house, let me beg of you to resume the same employment here, where every thing is at your disposal, Your compliance will exceedingly oblige me, as I propose laying out all my leisure hours in the improvement of our small estate. This, I do not place entirely in acts of general justice and benevolence; it is farther incumbent on me, to see and examine, whether by altering the distribution of the farms, by having an eye to the good economy of the schools, and by putting tillage and grazing on a better footing, the circumstances of our dependants may not receive very beneficial improvements. I have made myself acquainted with these subjects; for to one like me, born in the middle class of society, the culture of the mind, and the practice of most virtues, are besides being indispensible duties, considered as the sources of prosperity, and the surest means of advancement, and of this truth I shall ever retain the most pleasing sense, as I am indebted to it for the inestimable treasure of your love. Had I been born to the rank and fortune I at present possess, perhaps my ardour for acquiring a name would have been less strong. The greatest blessing that fell to my lot in the past years of my life, was the father which Heaven was pleased to give me; since had I been placed in another situation, never could I have found so wise, so faithful a guide of my youth. By the careful study of my mind, or perhaps in consequence of his knowledge of the human heart in general, he took care to conceal from me the greatest part of his wealth, in order to prevent that remissness with which the only sons of the rich apply to the sciences, and to preserve me from the temptations to which they are exposed: he justly presumed, that having once learnt to make a good use of my natural dispositions, and acquired talents, I should then make a judicious and wise use of the blessings of fortune. He therefore first endeavoured to make me acquire virtue and knowledge, with a view to render me good and happy, before he put it in my power to enjoy and share with others the pleasures and gratifications which it is in the power of wealth to procure.

The love and practice of virtue, and a taste for the study of the sciences, said he, impart to him who is possessed of them a happiness independent of accident, and the malignity or caprice of men; and at the same time the shining example of his amiable behaviour, the benefit and pleasure of his conversation, render him a very considerable benefactor to society. By such principles, and a suitable education, he qualified me for the happiness of enjoying the friendship of your brother, and I flatter myself, has rendered me in some degree worthy of the possession of your heart. Half my life, I may say, is now elapsed: God be praised, it has not been marked by misfortunes nor by any considerable faults: but the blessed moment, when the kind, the virtuous, the generous heart of Sophia P. was moved to countenance me, is that at which the plan of my remaining happiness receives its date. O my beloved Sophia, ever shall this heart be filled with the most affectionate gratitude and respect for you!

Here, ceasing to speak, he kissed me, and desired me to excuse his having talked so much. I could do no less than assure him that I listened with great pleasure, for my heart corresponded with my words; and I desired him to proceed, as I believed he had still something farther to say.

I should be very loath to tire my dear Sophia, but wish that you knew my whole heart; and therefore as you yourself seem to desire me, I will proceed in laying it open before you. It has been my custom, in all the stations through which I have passed, both in the college, in my military service, and in my situation here, to weigh and consider the several duties I am bound to perform in relation to myself, my superiors and others. According to the knowledge and convictions resulting from such reflections, I have divided my time and attention; and at the same time have been prompted by my ambition to perform every part of my duty with alacrity, and as completely as possible. When my task was done, I thought of procuring the relaxations most agreeable to my taste. A similar review I have taken of my present situation, in which four branches of duty occur to me. The first, those towards my amiable wife, are quite easy and delightful; for my whole heart rejoices in them. The second relates to your respectable family, and the rest of the neighbouring nobility, whom, without flattery or meanness, I shall study to convince that I am not unworthy of the Lady Sophia P's hand, and of being admitted into the baron's family. As to the persons of that class from which I have been raised, I hope they will never have cause to think that I have forgot the origin whence I sprung. In short there are duties to be observed towards those who are subject to me, and their welfare I shall endeavour to promote, and strive to reconcile their hearts to the state of subjection in which fortune has placed them, by rendering it easy and pleasant, and behave so as to make them cheerfully acquiesce in the distinction made by Providence between them and me.[9]

The worthy minister at P. has kindly promised that he will recommend to me a young man well qualified for my parish, with whom I may put in execution what has frequently employed my thoughts.[10] I would have the minister of my parish from a real concern for the ever-lasting happiness of his parishioners, and an animated conviction of his own duty, make it his primary care to instil into the minds of the people committed to his care, such a measure of knowledge, as may animate them in the cheerful and uniform discharge of their duties towards God, their superiors, their neighbours and themselves. The desire of wealth and sensual gratifications, are as natural to the poor as to the rich; and those desires frequently put them upon illicit practices; I would therefore have them well grounded in religion, and inspired with just ideas of pleasure and happiness. The contemplation of the natural world, I believe, is the best means of reaching their hearts, and the object by which they will be the most easily affected, since every look, every step leads them to make it the subject of their earliest observations. Thus disposed to acknowledge the hand of their beneficent Creator, I would have the minister endeavour to diffuse a sweet serenity through their souls by frequent comparisons between the circumstances in which they are placed, and the less happy state of other men, who like themselves are the creatures of God, he should then add a view of the moral world, show the obligations they are under to procure a life of comfort, to do good to others, and to secure their eternal happiness.[11]

I shall also carefully attend to the proper management of the schools, and to the salary and application of the masters; I would introduce into them two catechisms, one concerning the christian duties, with a plain and easy application of its several principles to their manner of life; the other should contain the approved principles of tillage, gardening and grazing, with, the management and improvement of all kinds of forest and timber trees, and the knowledge of all these should be considered as a duty belonging to their profession. Indeed I should be more desirous of seeing my dependants exact in performing all their relative duties, than in making a show of religion.

I shall employ an ingenious young man whom I met with at P. to assist me in gaining the confidence of my dependants, and a particular knowledge of all their circumstances, that I may the better superintend their concerns as a real father and a guardian, and on all occasions be enabled to give them good advice and friendly admonitions, as well as to lend them my assistance. And greatly deceived must my heart be in its benevolent hopes, if the careful observance of my duty, and a like zeal in the pastor and those I employ, do not produce the most happy consequences with respect to my dependants.

Here he ceased, desiring me to excuse his long-winded speech, as he termed it, and gently taking me in his arms, my dear Sophia, said he, must be quite tired out. When I in the warmth of my overflowing heart, embracing him with tears of joy, cried, How, my dear, can I be tired with the enlarged prospect of felicity you are forming around me! The benevolence and virtue of that dear heart, which can form such generous plans of goodness, ensures the happiness of my remaining life. — Blessed indeed is my lot, and O dear honoured mother, God long preserve you a rejoicing witness of it.

A more happy couple never lived than Colonel Sternheim and his spouse; who were idolized by their dependants; for equity and benevolence kept equal pace within the cheerful confines of their estates. Experiments for the improvement of husbandry, which, after being tried in the lord's grounds, had been found to answer, were communicated to the tenants, and such who, though poor, expressed a forwardness for putting them in practice, were freely supplied with what was necessary, *gratis*; for the colonel was sensible, that without such encouragement, they could not justly be expected to set about any thing, however advantageous it might appear, when it required expense, and the use of a piece of land; but he used to say, What I give them at first, in time yields me interest, and the good folks are best brought to believe by experience, that it is their own welfare we have chiefly in view.

I cannot forbear digressing a little from the capital object of my narrative, to give you, a specimen of the useful and benevolent institutions in which this excellent couple placed a part of their happiness, in a description of the poor-house at S. and this I cannot do better than by an extract of a letter from Baron P. to his mother.

How faithfully does my friend make good my promise to you, that our Sophy would be happy with him![12] How agreeable is that house! the most noble simplicity united with the most perfect order, gives everything an air of grandeur. The domestics are all with cheerful obsequiousness and diligence busied in their several departments. The happy looks of the master and mistress express the sweet felicity arising from uniform virtue and prudence, and they both join in cordial thanks for the share I have had in promoting their union. What a difference is there between my brother's two small villages, and those much larger and more populous which I lately passed through in my return from court! In the first alacrity and diligence put me in mind of two thriving bee-hives; and richly does Sternheim find himself recompensed for all his trouble in making a more proper division of the farms, each of the vassals being now provided with just as much as he is able to cultivate. But the use to which he has applied Count A's seat, which he lately purchased, and which lies exactly between the two villages must naturally be attended with signal benefits.

That structure he has converted into a poor-house for his vassals. On the ground-floor of one side lives a worthy man who was a schoolmaster; but being now disabled by age, from the proper discharge of that important office, he acts as superintendant of the behaviour of the people. Above is the appartment for the apothecary who has the care of the sick in the poor-house and both the villages. All the poor work according to their abilities, during the summer in a neighbouring field and kitchen garden belonging to the building, and the produce of both is applied to their own use. In rainy weather, and in winter, the women spin flax, and the men wool, which serve for linen and apparel for themselves, and other necessitous persons. Their diet is clean and wholesome, and every morning and evening divine service is performed by the master of the house. The men and women work in two different rooms, both of which are warmed by one stove. In that of the women, they have their meals, for as they dress the provisions and perform the washing and needle work, their room is the most spacious. Such poor widows, or aged single women as have the best character for industry and an exemplary behaviour, are invested with some little author-ity, as are the poor men of a like character, among their class. The dormitory is in the upper part of the house, and separated into two wards, each consisting of five chambers, and in each of these are two beds, and necessaries of all kinds. On the side towards the garden are the men, and on the other the women, two in each room, that if one be taken ill, the other may assist him, or procure help; and from the middle of the window a deal partition, some feet in length, runs between the bedsteads from the ceiling to the floor; so that both may be in some measure, alone, and when one is sick the other may breathe a less morbid air. Different pairs of stairs lead to these two wards, to prevent any disorder.

Under the master of the house are servants employed in husbandry, who being picked men, chosen for the goodness of their morals, and their skill in the practical parts of agriculture, have better wages than anywhere else.

Poor strangers here meet with relief, they are offered work at so much a day, and are allowed to break off an hour sooner than the usual time, that they may reach the next town before it be dark: but no lazy beggars meet with any relief. The farmers, after every harvest, contribute a quantity of corn to the poor-house, according to their ability, and unconstrained free-will; and thus all the really necessitous are provided for, and the donations not abused. Drunkenness, gaming, lewdness and idleness are punished, by the offenders being employed in hard labour without the usual allowance, or by fines, which are carefully appropriated to the benefit of the house.

The next month four men and five women are to be received into the house, and my sister goes every day to see that everything be prepared and made ready for their admission. The subject of the sermon on the Sunday before will be on real charity, and the proper objects of it; afterwards will be read an account of the foundation, and the duties to be punctually observed by all who shall be admitted under its hospitable wings. The minister will then call by their names the parties to be received, up to the altar, and give them a proper exhortation on the right use of the leisure and quiet of their last days; enlarge on their duties towards God and their neighbour, and conclude with a discourse to the like purpose, addressed to the master of the house, the apothecary and the housekeeper. All my family intend to be present at this ceremony, at least I will not fail to be there.

But to return, the nobility in the neighbourhood entertained such an esteem for Colonel Sternheim as to be solicitous for his taking into his family, their sons, on their return from their travels, in order that they might acquire that experimental knowledge of agriculture which it becomes a nobleman to be acquainted with. Among these was the young Count Löbau, who, by being at Colonel Sternheim's contracted an intimacy with Lady Charlotte, and they were soon married.

Colonel Sternheim readily condescended to give those young noblemen just ideas of the manner of governing their vassals, and their dependants, from the humane consideration, that he might, perhaps, instil into them the sympathy due to the indigent, whose toilsome and penurious life is often still more embittered by the haughtiness and severity of the great. Being persuaded that example goes farther than the most excellent precepts, he used to take his pupils everywhere abroad with him, conversing with them as opportunity offered. He explained to them the reasons of his conduct, and being acquainted with the income and nature of their respective estates, he added short personal applications. They were spectators of his several employments, and shared in his relaxations. From these last, he took occasion earnestly to recommend their forbearing such as hurt their poor vassals, and of these, one of the most detrimental, he observed, was hunting. This he allowed to be a manly and becoming exercise; but maintained that every humane and benevolent nobleman, would take care that his dependants should not be sufferers by his diversions. The love of reading was one of the dispositions he endeavoured to cultivate, and history, in particular, gave him an opportunity of discoursing on the moral world, its revolutions and evils; of expatiating on the duties of a court and military life, and of habituating their minds to reflection and deliberation. The history of the moral world, he used to say, qualifies us for conversation; to bear with other men; to make them better, and at the same time, to remain tranquil and easy in our station: but an attentive survey of the physical world raises us to the great Author of our being; it exhibits to us on the one hand, our own debility and impotence; and on the other, his wisdom and his goodness invite us to contemplate him with minds filled with a supreme love and reverence; besides, such contemplations will carry us placidly through the many cares and vexations, which in the moral world, frequently fall thicker on the great and opulent, than on the cottage of the peasant, whose cares seldom extend beyond his necessary subsistence.

Thus did he interweave instruction and exhortation with example; while in his house was seen the exalted happiness of a marriage between a worthy man and a virtuous woman. Love and esteem ran through every part of their

behaviour, and the respectful domestics were ready to lay down their lives
for their dear master and mistress.

It was also no small satisfaction to Sternheim that all these young
noblemen acknowledged his kindness and abilities, and after they left him,
were on all occasions, his most devoted friends.

His spouse at length brought him a daughter, a very fine and hopeful child,
who soon became his sole consolation; and the only joy he knew on earth,
death having dissolved the union which rendered him the most happy of
mankind. Young Sophia was nine years of age when she had the misfortune to
lose the most tender mother.[13] The colonel poured his grief into the bosom of
his friend; but he had soon other tears to shed. Baron P. had a fall from his
horse, which reduced him to a bad state of health, and a few months after
deprived him of life. He died without issue. In his will he duly remembered his
excellent spouse; but according to the law of the country, appointed his
younger sister, the Countess of Löbau, and the young Sophia Sternheim, as
daughter to his eldest sister, his chief heiress, which the count and countess
considered as a wrong done to them.[14] The will however remained good.

The old Baroness of P. who was extremely afflicted at her son's untimely
death, now took up her residence with Colonel Sternheim, and superintended
the education of her little grand-daughter. That gentleman by every mark of a
respectful affection, and by the example of his own resignation, alleviated the
weight of her sorrows. Meanwhile the worthy patron and his daughters were
almost the only company in which she found any consolation. Sophia received
an excellent education; one of the pastor's daughters who was nearly of the
same age, was placed with her to excite her emulation, as well as to prevent
her contracting a melancholy disposition, which she probably would have
done, had she no other company but that of her father and grandmother: for
both used frequently to lament their loss, and the colonel would lead his
daughter, now in her twelfth year, up to a picture of her mother, and talk with
such tenderness of her virtue and goodness of heart, that she once fell on her
knees dissolved in tears, and ardently wished to die, that she might be with
her dear mother. This excessive sensibility made the colonel apprehend that
her tender mind would imbibe too strong a propensity to melancholy, and
that the extreme delicacy of her frame would increase to such a degree as to
render her incapable of struggling with grief and distress. He therefore strove
to overcome himself, and show his daughter, how those misfortunes are to be
borne, which generally give the deepest wounds to the best persons, and the
young lady discovering an extraordinary understanding, he cultivated it with
history, several parts of philosophy, and the languages, of which the English
was that in which she made the greatest proficiency, and became almost as
much mistress of it, as of her native language. She perfected herself in singing
and in touching the lute. Of dancing she knew as much as became a lady.
Indeed she rather imparted a grace and ornament to that art, than derived any
from it; for everybody agreed that there was in all the young lady's motions
something inexpressibly charming, to which no degree of art could attain.

Besides these daily employments, she, with singular dispatch and facility, made herself mistress of all kinds of needlework, and the use of her pen, so that when she was scarce sixteen, she was entrusted with the whole management of the family, and her mother's diaries and books of account were put into her hands for her instruction. A natural love of order, and of an active life, strengthened by an enthusiastic veneration for the memory of her mother, whose resemblance she was ambitious of obtaining, made her succeed as much in this as in the rest. When any one mentioned the variety of her knowledge and attainments, she would modestly answer, I owe it to natural genius, good examples, and kind instructions, and with such a happy concurrence of circumstances, who could do otherwise. She was fond of whatever was said to be English, and her only wish was that her father would visit that island and give her an opportunity of seeing her grandmother's relations.

Thus was this young lady shooting up in the bloom of youth, when being a little turned of nineteen, a lingering illness deprived her of her excellent father, who with a fond anxiety earnestly recommended her to the care of Count Löbau, and the worthy pastor of Sternheim as her guardians. To the latter he, a few weeks before his death, wrote the following letter.

Col. Sternheim to the Minister of ———.

Soon shall I see her who was the dearest part of myself. My house and everything concerning my dear Sophia's fortune are settled. This was both the last and the least important office that remained for me to do for her. As to the first and most sacred duty of a father, that of giving her a good education, adapted to draw down upon her the blessings of heaven, if I may believe the testimony of my heart, I have not neglected it. Thus I do not fear that with a soul like hers, born with the love of virtue, she will ever be the cause of uneasiness to you my valuable friend, who will now succeed me as her father. Love, in particular, notwithstanding that extreme tenderness of disposition she has inherited from her excellent mother, will have little influence over her, unless she finds a *person whose virtue corresponds with her fantasy*.* Guard her, my dear friend, guard her, I conjure you, from being seduced by a *false virtue*. She searches with such eagerness to discover the good qualities of others, and glides with such candour and indulgence over their defects, that in this respect, and in this respect only, I have reason to tremble for her. Never, no never, will any humane mind be made unhappy by her; for I know that to promote the welfare of another deserving person, she would be ready to sacrifice her own; and that she would not give another a transient affliction to secure the happiness of her whole life. But alas! her tender and delicate feelings put her *too much in the power of others*. I have hitherto concealed my apprehensions from the Countess of Löbau's

---

* The meaning of this expression will become evident in the longer course of the narrative. It doubtless refers to a man, the subtlest lineaments of whose character most nearly resemble the particular ideal of virtue and moral perfection that has formed within her soul. – E.

temper, and the thoughts of Sophia being with her make me tremble. The mildness and goodness that appear in that woman are *not in her heart*, and the engaging wit, and soothing voice, she has learnt at court, are only a deceitful varnish that covers the vices of her soul. Yet I never communicated what I thought of her to my daughter; this I esteemed unnecessary while I lived. But when the Baroness P. shall sink under the weight of age and affliction, do you take Sophia under your care. Providence will soften the trouble of your office, and I hope God will make it easy to you, by his granting the last supplications of a dying father, who does not desire for his daughter riches and grandeur; but prays that wisdom and virtue may be her portion. Thus I resign her to the divine goodness, and commit her to the hands of a faithful friend. Yet more easily can I disengage myself from all my earthly concerns, than from the thoughts of my daughter. Here I recollect a conversation we had on the force of the impressions we receive in our youth: I actually feel a part of what I then advanced, and that with all the warmth which the circumstances I am in ought to add to that remembrance. My worthy father endeavoured particularly to impress upon my mind two things, the *certainty of a retribution*, even in this life, and the advantage we ourselves receive from *the good example we set to others*. His arguments on these heads were so strong and sublime, and his expressions so pathetic and affectionate, that they could not fail of being deeply impressed on so tender a soul as mine. How often did he say to me, that the uneasiness or joy I gave him, would be either punished or rewarded by my children! Praised be the bounteous giver of all grace, that my behaviour towards my worthy father obtained for me the blessing of so dutiful and virtuous a child; and this gladdens the last scenes of my life with the transporting remembrance, that I also crowned my father's last days with the most complete satisfaction which a truly paternal heart can feel. 'Never', said he, on his death bed, 'have you given me uneasiness by your evil inclinations, or your disobedience to me. No, your love of virtue; your constant application to useful and praiseworthy objects, have rendered you my comfort, for which may God bless you, and recompence you by your feeling in your turn the sweet satisfaction which the sight of you now imparts to a dying father; from the assurance, that in my son I leave a worthy member of society.' That sweet satisfaction, my dear friend, I now feel in myself, as I can bear the like testimony of my daughter. She has also been to me the source of another kind of satisfaction mingled with sorrow, since in presenting before me the lively image of her mother, she has revived the remembrance of my happiness, and the grief of such a heartfelt loss. How often has this sent me away from the table, or from company, especially in the two last years, when being grown up to her mother's stature, and, at my desire, wearing her clothes, all her mother shone out in her! and I found again in the sound of her voice, the manners, the amiable gaiety, and all the goodness of heart of my beloved wife! God grant that this example of filial piety may be continued from her to her latest posterity.

Thus affectionately did he lay open his heart to his worthy friend. It is with keen emotions that I recollect the last hours of that worthy man, and his various discourses preceding his death. The grief of his dear Sophia was too violent to admit of the consolation of tears. She kneeled by his bed; her countenance and attitude expressing the deepest sorrow: her father's eyes were fixed on her; with one of his hands in hers, and now and then a sigh escaped him, ending in, O my dear Sophia! One of the young lady's arms extended in silence towards heaven, while all the lineaments of her countenance expressed her love, her piety, her distress. Oh this scene of solemn grief, of virtue, of resignation, rent all our hearts!

Sophia, said he, we cannot complain, sixty years is not too hasty a separation. Death to me, so far from being an evil, will unite my spirit to its gracious Creator, and my heart to thine excellent mother. Congratulate me on such felicity, though it shorten the pleasure thy father's longer life might have given thee.

Overcoming in some degree her dejection, she herself attended her father with all possible care and composure. He observed her struggles to triumph over nature, and begged her to give him the consolation of seeing, in his last moments, the fruit of his endeavours, to enable her to possess herself at such a trying season. She fully answered his wishes, O best of father's! said she, after directing me how to live; you now teach me how to die! May heaven appoint you my guardian angel, and to be a witness of all my thoughts and actions. I will deserve your care.

When he had uttered his last sigh, the house exhibited the most affecting scene. It was crowded with weeping dependants; in his chamber the domestics accompanying their tears with fervent supplications: his daughter by his bedside, kissing his cold hands, unable to speak, sometimes kneeling, then rising with all the gestures of oppressive grief. – O my friend! how does the remembrance of that day penetrate my heart! How pregnant with the most important instructions is the death bed of a good man, to a sensible mind!

My father stood a silent spectator; he was himself too much affected to have the free use of his speech. At length, taking the distressed young lady by the hand, God grant, said he, that you may inherit the virtues of your worthy father, who is now gone to receive his reward! May he plant them in these afflicted hearts, (here he pointed to us) and by a dutiful remembrance of your respectable master, may you be induced to walk in his steps.

The old lady was likewise there, and this circumstance my father made use of to get Sophia out of the room, by desiring her to attend her grandmother, who was retiring to some other place to seek for comfort. When the young lady began to move we all made way. She viewed us with a look of tenderness, tears now trickling down her lovely cheeks. The family crowding about her kissed her hands and even her clothes; not by way of recommending themselves to the heiress; but as marks of respect for the only surviving remains of the best of masters.

The funeral was conductd by my father and the steward, and never had such a burial been seen. Col. Sternheim had directed that it should be at night, and with as little show as possible, in order to save his Sophy's seeing his body deposited in the mansions of the dead. But the church was crowded with people, and everyone in mourning, as it was illuminated suitably to the occasion. All expressed their eagerness to see once more their dear master and benefactor. The old, the young, all melted into tears, and blessed him, pouring forth their ardent prayers, that God would reward the daughter, for her father's great goodness to them.

The concern at Sternheim was far from being a transient ceremony, concluding with the funeral. Sophia's perseverance in her grief even gave my father some uneasiness, particularly as the old lady, overcome by this last affliction, grew daily more weak and infirm. Her affectionate grand-daughter waited on her with a tenderness which she thus acknowledged. O Sophy! you have all your mother's sympathy and goodness, with the strong sense of your father. A happier creature, surely does not exist on earth, as in you are united the endowments which so advantageously distinguished your dear parents. Now left to yourself, you enter on your independency by your assiduous attendance on your infirm grandmother, and believe me, child, to help and cherish age with such tenderness, is a virtue not inferior to the most liberal acts of charity.

The Count and Countess of Löbau paying them a visit, she earnestly recommended the orphan to them. They both seemed to behave with much courtesy and even tenderness towards the young lady, and were desirous of taking her home with them; but she entreated her grandmother, to allow her to stay the year of mourning with her.

In this interval began that intimate friendship which she afterwards steadily preserved for my sister Emilia. With her she used frequently to visit the tomb of her parents. These bones, these bones, said she, are now all my kindred. Lady Löbau is no relation of mine; she has no sentiments that I can approve. Our way of thinking is entirely different, and I only regard her as my uncle's sister.[15]

About this time the steward of the estate of Sternheim, who is a very worthy man, married my eldest sister; and his brother, a clergyman, being there on a visit, took a fancy to Emilia, and obtained both her's and my father's consent. This marriage, which separated the two friends, gave rise to a correspondence that will afford me an opportunity of frequently making her speak for herself.

But I must first draw you my young lady's picture, in which you are not to expect a perfect beauty. In stature she was somewhat above the middle size, and exceeding well shaped: her face oval, and full of expression: she had beautiful hazel eyes, beaming both vivacity and goodness: a fine mouth, and within it a very beautiful set of teeth. Her forehead high, but rather too large for a perfect beauty. In all her features there was something amiable, and in all her deportment such dignity, that wherever she appeared she attracted all eyes. Every sort of dress became her, and I have heard my Lord Seymour say, that in every plait of her robe resided some particular grace. In her choice of silks she constantly preferred those that made the least show, and yet she was always distinguished, however splendid was the company in which she appeared. Nothing could equal the beauty of her hair, which was of a chestnut colour, and of a great length. The sound of her voice had an engaging sweetness; and her expressions were well chosen, without being affected. In a word, it was her character and mind that gave charms to her person, and attracted the heart.

Such was Lady Sophia, when her aunt carried her to the court of D. Among the preparations for this journey, which my father concurred in persuading her to take, I cannot omit the following. She had enamelled pictures of her father and mother set in bracelets, which she constantly wore: she desired to have them unmounted, and accordingly gave orders to a jeweller. The portraits were brought back encompassed with brilliants; and two days before her departure, she went, accompanied by my sister Emilia, to the tomb of her parents and bidding a solemn farewell to their dear remains, renewed her vows of faithfully copying their virtues: she then took off her bracelets, which were contrived in such a manner, that a little vacant space was left under the pictures, that was discovered by means of a spring. When she had opened them, she filled this space with earth taken from the tomb, and while she was thus employed the tears trickled down her cheeks. My dear lady, said Emilia, what are you about? What is the meaning of your putting up that earth? Dearest Emilia, answered she, the wisest and the best persons esteem it a virtue to reverence the dust of the virtuous. This earth, which covers the sacred remains of my parents, is dearer to me than the whole world, and, as I am going from home, will be the most precious thing I can take with me.

My sister, troubled at this, told us she apprehended that some grievous affliction was impending, and that her mind had secret forebodings, that when the dear young lady was gone, she should never see her more. My father, however, endeavoured to remove our fears, and yet he himself was soon seized with them. He was informed that the dear lady had visited every house in the villages that belonged to her, and had conversed most affec-tionately with all the people, distributing presents among them, and exhort-ing them to be industrious and honest; that she had increased the allowance for the widows, the orphans, the aged, and the sick: was particularly earnest in her conversation with the schoolmaster; augmented his salary, and instituted prizes for the encouragement of the children: that she made my brother-in-law, the steward, a present of a gold snuff-box, and my sister of a ring, to keep for her sake, recommending to the former equity and tenderness towards her dependants. This account drew tears from every eye; but my father alleviated our grief, by saying, It is the way of all people of a melancholy cast, to throw a kind of solemnity over their actions. Yet it gave him much satisfaction, that she entered on the great world with such strong impressions of true goodness and humanity, as not a few of those sensations would be there moderated, by an imperceptible mixture of gaiety and spirit, and by her becoming better acquainted with the human heart, her enthusiasm would gradually subside, and be kept within due limits.

My sister Emilia had also her friend's picture, and a most elegant casket, the contents of which amounted to a little fortune. A servant she left behind, because he was married, and Count Löbau had sent her word that his people should wait on her.

A few days after came the count, her uncle, to fetch her away, and I, at her earnest desire, was permitted to accompany her. Her taking leave of my father was very affecting: you who knew him, must be sensible that he at the same time inspired love and esteem. We first went to the Löbau estate, and from thence, along with the countess, to D. and here begins the fatal period in which you will see this most amiable lady entangled in embarrassments and distresses which at once destroyed the beautiful plan she had formed of a happy life, and, by the severe trials they drew on her virtue, render her history a treasure of instruction to our sex.

It will now, I think, be the best way for me, instead of continuing the narrative, to lay before you a series of letters written by my beloved lady, from which you will form a better idea of her genius and temper, and of everything remarkable that happened to her during her residence at D. than by any extracts I could make from them. To these I shall join the copies of some letters which will serve to elucidate hers, and to complete these memoirs: for all these, by a train of circumstances, at length fell into my hands.[16]

LETTER I

Lady Sophia Sternheim to Emilia

My dear Friend,
I have now been here[17] four days, and this seems to me a kind of new world. The rattle of carriages and the bustle of the people is, indeed, little more than I expected, yet to an ear like mine, accustomed to the stillness of the country, it was at first very irksome; but a much more disagreeable circumstance, was my aunt's sending for the court hair-dresser, to put mine in the top of the mode. She was so complaisant as to come with him into my chamber, where, loosening my hair, she said, Here's a head on which you may do honour to your skill, and pray show it to the utmost; but be

exceeding careful that these beautiful locks are not injured by your hot
irons.

This little flattery in my aunt did not displease me; but the man's high-
flown praises nettled me, and my pride made me think it would better
become him to mind what he was set about, and keep his admiration to
himself. But still more insupportable were the mantua-maker[18] and the
milliner. Rosina can tell you all their idle tattle, and some remarks, a little
severe, that escaped me. The vanity of the ladies of this town, thought I,
must surely have very little delicacy, and be sharp set, when they can
encourage these people to bring it food, which to me appears so coarse and
insipid. But of what value are the praises dictated by interest? With the
disdain which I feel for general applause, it gives me no pleasure to be
remarked for any particular advantage.

This afternoon I have seen some gentlemen and ladies whom my aunt had
informed of her arrival, excusing her not waiting on them on account of her
being extremely fatigued with her journey; when, in reality, the sole cause
was the clothes being not yet ready, in which I was to make my appearance.
You know, my dearest Emilia, that my father was fond of seeing me in my
mother's clothes, and I was no less fond of wearing them: but here they are
all quite out of fashion, and, as it was my aunt's pleasure that they should be
laid by, I submitted to her will. The only gown I am allowed to wear is the
white tabby,[19] which was made for me at the conclusion of our mourning.
Ah! my dear Emilia! don't take this term in the literal sense: for though I
have laid aside the external trappings of sorrow, it still retains its former
residence in the secret recesses of my heart, and appears to have made an
alliance with my secret monitor, I mean my conscience: for amidst the
multitude of silks and trinkets lately brought me (this for the approaching
gala, that for the next ball, another for the assembly) the motion of my
hands present to my sight the picture of my mother, so plainly dressed, in
the bracelet, and that fixing my attention while I am preparing to adorn my
person, I could not forbear thinking, What a different figure from this shall I
shortly make? But God forbid this difference should ever extend beyond my
dress, which I consider as a sacrifice which the best and most sensible
people cannot sometimes well avoid offering, to custom, to circumstances,
and to their connection with others. This thought seemed to me a lesson
given me by my conscience and the remembrance of my parents. – So much
before my making my appearance: however, as you, my tender friend, are to
serve me instead of a parent, and have desired that I would give you an
account, as occasions offer, of everything in which I am interested, and of
the ideas which various objects excite in my mind, I am resolved to obey
you. I shall say very little of others, any farther than I myself am concerned;
besides, what I observe in them is not quite strange to me, as I know the
manners of the great, from the pictures of them which my grandmother and
my father often sketched out for me.

I now entered my aunt's room, where the company were assembled. I had on a white sack with blue Italian flowers. My head genteely dressed in the tip of the fashion. How it was with my air and complexion I know not, but I suppose I might look a little pale; for soon after the countess had introduced me as her favourite niece, a young gentleman, naturally no bad figure, came up with an indecent pertness, and inclining towards my aunt, with his face toward me, in an attitude of fear, cried, My dear countess, is this really your ladyship's niece? – Do you doubt it, sir? – Why, from her first appearance, dress, and fairy motions, I really took the lady for some lovely spirit. – Poor F.! said a lady, and, very likely, you are afraid of spirits.

The ugly ones, answered he, I mortally hate and abhor; but, with a spirit like this, I could trust myself alone for hours.

Thus, with this bright conceit, you would bring upon my house the disgrace of being haunted!

I wish it were, to keep all other gentlemen at a distance; but then I should be for conjuring away the pretty spirit.

Well said, Count F.! and all the room rang with Bravo! Bravo! – Now niece, continued my aunt, are you for being conjured away?

I know very little of the world of spirits, answered I; but am apt to think that every ghost requires a particular kind of conjuration, and the fright which my appearance gave the count, makes me think myself under the protection of a more powerful spirit than that which taught him his conjuration.

Admirable! excellent! Go on Count F. called out Colonel Sch.

I have, however, answered the count, found out more than any of you; for though the lady is not a mere spirit, I perceive she has an infinite deal of spirit.

O! that you might have guessed, and it was probably your penetration was the cause of your being seized with such a panic, said Miss C. maid of honour to the Princess W. who till then had not opened her mouth.

You are always severe upon me, Miss C. for by that you mean to say, that an inferior spirit began to be afraid of a superior.

There is more truth in all this raillery, thought I, than they imagine. I am a kind of apparition not only in this house, but in this town and at court. Spiritual beings are supposed to come into the world with a knowledge of mankind; they are neither astonished at what they see, nor at what they hear; but, like me, frequently compare this world with that from whence they came, and deplore the levity with which people think of a future state: men see them, they being clothed with the same form; but they belong to a different species of beings.

Miss C. had then a pretty long conversation with me, at the close of which she expressed her high esteem, and very obligingly wished to cultivate an acquaintance with me. She is very amiable, and a little taller than I, with something graceful in her walk and the motion of her head. Her face is rather long, but every feature is delicately formed. She has fair hair, and a most engaging sweetness of countenance: only I thought her beautiful eyes bestowed their looks too much on those of the men. She has a fine understanding, and all her expressions speak the goodness of her heart. In short, of all the persons I saw in that company, she pleased me most, and I intend to close with her kind proposal of cultivating an acquaintance.

At length entered the Countess of F. whom my aunt had desired me to treat with great respect, as her lord could be of great service to my uncle in a lawsuit then depending. I accordingly did so; yet that the niece was by her complaisance to the minister's spouse, to forward the uncle's claims, was what I did not relish. Were I in his stead, I should not employ either my own or the minister's wife; but it being men's business, should treat of it only with men. The minister, who is governed by his wife, I do not much like; but this is here the usual custom; hence the one makes no complaint, and the other forbears all airs of superiority.

Miss C. and Lady F. stayed to supper. The conversation was very lively, but so vague and confused that I could make neither head nor tail of it. Lady F. was very liberal of her compliments to me on whatever I said or did; but if she meant by this means to please me, she was grievously out in her reckoning; for my heart will never be inclined to love her, and I do not look on myself as under the same obligation of duty to get the better of any dislike to her, as I am with respect to my aunt, though we now and then have some little altercations. But for Miss C. I shall ever retain a cordial love. She was with me in my apartment, and we conversed together as freely as if we had been old acquaintance: she said a great deal of her princess, and how fond she would be of me, I being quite to her taste. Having, by my aunt's desire, played some tunes on my lute, accompanied with my voice, she gave me still stronger assurances of the princess's favour, and I came off with general applause. I believe that what renders the voice and accent of the courtiers pleasing, is the attention they pay to the self-love of others.

My aunt was pleased to say, that she liked me very much, for she had been under terrible apprehensions of my appearing a strange sort of a creature, and at least extremely rustic. I had also Lady F's praises, though not without the exception of my being something cold and reserved; and so I was, for I cannot prostitute the assurances of my friendship and esteem, and never can I give them when I do not feel them. No, my dear Emilia, I am above deceit, and my heart has not an equal sensibility for all. But don't think that I form a disadvantageous opinion of all who think and act contrary to my sentiments. I assure you I endeavour to do justice to everyone, and never put the worst construction on anything. I say to myself, a wrong education that produces false ideas, examples which confirm them, and the pretended obligation of living as others do, have warped these people from their genuine character. I consider them as persons labouring under a family distemper. I will behave kindly to them, but not with familiarity and confidence, lest I become infected with their disease.

Pray, my dear friend, for my steady continuance in right principles, and continue to love me. Heaven's choicest blessings on our dear father! How will he be able to bear his being separated from so fond a child as his Emilia? but how auspiciously do you enter the marriage state, crowned with the cordial blessing of so pious a parent! With my respects to the worthy man you have chosen, and who possesses a valuable treasure in the heart of my Emilia.

LETTER II

From Lady Sophia to Emilia

I am pleased, my dear Emilia, that this letter will likewise come to your hands in your father's house, as I am persuaded it will show a visible confusion in my ideas; but your father will be able to point out the best means of rectifying them. I have been presented to the Princess of W. and all the nobility, and am now personally acquainted with the court and am known to the great.

I have already told you, that I had some knowledge of them from the representations of others, and nothing that I first saw appeared strange; but imagine a person capable of observation and fond of speculation, to whom a capital picture, finely executed, has long been known; she has frequently viewed it and considered the plan, the ordonnance, the blending of the colours, and nothing has escaped her curious eye: when lo! this picture with all its parts is set in motion by a foreign power: this naturally fills the observer with amazement, and excites in her mind a variety of emotions. This amazed person am I. It is neither the objects nor the colours that strike me, but the motion so foreign to it.

Shall I tell you how I was received? Exceeding well everywhere; for on such occasions the court has a general round of phrases in which the most shallow are as fluent as the most sensible. The princess, who is near fifty, has a great share of wit, and an air of goodness in her expressions and behaviour, which from its indiscriminate condescension seemed to me habitual, and to have taken its rise at a time when she might think it of importance to gain the affections of all sorts of people. This I consider as the *only* motive capable of producing this effect; for it is little worthy of a soul truly noble, to show an equal benevolence to all without distinction of merit. She talked with me a long while, and said much in praise of my dear father, whom she had known when a captain, and afterwards on his being raised to the rank of colonel. She was pleased to say, I was the worthy daughter of an excellent man, and that she would often send for me. You can't but think, my dear

Emilia, that I love and honour this princess the more on account of her regard for my father's memory.

I shall here draw no more characters, there being such a general resemblance in most of them, at least, when they show themselves in the princess's withdrawing room, and in common visits.

Yesterday I was interrupted in my writing by being informed that there was to be an assembly at the princess's, where I was expected, and was therefore under the necessity of idling away at the *toilette*, an interval which I had promised myself I should consecrate to friendship. Believe me, honest Rosina is no more fit to be a modish chambermaid, than I to support the character of a lady of high rank; for I cannot contract the noble habit of consuming a great part of my life at my *toilette*, nor meditate long together on the choice of my dress. My aunt, to remedy our defects, sends me every day one of her women, besides the hairdresser: all their preparations, and the importance they give to their office, put my patience to a very disagreeable trial; however, for that time I was very well satisfied when all was over, because I was really well dressed.

This is a satisfaction which you never yet perceived in me, and to save you the trouble of surmises and conjectures, I will honestly let you into the cause. I was pleased with the elegance of my dress, because I was to be seen by two English noblemen, whose approbation I was very desirous of obtaining. One was my Lord G. the English Envoy, and the other Lord Seymour, his nephew, who under his uncle's conduct was qualifying himself for that branch of public business, and gaining a knowledge of the courts of Germany. The envoy by his figure, his noble and lively countenance, and a certain dignity accompanied with politeness, did honour to his character.

I was in company with the young Lord Seymour above half an hour. Miss C. who has a very high esteem for him, as he also has for her, introduced him to me, by observing that I was her new friend from whom she never would be separated while at her own disposal. My lord answered her with a bow; but his whole demeanour so plainly expressed his sentiments, that both his approbation of everything Miss C. said, and his favourable opinion of her friend were plainly visible. Were I obliged to draw a picture that should represent the happy union between an elevated soul, a penetrating mind, and a heart in which sweet humanity resides, I would form it entirely of the person and features of Lord Seymour, and I fancy that all who ever had any just idea of those three qualities, might perceive them plainly expressed in his form, look and demeanor. I shall not expatiate on the sweetness and charms of his voice, of his noble appearance, and of the tincture of melancholy which softens the vivacity of his fine eyes; but what distinguishes him from multitudes of men I have seen in the few weeks I have been here, is, if I express myself right, the sentimental look of modest virtue which gives no offence.

Miss C. wishing that I might never leave her, made him ask whether I was not to stay at D. to which I answered, I believed not, as I stayed only for my aunt the Countess of R's return, who was gone on a tour to Italy with her husband, and then I should go with them to their seat.

I can't conceive, said he, how your vivacity can reconcile itself to the simplicity and uniformity of a country life.

And I can scarce think Lord Seymour really believes that a sprightly, and consequently an active disposition, is in danger of wanting entertainment in the country.

I don't mean, miss, a total want, but the disagreeableness and lassitude of seeing our thoughts and observations perpetually confined to one kind of objects.

I own, my lord, that since my being here in town, I have found, on comparing both kinds of life, that in the country employments and diversions are as various as those I see here; with this only difference, that amidst the amusements and pastimes of the country, the heart is perfectly easy and at rest, which I see little of here, and such rest I account very valuable.

So do I; and addressing himself to Miss C. I am inclined to think from your esteemed friend's manner of expressing herself, that she would maintain that rest though she made thousands uneasy.

As his eyes were not on me while he said so, and Miss C. only smiled, I likewise was silent; for this politeness of his gave me some confusion, which I would not willingly have betrayed, and therefore, instead of holding him in talk any longer, left her the preference, as due to her former acquaintance; which I might the better do, as he had with great earnestness addressed himself to her.

Here, methinks, you say, Why *former acquaintance*? Was you then his acquaintance, though this first time of seeing him was but about half an hour?

Yes, dear Emilia, he was my acquaintance before I saw him; for Miss C. had given me a particular account of his excellent character, before his return from an excursion, in which he had accompanied his uncle, during the absence of the prince, and all the good things said of him were no more than was expressed in his countenance. Besides, Emilia, I was struck with the melancholy pensiveness in which he stood leaning against the side of the window, in which we were both sitting, and continued our chat. Making Miss C. observe her friend's thoughtful attitude, I softly asked her if he was often so? She told me he was.

She then asked me many questions about the kind of pastimes which it was possible for me to procure in the country, and I briefly, but with a full heart, gave her an account of the happy time of my education in my guardian's house, and protested that her friendship was all the satisfaction I had hitherto known at D. She kindly squeezed my hand, and said, she had no less pleasure in mine. I proceeded by saying, I could not bear the word *pastime*, as, during my whole life, time had never hung heavy on my hands, that is, whispered I, when in the country. In my opinion, a desire of what is called killing time shows an ill turn of mind; for life is so short, and we have so many subjects of observation in order to know this place of our abode; so much to learn, if we would make a right use of our intellectual powers, and are capable of doing so much good, that it hurts me to hear people talk so lightly of getting rid of what is of such concern. How lamentably people study to deceive themselves!

Your seriousness, my dear, amazes me; yet what you say gives me pleasure. You are, as the princess said, a most extraordinary person.

I know not how it was with me, Emilia. I perceived that this way of thinking did not pass current here; but that I could not help. I was seized with inquietude, with a desire of being at a great distance; I longed to be alone, and could even have shed tears, without being able to assign any particular cause.

Here my Lord G. came up to his nephew, and taking him by the arm, said, Seymour, you are like a child sleeping securely on a river's brink. Look about you! pointing to us; it is very happy for you that I awaked you. Very right, uncle; I was too much absorbed in the ravishing harmony I heard, to dream of danger. While he said this, his eyes returned to me with the most lively expression of fondness; so that casting down mine, I turned away my head. On which my lord said in English, Seymour, have a care! it is not for nothing that these beautiful nets are spread abroad so alluringly. At the same time I perceived his hand pointing to my hair, which made me blush as red as scarlet; for I was piqued at being charged with coquetry: but, to save both him and myself from more pain, I said to him, My lord, I understand something of English. This struck him a little; he however commended my candour, and Seymour changed colour, yet smiled, and immediately turning to Miss C. said,

Won't you learn English too? Of whom? she replied.

Of me, my dear miss, and of this young lady: my uncle also won't be against giving you some instructions, and you'll soon learn.

Never so well as from this dear friend of mine, to whom indeed it is natural, for she is half an English woman.

How so? says my Lord G. turning to me.

My grandmother was named Watson, and married Baron P. when he was envoy from this court to that of England.

Miss C. desired him to speak English. He did; and my answers were such that he particularly commended my pronunciation, and told Miss C. that I spoke it very well, and she could not do better than learn it from me. When he went away, my Lord Seymour persuaded Miss C. to take the trouble of learning to read English, which she promised, adding that she should not fail being with me every day that did not require her attendance at court.

Then there's an end of my service, said he with some concern.

You shall hear, once a week, how I go on.

To this he answered with a bow.

The princess soon after ordered me to be called, and desired me to go with her into her closet. Here, my dear, said she, when we were there, is my lute; everybody is at cards, and do you give me, now we are alone, a specimen of your voice and skill. She was not to be refused, and I obeyed, by playing the first tune that came to hand. After which she actually embraced me, saying, You are a very amiable young lady indeed, to have made yourself mistress of so many accomplishments in the country, which ladies brought up at court are utterly ignorant of. She then, in a most affable manner, led me by the hand into the drawing-room, where she kept me till the assembly broke up, and talked to me of a thousand different things. My Lord Seymour's eyes were often fixed on me (be sure, Emilia, you read this to my dear guardian) and the notice he took of me gave me pleasure: but I was also gazed at by the whole company, which greatly disgusted me; for I imagined that their looks expressed something little agreeable to my principles.

Today we paid a visit to the Countess of F. to whom I was desired to show great respect. It is pretty evident that her spouse is a favourite of the prince, for the marks of favour conferred on them was a principal subject of her discourse. She then mentioned the high regard her husband entertained for a lord and master, for whom too much could not be done. This was followed by a very high encomiums on the prince, the comeliness of his person, his many accomplishments, his refined taste in everything, particularly in his entertainments, his munificence, his liberality, virtues worthy of a sovereign. This lady, thought I, has sufficient cause to dwell so much on this last quality. As to his inclination for the fair sex, she observed, that we are all but human creatures; to be sure he has carried it in some things too far; but the misfortune is, that His Highness has not yet met with an object that captivated his heart as much as his eyes; for such a person would certainly have performed wonders, both for the good of the country, and for the prince's reputation.

My aunt agreed with her in all she said, while I sat silent, as in this portrait of a prince I could not remark one single feature of him whom my father's observations on the *true prince*, while I was reading history, had left on my memory. I was very glad that my opinion was not asked; but when the countess took me into her chamber to show me his picture, I could truly say, that he makes a fine figure on canvas, as he really does. My aunt is desirous of having my picture drawn; and I have consented, as I am sure of giving pleasure to my Emilia, by sending her a copy of it. I know you will thank me for this intended present.

P.S. I beg to know my guardian's thoughts of this letter.

LETTER III

Lady Sophia to Emilia

All that my last letter informed you of was, that my Lord Seymour had found his best friend in myself; and now you say my dear guardian offers prayers, as the only thing in the power of man to do for me.

You love me, Emilia; you know me; but little thought of the disquietude this causes me. But I understand how it is. The warm esteem I have expressed for so shining a character as that of Lord Seymour fills you both with apprehensions; but, my dear, I beg of my guardian and you, make yourselves easy, since all the part I can take in that nobleman arises merely from the affection I feel for Miss C. She is the person he loves; she is the person he designs to make happy. My participation is only the complacence which a generous heart finds in the happiness of its friends, and the contemplation of the good qualities of its fellow creatures. Besides, my dear Emilia, from my being at present convinced that there really exists a man who is possessed of goodness, wisdom, generosity, and all the happy endowments that adorn the heart and the mind; a *despicable* man, or he who has no other advantage than a *lively wit*, and a person and qualities merely *agreeable*, will never have any influence over my heart; and this, which I account no small advantage, I owe to my acquaintance with his lordship.

I am the more concerned at the accident which hinders your father from using his right arm, as it deprives me of the pleasure and advantage of receiving his letters. Don't think, my dear Emilia, that I am dissatisfied with yours; but I should know more of his own thoughts from himself, than from you. I hope his arm will soon be well, and then I beg he will kindly make me amends for this disappointment.

Yesterday we were splendidly entertained at dinner by my Lord G. where Count F. came to us in the afternoon, and late in the evening the whole company repaired to the prince's. The count has an agreeable person, and is distinguished by his abilities. His lady herself introduced him to me. There, said she, talk yourself with my favourite, and tell me, whether I am in the wrong to wish I had such a daughter. He then said a great many very polite things to me, yet eyed me with an attention which appeared so singular and out of the way, that it filled me with confusion.

The Lord Seymour placed himself at table between Miss C. and me, and confined his talk chiefly to us: amidst other gallantries, during coffee he presented to both some English verses written on cards, desiring me to translate them for Miss C. On Lady F's coming up to me with her husband, they withdrew, and talked a long while at another window. The count at length went from me to my Lord G. taking with him the Lord Seymour. Meanwhile Miss C. and I amused ourselves with viewing the pictures and engravings, till we were sent for to play. Count F. and the Lord G. then coming up to us, talked to me about my father, who was once well known to the former, and also about my grandmother Watson, whom he had seen at her first arrival in Germany, protesting that there was a very striking likeness between us. The Lord Seymour was all this while with Miss C. looking very grave and thoughtful, and, I thought, his eyes sometimes seemed fixed, with a kind of uneasiness, on me and the two lords. A sudden bustle of people in the street drew us all to the windows, and I went to that where Lord Seymour and Miss C. were standing. It was the noise of people returning from seeing the prince land, after his being engaged in a party of pleasure on the water. While I was considering the number of people who passed by, many of whom had the look and dress of indigence, while we were clothed with the most pompous ostentation, and the heaps of gold that were spread on the card tables, Miss C. gave me an account of a like entertainment on the water, calculated the expense, and said that then also an infinite number of people had run from all parts to see it. I could not help being affected at these ideas, and saying, How insignificant are such diversions to me!

Why so? Were you once to see them, you would be of a different opinion. – The Lord Seymour continued all the time dull and silent. – No, my dear C. never shall I think otherwise, while I see, on the one hand, the pomp of the entertainment, the splendour of the court, the heaps of gold on these card-tables, and on the other a multitude of poor wretches with emaciated looks and threadbare clothes that bespeak their wretchedness: this contrast would fill my soul with melancholy and pity; it would make me hate my own exterior splendour, and that of others; the prince and his court would appear to me as a set of inhuman beings, who seem to take a pleasure in the infinite difference between them and those unfortunate people who come to contemplate their proud magnificence.

My dear child, what a severe lecture are you giving us! Forbear running to such extremes! said Miss C.

My dear friend, my heart is in a ferment! Yesterday the Countess of F. dwelt with such parade on the prince's diffusive liberality, and today how many miserable objects have I seen!

Here the young lady snatched my hand, and cried Hush! hush! – My Lord Seymour, fixing a serious look on me, lifted up his hands, saying, What a noble soul! What an excellent heart! You cannot, Miss C. love your friend too much. Yet princes are not to be censured. Very seldom is the real state of their subjects laid before them.

I am ready to believe it, answered I; but my lord, did not the people crowd the banks where the barges passed? Has not the prince eyes, that would, without any information, show him a thousand fit objects of his compassion? Why did he not feel for them?

Dearest miss, how glorious is your warmth! Yet show it only to your friend.

Here the Lord G. called his nephew; and, soon after, we returned home.

Today an extraordinary scene passed between my aunt and me. Though but just dressed, I was reading, when she came into the room. I am jealous of your books, said she: you have been up early, and are dressed, why then will you not let me have your company? You know how fond I am of it. Your uncle is continually taken up with his plaguy lawsuit, and poor I must begin to prepare for my lying-in; yet you can unkindly spend the whole morning in your dry morality. Bestow those hours on me, and give me your author for security.

I would very willingly, aunt, wait on you; but I cannot forsake my best friends.

Come, come along with me! this point we'll debate in my chamber.

I followed her. She seated herself at her *toilette*, and I had about a quarter of an hour's chat with her two sons, who are fine boys, and were admitted to see their mamma. But on their going away I sat like one that could not help it; saw the extravagant pains she took in dressing herself, and was surfeited with court news, the intrigues of ambition, scandal, and magnified ideas of my uncle's interest and grandeur. Be sure, added she, to carry it very respectfully to the Countess of F.; you may do your uncle great service, and at the same time procure something very handsome for yourself.

That, aunt, I neither comprehend nor wish; yet nothing that I can do for you shall be wanting.

My dear Sophy, thou art a charming girl! but I am vexed to my very heart, that the old parson has infected thee with so many of his pedantic notions. For God's sake get rid of some of them!

I am convinced, madam, that a court life does not suit my temper; my taste and inclinations run quite counter to it; and I must be so free as to declare, that I shall return with more pleasure than I came.

As yet you know nothing of the court: when the prince is here we are all alive; and then I shall hear what you think of it. In the mean time, conclude that you are not to return into the country before the next spring.

Oh! with submission, madam, I go with the Countess of R. when she returns, next autumn.

Am I then to be left alone during my lying-in?

So saying, she cast a very tender look on me, and holding out her hand, I kissed it, assuring her that I would not fail being with her when the time came.

Before dinner I went to my apartment, and walking up to my book-case, was surprised to find it quite empty. How comes this about, Rosina? The count has been here, and ordered everything to be removed. He said it was a frolic of the countess's.

A coarse kind of frolic, which they will never be the better for. I shall only write the more: but I'll not buy any new books, that she may not be offended at my obstinacy. Oh that my dear aunt R. would come soon! With what pleasure should I fly to her! She is peaceable, affectionate, and seeks in the beauties of nature, in science, and in the love of order, that satisfaction which is here eagerly pursued, but never found; and on that account they are perpetually finding fault with human life.

Miss C. has entered on her English lessons, and I believe will soon learn. She already knows many affectionate phrases and kind expressions, by which I know her instructor. She dined with us, when I merrily complained to my aunt of my being robbed of my books, and Miss C. sided with her. A good contrivance, said she; we shall now see what turn our friend's mind will take, when left to itself, without a guide. I joined in the laugh, saying, I am of the same opinion as a worthy man of letters, who says, 'Women's feelings are frequently more just than the reasonings of men.'* – I however obtained permission to work, on my observing that I could not bear to be perpetually sitting all the morning at the *toilette*, or playing and idling away all the afternoons; and I have begun a fine piece of embroidery, in which I propose using great diligence.

Tomorrow comes the prince, and with him the whole court. This evening came the foreign ministers. The Lord G. who was late in his visit, brought with him, besides the Lord Seymour, the Lord Derby, another English nobleman, introducing him as his cousin, who, from what he had heard him and Lord Seymour say, was very desirous of becoming acquainted with me, and the more as he found that I was half his countrywoman. Lord Derby immediately addressed me in English. He is a very handsome figure, has much wit, and an agreeable address. Being invited to supper, he cheerfully accepted the invitation, and as there would be moonlight, and the evening was fair, my aunt proposed our eating in the garden.

The saloon was instantly illuminated, and my aunt very lovingly said at the door, as she was going out with Lord G. Sophy, my dear, your lute, by moonlight, would add to the pleasure of the evening, and we should be obliged to you.

I ordered it to be brought. The Lord Derby gave me his hand; and Seymour went before with Miss C. The saloon being at the end of the garden, near the water-side, we had a considerable way to walk. Lord Derby's discourse turned in a very respectful manner on the many things he had heard of me. My uncle joined us, and when we were but a few steps above half-way, he gave me a gentle push, saying, Look! look! How warmly the demure Seymour can kiss a pretty hand by moonlight! I looked, and, O my dear Emilia! it seemed as if I felt a shivering. It doubtless proceeded from the coolness of the evening air, on our approaching the water: but a doubt

---

* A remark with which the editor, having had much occasion to observe its application both to himself and other men, can only agree wholeheartedly. – E.

arising in my mind, whether it might not also proceed from another cause, as I felt it only at that time, I could not help mentioning it to you.

Now likewise came the young Count F. the minister's nephew, who seeing the servant with the lute, asked who it was for, took it, and began thrumming at the saloon door, till my uncle looking to see who it was, saw him, and brought him in. Before we sat down to table, I was desired to play and sing. Not being in spirits, I sung, more from instinct than choice, a song on the quiet, freedom and delights of a country life. I myself felt the air too moving, and my aunt called to me, Child, you'll throw us all into the vapours. Why are you for proclaiming how you long to leave us? Let us have some other song! I obeyed with a pastoral taken from an opera, and it was very well received. My Lord G. asked me, whether I was not acquainted with English music. I said No, but that I would endeavour to follow if I heard anybody sing. Upon this the Lord Derby sang. He has a fine voice, but was rather too quick. I accompanied him with my lute, and received many compliments on my musical ear.

The Countess of F. said many kind things to me; Lord Seymour not a word; he often walked into the garden alone, and returned with looks that showed violent agitations of mind, speaking to none but Miss C, who appeared very pensive. Lord G. eyed me very attentively, with satisfaction in his countenance. Lord Derby viewed me with the flaming eyes of a hawk, in which were expressed inquietude. My uncle and aunt loaded me with caresses. In short, about eleven we withdrew to rest, and I seized that opportunity of writing this letter. Good night, dear Emilia! Desire our respectable father to pray for me. That thought imparts tranquillity and joy.

LETTER IV

Lady Sophia to Emilia

I wish my aunt would frequently take little journeys into the country; for I should accompany her with much more satisfaction than I do in the perpetual round of our court and town visits. My uncle has a half-sister in the convent of ladies at G. with whom, on account of her great fortune, he is desirous of keeping up a good correspondence for the sake of his children. For this reason my aunt took a journey to see her, accompanied by her two sons. She also took me with her, and thus gave me the pleasure, which I gratefully acknowledge, of contemplating various scenes of nature and art. Had it only been the sight of the rising and setting sun, this, at a distance from D. would alone have given me pleasure: but I saw more. The way we travelled lay through no inconsiderable space of German land, which had frequently a rude and sterile appearance, notwithstanding the toilsome and patient culture of the laborious inhabitants. Tender compassion, and grateful thanks for my being freed from excessive fatigue, filled my heart at beholding their rugged labour, while with grave but resigned looks they viewed our splendid chaises. The respect with which they saluted us, as the favourites of Providence, had something in it that affected me; and I endeavoured to contract an humane fellowship with them, by means of some pieces of money which I tossed, unasked, to the nearest: particularly I gave to some poor women, who, while they were at work, had here and there a child sitting on the ground. My aunt, thought I, is on a journey, in hopes of reaping advantage for her sons, and these poor women undergo a deal of toil and trouble for theirs: I will be the means of their receiving an unexpected advantage.

The servant who rode after us, told us how rejoiced these poor people were, and that they called down blessings on us.

Rich fields, well fed cattle, and the large barns of the peasants, in other places showed the happiness of their situation, and I wished they would make a good use of these blessings. My sensations, as usual, were very agreeable at the first sight of these marks of happiness, till gradually entering into myself, I drew a comparison between their peace and tranquillity, and my own severer lot.

By the way we called in at Count W.'s seat, which I cannot forbear describing. It stands on the top of a hill, and has a very extensive prospect of a fine country, diversified with fields, meadows, and rich farms. Through the valley, in the front, flows a river that abounds with fish, and the adjacent eminences are crowned with woods. The hill on which the house is seated is laid out in gardens and walks, according to the refined taste of the former owner, who endeavoured to unite the agreeable and the useful.

This, with the nobleman's hospitality, his choice library, his set of instruments for experimental philosophy, the excellent economy of the house (equally remote from prodigality and penuriousness), the appointment of a physician for the whole manor, the support during life granted to all the good and faithful domestics, the abilities and probity of the officers of the household, with many prudent regulations for the good of the tenants, are so many shining monuments of the taste, abilities, humane views, and noble disposition of the late proprietor,[20] who, after filling with the highest reputation several important posts at a foreign court, closed his valuable life in this delightful recess. His heir seems to have inherited, with his estate, his affability and goodness, so that to his house the worthiest persons in the neighbourhood resort. During the six days we spent there, our playing at cards gave me an idea which I should have been very glad to have heard discussed by Mr. Br———.[21] Many strangers being come, card-tables were necessarily provided for their entertainment, as of twenty persons, many were of different geniuses and dispositions, as evidently appeared at dinner, and in our walks, where everyone, according to his own humour and ideas, discoursed of the objects that presented themselves; some frequently running counter not only to the finer sentiments of virtue, but to the plain duties of humanity: yet while at play, one soul seemed to reign in all, for all acquiesced in the known laws of the game without the least murmur or contradiction; nor was anyone affronted at being reminded that he transgressed the rules, but owned his fault, and, agreeably to the dictates of one more expert, strove not to relapse.

I could not help wondering, and admiring the contrivance of play, as a kind of spell which instantly knits together for several hours, in a pleasing intercourse, persons of different nations, that cannot exchange a single word, and of no less different characters and dispositions; when, without this expedient, it would have been next to impossible to have hit on any amusement so agreeable to the general taste. I cannot help dwelling on the thought. How is it that a person learns games of several kinds, and is so studious to avoid deviating from the laws of play, that nothing which passes in the room can make him forget himself; when, a quarter of an hour before, nothing could restrain him from speaking in opposition to the laws of decency and virtue? One of the company, who played extremely well, yet, with a smiling countenance, seemed perfectly unconcerned while he lost his money, had a little before, on a question concerning tenants, spoke of them as if they had been so many hounds, and cruelly advised a young nobleman, just come to the possession of his estate, to keep them in the utmost subjection, and not to fail, on any consideration, to make them clear their accounts once a year.

Why, said my heart, why is man more inclined to submit to the merely arbitrary laws formed by the inventer of a game, than to the plain and salutary duties prescribed by the most wise and gracious Legislator, with a view of rendering him happy? And why is it not permitted to put him in mind that he transgresses those duties? These thoughts I did not dare to reveal to my aunt, as she has on other occasions, with some asperity, censured my morals as too austere and strait-laced; and which, as she said, set me at variance with all the recreations of life. I cannot conceive why this is laid to my charge. I can be cheerful; I love company, music, and even dancing; but offences against humanity and decency I cannot bear, without showing my disapprobation; and it is impossible for me to find entertainment in mere spiritless chat, without either wit or sentiment, and in idly spending whole days in talking on the most frivolous subjects.

Oh that I could find in our great assemblies, or among the friends of our family at D. one person like the canoness I have been to visit, I should not then be taxed with being of a too reserved and gloomy disposition! That candid lady informed me that she had conceived an esteem for me, and, though a stranger, the treatment I received from her greatly exceeded that of a cold politeness. As I had the happiness to continue to please her, it procured me the benefit of a thorough acquaintance with her many excellencies. Never did I find such strength and elevation of mind as in this lady. Her genius and agreeable flow of wit qualify her for the best company. She is eminently possessed of an uncommon happiness of expression in whatever she says and writes, and all her thoughts may be compared to beautiful figures clothed by the Graces in easy and flowing robes. Whether she was serious, cheerful, or friendly, I was charmed with the justness of her thoughts, and the natural unaltered amiableness of her disposition. A mind filled with just sentiments, and warm feelings of whatever has real beauty and goodness, with a heart formed for the generous reciprocations of friendship, complete her amiable character.

It is only for the sake of this lady that I have wished, for the first time, that I was of an ancient noble family, to entitle me to a place in that protestant convent, that I might spend my whole life in her valuable company, where I am persuaded all the inconveniencies of a cloistered life would scarce be felt.[22]

Judge yourself, how nearly it went to my heart to leave this amiable lady, though she had the goodness, in some measure, to make up the loss of her delightful conversation, by the favour of promising me her correspondence. You shall see her letters, and then you will be convinced that I have said no more of her abilities than they deserve.

The modesty which forms a striking lineament in the character of her friend the Countess of G. shall not hinder me, as she will never see this letter, from saying, that it was this excellent lady who, next to the former, had the greatest share in the wish that it was possible for me to pass my life in that happy retreat. A sequestered merit, the more engaging, from its avoiding notice and parade; a refined genius, enriched with great knowledge and eloquence, and united with the most candid sincerity and goodness of heart, entitle this lady to the esteem and friendship of every noble mind: even the thick veil, under which her too great modesty concealed her pre-eminence, exalted her in my eye. She scarce ever lays this veil aside, except in the chamber of the Countess of S. whose approbation seems to have rendered her indifferent with respect to the commendations of anyone else. Enchanting as her skill on the harpsichord is, the only value she sets upon it is, that it pleases her friend.

Among the other worthy ladies of this convent, I cannot omit the Countess of T.W. who consecrates her days to the active virtues, and employs her talent, in instructing girls who have no fortune in all kinds of ingenious works becoming our sex. – Particularly, with a most affectionate respect, let me remember the princess who is at the head of this convent. Was anything capable of exciting my envy, it would be the real, the inestimable felicity of passing through life under the guidance of the experienced virtue and prudence of such an excellent, such a tender governess.

As for my aunt's chief view in this journey, I shall only observe, that it has

turned out entirely to her wish. We are now returned to D. and to the
multitude of visits which we have had to pay and receive, you will kindly
attribute the blame of your having been so long without a line from me.

LETTER V

Lord Seymour to Dr T.

Dear friend,
I have frequently heard you say, that from the observations you made, in
your travels through Germany, on the natural genius of that nation, you
wished to see united the profundity of our philosophers with the methodical
manner of the Germans, and that their phlegmatic temper had more of our
lively imagination. Hence you have for a long time endeavoured to temper,
by a happy mixture, my natural ardour, considering it as the only obstacle
which, notwithstanding my taste for the sciences, prevented my arriving at a
certain degree of perfection. You took none but the mildest methods with
me, and knowing my sensibility, imagined that you ought to govern my head
by my heart. How far you, my worthy friend, have succeeded in this, I
cannot determine; but you have brought me to know, and, I hope I may say,
to love real goodness. I would die rather than do anything base, or beneath a
man of humanity; yet I question whether you will be satisfied with me,
when you know with what impatience I bear my uncle's authority. It seems
as if my soul was bowed down under the weight of a triple yoke, which
constrains all its exertions, when I consider my Lord G. as my uncle, as a
man of great wealth to whom I am heir, and as a minister on whom the post
I fill renders me dependent. Do not, however, be under any apprehensions
that I shall forget myself so far as to quarrel with his lordship: I have so
much power over my emotions, that they only discover themselves by a
melancholy, which I endeavour to conceal or divert. But why do I use such a
multitude of words in preparing you for the subject of this letter, which is
to inform you, that I have seen a young lady in whom the two national
characters are most happily blended. Her grandmother, on the female side,
was daughter to Sir William Watson, and her father a person of the most
eminent merit, whose memory is still held in the highest veneration. This
young lady is intimate with Miss C. whom I mentioned in a former letter;
and it is but a few weeks since the lady, Sophia Sternheim, first came here,
she having before lived entirely in the country. I forbear making rapturous
exclamations on her transcendent charms; but believe me, I do not exceed

the truth in saying, that all the graces, of which the figure and motions of a female are capable, are united in her: a courteous gravity of countenance, a politeness full of dignity, an unreserved affection for her friend, a goodness perfectly adorable, and the most refined delicacy in her sentiments, are only what she inherits from her excellent English grandmother.* She has a mind free from prejudices, adorned with knowledge, and filled with the best principles; a noble firmness of showing these principles, and in maintaining them; in short, many talents joined to the most amiable modesty: all this she owes to the worthy man who had the happiness of being her father. From this description, dear Doctor, you may guess what an impression she has made on me. Never, no never, was my heart so filled with love, nor with the happiness we feel in loving! – But what will you say, when you hear that this lovely maid, with all her fine qualities, is intended to be the prince's mistress? That my lord has forbidden my mentioning my love to her, because Count F. one of the authors of this project, already apprehends many obstacles on her part, though it is very certain that she was brought to court only with that view? I expressed to my uncle the utmost indignation at Count Löbau, her uncle, having entertained so base a thought. I would have informed the dear lady of the execrable plot formed against her; I even begged his Lordship's leave to marry her, and thus save from ruin so lovely and excellent a creature. He bade me quietly attend to what he had to say, told me that he himself had a great value for the young lady, and was persuaded that she would frustrate the whole scene of iniquity; assuring me, that if she acted agreeably to her fine character, he should with pleasure crown her virtue. 'But while', added he, 'the whole court looks upon her as the destined mistress of the prince, I cannot consent to your taking any step in this affair. You ought not to marry a woman whose reputation is in the least suspected. Attach yourself to Miss C. By her you will be informed of the dispositions of her friend; and I will give her an account of the vile scheme with which Count F. is entrusted. I have good hopes, from the young lady's character, that this will end in an illustrious triumph of virtue; but it must be visible to the eyes of the world.'

My uncle excited in me the desire of seeing the prince mortified. I represented to myself Sophia's resistance and triumph, as a ravishing sight, and that thought determined me to follow his directions. My Lord Derby had also given me another motive for doing it: he, on seeing her, was immediately fired with her charms (for I cannot call it love) and has been before-hand with me in owning his tenderness. If he be able to move her,

---

* I have, in the preface, already described our heroine's slight bias towards the English nation as a blemish which I would have removed from this excellent work, had it been possible to do so without too many alterations. – For if we are to credit the wisest of the English writers, a lady of so beauteous a disposition as Sophia Sternheim is as rare in England as in Germany. However, the sentiments expressed in this passage are those of a young Englishman, whom we might expect to be prejudiced in favour of his own country, as well as those of the enthusiast, who must occasionally be allowed to hold unreasonable opinions. – E.

there is an end to my happiness. Yes, it would be nearly the same as if she gave herself up to the prince; for if she can love an abandoned libertine, she would certainly never love me. Meanwhile, how dreadful is my situation! I love the most worthy object, whom I unfortunately see everywhere hemmed in by the snares of vice. I am agitated by turns, by my hopes founded on her virtuous principles, and by the apprehension of her being lost by the power of human frailty. Today, my friend, today she is, for the first time, to be exposed to the prince's eye, at an opera at court. I am something indisposed, but I will go, though it should cost me my life.

*   *   *

I am all alive, my friend! Count F. is in doubt whether anything can be done with this virtuous young lady.

My lord ordered me to keep near him during the opera. Sophia and her worthless aunt came into Lady F.'s box. She was so ravishingly lovely, that I could not contemplate her without a mixture of pain; but the moment in which I bowed to the three ladies, at the same time with my lord, was the only look I ventured to take. Soon after flocked in all the other nobility, and the prince himself, whose libidinous eyes were instantly turned to Lady F.'s box. The young lady paid her respects with such a grace as must have attracted his notice, had she no other charms. He directed his discourse to Count F. and looking again at Sophia, bowed particularly to her. All eyes were now fixed on her: but she soon after partly hid herself behind Lady F. The opera began, during which the prince talked much with Count F. who at length removed to his lady's box, to reprove my lord and the two countesses for depriving miss of her place, though they had often been at the opera, and she was never there before.

It is not on the ladies account, said the young lady gravely to the minister, that I have chosen this place. I here see well enough, with the additional satisfaction of being less *seen*.

But you deprive so many of the pleasure of seeing you. – She answered only with an inclination of her body, as an intimation of the little value she set on his compliment. He asked her opinion of the opera, to which she answered, in a manner peculiar to herself, that she did not wonder at so many persons being fond of that entertainment.

But I desired to know how *you* like it. Tell me what you think of it! You look very grave.

I admire the assemblage of so many arts and talents.

And is that all? Are you not charmed with the heroes and heroines of the piece?

No, not in the least, answered she with a smile.

The prince, the envoys, and other strangers, among whom was Count Löbau, uncle to Sophia, supped at the Princess of W.'s. The Countess of F. presented that young lady with much ceremony to the prince, who for a long time affected to talk very highly of her father; but she was very brief in her answers, and her accent expressed uneasiness. At the table, a gentleman and lady were placed in regular order. Count F. a nephew of the minister's, sat next to Sophia, and she was placed opposite to the prince, who perpetually kept his eyes on her. I was upon my guard, and seldom looked at the dear lady, yet could perceive her something discomposed. The table was removed to make way for play, when the princess, taking miss with her, walked round the card-tables, and then seating herself on a sofa, entered into an affable and kind conversation with her; and the prince, after playing some time with my lord, joined them.

Two days after Count F. said to my uncle, I wish Count Löbau hanged for bringing this lady hither. She is every way formed to inspire love; but a young woman who derives no vanity from her charms, who at an opera minds nothing but the assemblage of so many arts and talents, at a luxurious table eats nothing but an apple and drinks nothing but water, who at court only sighs after the country, yet plainly wants neither wit nor sentiment, is a *rara avis*,[23] and not easily overcome.

Heavens grant it! thought I; for my present distracted situation is more than I can support.

Write to me soon! Tell me what you think of me, and what you would have me do!

LETTER VI

Lady Sophia to Emilia

O my Emilia! how do I want the reviving comfort of a tender and virtuous friend! Alas! it was an unfortunate day when I was persuaded to set out for D. It has drawn me out of the sphere in which I was moving with such sweet serenity and content. I am here of no use to anyone, and least of all to myself. My best thoughts and sensations I dare not disclose, I being already looked upon as *ridiculously serious*; and whatever pains I take to show complaisance to those among whom I live, whatever endeavours I use to adopt their language, seldom is my aunt pleased with me, and as seldom am I pleased with her. If I know myself, I am neither opiniated nor conceited. I do not desire anyone here to think like me, which I am persuaded is impossible. I take no offence that the morning is passed at the *toilette*, the afternoon in visits, the evening and night at play. This is the grand world, and such is here the established method of passing through life. My former wonder at seeing one who had lived with my grandmother so deficient in the most valuable kinds of learning, though far from wanting capacity, is greatly abated; for, my dear friend, it is quite impossible for a young person to acquire them, while carried away by the whirlwind of tumultuous diversions. In short, all here appear to adopt the reigning ideas, and the fashionable mode of life, with as much pleasure as I feel in conforming to the principles which instruction and the dearest examples have planted in my heart. My ideas and opinions are not relished: I must adopt their thoughts and sensations, pride myself in the elegance and richness of my dress, place my happiness in being admired, and be enraptured at an entertainment or a ball. The opera, which was the first I had ever seen, should have transported me out of my senses, and made me think myself in heaven; and I should have been no less enraptured by the prince's compliments. During the performance, somebody or other was perpetually saying, Now, miss, are you not highly pleased? How do you like it?

Pretty well, answered I, quite soberly: it perfectly comes up to the idea I had conceived of such exhibitions. This quite displeased, and I was looked upon as one who knew not what she said. Possibly my little inclination for such entertainments may proceed from a want of sensibility, though I rather think it an effect of the impression made on me by a very animated description of them I have read in an English author, who exclaims, What a ridiculous and unnatural figure does a general make singing on the field of battle? and an enamoured heroine warbling away her last breath?[24] I would not, however, censure those who are fond of this entertainment with having a bad taste. The combination of so many arts employed to gratify the eye and ear, is very pleasing, and nothing seems to me more natural than the passions being moved by an actress or a dancer. If the first plays with skill, if she enters entirely into the spirit of her part, if she expresses the tender, the noble sentiments that flow from a full soul; if, at the same time, she has beauty, and this is joined to a splendid dress, soft music, and all the various illusions of the theatre, it must be difficult for a young man, who with a feeling heart enters the theatre, to resist the united efforts of nature and art to seduce him.

The female dancer, surrounded with the laughing graces, has attractions in every motion – indeed, Emilia, who can wonder if she raises the passions! Yet I think the lover of the actress less inexcusable than that of the dancer. I have somewhere read that the line of beauty is nicely drawn for the painter and sculptor; if he goes beyond it he is lost, and if he does not reach it, so far his work falls short of perfection. So the line of moral beauty for the dancer seems to me to be no less exactly drawn, but she often steps over it.

Upon the whole, I am very well pleased at having seen one of these entertainments, which perfectly agrees with the idea I had formed of them; but very easy shall I be if I never see another.

After the opera I supped with the Princess of W. where I was presented to the prince. What shall I say of him? He is indeed a handsome man, and is very polite; he was profuse in the praises he bestowed on my father, and those praises did not please me. – No, my dear Emilia, I no longer felt the joy of hearing encomiums bestowed on him. The voice with which they were spoken sounded as if he had said, I know how conceited you are of your father, and therefore I will praise him. And then, my dear, the looks the prince cast at me, would have spoilt all the best things he could have said. – Such looks, my dear! God preserve me from ever seeing them again! – How I abhor that Spanish dress, which allowed me nothing but a tippet.[25] Oh! if ever I was proud of dress, I yesterday suffered a severe penance for it. I cannot express the anguish of my soul, at being the object of such odious looks. It signifies nothing talking; I cannot bear to be here any longer! I will hasten to you, Emilia, and the remains of my honoured parents. Lady R. too delays her coming.

Today the Countess of F. told me, with a tedious multiplicity of words, how the prince praised my person and wit.

Tomorrow the count gives a splendid dinner, and I am to be there. Never since I have been here have I enjoyed the solace of festivity, according to my own taste. The friendship of Miss C. was the only thing in which I rejoiced; but that is not what it was. She speaks to me with such coldness; she never visits me, and I am never her partner at play. If I come up to her or Lord Seymour, who are always together, they drop their discourse, and my lord, with a dejected look, retires, while miss, filled with confusion, still keeps her eye on him. What am I to think? Would not Miss C. have me speak to my lord? Does he withdraw to show his entire submission? Then he speaks to no other soul but her. Oh, what a stranger is my heart here! I, who am ready to sacrifice my happiness to that of others, have the vexation to see that they apprehend my being an obstacle to theirs. Dear Miss C. I will dissipate your fears! I will forbid my eyes the pleasure of looking at my Lord Seymour – and yet my looks were only fleeting. No more will I intrude when she is happy in the conversation of that amiable man – You shall see that your Sophia is far from seeking to rob you of his heart. At this thought, Emilia, my eyes are filled with tears: but the loss of a beloved friend, the only one I had here, the loss of the conversation of a worthy man whom I esteem, deserve a tear. No other will I shed at D. Would to heaven that I was to leave it tomorrow.

Why does your letter tell me nothing of my guardian, nothing of your journey, nothing of your husband? Pray repair this instance of your forget-fulness, as your letters, your love and affection, are all the blessings I have to expect.

LETTER VII

Lord Derby to his friend at Paris

Soon will I silence thy insipid prate; and indeed my bearing it so long was only to see what lengths thou wouldst run in boasting and vapouring even to thy master's face.[26] This very day shouldst thou feel the lash of my satire, had I not a mind to show the plan of a German novel, the completing of which takes up all my thoughts. What signifies thy Parisian conquests, purchased by the help of gold? For without that, what couldst thou do with even a French woman, with thy long face and spindle shanks? Besides, what are the conquests of your right honourables at Paris? A coquette, an actress; both allowed to be pretty, but so common that none but an ass would glory in their favours. Pray, loving countryman, have not I been there too, and don't I know, as certainly as such a thing can be known, that the well-bred daughter of a creditable family, and the good wife, distinguished by her wit and merit, are not the females within our reach? Therefore boast no more, good B. for such triumphs little deserve any *Io Peans*.[27] But to get possesssion of a masterpiece of nature and art, that has been consecrated to the gods; to lay asleep an Argus[28] of prudence and virtue; to deceive ministers of state; to baffle all the deep machinations of a beloved rival, without his being aware of the hand that works his confusion; this, this deserves notice.

Thou knowest that I never allowed love any power except over my senses, whose purest and choicest pleasure it is. Hence the choice of my eyes was always certain, and my objects continually varying. I have progressively subdued beauties of every class, and, satiated with the charms of the fair, have reduced ugliness under my slavery; after which I have reigned over different minds, and rendered all characters subject to my law. What a fine field for observation would it be for the moralist, did he but know all the subtile snares, all the nets artfully formed, with which I have caught the virtue, the pride, the discretion, the coquetry, and even the piety of the female world; so that, with Solomon, I have thought that to me there was nothing new under the sun.[29] But love, who laughs at my vanity, has brought hither from a country cottage a colonel's daughter, a paragon of beauty, whose figure, genius and character, are so new and alluring, that, should she escape me, it would be a blot on my escutcheon as a man of intrigue. But I must keep a good look-out; Seymour is in love with her, but can't move a step without my Lord G. while this rose is destined for the bosom of the prince, in order to get a law-suit determined in favour of her uncle. Count F.'s son, as a cloak, is willing to marry her; but if she loves him, he will marry her in earnest, and overset Count Löbau's and his father's designs. That pitiful scoundrel shall not have her; no, nor Seymour, who, with his melancholy love, waits for the triumph of her virtue; no, nor the prince himself – he is most unworthy of her. So fine a flower must be cropped by none but me; that is as fixed as fate. I have raised the posse of all my contrivances to find her weak side. She is full of sensibility, which I know from the looks she frequently casts on Seymour, while even I am talking to her. She is likewise frank and sincere; for she told me to my face, that she suspected my heart wanted goodness. Why, said I, do you think the Lord Seymour better than I? She blushed, and answered, He undoubtedly is. Though these words filled me with raging jealousy, they at the same time showed me the way to her heart. I am now reduced to a troublesome dissimulation, to bring my character to a unison with hers. But a time will come when this shall be reversed; I shall make hers buckle to mine: for with her I will grudge no pains, and certainly she will make new discoveries in the land of delight, when her pure and refined soul shall bend all its faculties that way. But praising her graces and accomplishments does not in the least move her; a certain sign that her heart is already engaged. An uncommonly sublime genius, and a noble soul, seem in the highest degree united in her; and in her person, all the charms of an enchanting figure are joined, with a singular lustre, to that gravity which naturally accompanies elevated principles. Every motion, the mere sound of her voice, begets love; and a look from her eyes seems to force us to silence, so much do they discover of the purity of her spotless soul. – But hold! How the deuce came I by all this foolish babble! – Shall this country girl make a sighing coxcomb of me? Yes, so far as to answer my purpose; but, by jove, she shall dearly pay for it. I have brought over to my side my Lord G.'s under-secretary, and that rogue is half a devil.[30] He has studied divinity, but his debaucheries have occasioned his being stripped of his gown, and obliged him to lay aside all thoughts of being one of the clergy, and since that time he has endeavoured to be revenged on all the pious. Through him I'll sift Lord Seymour, whom he can't endure on account of his morals. Thou seest that the parson has undergone a strange metamorphosis; but, as I cannot here act myself, I have need of a fellow of his shame.

So much for this time. Somebody is coming in.

LETTER VIII

Lady Sophia to Emilia

My troubles are now more than I can bear. My guardian dead! Why did not you write to Rosina or me, before all was over? Poor Rosina is in the deepest affliction, and I endeavour to comfort her, with a heart little less affected than her own. Now, my dear friend, the earth covers the richest presents heaven has given us, our good, our worthy parents. – No heart is so sensible of the greatness of your loss, as mine. I doubly feel your pain. Why was not I to hear his last blessing? Why were not my tears to moisten his holy grave? I am sure I have all the filial affection, the respect, the grief of a daughter. – Poor Rosina! she kneels by me, with her head resting on my lap, and her eyes shedding a torrent of tears. I embrace and weep with her. God grant that our grief may make wisdom flourish in our souls, and thus accomplish the last wishes of our fathers! May heaven also grant the prayers which my guardian offered up for my Emilia, when his trembling hand blessed your marriage, and committed you to the care of a faithful friend! May virtue and friendship be Rosina's portion and mine, till the laws of mortality successively remove us to a state of happiness! Then may some noble heart love me for setting a pattern of goodness that had influenced her conduct, and some poor, relieved by my hand, bless my memory! Then will the wise, then will the friend of mankind say, that I knew the value of life.

I am unable to proceed, nor can Rosina for me. She recommends herself to the love of her brother and sister, and will continue to live with me. I hope you are not displeased, as it will strengthen the band of our friendship, and reciprocations of benevolence will preserve it from abatement. I embrace my Emilia with tears. You cannot imagine how dreadful it is to close my letter without a respectful word to my guardian, who was indeed my paternal friend. Eternal happiness is his reward and that of my father! Let us, my Emilia, my Rosina, so live, that having imitated their virtue and friendship, we may be admitted to partake of their felicity!.

LETTER IX

Lord Seymour to Dr T.

Sophia, I think, grows every day more charming – I, every day more wretched. The prince and Derby strive to gain her esteem, which both see is the only way to her heart. This the twofold caprice which my passion has adopted, prevents my doing. I am wholly taken up with observing her, while she shuns both Miss C. and me. I now no longer hear her speak, but everything that is said of her by Derby, for whom she shows some regard, confirms the high opinion I have of her soul; since the first emotions of virtue ever felt in his heart, I am persuaded, owe their origin to her. He told me the other day, that going into her chamber, in order to wait on her to an assembly, he found her chambermaid on her knees before her; Sophia herself but half dressed; her fine hair hanging dishevilled over her neck and breast, her arms locked round the girl, and, in a most pathetic voice, speaking to her on the happy death of the righteous, and the future rewards of virtue. Tears streamed from her eyes; but soon she raised them to heaven, blessing the memory of her father, and of some other man, for planting those joyful truths in her mind. He stood amazed, when she instantly seeing him, called out, O, my lord, your conversation will not suit me at present! Be so good as to go and excuse me to my aunt: tell her I can see nobody today! Her solemn and affecting countenance embittered her reproof, and made him more keenly feel her contempt for his way of thinking. He accordingly answered, that could she see the respect which at that instant glowed in his breast; she would not think him totally unworthy of her confidence. But seeing that, instead of returning him an answer, she reclined her head on that of her chambermaid, he took his leave, and was informed by the Countess of Löbau, that this scene was occasioned by the death of the minister of P. who had a share in her education, and was her chambermaid's father; but Count Löbau and his spouse were not a little pleased that the enthusiastic correspondence, as they termed it, between him and Sophia, was at an end, as she might now be brought to embrace ideas more suitable to her birth and station. They both went along with him to their niece's chamber, blamed her grief, and censured her for declining to go to the assembly. Dear aunt, she replied, after sacrificing so many weeks to the compliance I owe you, and to the manners of the court, surely the duties of friendship and virtue may claim one poor day! Yes, returned the Countess, but your love has ever been confined within *one* family, and you are not duly sensible of the esteem and affection shown you here. Dear aunt, she replied, I am sorry to be accused of ingratitude but surely he who has filled my mind with good principles, and useful literature, deserves a greater share of gratitude from me, than the polite stranger who obliges me to share in his transient diversions. This the countess took to herself, and after some ill-natured sneers, told her, that since it was her humour, she might stay at home that day.

This account Derby gave me with an air of levity, yet had an eye to all my emotions, which, you know, I am not skilful in concealing, and in this case it was beyond the power of man. I was extremely moved at Lady Sophia's behaviour. I envied Derby's happiness in having seen and spoke to her; and the bitterness of my displeasure against him, the prince, my uncle, and even myself, carried me so far as to say, Sophia is a most lovely young lady. Such virtue! such a mind! Curse on the wretch who has any bad designs against her! You, said he, are as extraordinary in your way as she is in hers. You seem made to be her lover, and I to be your confidant and historian. No, my lord, said I, I believe that neither Sophia nor I would have made you any such offer. At this answer he wore a kind of horrid pensive smile, at which I could not help saying to myself, So looks Satan when bent on mischief.

LETTER X

Lady Sophia to Emilia

Your long silence, my friend, gave both Rosina and me no little inquietude, yet the only revenge I will allow myself is, that the next journey I take of any length, I will write to you when it is half over; for as I know your love to me, I could not bear the thought of giving your gentle soul that concern which mine has, on this occasion, felt for you. But your happy arrival at W. and your agreeable prospect of futurity, made me ample amends. At the same time, my Emilia, I am rejoiced at having an agreeable subject for some letters to you; for had I been obliged to go on with my complaints of disagreeable events, I should have trespassed on your repose; so tenderly does your affectionate heart interest itself in whatever concerns me, or affects my sensibility, which I own is rather too quick. In this country, so barren of moral entertainment, I have met with two resources and an interesting discovery which prevents my considering the time as lost during the three months I have been here. You know that the education I have received has turned my taste not to pompous and frivolous pleasures, but to such as are plain and useful. Never was my mother's sensibility so much excited as at the relation of a noble and generous action; or at hearing an instance of humanity, or some other virtue; and never did she embrace and clasp me with such ardour to her bosom, as when I undertook a kind office for an acquaintance, a servant, or a poor tenant. Often have I observed that when, as is usual with children, I have happened to make some just remark, or to say something witty and sensible, she has only given a faint smile, and immediately endeavoured to turn the attention, and the praises the company bestowed on me, to things relating to active life, commending my application to the study of languages, my progress in drawing or music, and more particularly my having sollicited favours, or performed acts of kindness for others; thus intimating to me, that *good actions* are far preferable to the most *ingenious thoughts*. How agreeably did my father illustrate this truth, by observing to me, from the vegetable kingdom, that the several kinds of flowers which only exhibit entertainment to the eye, are neither so numerous, nor so fruitful as the plants of real use, that afford food for man and beast.* Every day of his life corresponded with this maxim. How studious was he to render his genius and knowledge of use to all with whom he was acquainted? His acts of kindness to his servants and inferiors can scarce be numbered. Under his guidance, Emilia, and with such principles and inclinations did I enter the gay world, where the general way of life is solely calculated to flatter the senses, and where a superior genius is allowed to show itself only in momentary flashes of wit and smart repartees.

My former ideas, thus planted, have not however entirely left me, and I never observe them more busy, than when I am filled with displeasure at opposite sentiments and proceedings. You yourself shall be judge. My love of Germany engaged me the other day in a dispute, in which I vindicated the honour of my country with such zeal, that my aunt exclaimed, that I had given a fine proof of my being a professor's grand-daughter. This censure nettled me; the ashes both of my father and grand-father were violated, my self-love was wounded by the contempt thrown on them, and I instantly answered, That I had rather my dispositions should prove me descended from persons of a noble way of thinking, than that only some fine sounding name should cause me to be thought of an illustrious lineage. This occasioned a coldness between us for some days; however we insensibly became reconciled. My aunt, proud of her noble blood, was, I believe, sensible that it was being too severe to reproach anyone with a defective ancestry; and I was displeased at my spiteful answer, which degraded me in my own eyes. But it is time for me to lead you to one of the resources I have mentioned at the beginning of this letter.

* It can hardly be claimed that there are species of flowers and plants that 'merely exhibit entertainment to the eye'. Moreover, there exists, to my knowledge, no species that is not either economically or medicinally beneficial to mankind, or essential to the sustenance of some animal, bird, insect, or reptile; no species, in brief, that does not fulfil a purpose within the total design of our planet. – E.

I discovered the first, in the visits I received and paid with my aunt, which have afforded me an opportunity of making a multitude of observations on an infinite diversity of tempers, dispositions and characters, a diversity that appears in the things related, in the judgment passed upon others, and in wishes and complaints. At the same time what a circle of trifles are run through! and how eagerly do people endeavour to get rid of a day! Accustomed to prize things according to their real value, I cannot see without grief and pity, that thirst of pleasure, that taste for dress which reigns here. I omit that false ambition which plots base intrigues, meanly crouches at the foot of fortune, despises virtue and merit, and without remorse renders others wretched. – How happy are you, my friend! Neither your birth nor circumstances have warped you aside from the moral line prescribed for us. You can, without apprehension, without obstruction, proceed in an uniform course of virtue, intermixed with the most valuable, the most useful accomplishments, and in the day of your health, in the season of active life, do all that good which most of the great world, in their last hours, ardently wish that they had done.

Religion and virtue are however treated with a show of respect, the churches frequented by the court are finely ornamented; great orators preach there; divine service is performed with solemnity and decent attendance. Loftiness of words and proper actions are carefully observed: no vice must appear without a mask. Nay the christian duty of love to our neighbour is in some measure considered as a present, which from a delicate and refined flattery, the self-love of one pays to that of another. Now all this is to me a copious source of moral reflections, so far useful, as it confirms the principles of my education. Often do I employ my imagination on the means of uniting the duties to which a court lady is called by her rank, with the duties that are the foundation of our eternal happiness. I have a faint view of the possibility of their being united: but it is so difficult to make them always consistent with each other, that I am not surprised at seeing that few make the attempt. How often have I thought that if a person like my father had the post of prime minister he would be the most beloved, the most happy man in the universe.

'Tis true, his days would be attended with care and fatigue; yet the consideration of the extensive sphere of action it would afford his abilities and his benevolence, in promoting the welfare of many thousands, both living and yet unborn; this animating prospect to a pious and good mind, would render everything light and agreeable. His knowledge of the human heart would make him find the most proper means of gaining the confidence of the prince; while his probity, his natural superiority and strength of mind would give such support to his authority, that the courtiers and placemen would be as ready to show their obedience to the able and virtuous minister, as they too often are to the weakness of the head and the vices of the heart in him from whom they expect favours and preferment. Thus my Emilia do I frequently amuse myself, since my being acquainted with the character and circumstances in which this or that person is found. My imagination places me in the rank of those I judge: I compare the obligations imposed on all men by the great Creator, with the power and means he has given of fulfilling them: I think what they are, and what they ought to be. Thus have I been by turns a prince, a princess, a favourite, a minister, the mother of such children, the wife of such a husband, and in each situation have found different ways of doing good, by following the rules dictated by prudence. I have discovered among many persons such just ideas, and such laudauble actions, that I have heartily acknowledged their superiority; while in comparing myself with others, I have been more satisfied with the dictates of my own head and heart than with theirs. After these ideal excursions fancy has naturally led me to a retrospect on myself, and the duties assigned *me*, and I have resolved to be no less strict in that enquiry than I have been with respect to others; and thus, Emilia, have I discovered a source of reflections on *myself*, for more deeply engraving on my heart, knowledge, sentiment, and a conviction of what is good; but at the same time I am more and more convinced how much a great observer of human actions was in the right in asserting, that very few duly exert all their physical and moral strength: for indeed I have found many void spaces within the circle of my life, and others filled with what I disapprove, or with trifles of no use. This shall now be remedied, and as I am not one of those happy beings who enter into life complete in soul and body, I will enlist among the people who are grown wise by observing the faults of others, that my lot may not be among those who can only be reformed by their experience and their sufferings.

LETTER XI

Lady Sophia to Emilia

You are indeed a real friend, and most sincerely do I thank you for sending me back to that part of my education which led me to put myself in the place of those I was inclined to censure; not only for the sake of seeing how I would have behaved in their situation, but to acquire that humane disposition which is so just and reasonable, of not branding everything as base and wicked, that contradicts my principles, or crosses my inclinations. What prompted you to this was, it seems, your thinking my dislike to the courtiers too hasty, too severe, and, as you intimate, bordering on injustice. I have followed your kind advice, and have seen the court in a new point of

view, that has moderated the disadvantageous impression I had entertained
of it. I say to myself, that as in the material world every species of beings has
its appointed circle, within which those beings find everything necessary to
their perfection; perhaps also in the moral world, a court may be the only
sphere in which the perfection of certain faculties, both of soul and body
can be unfolded: for example, the highest degree of refinement and perfection in the taste, with respect to whatever affects the senses and depends on
the imagination. The court is also the most proper stage for showing the
extreme subtleness of which the mind and body are capable; a quality which
is perceived in the manners, in the delicacy of expressions, in the happy turn
given to thoughts; and, what is more, in the conduct according to which
politics, fortune or ambition, agitate, in some degree or other, the air we
breathe there. The fine arts are there not only brought to perfection, but the
manners and the language are polished where the graces reside. These are
important advantages that contribute to the happiness of the human race.
We admire in the vegetable and animal kingdoms the traces of elegance and
beauty in shape, symetry, and mixture of colours; even the most rude and
savage nations are not without ideas of beauty, and it is not for nothing that
the sight, taste and feeling have such sensibility in comparing, choosing,
rejecting, and combining, according as they affect our senses: but it were to
be wished that people were not so ready to step beyond the boundaries
prescribed for all! Yet who knows whether the excess of which I complain,
may not spring from a desire of increasing the perfection of our being? a
desire, which, however it may be bewildered in the days of health and
happiness, by fixing on false objects, is however the strongest proof of the
Creator's goodness, as under the calamities of life, and at the period of the
dissolution of our bodies, every prospect and every hope of happiness is
fixed on a better world, when the reflection of every transgression fills the
soul with shame and remorse, and virtue alone imparts consolations which
nothing on earth can yield. You, my Emilia, will easily conceive that the
subjects I have here only skimmed over, have afforded me many hours of
reflection; and you may likewise conclude, that with these, and the avoca-
tions I meet with at my aunt's, no part of my time hangs heavy on my
hands.

I shall now lead you to a discovery which affords me a pleasing source of
amusement. On Count F.'s estate is a mineral spring, and the countess being
recommended to drink the water, occasioned our bestowing two days on a
visit thither. My aunt had bespoke Countess B. and Miss R.'s company, and
for that of Lord Derby we were indebted to chance. The house and gardens
are very fine. The ladies having several petty female affairs to adjust, Miss R.,
Lord Derby, and myself, were dismissed to take a walk. We first rambled all
over the house and gardens, where my lord was, indeed, a most agreeable
companion, entertaining us with the difference which the national temper
of every nation produces in its architecture and decorations of buildings. He
gave us a comparative description of the seats and gardens of the English,

Italians and French, and two or three he instantly sketched out in a very pretty manner. In short, we were so well pleased with our walk, that we agreed to range the next day, after breakfast, through the village and the neighbouring fields.

Two delightful days were they to me. The country air, the fine prospects, the tranquility, the beautiful appearance of nature, the Creator's bounty in the meadows and fields of corn, the industry of the peasants – With what tender emotions did my eyes fix on these objects! How many past occurrences did they bring to my mind! How many fervent wishes did I pour forth for a blessing on the labours of my tenants, and for the return of my aunt R.! You know, my dearest Emilia, that my countenance always expresses the feelings of my heart. I must have been extremely affected, for the accent of my voice was in unison with my soul. But Lord Derby almost frighted me, by eagerly looking at me, then suddenly seizing my hand, and saying in English, Good God! should love once heave this breast, and take place of those tender expressions in that countenance, how blessed would be the mortal that ——

My confusion, and the fear he excited in me, being now no less visible than my former emotions, he dropped his passionate exclamation, respectfully drew back his hand, and strove, by his whole deportment, to moderate the impression he had made on me by the impetuosity of his temper.

We entered the principal street of the village; but we had scarce got half way through it, when we were obliged to make way for a cart that came behind us, in which we perceived a woman with three young children. The moving dejection which appeared in the mother's countenance, the wan meagre appearance of the children, and the cleanly but mean clothing of them all, sufficiently expressed the poverty and affliction of this small family. I felt my heart affected: the idea of their indigence, and the desire of relieving them, were equally strong. Glad to see them alight at the inn, I was not long in resolving what to do; but saying that I had some knowledge of the woman, and wanted to speak a few words to her, I desired Lord Derby to entertain Miss R. till I returned; upon which, smiling, he kissed that part of his sleeve on which, in the heat of my forwardness, I had laid my hand. I blushed, and hasted to the poor family.

On my entering the house, I found them all sitting on a bench in the passage. The woman, with her eyes bathed in tears, drew out of a little bag a silk handkerchief and an apron, which she offered to sell to the landlady, to raise money to pay the man who brought her in his cart. Two of the children at the same time called out piteously for bread and milk. Though I was deeply affected, I had the presence of mind to step up to the poor woman with the cheerful look of an acquaintance, saying, I was glad to see her again. This I did to save her the confusion which a sensible heart is apt to feel at having many witnesses of its affliction, and because the distressed think any mark of respect shown them by the wealthy, a real favour I desired the landlady to show me a room where I might speak a word to the good woman alone, and ordered that the children should immediately have their supper. While the landlady got ready a room, the poor woman stood with the youngest child in her arms, looking at me, and appearing wild with astonishment. I took her by the hand, and desiring her to step in, followed her, leading in the two eldest children. Having obliged the trembling mother to be seated, I desired her to look on me as a friend, who, as she was in a strange place, intended to relieve her. Unable to speak, she viewed me through her gushing tears, with a look of hope and affliction. I seated myself by her, and reaching out my hand to her, full of concern, I said, You are under a very heavy affliction, both on your own account, and that of your poor children. As I am in easy independent circumstances, and my heart is no stranger to the duties which humanity and religion require, indulge me in the satisfaction of fulfilling those duties, and relieving your distress. I then gave her a little money, which I desired her to accept, and to acquaint me with the place of her abode.

The good woman sliding from her chair on her knees, exclaimed, with the most affecting emotion, O God! what a generous heart hast thou brought here to relieve me! The two biggest children flying to their mother, threw themselves about her neck, and began to weep over her. I embraced her, helped her to rise, caressed her children, and desired her to be calm and easy. Nobody here but myself, said I, shall know your situation, and what passes in your heart. Be assured that I think myself very happy in being able to serve you; but at present I would only know where you live, and will give you my name. This I immediately wrote with a pencil, and put the paper into her hand.

She told me, that she was returning to her husband at D. after having met with a severe repulse from her brother, with whom she had begged to take refuge; and that, if I pleased to allow her to give me an account in writing of the several causes which had reduced her to distress, she would submit her case to my impartial judgment. She then, casting her eye on the paper I had given her, cried, And are you Lady Sternheim? What a blessed day is this! The unfortunate Counsellor T. is my husband. If you should mention my name to your aunt, the Countess of L. it may lose me your pity; but, for Heaven's sake, do not condemn me unheard! – This she spoke with folded hands. I readily gave her my promise that I would not, and embracing her and her children, took my leave, desiring her not to say a word about me, but to leave the landlady in the belief that we were acquainted. At going away, I desired the mistress of the house to let the mother and her little ones have a supper and a good bed, and the next morning provide them with a carriage, and I would take care that she should be paid.

My lord and Miss R. were in the garden belonging to the inn, where I joined them, and thanked them for their great civility in staying so long for me. My countenance, it seems spoke the pleasure of my having done some good; yet were my eyes still red with the tears the above scene of distress had drawn from me. The English nobleman eyed me frequently, and with much earnestness, but during the remainder of our walk scarce spoke a word to me, he conversing solely with Miss R. which was the more agreeable, as it left me at leisure to think of relieving this unhappy family, to the utmost of my power.

You have here, my Emilia, the interesting discovery I have mentioned, which seems to me like a rich land which I am called to cultivate, which I will do with the utmost zeal, care and assiduity, and the produce will be the good of three poor children; for I hope that their parents will not so far neglect the duties of nature, as to apply my assistance to any other use than the advantage of their innocent babes. If all the purposes of my heart are answered, and things turn out hopefully, I shall rejoice at my staying here; for now I no longer look on the time as lost, as I most sincerely did before this opportunity offered itself. In a few days I shall receive a particular account of the cause of this family's misfortunes, till when I shall not properly know what I have to do. Counsellor T. is very ill, which hinders his wife from writing. We returned the day before yesterday.

LETTER XII

Lord Derby to the Lord B. in Paris

Thou longest to know how my intrigue goes on. Well, I will tell thee. As there is no doing without a confidant, that honourable post I confer on thee.

Come, let's have none of thy stupid bursts of laughter, at my owning that I have gained some ground, which I don't owe so much to contrivance and the masterly strokes of my policy, as to mere accident and chance. With this I am well satisfied; for the history of my love is thereby brought into the predicament of court affairs, where chance is the grand agent: the sum and substance of many a minister's sagacity consisting only in taking advantage of his knowledge of the history of other states, to improve a lucky accident, and then making the rest of the world believe that all is performed by his penetration and address.* Thou shalt see by and by in what I resemble him, and how I have had the address to improve an unforeseen event, from my knowledge of the passions, and my acquaintance with the female heart.

---

* None the less, considerable penetration and address are required to take maximum advantage of accident or chance; more perhaps than would be necessary for the execution of a carefully laid plan. But the common multitude is quite incapable of grasping this, which is perhaps why it is usually left to believe whatever it considers most to redound to the credit of its rulers. The world is so often deceived simply because it wishes to be deceived. – E.

I was for some days consumedly perplexed about the means I had best use to gain this lovely girl. Were her sense and virtue no more than what is common, my task had been easy. But as her thoughts and actions are peculiar to herself, every method I have taken with others would have been lost upon her. Yet she shall be mine, and that with her own consent too; but in order to accomplish this, I must gain her confidence, and dispose her inclinations in my favour. The only remaining difficulty will then be, minister-like, to improve accidental circumstances. This I have endeavoured to do. Knowing that Lady Sophia and her aunt were to spend some days at Lady F.'s, I took care to be of the party, and when there, had the happiness of twice taking a walk with my charmer and Miss R. An opportunity offered of introducing my travels. You know that I can see as far into a millstone[31] as another, and that my tongue will run with some mettle for an hour or two. The subject was buildings and gardens, and the young lady delighting in sensible and instructive conversations, I availed myself of her attention to some purpose, and so far riveted myself into her esteem of my skill, that she kept a design which I hastily drew of a garden in England, while I was giving her a description of it; telling Miss R. that she would keep that paper as a proof that there are gentlemen, who by travelling improve themselves and their acquaintance. An important step this, which will carry me very far. Let me now have none of thy stupid grins, at seeing me so elated at such a trifle. The young lady is extraordinary in everything, and I perceive by her questions that she has an inclination to see England, which will forward my cause, without giving me the least trouble. The conversation, which turned on different subjects, was kept up with an air of confidence and gaiety; but I took great care not to discover my love, or any particular attention to please her. But soon was I put off my guard, by a change in Sophia's voice and countenance. She seemed moved; yet I continued as well as I was able, talking with Miss R. with an air of indifference, but kept a watchful eye on Sophia. At length an eminence in the garden afforded us a view of the distant country. We stood still. The enchanting creature directing her looks to a part of the landscape, a beautiful red flushed in her face and breast, which seemed to beat with unusual rapidity, from a sensation of pleasure, and her whole aspect expressed a fervor of soul that brought tears into her eyes. All the charms I ever saw in the rest of her sex were nothing in comparison with the delightful impression of the sensations diffused over her whole person. Scarce could I restrain my ardent desire to clasp her in my arms; but to be wholly silent was impossible. I seized one of her hands, and trembling with desire, said something to her in English, but, faith, I can't tell what; but certainly the rage of love must have been expressed in my voice; for she was instantly seized with terror, and turned as pale as death. It was then time for me to recover myself, and through the rest of the evening I was so much upon my guard, as to behave with perfect compo- sure. My dove is not yet tame enough to stand the fire of my passion near at hand. It flamed in my soul all night, and not a wink of sleep could I get. The young lady was perpetually before me, and my hand shut itself, at least, twenty times, with the same ardour with which I had laid hold of hers. I was on the rack, and imagined I had perceived in her love and desire for some absent object, but I vowed that I would have her at any rate, with or without her consent. Should she conceive a love, a passionate love for me, she may perhaps *shackle* me; but let her be as cold as she will she shall not escape me.

The morning came, and found me like a frantic, amorous fool, open-breasted at the window. In the looking-glass I resembled the devil himself, and might have frightened the timerous young lady from ever having anything to do with me. Mad at the power she had over me, and resolved to make myself amends, I threw myself on the bed, and sought to rid myself of these new sensations, and to recover my former maxims. I prepared to pursue with patience the rugged way I saw before me; not being able to foresee what might happen in the afternoon. On my coming again into her company I was all gentleness and respect, and the young lady was silent and reserved. After dinner, we young folks were dismissed, while the aunt and the Countess of F. laid their hands together, to consult how they should deliver up Sophia to the prince. According to our agreement the day before, we went into the village, and on our coming opposite to the inn where my people quartered, a small carriage, in which was a woman and children, moving slowly before us, hindered our getting forward. My Sophia (for she shall be mine) looked wishfully at the woman, reddened, instantly assumed a pensive air, and with a melancholy look followed the carriage, which stopped at the inn, and its passengers came out. Sophia could not take her eyes from them; inquietude and concern were painted in her countenance; she looked at me and Miss R. then turned aside. At length, laying her hand on my arm, she said, in a tender and suppliant voice, in English, Pray, my dear lord, be so kind as to entertain Miss R. a few minutes; I would fain exchange a few words with that woman. I stopped and bowed assent, kissing the place of my coat where she had laid her charming hand. Of this she took notice, and blushing, hasted from me in much disorder. What the deuce, thought I, can Sophia have to do with that woman? She may have been formerly her letter-carrier, or a go-between in some private intrigue. Yesterday, after all my tender speeches, the slut was shy; and today, she is so reserved, that she will scarce bestow a single look on me, but a beggar's cart, with a bawd in it, passing by, she suddenly changes colour, and then I am her *dear lord*, on whom she lays her fair hand, affects a moving voice, and suitable looks, in order to be at liberty to talk to that wretch. Well, most willingly would I throw Miss R, into the horse-pond, that I might conceal myself in the inn, and listen to what passes. The latter, who had followed her with her eyes, now asked, What was become of Lady Sophia, I only answered, she told me she had something to say to that beggar woman. She shook her head with an apish grin of jealousy, at her acquaintance's superiority of beauty and accomplishments, and hugging herself that here was room for scandal, It may be some good old acquaintance of one of her villages, hissed the snake, looking as if fully informed of everything. I answered, that I would set one of my people to listen, for I knew not what to think of a thing so much out of the way. Accordingly I sent one after her, while I, in the mean time, went hard to work to sound Miss R. and asked her what she thought of Sophia.

She has an odd mixture of the manners of the citizens and the courtiers, and makes a mighty fuss about delicacy, which she does not know how to keep up to; for does it become a person of fashion to break from a lady and gentleman to – really I am at a loss what to say – to talk to a wretched creature, and perhaps to give her money beforehand, to teach her how to gain your heart, without the trouble of laying such a formal siege to it.

I made no farther answer than was necessary to keep her in breath, and to prompt her to go on. Now the young lady's genealogy was brought upon the carpet, in which her father and mother were not spared, and an abundance of ridicule was heaped upon their incomparable daughter. The particulars I don't remember, but I had much ado to forbear paying the venomous holder-forth in her own coin. Sophia stayed away pretty long; but at length she came with a pleasing emotion in her countenance, though her eyes were a little wet, and addressing us with a placid smile, and the sweetest tone of voice, I became more enflamed than ever, and knew not what to think.

Miss R. gave her an insolent look, at which my goddess was doubtless offended, as she became thoughtful, and did not utter a word till we got home. I immediately went out for intelligence, and my servant informed me, that he found both the landlady and the woman in tears, at the goodness of a young lady to whom the woman was absolutely unknown. She was amazed at her accosting her, and followed her with an anxious heart into a room to which she led both her and her children. There the lady spoke to her, begging pardon for her intrusion and offering her relief: she actually gave her money, and finding that she was going to D. where she usually lived, gave the woman her name and residence in writing, assuring her, in the most affectionate manner, of farther supplies, and even directed the land-lady to furnish the woman with a coach to carry her and her children home.

On hearing this account, I thought that either my fellow or I must be a fool, and therefore contradicted his whole tale; but he swore that it was exactly true, and I could not help wondering at the girl's extraordinary turn of mind. Why should she blush and appear confused, when about to do a good action? Was she afraid that we should have a share with her in this act of humanity?

But this discovery, this accident, will I turn to my own advantage. I will find out this family, and do them good without letting them know anything about me. But depend upon it, I'll not take a step that Sophia shall not be acquainted with. Through my liberality on this occasion, I shall assimulate myself to her character, and as pity and humanity always imply tenderness of disposition, she must necessarily conceive an esteem and regard for him, who without making a merit of it, contributes to the happiness of a poor family, and it will not be long before I shall be able to tell her, that I am influenced by her noble example, and having gained an inch on her self-love, I will proceed by spans and feet.

She watches me closely when I am engaged in discourse near her; but this little artifice, by which she endeavours to know me thoroughly, I combat with another. I always, when she comes within hearing, say something bright, or break the thread of my discourse, and assume a philosophic phiz. But though her reserve to me abates, it is not yet time to talk of love, for the turn of the scale is still for Seymour. I would fain know how it comes to pass, that this girl in the flower of her age and health, can prefer that pale dull mortal to a young fellow of my shape, complexion and sprightliness; and why she watches his sudden unmeaning looks, while at the same time she avoids mine, which are so full of life and expression. Is it owing to the coldness of her constitution? This we shall see at the ball, for which preparations are making, where nothing will be omitted that can rouse the most torpid to life and joy. Thy friend shall join in the task of intoxicating her with pleasure, and then let me alone for preventing a relapse.[32]

LETTER XIII

The Lord Derby to his friend the Lord B.

I now write to thee to give vent to the joy of my heart, which I dare not here reveal to anybody. But I am delighted to see that all the preparations made to please the prince, have turned out only to drive the beautiful timerous bird into the net I had concealed.[33] Count F. who on this occasion was the principal fowler, gave lately, at his seat, a very splendid entertainment to all the nobility, and we were to appear in the habits of peasants.

We assembled in the afternoon, and most excellently did our rustic dresses show the advantage which natural graces have over borrowed ornaments. How many of them, had they been furnished with a spade or a plough, might have been really taken for the boobies they personated; and among the ladies were more than one, who with a basket of fowls, or a milk-pail on her head, would not have had the least appearance of nobility or breeding. I was a Scotch peasant, and gave to the bold and resolute character of the Highlander my natural elegance, without deviating from what I represented. But that enchantress Sophia, in her disguise, was nature in its beautiful simplicity, and every feature expressed rural hilarity, with its attendant innocence. She was in a clear blue taffeta, striped with black, which seemed to improve her fine shape, and to show that she did not stand in need of any artificial ornament. Every motion was accompanied with an inimitable charm, which excited envy or desire, according to the difference of the sex. Her hair, divided into tresses, and tied up with ribbons, for fear it should fall down to the ground, gave me the idea of seeing her one day in the state of the Eve of Milton, when I shall be her Adam. She was very lively, and conversed, in a most graceful manner, with all the ladies. Her aunt and the Countess F. loaded her with compliments, to keep up her spirits till the prince's arrival, in order that her complaisance might extend to him.

Seymour felt all the power of her charms; but according to his uncle's political advice, concealed his passion, pretending a fit of the spleen, and the sour-looking chough, wandered, glum and silent, from tree to tree, followed constantly by Miss C. his female peasant, who attended him like his shadow. As for me, it required an Herculean strength to bridle in my passions; but I seized every opportunity of passing near Sophia, and expressing my admiration in English, though I sometimes put her out of countenance by catching her stealing a look, with all the anxiety of love, at Seymour. But suddenly she slid through the midst of the crowd, and directed her steps to the gate of the parson's garden, entered in and disappeared. Everybody now began to prate about her. As for me, I concealed myself near the corner of the dairy-house, to observe her return. In less than a quarter of an hour she made her appearance. The most lovely blush, and the most delicate expression of pleasure glowed in her face, and with a look of the sweetest satisfaction, she kindly thanked several of the spectators of the entertainment who gave way to her. Never did she appear so charming as at that instant; her very walk appeared more light and graceful than usual. Every eye was fixed on her, which she observing, cast hers on the ground, and blushed still more. Almost at the same instant appeared the prince, who proceeded through a crowd of people, coming also from the parson's garden. The countenances of the coquettes, prudes, and devotees, all agreed in expressing the most malicious suspicions. The prince's transport on seeing Sophia, covered her with confusion; the looks of both appeared a sufficient proof that they had seen each other at the parson's and the current whispers of the men were, that they were assembled there to celebrate the surrender of a beauty that was looked upon as impregnable. The graceful manner in which she presented some refreshments to the prince; his emotion in rising to come up to her; his eagerness to make her sit by him; the ardour with which he viewed her face and person; the joy of the old Count F. and the pride of her uncle and aunt, which already blazed out, confirmed our conjectures. I was seized with rage, and in the first transport of my passion, took hold of Seymour's arm, to descant on this pretty scene. He, quite beside himself, expressed the most violent contempt for her dissembled virtue; for the impudence with which she exposed herself before all the nobility, and to complete her shame, did it with a look of triumph. The last stroke of his censure brought me to myself, and I could not help thinking, that consider-ing her behaviour in this light, was entirely inconsistent with her whole character, and was too barefaced: the scene at the inn at F. then came into my mind, which increasing my doubts, I ordered my dexterous fellow Will to be called, and promised him a hundred guineas[34] to fish out the real truth of what had passed at the parsonage between the prince and Lady Sophia. In an hour's time, of which every minute seemed an age, he brought me word, that she had not so much as seen the prince there; but had only a little talk with the pastor, into whose hand she put ten carolines[35] to be distributed among the poor of the village, earnestly desiring him not to mention a word of it to any soul living. The prince came thither after she was gone, and stood a moment, at a distance, to see how the nobility were diverting themselves.

I here began to curse the fanatical jade, who had made us form such false conjectures, when, in reality, she had more generosity than all of us put together. While we were thinking only of pleasure, her heart was open to the poor of the village, whom she resolved should share in the joy to which the day was dedicated: and how is she rewarded for it? Why her character is traduced, in the basest manner, by censures which the most despicable amongst us think themselves justified in making. A fine encouragement to virtue truly! But thou wilt perhaps say, that inward satisfaction is the reward of this good work; but to prove thy mistake, I need only make thee call to mind, that the satisfied air the angelical Sophia brought from the parsonage, appeared a proof of her guilt. But how glad was I that I had found her out; for thus I, an arrant villian, was the honestest fellow in the whole company, and had not condemned her in form, till I had searched into the affair; and now am I recompensed for this virtue, with the hopes of taking to my arms this charming creature, pure and spotless: for now nothing but her death, or mine, can prevent my putting in practice all the expedients of my fruitful genius, and employing my whole fortune to give success to my design.

With a triumphant look I hasted back to the company, forbidding Will to mention a word of his discovery, and promising him, on that condition, to give him another hundred guineas.[36] Thou wilt say, perhaps, that for the honour of my Sophia, I should have communicated what I had heard, and that then my triumph would have been truly noble. But, fair and softly, my lord; I could not proceed so fast in the way of good works, and much less could I have sacrificed all my satisfactions: for what purpose could my discovery have answered, except to have increased my difficulties, as well as those of the prince? Besides, of what amusement should I have deprived myself, if I had interrupted the fine things said on this subject? During my absence an answer made by the prince had confirmed the first suspicions. Count F. having asked him if he had seen Lady Sophia in the parson's garden; he answered, Yes; and at the same time fixed his eyes on her. Nobody had now any doubt; and already many of the courtiers showed her an extraordinary respect, as the future distributor of favours. Count F. his lady, Sophia's uncle and aunt, were in the van of these wrong-headed people, and even Lord G. was among them; but in him it appeared somewhat forced. As to Seymour, whose love was wounded, and who imagined that he saw disfigured, that beautiful model of perfection he had admitted in Lady Sophia, I beheld him so transported with rage, that he could scarce conform to the rules of common civility, in dancing a minuet with her. The cold and forbidding air with which he returned the softest and tenderest looks, made her turn her eyes from him; but at the same time spread over her a dejection which gave an inexpressible charm to her inimitable manner of dancing. I was set in a flame, at the visible preference her heart gave to him; but at the same time redoubled my vigilance, in seizing whatever could conduce to accomplish my end. I also perceived that she was displeased at the flattery, and excessive officiousness of the courtiers, on which I only treated her with a natural modest respect; and this succeeded to a miracle. She conversed with me in English, with great sprightliness, on dancing, as the only diversion she loved, and on my praising her performance of the minuet, she wished I could say as much of her in English country dances, which she preferred to the German, on account of the mixture of sprightliness and decency which characterise them, and which will not permit the nymph to forget herself, nor the swain to take any improper liberties. The delight I received from this little bit of chat, acquired an incomparable relish from the visible pain it gave Seymour. The prince, to whom it was as little agreeable, came up to us, on which I withdrew, to tell Count F. that Lady Sophia preferred English dances. The music instantly began, and each chose his lass. Sophia who was that of young Count F. was led by him to the middle of the row. But the old count threw all into confusion, by placing her at the head: though much surprised at this, she began the dance with a surprising lightness of step, and all the proper graces. I had particularly avoided dancing this time, and therefore walked up and down with Lord G. and the prince. The latter minded only Lady Sophia, and could not help crying perpetually, Does not she dance like an angel? Lord G. declaring, that no Englishwoman could perform either the step or the figure better, the prince said he could like to see her dance with an Englishman. I retired to a window, to attend to the choice she should make, and after an interval of rest, the prince desired Sophia to oblige him so far as to join in another country dance, and to take for her partner one of the two Englishmen, pointing to us. A graceful curtesy, and her eyes turned to us, expresed her consent. With what an entreating look did she invite the frigid Seymour, to whom Count F. made the first offer, on account of his being nephew to Lord G. but he refused to dance. The blush with which this disappointment deeply tinged Sophia's face and bosom, gave way to a benign mien, on her seeing the respectful eagerness with which I offered her my hand; but this, instead of putting an end to my tortures, only increased them. O Sophia, thought I, such sentiments for me would have secured my heart to you, and virtue, forever! but my trouble in wresting you from others abates my fondness, and fills my heart with nothing but desire, jealousy, and revenge. – But I suffered nothing of this to appear, and my whole conduct showed respect. She surpassed herself in dancing, which was attributed to her desire of pleasing the prince; but I alone knew it to be the effect of her offended self-love, which strove by redoubling her gaiety to punish Seymour for his refusal. And indeed he was punished, for his heart laboured under such anguish, that he was glad to vent his complaints to me, and cursed himself for being too sensible of her charms, in spite of the indignation with which she had filled him.

But why did not you dance with her then?

God forbid. I should not have been able to support the struggle it would have caused between my love and contempt, and must have sunk under the former. I laughed at him, and bid him love as I did, and then he would find more satisfaction in it than he would reap from his high flown notions.

I find, said the fool, that you are the happier of the two; but I can't change my nature. A plague on this love, thought I, which makes such miserable dogs of us both: Seymour because he is ignorant of the innocence and tenderness of the object he adores, and I, who can neither refuse her my esteem nor my love, am a prey to envy and the desire of revenge, and feel no other joy but that of disturbing theirs. I have the devil and all to do! All my past experience, all my address in laying snares are here of no use from the indifference she shows to sensual gratifications. At a ball, where most women are coquettes, and the best of them filled with the desire of pleasing, Sophia's thoughts run upon doing good. Others are infatuated with the company, and the tumult of the entertainment; they are dazzled with the finery of dress, and softened by music; in short, they are every way exposed to seduction. Sophia, in her turn, suffers herself to be moved; but with what? With pity for the poor; and this impression is so strong; that she leaves the company, and all their amusements, to perform a benevolent action. Ah! When this sensibility, so strong and so active, shall be dedicated to pleasure, and exerted in my favour – then, B. then I shall experience the delicate voluptuousness imparted by Venus, when she is attended by the Muses and the Graces! But I must prepare for it, before I can enjoy it. As those enthusiasts who aspire to a personal intercourse with spiritual beings, prepare themselves by fasting and prayer; so must I to humour this sweet enthusiast, renounce all my favourite pleasures. That is not all, I must let her know that I have adopted her taste. The accidental discovery of my kindness to the family, for which Sophia interests herself, has already been of considerable service, and now the business is to surprise her at the counsellor's, where she frequently goes, merely to give instruction to the children, and consolation to the parents; yet all her morality cannot prevent the influence of my guineas; for through these people, I shall find an opportunity of seeing her, and of getting access to her heart. On the other hand I shall leave no stone unturned, to prevent that magical sympathy that may arise between her and Seymour, if ever they come to such an explanation, as to know that their souls are in perfect unison. But this I have pretty well obviated; for Seymour's grand instrument in procuring intelligence, is no other than his uncle's secretary who is devoted to me: the news he gives him, is communicated to me, without our ever exchanging a word; for we write to each other with the precaution of hiding our letters behind an old picture. This imp of Lucifer is an admirable blade. However, I must do justice to Seymour, who as much as possible, avoids giving us trouble; for he shuns Sophia as one would a serpent, tho' he carefully informs himself of all her motions: but these, by the colours which my new lights give them, are sufficiently equivocal to produce in his prejudiced mind all the effects I could wish. Of the prince I am not in the least afraid; for every step throws him farther from his bias; for Sophia is not fond of anything that princes can give; indeed, she is entirely a new character.

LETTER XIV

Lord Seymour to Dr T.

I am just come from a splendid and well-contrived entertainment, and since it is impossible for me to sleep, notwithstanding the violent emotions my animal spirits have sustained, I will, at least, endeavour to make myself amends by the tranquillity which the conversation of a worthy friend conveys to a troubled mind. Why, O my instructor! is your experienced wisdom at a loss for the means of fortifying my soul against the force of good impressions, where you have so successfully armed it against the seductions of bad examples? I will lay the cause of my inquietude before you, and then you will see how happy a reasonable degree of indifference would render me.

The prime minister gave the nobility, or more properly the prince, under the name of Count F. gave the Lady Sophia Sternheim, a grand entertainment; in which the dresses, the music, and the place where it was exhibited, were rural, and perfectly conformable to a country festival. In the midst of a meadow were erected some cottages, and a barn for dancing. The thought, and the execution, transported me during the first two hours, when I was wholly taken up with the elegance and taste of the festival, and Lady Sophia's inexpressible charms. Never, my friend, no never shall I for the future contemplate such a lively image of lovely innocence and pure joy, as that which was afforded us during these two hours, in the elegant and noble figure of Sophia! Cursed be the guilty arts that could rob her of that divine character: but it was impossible she should be deceived: it was impossible that it should be the effect of the delirium with which the music and dancing involved her senses. I know what sometimes happens in the like circumstances, that we are insensibly drawn from the path in which we are guided by our moral sentiments: but when she rejected the last admonition of her good genius, when she, some minutes after, hasted to a place agreed upon, to have a secret interview with the prince, and thus exposed herself before every eye, it was then that I felt the pain of dissembling the profound contempt I had conceived for her. But it is necessary for me to inform you, what I mean by the last admonition of her good genius: there was a picture shop where the ladies drew tickets in a lottery; now tell me pray, was it merely by chance, or by a providential interposition, that Sophia, drew Daphne pursued by Apollo.[37] The cabal belonging to the prince, seemed disconcerted at this little incident; and I believed their vexation was well-founded; on my observing that she was pleased with the picture, and showed it to those who surrounded her, talking like a connoisseur on the design and colouring. My joy was inexpressible, and I became confirmed in the opinion, that in the sequel she would imitate Daphne. But how dreadfully was I deceived by her false virtue, since a moment after she threw herself into the arms of Apollo. I saw her walk some time with her worthless aunt, and the Countess of F. attending to the flattery those two procuresses lavished on her. At length I observed her look with a kind of tender thoughtfulness, sometimes on the company, and sometimes at the door which leads into a clergyman's garden: then suddenly she took her resolution, and skimmed with the most graceful agility, through the crowd of spectators, and entered the garden. She did not stay long, but her absence had already excited the attention of the company. But what remarks were made, when they saw her return with a mingled air of confusion and complacency, and on her being soon followed by the prince? That passionate lover could not retain his joy, and his passion broke out in its full blaze. With what abject complaisance did she present him with sherbet, converse with him, and to please him, dance some English country dances, and that with a spirit which she had before only shown in the cause of virtue. But, O heavens! How ravishing did she appear! What charms were there in her dancing! All the graces were united in her, as all the furies were assembled in my heart! How distracting was this thought, that I who had adored her virtue, who desired to be united to her, was a witness of the sacrifice she had made of her innocence, in the face of heaven and earth; and far from showing the marks of remorse, would you believe it? She behaved with an air of triumph! I now curse Sophia and her charms: her image, and my tenderness, are deeply impressed on my heart; yet I hate them both: I hate myself for being too weak to obliterate them.

My uncle, while we were returning from this ball, talked to me like a man whose passions have long been satiated; and like a minister who, thinking nothing of a thousand victims sacrificed to the vices of his prince, must imagine the ruin of a girl of little importance, when she gratifies the passion of a great man, by asking him a sacrifice of her honour. O had she been only a girl of the common stamp; if she had only personal charms, and an agreeable address, I could have considered it in the same light as he. But with a soul so noble, with such endowments, that she had a right to the esteem of the whole world, to deliver herself up thus! – Everybody concurred to flatter her; but you, who know me, may judge whether I was of the number. Never will I return to court till I feel more tranquility. Indeed I was never fond of the life that is led there, and now I abhor it. I will follow my uncle in his travels; but I hope that my mother will never more desire me to accept of a place at court, or persuade me to marry. Sophia has now rendered me averse to both. Derby, the licentious Derby also despises her; but he assists in seducing her, and treats her with more respect than ever. What a villain!

LETTER XV

Lady Sophia to Emilia

Come, my dear Emilia, for once you shall have a sprightly letter from me. You know my fondness for dancing, and that Count F. was to give us a ball. He has done it, and so much to my satisfaction, that I really take a pleasure in thinking of it. All the dispositions of this truly grand entertainment were entirely conformable to my taste, and agreeable to my notions. It was a mixture of rural simplicity and courtly splendour, so happily blended, that they could not be separated without depriving the one or the other of its principal ornaments. I will try whether, in giving you a description of it, I can make good this character.

Count F. to express his joy for the recovery of his lady, and in acknowledgment of the regard that had been universally shown her, gave us a ball at his seat, to which she had withdrawn in order to complete her recovery, and where she had received the visits of all the nobility. We had been invited a week before, and desired to appear in couples, and in the habits of the peasants, it being intended to give us a rural feast. The dresses were various, and each couple was chosen beforehand; that of young Count F. was a shepherd, and I an Alpine shepherdess. The colour of my habit was a clear blue striped with black, and the simplicity of its form was of advantage to my shape: my hair hung in tresses without art, and a straw hat, put on in a careless air, did honour to my character. I am very fond, you know, of the plain artless ways of the country folks, and therefore when I was dressed, cast a glance on my elegant and simple habit; I found it more agreeable to my disposition than to my figure; I felt myself delighted with my country look, and sincerely wished, that after having laid aside that disguise, I might forever preserve in my heart, that innocence, candour, and artless benevolence, which can alone fill it with solid joy. My uncle, my aunt, and Count F. never ceased while we were on the road to commend my dress and appearance. On our reaching the seat, we turned down a vista which led through a delightful meadow, and alighting from the coach, heard the sound of flageolets; several agreeable couples of peasants then appeared, and on our advancing, sometimes a bagpipe, and at others an oaten-reed, or some other instrument of that kind, proclaimed the feast. Wooden benches of a very artless construction were placed under the trees, to serve for seats, and on each side of the walk were erected two pretty cottages, in one of which was milk prepared different ways, and in the other were served refreshments in little earthenware bowls, with a spoon of the same kind, and wooden trenchers. At the door of this cottage was Lady F. dressed like an hostess, who received everybody with the most obliging complaisance. All the count's domestics had laid aside their liveries, and their dress, as well as that of the musicians was agreeable to the rest. There was also a pastry-cook's shop, and a print-shop. Our peasants lead us to the former, and offered us cakes, which on breaking, discovered a piece of lace, a ribbon, or some other pretty trifle. At the other shop we drew a lottery of pictures in miniature. I had for my lot Daphne pursued by Apollo, a charming piece, which seemed to be the best, as it appeared to excite the envy of the other ladies, and I thought I perceived, on this occasion, a change in several countenances.

When all the nobility were assembled, we young folks were desired to assist in serving the ladies of a more advanced age, and the noblemen with refreshments. This employment had a very agreeable effect; but a stranger, who was a spectator, would have had more than one remark to make, on the inquisitive looks, which the ladies cast by stealth at each other. Your friend's heart was open to joy, my feet pressed the verdant sod, I drank milk under the shade of a tree, I breathed a pure air, and enjoyed a clear blue sky: at twenty paces from me ran a limpid brook, and I had the view of well cultivated fields that promised an abundant harvest. It seemed as if the unlimited prospect of the works of nature rendered my sensations more lively, and gave a freer course to my spirits. Escaped from the narrow enclosure formed by the walls of a palace, I saw myself transported into my own element. Hence I talked more, and with greater gaiety than usual, and was one of the first in mingling in the dances under the trees. All the inhabitants of the village had left their cottages to see us dance; and during an interval of rest, I took a turn with my aunt and the Countess of F. casting my eyes sometimes on the brilliant throng of joyful village courtiers, and sometimes on that of the peasants who were spectators, among whom I perceived several that had a look of poverty and distress. I was affected by this contrast, and at the part these good people took in our pleasures. At the moment when I thought I was least observed, I slipped into the parsonage garden, which joins to the meadow, and putting into the pastor's hands some money for the poor of the parish, went and rejoined the company with a satisfied heart. It seems the Lord Derby had watched all my steps; for, at my return, I saw him at one of the corners of the dairy-house, with his eyes fixed on the garden gate: he hasted to me, and, with eager and curious looks, talked very strangely, and, I think, made use of some rapturous expressions. This language, joined to the extraordinary manner in which everybody stared at me, made me blush and cast down my eyes; and when I lifted them up, I found myself near a tree, against which the Lord Seymour was leaning with a distracted look. I then thought he might have heard the expressions uttered by the Lord Derby, and that apprehension, I do not know why, ruffled me. But what was my surprise, a moment after, at seeing everybody rise on the prince's coming from that very garden door through which I had just passed. The idea that it was possible I might have met him there, seized me in such a manner that I ran to my aunt, as if I had been afraid of his finding me alone. In the mean time, the satisfaction I felt within, helped me to recover myself, and I made my curtsy with a calm air. He viewed, and praised my dress in very lively terms; but, Lady F. by urging me to present him a bowl of sherbet, embarrassed me very much; for on my doing it, he insisted on my sitting down on the bench by him, and I was obliged to bear all the strange things he was pleased to say both of me and other people. In the mean time the company separated, and the greatest number began to walk in parties. The prince seeing that I followed them with my eyes, asked if I preferred walking with them; I answered, that I imagined they were going to begin again the dances, and I should be glad to make one among them, upon which he arose, and conducted me to the others. I applauded myself for this thought, and mingled with the young folks, who were standing all together. They smiled at my eagerness, and all behaved to me with great politeness, except Miss C. who with an affected air turned away her head. I turned also, and perceived the Lords Seymour and Derby arm in arm, walking with hasty steps by the side of the brook. Meanwhile the day declined, and we began supper, which was served up in one of the cottages. It was soon over, for everyone was desirous of going to the ballroom, which was built in the form of a barn. Nobody was more glad to leave the table than I, for in drawing the lots, my adverse fate had placed me next to the prince, an honour for which I severely suffered; for he incessantly talked to me in the most extravagant terms, and treated me with all possible marks of respect. This pretended advantage, which I owed entirely to chance,* made me see the courtiers in a very mean light; for their

* Few readers need be informed, that Lady Sophia's innocence, and little knowledge of the world, made her attribute to chance, what was done with an express design, in consequence of the plot they had formed against her. None are better acquainted than a court, with the art of producing unforeseen events, in order to flatter, in an artful manner, the passions of the sovereign. – E.

conduct, with respect to me, seemed to say, that I had acquired a very great merit in their eyes, and therefore none of them failed to lavish their flattery on me, whether well or ill founded, except my Lord Seymour, who did not so much as open his lips. His uncle and the Lord Derby, on the other hand, gave me the most delicate praises, and the last especially treated me with a respectful complaisance. He talked of dancing with great propriety, and I had reason to admire his talents, and to complain of the abuse he had made of them. I found during the ball that he was not of the general opinion, that it should begin with minuets, which require such grace in the movements, and such exactness in the step, that few can do them justice. The extraordinary applause I received led my heart to an affectionate remembrance of my parents, who, amidst all the care they took of my education, had me early taught to dance. From the quickness of my growth it was thought I should be very tall, and to such, my father used to say, that dancing was a particular advantage, as it communicates to all the motions a peculiar harmony; and that we seldomer see the graces accompany those who are tall, than those of middling size. For this reason he would have me dance every day, and sing my minuets when I was at work with my needle; which, he was of opinion, would insensibly give a natural grace to all my motions. If I could believe the praises lavishly bestowed on the air and dancing of his daughter, my father's opinion would be justified. It appears to me too, that he had good reason to prefer a genteel figure to beauty; for I have remarked, for instance, that the fine features and complexion of Miss B. were much less admired than the enchanting graces of the Countess of Zin to whom nature, however, has given rather an ordinary person; and among those who seemed to envy her, were many women of merit. How comes this, Emilia? Is it because they have a more lively feeling than others, of the advantage which a graceful figure has over beauty, and therefore the more ardently desire to be possessed of it? Or had this desire its source in the approbation which all the men of distinguished merit gave to the amiable countess? However this be, I believe that a proper well founded self-love ought to attach itself to the worship of the Graces; they never withdraw their favours, and time cannot deprive us of them. For my part, had I lived in the happy times of Greece, I should have presented on their altars my richest offerings. – But I guess my Emilia's thoughts, and imagine I see your looks, which seem to say, Is my friend Sophia exempt from faults, while she so freely censures those of others? It is not envy that I suspect her of; no, her vanity makes her believe that she has nothing to fear, and the gratitude she feels for having her talent for dancing so well cultivated, is a proof of this. But our security from envy is frequently no virtue, but the effect of an excessive self-love.

Be easy, my dear and severe friend! I am sensible that you are in the right. I was vain, and well satisfied with myself; but I did penance for it. I have thought myself amiable; but have not appeared so in the eyes of him I most wished to think me so. I had used all my skill in a country dance, and had succeeded so well, that my Lord G. and Lord Derby told the prince that an Englishwoman could not have done better. They at length would have another country dance, with an Englishman for my partner, and proposed the Lord Seymour: but (would you believe it, Emilia?) he refused it, and that in so uncivil, I might say contemptuous a manner, as struck me to the heart. My pride strove to cure this wound; but what more particularly contributed to calm me, was the gloomy and angry air with which he behaved to the whole company; for, except to his uncle and the Lord Derby, he spoke to nobody. The latter received the invitation to dance with me with the most lively eagerness, and I did my best, both to recompence him, and at the same time to show Seymour, by my gaiety, how little his behaviour had affected me. You who know me, Emilia, must be sensible that this moment was not the most agreeable to your friend: but my precipitate inclination for him deserved chastisement. How could I suffer myself to be so prejudiced in favour of my Lord Seymour, by the praises of a woman who loves him, as to be unjust to others, and almost to forget the regard due to myself! But I have reason to thank him for having brought me to reflect. I feel myself at present more tranquil and more just. Here is a new reason for congratulating myself on this entertainment; I have discharged a duty of benevolence towards my neighbours, and for my own benefit learned an important lesson of prudence. Thus I hope my Emilia is satisfied, and that she loves me as much as ever.

LETTER XVI

Lady Sophia to Emilia

At last I have received poor Mrs T's letter, which she promised me when I first saw her at the inn, and in which she gives me an account of her misfortunes; but it is so long, and the paper so thick, that I cannot enclose it in this I now write: but the extract I will here make of it, and a sketch of my answer, will give you sufficient satisfaction.

She is of a poor but reputable family; her mother, who was of an irreproachable character, and a great œconomist, would not allow her daughters either luxuries or recreations, but obliging them to be constantly employed, continually reminded them of the straitness of her circumstances, which would not permit their living like those who were more plentifully provided for. The children submitted with reluctance. The mother died: Counsellor T.[38] payed his addresses to the second daughter, and easily obtained her, as they knew that his parents had left him a considerable fortune. The young man, to show his riches, made his wife handsome presents, lived in an expensive manner, visited and entertained a great deal of company; and the young woman, who had hitherto been unacquainted with the enjoyment of wealth, indulged her taste for dress, company, and dissipation. She became a mother, their expenses increased, and their fortune was consumed. They contracted debts, and with the money they borrowed, continued to live with the same profusion. Soon the sum they owed became so considerable, that their creditors losing all patience, paid themselves by seizing on the house and furniture. The habit of enjoying the luxuries of the table, and a fondness for dress, completed their ruin. The income of his office was spent in the first months of the year, and the remainder was passed in care and want. The husband could not now gratify his vanity, nor the wife her fondness of ease: the one had neither the will, nor the other the wisdom to live within their income. They sought for benefactors; some they found; but soon they withheld their assistance. Their refusal embittered Mr T's mind, and he loaded with reproaches those whom he had found his friends; this they resented, and to be revenged on him, caused him to be deprived of his employment. Having thus lost every means of support, distress and despair became their portion, which was aggravated by their having six children. All their relations refused to assist them, and the extremity of their distress frequently compelling them to commit little mean actions to obtain subsistence, they at length became objects of hatred and contempt. They were in this situation when I came to know them, and offered them my assistance.

I began with furnishing them with money, clothes, and the necessities of life: but I plainly see that this will be of little use without plucking up the evil by the root, by removing their false notions of honour and happiness. I am employed in forming a plan for their conduct, and desire Mr Br. your worthy husband, to perfect it: for I am convinced that the experience and discernment of a girl of twenty years of age, is not sufficient to enable her to furnish a right rule of conduct for his family. In those I venture to give them, you, my dear Emilia, will recollect many drawn from the writings that were used in my education, and which I have endeavoured to adapt to their circumstances. But it is difficult for the rich to give to those who are not so, such advice as they will relish; for the latter always doubt the sincerity of the moralist, and when they exhort them to use industry, moderation, and œconomy, suspect that they are weary of relieving them, and this idea is sufficient to destroy the effect of the wisest maxims.

Some days of distraction have prevented my continuing this letter, but not my employing myself about Mr T. Would to God I was able to enrich him, and had nothing more to do, than to entreat him to make a good use of the money. The welfare of that family has cost me more than if I had given them half my estate. For their sakes I have acted contrary to my principles. The counsellor earnestly solicited me to procure him another employment, by engaging my uncle to speak to the prince in his behalf: but on my acquainting him with the counsellor's request, he answered, that he could not make use of the favour he began to recover with the prince, for any other purpose than for the advantage of his children, and his great concern now was to gain his cause. On my appearing dejected at this refusal, my aunt said, that I should seize the first opportunity of speaking to the prince myself, and you will see, added she, that he is inclined to be generous, provided the person proposed to him be worthy of his favour, and in that case you have no reason to fear a refusal.

After dinner the Count and Countess of F. paying us a visit, I addressed myself to them, and desired them to solicit the prince in favour of this poor family; but they told me that nobody could obtain that favour more easily than I, since it would be the first favour I had asked of him; besides, it would be granted, on account of the rarity of the thing; a young lady of my age, being never known to interest herself so warmly in behalf of the unhappy, and this new instance of the tenderness of my disposition, would increase his highness's esteem for me. I was sorry to find that none would concur with me in this good work. The thought of addressing myself to the prince gave me pain; indeed I could depend on my success, for I had too well perceived his inclination for me; but that was the very thing that caused my irresolution. I was willing to treat him with the greatest reserve, and to keep him at a distance; but instead of that, my solicitation, his favours, and my gratitude, would draw me nearer to him, and expose me to fresh compliments, and fresh declarations. For some time I struggled with myself; but on the fourth day having visited the inconsolable family, and seen the parents rejoicing in my favours, but the house still in want of many necessaries, and filled with six children, one very young, and the others fit for instruction, all my ideas in relation to myself became weakened. The delicacies of self-love, said I, ought surely to give way to the duty of assisting those like myself, whom I find still suffering; and can the vexation the prince's growing passion gives me, efface from my heart the joy reflected from that of this family? I am sure of procuring him an employment, for they have warranted my success. On the other hand, I am certain that the prince cannot hurt me, without my own consent. I then fixed my resolution, and executed it the next day at the Princess of W's, where I was obliged to sing and play. The prince seemed quite in raptures, and repeatedly desiring me to walk with him in the saloon, I at last complied. You may guess that he said some fine things on the sweetness of my voice, and the lightness of my fingers, and that I returned his praises with very modest answers; but when he came to express his wishes that it was in his power to prove his esteem otherwise than by words, I told him that being convinced of his noble manner of thinking, I presumed to implore his favour for an unhappy family, who stood greatly in need of the assistance of the father of the country, and who appeared to me to be worthy of obtaining it.

He stopped, and giving me a lively and tender look, said, Pray, what is this family? What can I do for them? I then painted in a few words, but clearly, and in as affecting a manner as I was able, the distress in which the counsellor and his children were plunged, and besought him, for their sake, to provide for their father, who had expiated his imprudence by his long sufferings. He promised that he would; commended my charitable zeal; and added, that it afforded him a real satisfaction to be able to relieve the unfortunate; but that he plainly perceived that all those who were about him were governed by private interest, that therefore I would sensibly oblige him, by offering him new objects on whom he might exercise his beneficence.

I assured him, that I would not abuse his goodness, and in two words renewed my petition. He took my hand, pressed it between both his, and cried with an air of emotion, I promise you, my dear zealous intercessor, that all the wishes of your heart shall be fulfilled, as soon as I find that you think favourably of me.

At this moment I almost hated my compassionate heart, and the family that had inspired it with pity; for the prince looked at me in the most expressive manner, and when I would have withdrawn my hand, held it fast, and raised it to his breast: Yes, repeated he, I will make use of every means to obtain your favourable thoughts.

This he spoke so loud, and with such an ardent and disordered look, as drew many eyes upon us. I was seized with a trembling, and snatching my hand from between his, said, with a hesitating voice, that I could not avoid having a good opinion of a prince so disposed to bestow favours on an unfortunate subject; at the same time making him a low curtsy, went in great confusion, and seated myself behind my aunt's chair. The prince, it seems, followed me with his eyes, and threatened me with his finger. Let him threaten if he will, never more will I walk with him, and when I thank him for his favour, it shall only be in the great circle, which at court is always formed round him at his first appearance.

Attention sat visible in every face, and never did I hear at the card table such complaints of the carelessness of the players. I perceived that the prince and I were the cause, and found it very difficult to get over my confusion. In Lord Derby's looks there was something gloomy; he seemed to view me with concern, and his lips moved as if he was talking with great agitation to himself. He walked up to the table where my aunt was at play, just at the moment when she cried, Sophia, you have been certainly speaking to the prince in favour of poor Counsellor T. for I see that you are moved.

Never did I love my aunt better than at this moment, when she gave me an opportunity of telling the whole company the subject of our conversation. I therefore cheerfully answered, Yes, my solicitations have been attended with the most favourable success. Lord Derby's gloom instantly vanished; yet he preserved a thoughtful but serene look; the others, by their gestures, or their words, expressed their approbation. But how does my Emilia think it was with me, when undressing myself after the assembly, I went with Rosina in a sedan to Counsellor T's, who lives at no great distance from us. I was willing to give the good people a peaceful night, by letting them know the favour the prince had promised to grant them. I had there seated myself in a window, which looks into a little street. The parents and their children were assembled round me. The husband, by my desire, had seated himself by my side, and with one hand I drew the wife to me, saying to both, Soon, my dear friends, I shall see here none but satisfied looks, the prince has promised the counsellor a post, and to give his assistance to the rest of the family.

The mother, and the two eldest children, fell on their knees, and burst into exclamations of gratitude and joy. At the instant we heard somebody rap at the window, which the counsellor hastily opening, a purse of money, to the amazement of us all, was thrown in, and fell heavily on the floor. I hastily put my head out of the window, and distinctly heard the voice of my Lord Derby, who said in English, Thank God, I have done some good, though on account of my gaiety I am esteemed a rake!

I must confess, that I was moved both by the action and the words, and my first thought was, perhaps the Lord Seymour is neither so good, nor the Lord Derby so bad as he is thought. Mrs T. had run to the house door, and called out, Who is there? But he hastily flew away. On opening the purse there were found fifty carolines. You may guess the joy this sight gave both the father, mother, and children; all wept, and took it in their hands by turns: they were almost ready to kiss the gold, and to press it to their hearts. I there saw the difference between the effect of expectation and actual possession: the prospect of an employment had given them great joy, but it was allayed by fear and distrust: while the fifty carolines which they had handled, counted, and grasped in their hands, filled the whole family with transport. They asked me how they should employ that sum. I tenderly answered, my dear friends, take as much care of it as if you had acquired it by much labour, or as if it was the remainder of your fortune; for we cannot yet know when, and in what manner the prince will perform his promise. I then left them, and returned home very well pleased with my day's work.

I had by my solicitations fulfilled a duty of humanity, by inducing the prince to exert his beneficence, while others solicit him for gifts, which only tend to the gratification of luxury and voluptuousness. I had filled the hearts of the distressed with gladness; and had the satisfaction of being witness to a good action done by a man, whom people thought incapable of it. For with what speed had the Lord Derby seized an opportunity of doing good? He by accident hears at my aunt's card-table, of a family worthy of compassion; he immediately makes enquiries, and the same evening, like a true Englishman, conveys to them a generous supply.

Little did he think that I was there; but that I was at supper at my uncle's, or else he would not have spoken to himself in English. In company I have often heard him utter good sentiments; but I have taken them for the hypocritical language of an artful, wicked man. At present it is impossible that I should suppose this in a good action, performed in such a manner as to be concealed from the whole world. Oh, should he obtain a taste for virtue, and to it consecrate his abilities and his knowledge, he will be one of the most worthy men I know!

I cannot now help showing him my esteem, since he has proved himself worthy of it. Never could his respect, his praises, his wit, obtain my favourable opinion. It often happens, that by external attractions we obtain the homage of a vile and debauched man; but how despicable is the woman, whose vanity is pleased with it, and she weakly thinks she owes him her gratitude! But, never will I profane my esteem: it is a tribute which shall only be paid to merit.

It is now proper to inform you, that when the counsellor's family has received a fixed revenue, my whole plan, with respect to them, must be new cast: I desire that your husband, as a wise man, acquainted with every class of moral duties, will form the model, and beg he would use dispatch. Now, my dear Emilia, as sleep is weighing down my eye-lids, I wish you a good night.

LETTER XVII

Lady Sophia to Mrs T.

I thank you, madam, for the pleasure your confidence has given me, and, in return, I assure you of my real friendship, and unwearied readiness to serve you.

I informed you in my last visit, that the prince has been graciously pleased to comply with Mr T's request. I need not tell you, how much I am rejoiced at the thought of soon seeing you freed from the anxieties under which you have laboured; may I be permitted also to say, that my joy is accompanied with the wish that you will make use of your endeavours to render your happiness *durable*, both for your own sake, and that of your children. The comparison between that you formerly knew, with the years of unhappiness which followed, may serve for the foundation of a new plan of conduct, directed by prudence. The Lord Derby's present has enabled you to buy the clothes and furniture you wanted, so that the whole produce of your income may be entirely applied to your support, and the education of your children.

My years being unequal to the task of forming a plan for this purpose, I have begged the assistance of a clergyman of my acquaintance, who has favoured me with the following:

From the informations I have received, the three eldest children are capable of attending to the voice of reason; therefore inform them that God has appointed for us two kinds of happiness, one of which is eternal, and can be only obtained by a life of virtue; the other, which relates to the present life, must be acquired by industry and prudence.* Talk to them of the order which God has established in society, by diversifying their stations. Give them a transient view of the classes that are higher and more wealthy than theirs; and bring back their attention to those who are poorer, and enjoy fewer of the means of happiness. Show them the inconveniences and advantages of each state, and thus lead them to the exercise of humble gratitude to their Creator, who has placed them in a situation in which they may enjoy happiness, and that this solely depends on their performance of the duties of life. Make them sensible that those of religion and virtue are as binding to the prince, as to the lowest of mankind.

The duty of those who hold the first rank in a private station, is to render themselves of advantage to society, either by cultivating the sciences, by the discharge of public employments, or by rendering themselves useful by commerce: engage therefore your sons, to perform the duties that lead to eternal felicity, and then to acquire the qualities and knowledge proper to render them useful members of society. Tell them, that nobility is the reward of those, who by their virtue, have served their country; that riches are the fruit of labour and industry, and that thus it is, in a great measure, in their power to rise above their equals; since extraordinary abilities, joined to virtue, seldom fail of being the foundation of honour and prosperity.

Tell your daughters that they should join to the duties religion requires, all the accomplishments that can render them valuable and amiable women.

Our hearts and understandings are not subject to the vicissitudes of fortune. We may have a *noble soul*, though our origin be mean; and a superior mind, without being of high rank: without the lustre of wealth, we may be happy; and by our temper, sense, and personal accomplishments, make a very agreeable figure, without the aid of expensive ornaments; and thus, by our attainments and engaging qualities, obtain a general esteem, the first and surest step to advancement and honour.

After having made them fully sensible of the truth of these principles, lay before them an account of your income, and the use to which you will apply it; that here you have two principal objects, the support of the *body by food and raiment*, and the improvement of the *mind* by *books*, *masters*, and *company*. Remind them too, that prudence requires you to lay by a part of your income, as a provision for unforeseen events.

If we attend only to the voice of nature, and what health requires, and

---

* The editor must concede the task of justifying this statement to the reverend gentleman from whom it supposedly derives. His own opinion, which is hardly new, is that neither individual nor general happiness is thinkable in this life here on earth without the practice of virtue, and that Revelation teaches us that something more than mere virtue is required for the attainment of everlasting bliss. – E.

not to the fantastic wants of the imagination, the most simple food will be sufficient, and this may be obtained at a small expense. And since the rich man, after having injured his constitution by a luxurious intemperance, is obliged to have recourse to water and the plainest diet, why should we murmur that our station obliges us, in the midst of health, to be satisfied with mere necessaries? As to clothes, a cheap stuff may be of the same service as the most valuable tissue: the choice of the colour, and the elegance of the make, are the principal things to be consulted in all kinds of dress: a genteel walk, a graceful air, a countenance such as nature made it, sets a value on the plainest clothes, and gives an advantage, which the expenses of the rich, though loaded with ornaments, cannot always procure; and in the opinion of the most sensible people, moderation in those who possess a middling fortune does them as much honour, as the rich endeavour to acquire by all the extravagance of external decorations.

If we are obliged in the furniture of our house, to do without many ornaments and conveniences, we may make ourselves amends, by the highest degree of neatness, and, like the wise Arabians, rejoice that we can be happy without superfluities. Besides, the counsellor's daughters will, in time, contribute to adorn the place, by decorating the walls with their drawings, and the chairs with needle-work. In the mean time, if, notwith-standing this noble submission to your lot, the view of the possessions of the wealthy should lead you to make gloomy comparisons between their situation and yours; stop not at the mere enjoyment of riches, but extend your thoughts to the benefits which arise from their expenses to the merchant, the artist, and the tradesman: for though the first thoughts may produce only discontent at your lot, under the other you will possess the satisfaction of a generous mind, which rejoices at the welfare of his neighbour, and the more scanty the share you have in the public happiness, the more noble and praiseworthy will be your joy.

Carefully weigh and examine the capacities of your children, and let none of their talents remain uncultivated: in proportion as you are sparing with respect to everything relating to external appearance, consecrate your care and expenses to everything that relates to their education. Let your daughters learn drawing, music, some of the foreign languages, and all the works proper for their sex; and let your sons acquire all the knowledge proper for men of a liberal education, Inspire them with a love and taste for reading the most valuable books, particularly those which treat of natural history. It is the duty of a reasonable creature to endeavour to become acquainted with the works of his Creator, from which we receive so many enjoyments. The works of nature everywhere display the goodness of the Almighty; the view and knowledge of them impart to the soul the most pure and refined pleasures, pleasures subject to no accident, and under no human control. The more your children are charmed with the natural history of the earth we inhabit, the more they are acquainted with its products, their use and beauty, the more gentle will be their dispositions, passions, and desires; the stronger will be their taste and attachments to what is truly beautiful, and the farther will they be from the idea that felicity consists in sensuality and show.

Let your children also apply themselves to the history of the moral world: the revolutions of states, and the reverses of fortune among the most illustrious persons, will make them see charms in the middle and peaceful rank of life, and doubtless inflame their zeal for virtue, and their eagerness to acquire useful knowledge; for history will convince them, that knowledge, wisdom, and virtue, are the only goods of which neither fortune nor mankind can deprive them.

This very evening, Madam, your children shall receive the books proper to furnish them with these instructions. My heart's best wishes accompany them; may they, in reading these works of the benefactors of society, become enlightened with the rays of truth, and find, as I have done from experience, that study is a perpetual source of solid pleasure.

Permit me, Madam, to make you one or two requests farther; seek no more to form connections with the friends of the table. Show to those who have served you in your misfortunes, all the testimonies of gratitude, esteem and friendship, that is their due: be as kind to the unhappy as your abilities will permit; and till your acquaintance is sought by persons of merit, live with your children in a tranquil retirement. The more beauty and accomplishments your daughters acquire as they grow up, the more you ought to keep them at home. The praises of their masters, the wisdom and modesty of their conduct, will give them a reputation that will excite the desire of knowing them. I am sure, Madam, that you will soon rejoice at your having followed the advice of your friend. Adieu, Madam, I reserve some other particulars for my next visit.

LETTER XVIII

Lord Derby to his friend at Paris

Now for it, brother, is the word with my dear Sophia's countrymen, when disposed to be joyous. As I have spread my English net on German ground, I'll draw it close; for my success is now no longer doubtful. The wings of my bird are already entangled: 'tis true her head and feet are still free, but the other fowlers, who would make her their prey, are driving her into my nets; and what in all this is most wonderful is, that the bird herself will look upon me as her deliverer. What a happy thought was that of dressing myself in her virtues, and imitating her beneficence, without the appearance of wishing to be known! But I was almost too late in putting it in practice, and had like to have let the finest opportunity in the world escape me: but her aunt's tattle set everything right.

In the last assembly at court a mysterious conversation between the prince and Sophia, excited everybody's attention. I observed that the sound of her voice, besides its natural sweetness, had something soft and soothing. – While I was endeavouring to discover what she could be saying to him, I saw the prince seize her hands, and I think he kissed one of them. My head grew dizzy, I flung down the cards, and full of spite, went and leaned against the window: but soon seeing that, filled with confusion, she left him and hasted to her aunt's card-table, I drew near, and cast upon me an animated and somewhat timorous look. I guess, said her aunt, by your looks, that you have been speaking to the prince in favour of Counsellor T. Sophia acknowledged that she had, and that he had promised to take care of him, adding something about his unhappy family. I immediately took the resolution to do something for them the next day, before the prince could fulfil his promise. According to my custom, I went that very evening in my fellow's topcoat, to the window of Count Löbau's dining-room, to get intelligence who supped with my charmer; but scarce was I got into the street, when I saw two sedans stop at the door. Two women instantly appeared, and I heard Sophia's voice, who said, Go to Counsellor T's at S. Gardens. Knowing the house, I flew to my apartment, fetched a purse of money, and going to the counsellor's, threw it into the window at which the lady was sitting; then muttered a few expressions of joy at the good I had done; and when they opened the door I was at a good distance. Surely there was some magic in the words I had uttered, for two days after, going as usual to pay my respects at Count F's, I observed Sophia's eyes fixed on me with a countenance expressive of esteem and complacency; and she began to enter into a conversation with me in English; but as she had come very late, the young Count F. immediately begged her company at cards, and gave her them to cut. She looked about as under some apprehension, and immediately turned up a king, by which she became the prince's partner.

Could I turn up none but this? Said she in a discontented accent; but had she chosen ever so long, she could have turned up none but kings, Count F. having no other in the heap. Her aunt had come late on purpose, when all the other parties were engaged; and the prince entered without the appearance of being expected, and being too polite to take any one's hand, he waited till chance, under the direction of the discreet Count F. should direct who was to be his partner. The French envoy, and the Countess of F. also joined in the party. I was at pharaoh,[39] which allowed me sometimes to rise; I then fixed myself behind the prince's chair, and allowed my eyes to speak for me. She on whom they were fixed, had an enchanting grace in all her motions; the prince was so sensible of it, that seeing her fine hands employed in gathering up the cards, he held out his to seize one of her fingers, crying, Is it possible that so many graces should be born at P**!

Certainly, Monsieur Le Marquis, France itself cannot produce anything more lovely.

The envoy must have been neither a Frenchman nor an envoy, had he not seconded the compliment, though he had thought otherwise. But my Sophia's vexation appeared as visible as her charms; for I suppose the prince's looks expressed no less love than the sound of his voice. My dear girl shuffled the cards with a dejected look. While she was dealing, I turned about, and on her lifting up her eyes to me, I showed her a countenance of indulgent melancholy, and then casting an expressive look at the prince, returned to the pharaoh table, where she could see me playing; I set high, and played with visible distraction, in order to make her believe that the prince's passion had occasioned my confusion, and disregard to my own interest. This could only be attributed to the violence of my love; that was the turn it happily took, and Sophia was attentive to all my actions. When they had done, I went up to the table where she had been playing at piquet,[40] at the moment when she was collecting what she had won, which was considerable; but she owed her good fortune less to chance, than to the prince.

This evening, said she, the Counsellor T.'s children shall have this, and I will tell them, that your highness generously lost it to serve them.

The prince answered with a smile and an air of satisfaction. I now abruptly left the room, fully resolved to watch her going to Counsellor T.'s in order to gain admission there, and speak to her. She had perceived me during the whole evening, dejected and agitated by turns, and my intrusion into the counsellor's house, might naturally be imputed to my ungovernable passion. During my stay in Germany, I have found, on other occasions, that there prevails here a strong prepossession in favour of the English, which putting the most favourable constructions on our most extravagant actions, considers them as a proof of a great and free soul.

By the art of properly seizing the critical moment, I have gained more than I could have done by a whole year spent in sighs and whining. Read the scene I am going to describe: admire my presence of mind, and command of my passions, formerly so unruly, during a close conversation of a full half hour with my goddess, whom I saw before me in the most attractive form. On her leaving the court, she had returned home, to lay aside her robe and head-dress, and was carried to the counsellor's only in a large cloak and plain cap. Her taking off her head-dress threw her fine auburn locks into some disorder; this, with a close jacket, and the colour which the sight of me, and my conversation, gave her, rendered her charming beyond expression.

When she had been there a few minutes I knocked at the door, and asked softly for Mrs T. She came, and I told her that I was secretary to my Lord G. who had intrusted me with a present for her family; but I was to place it in Lady Sophia's hands, and to talk to her about it. The woman desired me to stay a moment, and then ran to get her husband and children out of the room. She then beckoned to me, and I, like a foolish ninny, could scarcely forbear trembling at the very first step within the door; but the anxiety the fair one was in, reminded me of the superiority of a manly spirit, and some remains of confusion seemed to apologize for my intrusion. Before she could recover from her surprise at seeing me, I was at her feet, and made, in English, some warm excuses for the surprise and fear into which I had thrown her; but added, It is impossible for me to live without professing the most respectful, and at the same time the most ardent love; and since my Lord G. has forbid my making frequent visits at your uncle's, and I have seen others have the boldness to entertain you with their passion, I have been ambitious of obtaining the liberty of telling you, that being a witness of your virtues, I cannot help admiring so extraordinary a character. You alone have made me feel the truth of that maxim of one of the ancients, that if Virtue was to appear visible to human beings, none of them could resist the force of her charms. Yes, I consider this house as her temple; I come here to pay my homage at the feet of her who has made me know her in all her beauty. I am come hither, to declare that I did not think myself worthy of mentioning my love, till I had conformed myself to her example, and become worthy of her, by imitating her perfections. My sudden appearance, and the warmth with which I expressed myself, had in a manner confounded, and at first ruffled her; but the word Virtue, which I took care to pronounce several times with particular emphasis, was the charm with which I appeased her resentment, and procured all the attention that was necessary to make me gain over her vanity to my interest. The philosopher Plato, and the virtue which appeared visibly by degrees, dispersed the clouds which hung on her brow; and in her eyes, which were cast down, I could discover the expression of a delicate pride. I was satisfied with this remark, and concluded my speech, which had taken a very tender turn, by repeating my excuses.

She said, with a somewhat tremulous voice, that she owned both my appearance and discourse had been very unexpected, and that she could have wished that the sentiments I professed to have entertained for her had prevented my surprising her in a strange house.

I made some tender protestations, and my face expressed the fear of my having offended her. My lord, said she, giving me a look of inquietude, you are the first man that has talked to me of love, and with whom I have been alone; and both give me pain. I beg therefore you would leave me, I shall consider your retiring as a proof of the esteem you pretend to have for my character.

Pretend! O Sophia, were my sentiments only feigned, I should have had the prudence to avoid your anger! Love and despair have rashly brought me hither: say that you forgive me, and that you do not reject my sincere adoration.

No, my lord, never shall I reject the real esteem of a worthy man; but I repeat it, if I have obtained yours, leave me.

I seized one of her hands, which I kissed with a tender ardour: Adorable creature! angelic maid! cried I, I am the first man that has spoken to thee of love, oh may I be the first that has made thee feel it!

Seymour then came into my thoughts: it was time for me to retire; I left my purse at the door, and looking back, desired her to give it to the family.

She followed me with her eyes, which had a look of goodness. Since that time I have seen her twice in company, but took care to observe a respectful distance; dropping seasonably a few tender expressions, and some words expressive of my sufferings; and, besides, when she either hears or sees me, I take care to behave with the utmost prudence.

I know from my Lord G. that at court all imaginable measures are taken to gain over her understanding; for, as to her heart, they already think themselves sure of it, because she is fond of doing good, and the prince is willing to oblige her in everything she desires. All the talk before her continually turns on love and gallantry. But nothing can be more favourable to my views, than this method of proceeding; for the more they exert their endeavours to destroy her ideas of virtue and honour, the more will her female obstinacy make her steady to her principles. My Lord G.'s stoical politeness, and Seymour's suspicious and reserved looks, wound that delicate soul which knows what right it has to the esteem of others; but, on the contrary, I always treat her with the utmost respect. I admire her singular excellence. I hold myself unworthy to speak to her of love, till I have formed myself by her example; and am thus become worthy of her: hence everything she opposes to their seductions, and even her very virtue and self-love, are in my interest; I shall surprise her in complete armour, and my Sophia will be in the case of the knights of yore, who, embarrassed with their gorgeous and heavy coats of mail, became the prey of the conqueror. Say no more of my being so soon satiated with the pious and lovely Orphisa, notwithstanding all the trouble her conquest had cost me; nor any longer imagine that the scene with this immaculate nymph will be closed in the same ridiculous manner. Thou art far wide of the mark in thy notions of this transcendent creature. A devotee, of lively feelings, has no less extravagant ideas of virtue, than those of my Sophia, and there is a satisfaction in driving away all such hobgoblins from the imagination of a pretty woman. But here lies the difference between them. It is from self-love that the devotee ardently strives to avoid torment, and to gain an entrance into Paradise; consequently, it is from interest that she is virtuous; that she dreads the torments of the infernal regions, and desires a state of felicity; hence, at bottom, her piety is merely sensual. If, after this, she sacrifices herself to the desires of a lover, it is doubtless from the same principle, to taste the pleasures that spring from love; for it appears, from their descriptions of celestial joys, from their choosing at table the most delicious morsels, and relishing them with a luxurious satisfaction, that the senses have great power over the devotee.

But it is quite otherwise with my lovely moralist, who makes her virtue and happiness consist in doing good to her fellow-creatures. With her neither the delicacies of the table, splendor, diversion, adulation, nor the most flattering respect, can out-balance the pleasures of a benevolent action; and the same motive which leads her to render those objects happy to whom her beneficence extends, will doubtless engage her to invent every day new pleasures for her lover: thus I cannot conceive that one can be ever tired of her. However, I shall soon be able to send you more news, for the plot is ripening apace: the violence of the prince's passion makes them in haste to conclude the comedy, and I am told, that to seduce the lady, nothing but entertainments upon entertainments are proposed.

LETTER XIX

Lady Sophia to Emilia

Could you have believed, my dear Emilia, that the time would ever come when I should repent of my having done good? Yet it is come, and I reproach myself for my too ardent zeal in serving others, and am myself become a victim of it. You saw in my last letter, the difficulties I had to get over in conquering my reluctance to intercede with the prince for Counsellor T.'s distressed family. You know also the reason of my dislike to it, and the motives which induced me to comply. The consequences of that unhappy step have involved me in distress and perplexity, and have made me thoroughly dissatisfied with myself. This is owing to the behaviour of the prince and Lord Derby. The prince, since that time, has importuned me by his looks and discourse, and went so far, that while we were playing a game at piquet, his exclamations on my charms, and the like nonsense, fixed the attention of the whole court. In the midst of the anger and confusion I was then in, I accidentally cast my eyes on my Lord Derby, who was just come to us from the pharaoh table, and plainly perceived in his countenance the marks of a violent emotion; then casting a furious look at the prince, he went and played like one who scarcely knew what he was about; but I little thought that very night he would fill me with the utmost distress and inquietude. I won a good deal of money of the prince, which was not owing to chance; for I several times perceived that he played ill with a design to lose; but whatever view he proposed to himself in this, my winning gave me no pleasure, and this I made him sensible of, by saying, that I would go that very evening to give the money to Mrs T.'s children. Derby must certainly have heard me, and immediately have formed the scheme of watching for

the moment when I entered that house. To introduce himself, he made use
of a cunning artifice. I had been there but a little while, when he knocked at
the door, and asking for Mrs T. told her, he was Lord G.'s secretary, and
was entrusted with a present which I was to give to her family. The good
woman, delighted with the hopes of receiving another considerable present,
came and took out of the chamber her husband, her children, and even
Rosina. Before I could know what she was about, she conducted in the
pretended secretary; and having just mentioned the commission with which
he was entrusted, disappeared. I was so filled with surprise and vexation, at
the sight of the Lord Derby, that he had time to kneel before me, and to
apologize for his conduct, before I was able to complain of it. When I could
recover my voice, I reproached him for his intrusion in a serious manner,
and in few words; on which he began to talk of a passion which he had long
concealed, of the despair to which he was reduced by Lord G. who had
forbid his frequent visits at our house, while he saw others presume to
entertain me with their love. My Lord G.'s prohibition surprised me, and
made me thoughtful. My Lord Derby continued to express himself with
great warmth, and I recollected the agitations I had observed him under
during the whole evening, and this served to increase my distress. I desired
him to leave me, and walked towards the door. He opposed my going out,
though in a respectful manner; but the sound of his voice, and his looks,
expressed such softness, that I was extremely frightened and displeased. At
this moment I was out of humour with the sensibility of my heart, and
regretted the emotion of humanity which had led me that evening with my
card money to that house, and thus exposed me to this distress.

I, however, at length recovered myself, on his entreating me, in the
sacred name of virtue, to consent to hear him a moment. I cannot repeat
what he said; but recollect that he said little on my exterior form; though
much on my character, which he pretended to be well acquainted with, and
concluded in an affecting manner, by promising to consecrate his life to
virtue and to love.

Fluttered, confused, and dissatisfied both with myself and him, I entreated him, as a proof of his sincerity, to leave me. He at length went, after
repeating his excuses, and left near the door a heavy purse of money for the
poor family.

An unusual weight oppressed my heart; and at that moment the only
happiness I wished for was solitude. Mrs T. coming in, I gave her my lord's
present, with my card-money. Her joy relieved me a little; but I left the
house with the firm resolution of never entering it again while the Lord
Derby remained in D. At my return, my uncle and aunt were still at play,
and I retired to bed. The loss of parents and friends dear to my heart, had
made me pass melancholy nights; but till this time, sleepless hours of painful
solicitude, and anguish of soul, I had never known; gloomy thoughts on the
opposition between my character and my lot, on the contradiction of all my
wishes, employed the hours destined for sleep. It had always been my

principal care to preserve an irreproachable conduct, yet the Lord Derby
had exposed me to the suspicion of having given him a private meeting. My
Lord G. whose esteem, I flattered myself, I deserved, forbade his relation to
visit me. I desire the friendship of a virtuous man, he shuns me, and I see
myself exposed to the pursuit of the prince and Count F. What shall I say of
the Lord Derby? I confess that I am prejudiced in favour of the English; but
– Yet why should I prefer the one, and reject the other, before I know
them? Certainly I have been unjust, and too precipitate. Derby is impetuous
and inconsiderate; but is a man of wit and sensibility. His heart cannot
surely be corrupt, since he is so ready to do good: he is capable of loving me,
and appears to be charmed with my principles. However he passes for a
wicked man, and an opinion so generally received cannot be without
foundation; yet virtue still bears some sway in his heart. O Emilia! if love
should draw him from the path of error; if I should be destined to conduct
him to that of virtue, should I not be obliged to sacrifice my preference of
him who never asked it, to him who is the object of this change? But at
present I could wish that my choice was superseded by the arrival of my
aunt R. Vain wish! she is at Florence, and stays to lie-in there.[41] Thus you
see that everything is against me. Add to this, the importunity of young
Count F. an union with whom, even though I could like him, would not be
agreeable to me, as it would chain me to the court; for however these fetters
were gilt and adorned with flowers, they would not be the less galling and
insupportable. I suffer by the thought of depriving anyone of the hopes of
the happiness it is in my power to procure; but why will not they
condescend to compare their way of thinking with mine? they would then
see the impossibility of making me conform to their measures. My uncle and
aunt astonish me. They, who knew my parents, and the education I have
received; they who cannot but be convinced that I am steadfastly fixed in
my ideas and sentiments, think of decoying me into a surrender of my heart
and hand, by the glittering toys of splendour, rank, and diversions! Yet I
cannot be angry with them: they desire that I should be happy in their way,
and they take all imaginable pains to show me the court in a most tempting
light; even my inclinations to benevolent actions, they have mentioned as a
motive that deserves my utmost regard. While Count F. imagining that the
prince has an extraordinary value for me, would, with pleasure, grant any
request I should make, has, I have reason to believe, set some people on
applying to me to obtain favours. If they thought by this means to expose
me to the greatest temptation to which I could be subject, they were right;
for to have the power of doing good, appears to me the only happiness
worth wishing for.

Happy was it, that the first request made to me proceeded from vanity,
and they desired what they could very well do without. I then said, I had
resolved, that I would never more importune the prince, and that had it not
been for the extreme distress of the counsellor's family, I should never have
done it at all. Indeed, had it been a person really necessitous, who applied to

me to speak in his behalf, I should have fallen into a painful perplexity, between my desire to serve another, and my reluctance to lay myself under any obligation to the prince. Yet I must be obliged to speak to him of my uncle's lawsuit, and I am to do this at a masked ball, for which great preparations are making: invention has been set on the stretch ever since it was first mentioned; both the courtiers and the citizens are invited, and all are determined to distinguish themselves by their habits.[42] I must confess that I am pleased with the plan, because it will not only be a lively representation of the Roman Saturnalia,[43] which may be called the feast of equality; but I promise myself that I shall be entertained with seeing the various effects of fancy, in the choice of dress, in so many persons. The young Count F. my uncle, my aunt, and I, are to personate a band of Spanish musicians, who rove all night about the streets, singing and playing under the windows of some admired Dulcinea.[44] It is a happy thought, and our clothes, which are to be scarlet and black taffeta, will appear very fine. But my being obliged to make my voice heard before so many people, must destroy all my pleasure; because it is showing such confidence in one's talents, and such an odious thirst of praise. But they are resolved to please the prince, who loves to hear me sing, and persuade themselves, that by this means, my uncle will gain his suit. I own I had rather sing before the whole world, than renew the scene of yesterday, when I was forced to sing before him in our garden; to allow him to walk with me, and to hear him all the while talk of his love. He expressed his admiration of my wit, and of my being so mighty clever in everything; and said, that my whole form had thrown his court into such disorder, that he was scarce able to bring business into a right channel, the power of my charms having spared the master as little as his servants.

My going away, said I, will then be the best means of remedying this disorder.

No, that must not be; my court shall not be deprived of its most lovely ornament: You shall make your choice, and render one man happy; and never – never shall you leave D.

I was pleased with his stopping here, which he doubtless did, from his observing that I suddenly looked very grave and pensive; for on his mentioning my making choice of the happy man, he turned to me with such an eager and passionate look, that I was really afraid he was going to make a more full declaration. He asked me in a very tender manner, what made me so serious? On which, recovering myself as well as I could, I answered with some spirit, that it was the thoughts of my choice, as I did not know any one in D. whom I could fancy.

How, nobody! Then take him who loves you best, and can best prove his love. We then joined the company. Every eye seemed to study the prince's countenance. He behaved with great politeness, and retired soon after, saying to me with a smile, Do not forget my advice.

I talked very seriously to my aunt on the disposition the prince discovered with respect to me, and told her I would not feed any person's love, where I could not return it, therefore I would not sing at the ball, and entreated her to let me return to Sternheim.

She exclaimed at my fantastical notions. I had such strange principles, and was so foolish as to be disgusted at what was no more than mere politeness; but for heaven's sake, and for the sake of her children, I must not refuse to be at the ball; and if anything happened there that I did not like, she herself would go with me to Sternheim, and stay there the remaining part of the year. I told her that I would put her in mind of her words, and renewed my promise of compliance. Thus this is the last act of tyranny to which complaisance shall make me submit; and immediately after it, I will return to my dear abode at Sternheim. O my dear Emilia, with what a transport of joy shall I enter that house, where everything will recall to my mind the virtues of my parents, and everything invite me to follow their steps! I can neither adopt the virtues nor the vices of the great: the former are too glittering, and the latter too dark. A round of peaceful employments proper to satisfy the mind, and to sooth the heart, is the kind of happiness for which I feel myself born, and that I shall find on my estate. Once that happiness was increased by the company of my Emilia; but Providence has called her to exercise other virtues; her friendship remains, and her letters will give me pleasure.

Glad am I that I know the great, and am acquainted with the vanity of all their splendour. From this knowledge I have obtained some advantages: my mind and my taste are improved; their luxuries; their alarming, their tiresome pleasures, will make me find more charms in the noble simplicity, the tranquil delights of my late father's house. I have not found in the world the enjoyments of friendship, for which my heart longed; but it has taught me to set a higher value on that of my Emilia: I have felt the power of love, but I have also found that virtue has preserved its empire in my heart; and an object that would banish it from thence, shall never possess my tenderness.

Beauty and wit, though I am no stranger to their value, have no influence on me; as little have the tenderest speeches; and less still praises of my person; for then I discover in my admirer only the love of pleasure. By an esteem for the good dispositions of my heart, and by applauding my assiduous endeavours after mental improvements, I may be moved, as it is a sign that the person possesses a soul that is at unison with mine, and is a proof of a real and lasting love: but of this I hear nothing from any one from whom I could wish to hear it. Derby has endeavoured to assume a similar sound, but not one string of my heart has returned it. Even his love, or whatever it be, only increases my longing after a tranquil solitude. This day se'nnight[45] brings on the ball; and, perhaps, I shall write my next letter to you, in my closet at Sternheim, at the foot of my mother's picture, the sight of which will invite my pen to entertain you on another subject.

LETTER XX

The Lord Derby to his friend

The comedy of the prince, and my Sophia, which I made the subject of my last letter, has, through a romantic freak of my cousin Seymour, assumed such a tragical appearance, that nothing less than the death or flight of the heroine can unravel the plot. From the first, I hope that the God of youth will preserve her; and to accomplish the latter, I trust that Venus will provide for her by my means.

As Sophia loves dancing, they flattered themselves that the amusement of a ball would render her more compliant and tractable; and as she had never seen a masked ball, preparations were made for giving one on the prince's birthday. She was prevailed with to promise to sing, because she and her company were to personate a band of Spanish musicians. The prince getting intelligence of this, desired Count Löbau to indulge him in the satisfaction of providing Sophia's dress, that he might make her a present of it, without her knowing it. The uncle and aunt consented to it, and employed themselves in providing their own habits; but two days before the ball, a report spread throughout the court and city, that the prince had given jewels to Lady Sophia, and that he himself would wear her colours. Seymour, on hearing it, was filled with the utmost rage and indignation; I myself had some doubts, and resolved to watch her more narrowly than ever. Nothing could be more whimsical than their entering the ballroom, headed by the Countess of Löbau, clothed like an old beldam, with a lantern, and some scrolls of music. She was followed by old Count F. with a bass viol; Löbau had a German flute, and Sophia, who had a lute, was in the rear. Being drawn up before the prince's box, they began to tune their instruments, the music for the dancing ceased, and my charmer sang an air. She was in crimson trimmed with black taffeta; her fine hair flowed negligently on her shoulders; her breast decently covered, yet rather more shown than usual; and, in general, she was dressed with much taste, and in a manner that seemed designed to display alternately all her personal charms: they had invented, for instance, very wide sleeves, which falling back while she played on the lute, discovered the lovely proportion of her fine arm; while, an half mask, discovered the prettiest mouth imaginable, and her self-love, inducing her to sing well, she made us hear the most harmonious strains.

Seymour, in a black domino,[46] leaned against the wall viewing her with convulsive emotions. The prince, in a Venetian cloak, gazed on her from his box, with eyes sparkling with hope and desire, clapped her singing, came out to dance a minuet with her, and bestowed a profusion of praises on her skill, and the celerity of her fingers. My head began to grow giddy, and I ordered my friend John, the clerk to Lord G.'s under-secretary, to redouble his attention; my blood being in such a ferment as to throw all my thoughts into confusion. However, I made this remark, that the countenance is the proper expression of the soul; for my Sophia being unmasked, was always the image of modest beauty, a nobleness and purity of soul shining in her air and looks, that confined the desires she inspired, within the bounds of respect: but now her eye-brows, her temples and half her cheeks, being concealed by her mask, her soul became invisible; she lost the moral characters by which she was distinguished, and was no more than a fine woman: besides, she owed all her splendour to the prince; she had had the complaisance to sing to please him, though she had long known that he loved her; all this made us consider her as his mistress.

This opinion was confirmed, when, within a quarter of an hour after, the prince appeared in a habit of the same colour as hers, and after a few German dances, came up to her, who stood by her aunt, with whom she was talking, and throwing his arm round her waist, made her run dancing to the other end of the hall. This sight rendered me furious, though I observed that she frequently strove to disengage herself from his arm; but at every effort, he pressed her more closely to his breast, and at last led her back, when Count F. taking the prince aside, talked very earnestly with him. Soon after a white mask, placed himself close to Sophia, who suddenly made a violent motion with her right arm towards her breast, then stretched her left towards the white mask. He escaped in the throng, and she ran through the hall with inconceivable swiftness. I followed the white mask to the corner of a passage where he threw off his habit, and who should it be but Seymour, in his black domino, who flew downstairs, and disappeared, leaving me extremely anxious about what he had said to Sophia. John, who did not lose sight of her for a moment, had followed her, and seen her enter a room, where she found her uncle and the Countess of F. where instantly tearing from her head all the jewels with which it was adorned, with the utmost anguish and contempt, she threw them on the floor, and looking at her uncle, cried with the voice of distress, How have I deserved to have my honour and good name sacrificed to the prince's detestable passion?

With trembling hands she untied her mask, tore the lace of her neck and ruffles, and scattered them on the floor. John had slipped into the chamber, and was a witness of all these extravagancies. Soon after the prince came in with Count F. and her aunt, whereupon John concealed himself behind the curtain of the door, which they took care to lock. The prince fell at her feet, and entreated her in the most tender terms to explain the cause of her terror, she answered with a flood of tears, and endeavoured to go away; but he held her, and renewed his entreaties.

What signifies that humble posture? Will it repair the loss of my reputation? O, aunt, how cruel are you to the child of your sister! – O, my father, to what hands have you entrusted me!

The solemn voice of agony with which she pronounced these words, seemed to move the prince extremely. Her aunt then began: She did not understand one word of her vexation and complaints; but wished to be no longer troubled with her.

Grant me then one last favour, and send me from hence; I shall not be long a trouble to you.

This was said by my Sophia, with a stammering voice. A violent trembling had seized her; she leaned upon a chair, and was scarcely able to stand. The prince, with all the tenderness of a lover, endeavoured to calm her, and protested, that there was nothing in the world which his love would not make him do for her.

Oh, it is not in your power, said she, to restore me that peace of which you have deprived me. Pity me, O aunt, pity me, and send me home!

Her trembling increased; at which the prince was so deeply concerned, that he went himself to order a coach to be sent for a physician.

Lady Löbau had now the barbarity to give Sophia some harsh words on account of her behaviour, to which the distressed lady only answered by a torrent of tears; at the same time raising her eyes to heaven, and wringing her hands.

The prince entered the room with the physician, who looked at her with surprise, felt her pulse, and then observed that she was in a violent fever, with strong convulsions; on which the prince earnestly recommended her to his particular care. On its being mentioned that the horses were put to the coach, Sophia looked around her with fresh terror; fell on her knees to the prince, and holding up her hands to him in a supplicating attitude, cried, Oh, if you have really any love for me, let me be carried no where but to my own house.

The prince raised her up, and said, with great emotion, that she might depend on his most sincere respect, and that he had no thought of deceiving her; but only entreated her to keep herself composed, for the doctor himself should accompany her.

Having thrown her handkerchief about her neck, she gave the old gentleman her hand, and left the room with tottering steps. Her aunt stayed, and began to talk about her niece; but the prince silenced her, and said, with anger, that they had all of them deceived him with respect to the lady's character, and had concurred to mislead him. Then leaving the room, the countess did so too, and John was released from his confinement.

They continued dancing in the ball-room, but not without whispering their remarks on this adventure. Almost all blamed Sophia's conduct. 'She might be virtuous without making such a racket about her virtue. – Don't they say that the prince was never in love with any woman before her? She might defend her honour in a more prudent manner, without calling the public to be witness to it, etc.'* Others looked upon it as all a farce, and were curious to know how long she would play her part.

As for me, being persuaded that Seymour must have been the cause of her virtue being put into such a violent ferment, I eagerly longed to know what he had been able to say to her, and the impression it had made, in order to regulate my conduct accordingly. I, however, concealed my uneasiness, and laughed and jested with the company, while I waited for John's return; for he had hasted home to watch Seymour.

But imagine, if you can, how greatly I was surprised at hearing from my emissary, that Seymour had just set off in a post-chaise and six, followed only by a single domestic. What could this mean, if it did not proceed from a concerted scheme. I drew John out of the ball-room, and throwing my mask into the street, put on his surtout, to run to the Count Löbau's, to get, if possible, some intelligence of my actress. Jealousy, rage, and love, made such a commotion in my brain, that it would have cost the life of him who had told me she was abroad; but in less than a quarter of an hour a person ran from the house to an apothecary's, and the door being left open, I slipped into the court, and saw a light in Sophia's chamber. This gave me comfort; but a thought arose in my mind, that this light might be only a blind. I ventured therefore to go in, and found my way in the dark to her servant's chamber, where a closet door, which led into Sophia's room, being open, I heard her voice. Seymour was therefore gone alone. I thought, for a moment, how to excuse my intrusion, and had the courage to show myself, and beckon to Rosina, her maid, to come and speak to me: the girl did not know me; she came out with a candle, shut the door after her, and hastily asked me, Who are you? What do you want?

I made myself known, entreated her, with a respectful earnestness, to inform me how her divine lady did, and begged of her, on my knees, that she would every day inform one of my men. I told her that I had been a witness of the young lady's adorable character, and was ready to offer up my life to serve her; but that having heard that the physician had said something about a fever, I was extremely alarmed.

Highly pleased was the Abigail[47] to hear from me what had passed that evening; for her lady had done nothing but weep and tremble. I took great care to embellish my account with everything that might serve to exalt my heroine. When I mentioned the white mask – Oh! it is that mask (cried she, interrupting me) that has made my lady sick; it is he that peresumed to say, that she trampled under foot all the laws of honour, in appearing in a habit and with jewels that were to become the price of her virtue: all the masks, added he, will tell you so; they all despise you, and expected a very different conduct from a character like yours, and the education you have received.

And who, cried the girl, was this mask! My mistress don't know; but she

---

* And those who spoke in this way were perhaps not entirely in the wrong. – E.

says he has a noble and beneficent soul, though his discourse pierced her heart.

Heaven bless, thought I to myself, the beneficent Seymour, for his folly! He is willing to perform good offices for a man of wit. I promised the servant to make enquiries who this mask was: I also told her the various opinions of the assembly, adding that I had been her mistress's defender; that I would always defend her at the hazard of my life; and that I only entreated her to let me know what I could do to serve her. Rosina appeared affected. Girls are delighted at seeing the power of love, and are so charmed at the empire their sex has over ours, that they heartily assist in forming the garland that is to crown our constancy. She promised me a second interview the next evening, and I retired in high spirits, turning a hundred projects in my head.

My most important care was now to conceal from the soft-headed Seymour, the heroic effect of his ungenteel reproof; but being ignorant of the place of his retreat, I was obliged to have recourse to my guineas, and by virtue of them I prevailed on a clerk of the post-office to deliver to me all the letters directed to Lady Sophia Sternheim, Count Löbau, or any of Seymour's and Sophia's acquaintance. I am at least very sure, that she can receive none at that house. She was for setting out immediately for Sternheim; but her uncle has declared, that he won't let her go. Her fever continues; she wishes for death, and permits nobody to approach her but the doctor and her maid, who is entirely in my interest. I go there every night, and am obliged to hear a great deal of her lady's virtues – 'She is of a very tender disposition, but will never love anyone but a husband.'

Do you mind the hint? – Was she never in love? said I, with an innocent air. No; never did I hear her say a word about it, nor praise one man more than another, except my Lord Seymour, on our first coming hither; but now it is a long while since I heard her say a word about him. I know, my lord, that she esteems you for your beneficence.

I behaved to the creature with great modesty and discretion; and as she, in her lady's name, forbade my taking any of the steps I proposed for the defence of her honour, I cried, in a plaintive voice, Will she also reject the offer of my hand? I should act without the consent of Lord G. but no matter, I would hazard everything to deliver her out of the hands of her unworthy family, and to present her in England to more worthy relations. This string I could not avoid harping on, she herself having begun with it, and I was willing to avail myself of her aversion to D. and her attachment to England, before Seymour's return, who on his being undeceived, would be as extreme in his enthusiastic passion for her, as he was unjust in his contempt. She had formerly praised him; but now she did not so much as mention his name; nor did she take any notice of Lord G. which were evident signs of a glimmering passion. I found out the means of conveying to her short sarcastical letters, in which her sickness, and the scene she had acted at the ball, were ridiculed; in which were, also mentioned the little

value Lord G. expressed for her; and I did not fail every day to repeat the
offer of my hand, leaving it to her choice, to make the marriage public, or to
trust to my honour and tenderness. I leave to fate the effect which this mine
will produce: It is difficult for me to continue long sneaking about this house
without being discovered. I have already done it a fortnight, and had it not
been for the preparations that are making at court for the reception of two
princes, they would perhaps have interrupted my work. John is an admirable fellow; he intends, should it be necessary, to learn the marriage service
by heart, and to personate the chaplain to the English envoy. My last scheme
must be attended with success; for with all the lustre of her perfections, she
is but – a woman. Her pride is offended, and it is difficult to refuse the
pleasure of revenge. No soul but me interests himself in her behalf; she has
also found out that I am generous, and she sets a value on the sentiments I
discover. Never could she have believed that she should find herself in such
a situation; but she would not render me unhappy: She would not involve
anybody in her calamity.' My forbearing to intrude so far as to visit her in
her chamber, pleases her extremely; that is, perhaps, because she would not
choose to be seen with the colour of the fever.

Within a few days the mine will be sprung, and I have reason to believe
that it will succeed. Won't you wish it success?

LETTER XXI

Lord Derby to his friend

She is mine, irrecoverably mine[48]; there is not one of my shot that has not
taken effect. I stood in need of a devilish deal of cunning to keep up her
favourable dispositions, and to hinder others from taking advantage of her
weakness. But her guardian angel must either have left her in the lurch[49], or
be a phlegmatic torpid being; for not one single good turn has he done for
her. – Did not I tell thee, that I would bring over her very virtue to my
interest. I touched her greatness of soul, by offering to sacrifice myself for
her. She could not bear to be in my debt, and therefore sacrificed herself to
me. Couldst thou believe it? She consented to a private marriage, which
was, however, on certain conditions, which none but such an enthusiast
would have dreamt of. My satirical letters had said, that her uncle had
resolved to sacrifice her to his lawsuit; which sat the easier on him from the
public tattle, that on account of her mother's marrying below herself, she
ought not to be treated with the respect due to a real Lady.

Every passion was now set in motion, her virtue, her self-love, her vanity; and I was permitted to read the whole bundle of satirical letters; for I received a packet containing all those libels, with a note written by her own hand, in which she asked me, Whether my observations on her disposition and manner of thinking, were sufficient to convince me of the falsity of those accusations? She was not ignorant, she added, that in England a man of honour, by his marriage, did not expose himself to censure, for only consulting his heart, and the merit of the object beloved. She had no doubt of my generosity, as she had seen several instances of it; that since she was called by her lot to put it to the proof, she accepted of the assistance I offered her, and in return, promised me an eternal esteem and gratitude: that she foresaw all the inconveniences that would attend a public marriage, and should be glad that everything should be passed over in silence. She only desired me to subscribe to four conditions, the first of which was difficult to accomplish, but was esentially necessary to her peace of mind; that is, of its being performed at her uncle's house, she being resolved not to leave it but with a husband worthy of her. The second was, that I would permit her to make over the income of her estates for three years. The third, that I would conduct her to her uncle Count R. at Florence, to whom she would first declare her marriage: but that as to her relations at D. they were unworthy of her confidence. At the moment of her arrival at Florence, she would be mine without reserve, and during the rest of her life, would have no other will but mine. Fourthly and lastly, she desired me to let her have her chambermaid with her.

I objected to the first article, the impossibility of accomplishing it, without the prince and my Lord G. being informed of everything; and said, we would therefore have the ceremony performed in some other secure place. But she replied, that then everything was over, and she would wait for her destiny. – John now came to my assistance, and two days after I wrote to inform her, that I had gained the envoy's chaplain; and, if she chose that her chambermaid should speak to him, she might send her the same evening. The girl, in fact, came with a letter written in English, in which my heroine gave the particular reasons that obliged her to consent to a private marriage, and concluded with recommending herself to his prayers. This letter was accompanied with a valuable ring.

That devil John had on the doctor's canonicals, and an ample wig: he talked bad German, but very pathetically, at which the wench seemed to eye him with great edification. I put into her hand a paper, signed by John, and desired her to tell her mistress that the approaching entertainment given by the prince, would afford the most favourable opportunity of accomplishing our design, since, on account of her illness, she would be neither invited nor observed.

Everything succeeded to my wish; she was highly pleased on reading the paper, to see that I had the complaisance to agree to all her conditions. Why are all good people so shallow, and women so very imprudent, after so many examples of our knavery? But vanity has such dominion over them, that each of them imagines that she has a right to think herself an exception, and believes she is too amiable for anybody to desire to deceive her. They, therefore, are obliged to submit to the natural punishment of their folly, while we enjoy in peace, the rewards of our genius. Certainly, if my Sophia cannot be an exception, no woman on earth ought to flatter herself with being so. Meanwhile her ruin is not yet resolved: if she loves me, and I find in possessing her that variety of pleasures with which I flatter myself, she shall, in earnest, become Lady Derby, and shall render me the father of the most singular race that ever existed, from the mixture of good and evil that will be found in it. It will be happy for my first son, that his mother has such a soft, pious soul; for if she was animated with the same spirit as I, it would be necessary, for the good of society, to strangle the little devil as soon as it was born: but now, instead of this, all the boys in the family will be distinguished by a charming mixture of wit and sensibility. How the deuce came I to treat of this point of matrimonial philosophy. Friend, this is a bad sign; however, I will try it to the utmost.

My virgin made up some medicines, and filled a trunk with linen, and some light clothes which John and I carried away in the evening. She wrote a long letter in the high-flown style of lofty virtue, in which she declared, that she fled with a husband worthy of her, from the danger and guilt that threatened her; that she left to her uncle the produce of her estate during three years, in order that he might make use of it in carrying on his lawsuit, and hoped that it would procure greater advantages for his children, than he had obtained for them by his cruelty to her. − Her rich clothes she left to the parish, to be sold for the use of the poor. − In short, she made two copies of this kind of will, and sent one to the prince, and the other to Lord G.

On the day of the grand entertainment, which was kept in the country, I had taken all my measures for the execution of my schemes. I was at court the whole day, and had shared in all its amusements, till the bustle and confusion becoming disagreeable, I slipped into my chariot, and drove away to D. John hasted with me into the little saloon of Count Löbau's garden, where I own I waited, for the first time, with a throbbing heart, for my pretty Sophia. At length she came, tottering and leaning on her maid's arm, neatly dressed from head to foot, an assemblage of dignity and graces. She cast an eye towards the door; I hastily ran to meet her; she made a step forward, and I kneeled to her with a real emotion of fondness. She gave me her hand, without being able to speak, and the tears flowed from her eyes, though she endeavoured to smile. I could, without the least difficulty, have imitated her embarrassment, for I felt myself a little depressed, and John told me afterwards, that it was high time for me to give him the signal, for had I stayed longer he could not have answered for himself, his resolution beginning to fail. But these were only silly qualms, owing to the tender prepossessions of youth being not yet properly subdued.

I pressed my Sophia's hand to my breast, saying, with a soft voice, Is this hand, fraught with bliss, mine? this celestial hand, mine? Do you consent to make me happy? She answered, stammering, Yes, laying her left hand on her heart. John observing my signal, came forward, pronounced a short discourse in English, babbled over the marriage service, gave us the benediction[50], and I – with a triumphant air, lifted up the half-fainting Sophia; for the first time pressed her in my arms, and kissed the loveliest lips mine had ever pressed. I then felt an emotion of tenderness which I had never before experienced, and endeavoured to inspire her with courage. She seemed, during some minutes, wrapped in silent amazement: then, with an adorable confidence, reclined her head on my breast, raised it a moment after, and pressing my hand to her bosom, said, My Lord, I have nothing left upon earth but you, and the testimony of my own conscience. Heaven will reward you for the consolation you have given me, and this heart will be filled with everlasting gratitude.

I embraced her, and made her all the protestations proper to give her courage. It was then necessary that she should retire with her maid to put on man's clothes. I did not follow her to her *toilette*, fearing to trust my passion; and besides, I had no time to lose. We went out of the house without being perceived: the great number of carriages going and coming on account of the entertainment given to the princes, prevented mine being observed, in which I hastily put my lady, and her servant. John, who had quitted his disguise, was her ductor. Having agreed with him that they should put up at a village not far from B. I hasted back to the ball, where nobody had observed my absence. I gaily mingling with the dancers, frisked about, and could not help laughing at seeing, that the prince would not look at the English dances, from his being galled at the remembrance of my Sophia.

The tumult, the conjectures, the pursuits of the next day, shall be the subject of another letter. I shall now make an excursion to spend a week with my Lady, who, John writes me word, is very thoughtful, and often observed to be in tears.[51]

LETTER XXII

Lord Seymour to Dr T.

Two months have passed since I wrote to you; since tormented by doubts and apprehensions, I have sequestered myself from society, till by a mistaken zeal for virtue, I became the most miserable of all human beings. Oh! If I alone was unhappy, my state would be worthy of envy, when compared with what I now feel; but I have led the most noble, the best of women to form the most desperate resolution! I have caused the most dreadful misfortune to befall my adorable Sophia! Nobody, however can inform me of her fate; but my heart tells me that she is unhappy; and this thought corrodes the heart which entertains it. – But, alas! You cannot comprehend my complaints, and I must endeavour to make myself understood. You know how ruffled and dissatisfied I returned from the rural entertainment provided by Count F. and that from thenceforward I resolved to avoid all company. My love was wounded, but not destroyed. I had flattered myself that contempt and absence would produce my cure. I would not even hear the name of Sophia mentioned. While I was in this situation, my uncle came to extinguish my passion, by informing me, that on the anniversary of the prince there would be a masked ball, and that Sophia would receive from him her habit and her jewels. He added, that she had certainly sacrificed her virtue to him: she had already solicited him for favours, and had obtained them; besides the prince had gone in the evening to Count Löbau's garden, where he had enjoyed the company of his favourite. By this discourse my uncle gained his end: the ardour of my passion vanished with all the blind esteem and hope I had hitherto cherished. But I was not yet entirely indifferent: far from it, my heart was torn by the remembrance of her wit and her virtues. How happy, O my God, cried I, how happy might she have made me, had she but continued faithful to her principles! I will not, however, abandon her, without making her the reproaches she deserves, and this masked ball will afford me a favourable opportunity of executing my design. I provided myself with a double mask, and resolved first to be convinced of the truth of everything that was said against her.

When the time arrived, Sophia entered the hall, led by all the graces; but she wore the diamonds which the jeweller of the court had shown to my uncle, and she was soon so meanly complaisant as to let her harmonious voice be heard. Ah! had I then the power of depriving her of all her talents, and of the enchanting charms of her person, I should have done it at that instant. Yes, I had rather have seen her disfigured, unhappy, or even dead at my feet, than to be a witness of her fall from virtue. I was involved in the most profound melancholy, while she sang and danced minuets with the prince, and some others; but when he threw his arms around her, when he pressed her to his bosom, in the free and indecent dance of their nation[52] – my mute affliction was suddenly kindled into an impetuous flame of rage. I ran out, put on my second mask, and no sooner returned, than I went up to her to load her with the bitterest reproaches. I exclaimed at her having covered herself with disgrace, by her effrontery in having adorned herself with those shameful ornaments presented by the prince; and added, that everybody despised her whom they had adored. These words threw her into the most extreme astonishment. Who I – I was all that she could say, at the same time putting one hand to her breast, and with the other endeavouring

to take hold of me. But, stupid wretch that I was, I fled without waiting to
see the effect produced by what I had said. I hastened home, caused six
horses to be instantly put to my post chaise, and followed only by Dick, my
old servant, I travelled six hours, without knowing where I was going. At
length I stopped at a village, where I excluded myself from all society, and
strictly charged Dick not to mention a word of what passed in the world. It
is impossible to describe the state of my soul: I was senseless, oppressed,
vexed restless, and yet refused to hear any news from D. the only relief my
torments required. This unhappy obstinacy was the foundation of the deep-
rooted sorrow which will now lead me to the grave; for while I went to
conceal the rage of my unconquerable passion in a lonely village, to avoid
being present at the prince's triumph, the Lady Sophia Sternheim opposed
him, by the most noble resistance. The violence of her astonishment and
grief, at what I had said had almost deprived her of life: at length she found
means to escape from her uncle, because he refused to let her return to her
own estate. A month after this last event, I came back to D. with a gloomy
countenance, and a mind worn out with grief. My uncle received me with
paternal goodness, and told me, on mentioning the inquietude I had given
him, that he had suspected me of having carried off Sophia.

Would to God that you had allowed me to do it! cried I, I should not
have been then so unhappy. But, pray, say not a word more about her.

My dear Charles, said he, it is however necessary that you should know
what has happened. She was strictly virtuous; everything said against her
was false; and now she has disappeared.

At this, my desire of knowing everything was equal to the fear I had
conceived of hearing her mentioned.

Sophia, resumed my uncle, who was accused of having received the
jewels from the prince, believed that her aunt had caused her own to be re-
mounted, and that she lent them to her to wear at the ball; for the habit
with which she was dressed, she thought herself in the tradesman's books;
her singing at the ball was on her side, a forced complaisance; and in a letter
to the prince, she called for a thousand blessings on a white mask, who had
revealed to her the base and odious plot which had tarnished her reputation.

O my lord! cried I, I myself, wore that white mask! I spoke to her, I made
her the most bitter reproaches: but immediately after I hastily fled.

At the ball itself, cried my lord, Sophia threw all the prince's jewels at his
feet; she returned home in a deplorable situation, and during eight days was
extremely ill, and would see nobody. As soon as she was recovered, she
earnestly desired to return to Sternheim; but her uncle refused to let her go,
and eight days after, while an entertainment was given to the Prince of P,
she and her chambermaid disappeared. Neither the Count and Countess of
Löbau, who had continued at that entertainment till the morning, nor their
servants, who did not rise early, thought of Lady Sophia till the hour of
dining, when on laying the cloth for the count, they remarked that neither
she nor her maid had been seen, and running to her apartment, found in her

stead several letters: one of them directed to the prince, another to me, and a third to her uncle, in which was enclosed a list of her most valuable apparel, which she had sent to the minister, that it might be sold for the advantage of the poor of the parish. In her letter to the count she expressed, with a proper dignity, and in very moving terms, her complaints against him and his lady; with the reasons which had obliged her to put herself under the protection of the husband she had chosen, and who had received her hand, before she had left their house. She was going, she said, to reside with him at Count R's, at Florence, whence they should hear from her: meanwhile she left them for three years, the produce of her estates, to enable them to carry on their lawsuit, with more innocence, than their attempt to gain it, by sacrificing her honour, She wrote to the prince, that she fled with a generous husband to deliver herself from the pursuits of a guilty and odious passion; that she left her uncle the enjoyment of her estates for three years, at the end of which she hoped, from the justice of the sovereign, to enter again into the possession of her rights. In short, she observed to Lord G. my uncle, that his merit had always engaged her respect, and made her desirous of obtaining a share in his esteem; that it was evident, the circumstances in which she had been placed, had spread a false light on her character and conduct, which prevented his obtaining a just idea of them; but that she could, however, assure him, that she had not rendered herself unworthy of his esteem, which she was ambitious of obtaining, and had done nothing to merit his condemnation. She concluded with entreating him to read that letter to his nephew Seymour. He added, that Count Löbau no sooner discovered that she was fled, than he hasted to the prince, who, astonished at the news, resolved to send everywhere in search of her, but was persuaded from it by Count F. and they were satisfied with sending a courier to Florence, from whence they had not yet received any news of her.

While my Lord was giving me this account, all the faculties of my soul were suspended; but when he stopped, they were all in motion. My uncle was obliged to hear the most bitter complaints of his barbarous policy, which had prevented my being united to that spotless soul. Her generous behaviour to her uncle; her noble revenge of the most shocking outrage; her remembrance of the poor; her desire of justifying herself to me, wounded my heart. How odious then became my abode in that hated city! With what pain did I restrain my indignation, when I saw her enemies, or when they presumed to mention her to me! For the courageous step she has taken to procure her deliverance, is universally blamed: they seek to degrade her excellencies, and suppose her guilty of faults and ridiculous follies, of which she is utterly incapable. How base and shameful, and yet how common is it to take pleasure in obscuring merit! A thousand people stoop to the baseness of discovering in a person, distinguished by eminent qualities, the weaknesses of humanity while there is scarcely to be found an honest heart, who knows how to render a noble and sincere homage to another's superiority.

I dispatched a courier to Florence, and wrote to Count R. the history of his admirable niece; but learnt by his answer, that he was ignorant of her abode, and that all his enquiries after her were fruitless. How did this add to the reproaches I cast on myself for my too precipitate departure! Why did not I stay to see the effects of my expostulations? – Is outrage alone sufficient to recover the guilty? – My heart would be shocked at seeing a suffering being treated ill – Yet a person whom I loved, whom I considered as blinded, I had hastily abused in a manner, that must have wounded her very soul! But I thought she had voluntarily degraded herself; that she was unworthy of all regard, and imagined I had a right to treat her thus. Oh! How barbarous was I to this amiable girl! At first I had resolved to conceal my love, till the moment in which she was to show herself in the full lustre of triumphant virtue. Sophia proceeded without turning aside in the fair path which lay before her, and because she did not follow my chimerical plan, I assumed to myself the right of punishing her in the most cruel manner. We all presumed to judge, to condemn her: but how great, how noble was she, at the very instant when I thought her sunk and debased, she blessed me, who, in the white mask, like a frantic fury, dug in her innocent path an untimely grave. – O what must she think, if she be still alive, of the inconsiderate wretch who has driven her to a precipitate, and doubtless a wretched union; an union which perhaps she already laments, and cannot break! Yet stilll Sophia writes my name – she still desires my esteem! O Sophia, in the midst of the distress I have occasioned, thy innocent, thy generous soul would pity my misery, couldst thou but see in my heart the image of its first hopes, joined to the pangs of its having lost thee!

Derby is returned after an absence of two months. He treats me with great respect; filled with my pains I poured them into his bosom; he laughed at me, and still maintained, that with all his reputation for profligacy, he had done less mischief than I with my zeal for virtue. His wickedness, he said, admonished people to be upon their guard; while the severity of my morals led me to judge of seeming faults, and those which are inevitable, with a severity adapted to increase the obstinacy of the vicious, and to drive the virtuous to despair. How could this truth come from the mouth of Derby! Ah! I feel – I feel that he is in the right! I have been cruel – Yes, I feel that I have – Unhappy that I am, I have rendered the best of women miserable!

O my friend, my instructor, learn a dreadful circumstance of my sorrows, that will embitter all the hours of my life. John, our secretary, disappeared before Sophia's flight, and has not been heard of since. The young lady's chambermaid was once with him, and among his papers has been found part of a letter written by the hand of my Sophia, which contains the following words: 'I approve of the reasons you allege for keeping our union secret; only think of the means of our receiving the nuptial benediction; for I am determined not to go till that be performed, though an alliance with an Englishman appears to me preferable to that of any other.'

Thus she is become the property of one of the worst men any nation can produce. Oh cursed be the day when I first saw her! – when I perceived between us a sympathy of souls! – and may the villain into whose arms she has thrown herself, forever perish! What execrable artifices must he have employed! Her affliction must certainly have disordered her brain; since without this the whole is inextricable. But the letters she has left are so worthy of her, so full of sense and spirit! – Adieu, my dear friend, pity your unfortunate friend; it is he whom grief has rendered distracted.

LETTER XXIII

Lady Sophia to Emilia

Here, in a lonely village, unknown to all who see me, and from those that know me concealed, lives your friend. It is here I find myself, after my self-love, and my excessive sensibility have led me to take a step, which in my days of calm tranquility, I should have beheld with terror. Oh that I could not say to myself, Oh that my Rosina, that my Lord Derby himself, were not obliged to bear testimony, that affliction and sickness had weakened, and in a manner annihilated all the powers of my soul. Where, oh where, my Emilia, shall I find a moment's satisfaction and peace in thinking that I have engaged in an intrigue; that I have entered into a clandestine marriage; that I have fled from the house which my second father had assigned for my abode?

'Tis true, in that house I was treated cruelly, and it was impossible for me to stay there with pleasure or confidence. My resentment was certainly not unjust: for was it possible for me to think without terror, of relations who joined in laying snares for my virtue, who basely strove to sacrifice me to their private interest?

Besides, I had no friend at D. and my heart was averse to the bare idea of seeing again persons who had long been informed of the designs carried on against me at court, and had laughed at my distress and resistance. Yes, nobody was ignorant of them, not even Miss C. whom I believed to be my friend; nobody was so kind and generous as to inform me of them; yet I had never offended them; for I had carefully concealed my sentiments, when I perceived that they would condemn them! But they thought the loss of a girl, the issue of an unequal marriage, of little consequence. Could I, oppressed by the weight of so many offences, whose character was tarnished by my birth, and the loss of my reputation, refuse the only consolation offered me, the esteem and love of my Lord Derby? The distance of the

Count and Countess of R. their not answering my last letter, my being refused to set out for my own estate. – In short, my Emilia, I must confess, that my inclination for England, and the distinguished rank to which the alliance, and the generosity of my lord would raise me, contributed to seduce a mind already prepossessed. I was, however, so prudent, as not to leave the house where I was, without having fixed my lot, by receiving the hand of Lord Derby. I wrote to the prince, to my Lord G. and to my uncle, without naming my spouse; he was, however, so generous, as to leave this to my choice, though my mentioning him would have made him lose the favour of the minister and the court, because it might be suspected that my Lord G. had promoted our marriage, a suspicion that might have been attended with fatal consequences: I was therefore obliged to be so generous as to be silent with respect to him, for fear of exposing to vexation a man by whom I was beloved, and to whom I was to owe my deliverance. It was sufficient that he could bring over the Envoy's chaplain to our interest: I wrote to that gentleman all the reasons which obliged me to consent to a private marriage, and my Lord settled a pension upon him, as a recompence for his losing his place, should the minister deprive him of it.

Conducted and suported by the motives I have here alleged, I set out from G. with a cheerful heart, attended by only one of my Lord's most faithful servants; for to avoid all suspicion, he was obliged to be present at an entertainment given at court. This was very agreeable to me. I should have trembled and suffered extremely had I sat by the side of my husband; but with Rosina, I made a happy and tranquil journey to this little village, where I have been a month without my Lord's having found a convenient opportunity of coming to me. I intended to have prosecuted my journey to Florence, and to have waited there for my Lord: but I could not prevail on him to consent to it, and at present he would disengage himself from all his connections with Lord G. before he takes me to Count R's, and on his leaving Florence, he will make the best of his way to England.

During these four weeks of solitude, I have kept myself closely confined without any other English book but some belonging to my Lord, which I have not read, because they were testimonies of the disorders produced by corrupt principles and examples. Therefore, on the first cold evening which obliged me to have a fire, I threw them into it; not being able to suffer those books and me to have the same master, and the same house. The days seemed long; Rosina asked needlework for herself from our landlady, and I recovering by degrees the exercise of my mental faculties, turned them on myself, and employed then on reflections on my own destiny. These reflections are all gloomy, from the contrast which has for a long time subsisted between my inclinations and the circumstances in which I am placed.

Oh that my father had lived to dispose of my hand to some virtuous man whom he approved! My fortune is considerable, and as my husband and I should have imitated the examples of beneficence my parents have set us, the consciousness of a life, well spent, and the prospect of the happiness diffused around us, would have crowned my days with a solid and pure felicity. Why did I not attend to the voice which restrained me, when my disturbed mind refused the solicitations of my uncle and your father? I imagined that my aversion might spring from unjust prejudices, and consented to exchange a peaceful and uniform life for my aunt's confused flutter of vain amusements. You know how I suported them. At last, I learnt, that people had conspired against my virtue and honour, and then that extreme sensibility which I received from nature, was directed entirely to my defence. Oh how often have I learnt to distinguish by their effects, the difference between the sensibility which relates to others, and that which has no other object but ourselves. The latter is lawful, and natural to all human beings; but it is the former alone that is noble; it is that alone which justifies that expression of the holy scriptures, that man is created after the image of his Maker: since this sensibility to the welfare or sufferings of our fellow creatures is the source of that beneficence, which is the only quality that bears a just, though imperfect, impression of the divine image; an impression not only imprinted on all rational beings, but on the lifeless parts of nature; so that the most feeble plant, or blade of grass, by contributing to the nourishment of animals, is according to its sphere, as beneficent as the large tree, that is so many ways of use to us. The least grain of land, which by its lightness serves to make the earth yield to the labour of the husbandman, as usefully fills its destined place, as the rock, which by its size, fills us with astonishment, and which serves to fix the foundations of the earth. Do not the animal and vegetable kingdoms offer on all sides the gifts with which they enrich our lives? The entire physical world faithfully discharges these duties, and every spring they are renewed. Man alone degenerates, and effaces that sacred impression, which in us would shine with a much stronger lustre, and in greater beauty, from the various ways in which we are capable of exhibiting it.

Here, my Emilia, you recollect my father's principles: my melancholy warmly recalls them to my mind, when in the peace of solitude, I turn back to view the path which my sensibility had pointed out to me; a path so far from that into which I have been hurried. Oh! I have failed in one of the duties of beneficence, that of doing good to others, by setting them a good example.* Nobody will say that my resolution has been influenced by vexation and despair; but all mothers will make use of my fault to guard their daughters from committing the like error; and each maid will persuade herself, that was she in my situation, she could have found a more lawful and more prudent means of extricating herself than I have discovered. I myself know that I might, but then I did not see it, and nobody condescended to point it out to me.

---

* But do not her mistakes themselves become beneficent in virtue of the cautionary effect of their example? Why does she fail to find consolation in this thought? – Perhaps because even the noblest of souls is unwilling to owe its beneficence to the loss of its self-esteem. – E.

How unhappy is it, my dear Emilia, to be reduced to seek for excuses! and how dreadful is it to find none but such as are weak and insufficient! While I was insensible only with regard to others, I offended only those cold souls who are void of feeling; and if I carried my notions of beneficence to an extreme, that sensibility justified the excess. But when it had no other object but myself, I offended against prudence; I failed in the social duties of a maid well born. Oh how dark is this part of my life! With what a gloom is it encompassed! What remains for me, but to raise mine eyes, to keep them fixed on the way before me, and to proceed with courage.

I have owed the first hours of my consolation to my being employed in teaching two poor girls, to work and to think. You know, my Emilia, how I love to be employed: my reflections, and the use of my pen, made me melancholy. – I could not remedy what was passed, and was obliged to consider whatever was blameable in my conduct, as a natural consequence of my erroneous self-love, and to seek for consolation out of myself, either by endeavouring to render my husband happy, or by continually striving to do all possible good to my fellow-creatures. I made enquiry after the poor of the place, and relieved their distress. This induced the tender-hearted Rosina to recommend to me our landlady's two nieces, who are orphans, whom our landlord and his wife do not love, and who make them pay for their subsistance by the harsh treatment they receive. I sent for them, sounded their inclinations, and enquired into what they knew, and of what they were ignorant. Both of them were willing to be taught by Rosina, and I shared with her in instructing these young children: the next day they assisted at my *toilette*, to receive lessons from me, and a fortnight after they served me by turns, while I talked to them of the duties of the stations in which God had thought fit to place them, and also of those which he had been pleased to confer on me. This I did to such purpose, that I brought them to think themselves much happier in being chambermaids, than if they had been ladies, on account of our being obliged to answer for the wealth, and all the advantages we enjoy. Their hopes and desires are otherwise very limited, and the little prospects I lay before each of them suitable to their particular tempers and capacities, give them singular satisfaction, and they imagine that I can read their very thoughts. I pay for their board, have provided new clothes for them, and purchased everything necessary for their learning. I assign them hours for writing and accounts, and take no small pains in teaching them to support, with propriety, the characters and situations in which they may be placed. The landlady, and her nieces, consider me as their guardian angel, and did I permit them, would frequently fall on their knees to thank me. How sweet and happy are the hours devoted to these children! and how often do I call to mind those words of a modern author. 'Art thou plunged in melancholy, and seest nothing around thee that can give thee comfort? Read the Bible: strive to eradicate a vice from thy heart; or seek to do good to thy fellow-creatures: then will thy melancholy disappear.'

Resources as noble as they are infallible! With what pleasure do I take my walks with my pupils, while I entertain them with talking of the goodness of our common Creator! How pure is the joy that fills my heart, when I see their softened eyes lift up towards heaven with sensations of awful respect and gratitude, and at length press my hands, and imprint on them their kisses. In those moments, Emilia, I rejoice even in my flight, since had it not been for that, I should not have found these children.

LETTER XXIV

Lady Sophia to Emilia

Since the arrival of my lord, my pupils have become twice as dear to me as ever; for the happy hours I passed with them had strengthened my mind, and inspired my heart with courage. My lord is not pleased with the gravity of my disposition; he is in love with nothing but sallies of wit; and my soft and timid tenderness is not the return which his flaming and impetuous love demands. All his sensations are violent, and my burning his books threw him into a rage. During the three weeks he has stayed here, I have not dared to see my scholars: his temper appears extremely unequal; sometimes gay and affectionate, sometimes cold and gloomy: he fixes his eyes on me, sometimes with a smile, and at others with a look of secret discontent. He has required me to give him the reason of the aversion I first felt for him, and the motives of my change. He has even questioned me about my Lord Seymour; and my blushing at hearing his name, produced a look that struck me with terror, and which I cannot describe. On a much more delicate occasion I had perceived that he was jealous of Lord Seymour: thus am I constantly to suffer for others. My Lord loves splendour, and has already made me a present of some valuable ornaments, though I prefer a noble simplicity to all the pomp of dress. God grant that this may be the only point in which we shall differ: but I fear – O Emilia, pray for me! – My heart is distracted with apprehensions – I will, however, spare no pains, no complaisance to please my husband: but oh, I find that I shall have to be devious if I am not to sacrifice my character and principles.

I have chosen him; to him I have entrusted my honour, my reputation, my life. I owe him more respect, more submission, than I should owe to a husband whom I had married in other circumstances.

Oh that I were once in my own house in England, and my lord engaged in affairs suitable to the boldness of his character, then I dare hope, that in the midst of his family, his mind would take a more peaceful course; that his pride would change to dignity, his petulance to a noble ardour for praise-worthy actions. That ardour I would endeavour to excite; and since I cannot have the happiness of being an ancient Greek, I will endeavour, at least, to be ranked among the best of the English ladies.

LETTER XXV

Lord Derby to his friend

A plague of thy predictions. What hast thou to do to interfere in my adventures? 'The enchantment will not be durable!' Sayest thou. How the deuce hast thou, with thy shallow capacity, been able to see that at Paris, which I could not see here? But suspend a little the impulses of thy vanity, for thou art not entirely in the right. Thou mentionest satiety, but that is not the affair in question. I have it not, and don't know that I ever shall have that satiety: for many things are wanting to form the idea I had affixed to the possession of her; and yet I can no longer bear the sight of her. – What, not bear the sight of my Sophia, my own supposed lady! She whom I have loved five months even to distraction! But her destiny has placed my pleasures, and her inclination, in opposition; and my heart has been buffeted between them. Sophia makes no other return to the warm embraces of her lover, than the feeble affection of an insensible wife; and she whose compassion is so lively, whose zeal is so ardent, and so active for mere ideas and phantoms, treats me with a cold salute, interrupted with sighs. What a value have I set on her tenderness, and the happiness of possessing her! Proud of my conquest, I looked with contempt upon the prince and his agents. – With what impatience did I wait for the moment, when I should see her again! I would have sacrificed horses, postillions, domestics, to hasten my course. My heart leaped with joy on my discovering the village which contained my treasure, and I was very near pistolling the unhappy wretch who did not instantly fly to open the chaise. In five steps I was at the stairs' head, where she stood in a white English dress, majestically beautiful. I embraced her with transport. She welcomed me, stammering, blushing, and turning pale by turns. Her dejection would have rendered me happy, could I have discovered in it one symptom of love; but an inward anxiety and constraint were visible in all her features. I left her to change my clothes. At my return I stopped at the door, and it being a little open, saw her sitting in the seat of the window, her arms wrapped in the curtains, all the muscles of her face agitated; her eyes lifted up to the ceiling; a strong and short respiration slowly moved her lovely bosom, and, in short, her whole frame expressed the image of silent despair. Judge what an impression this must make on me, and what I ought to think of it. My arrival, indeed, might fill her with new and unknown sensations; but whence this disorder and distress? She might be a little afraid; but if she had any love for me, would so violent a conflict have been natural? I was seized with indignation; I entered the chamber; she changed her attitude, and let her arms and head sink in sadness. I threw myself at her feet, and grasped her knees with my trembling hands.

Smile, Lady Sophia, cried I, smile, if you would not have me lose my senses.

A flood of tears gushed from her eyes; my rage increased, but she put her arm about my neck, and inclined her head on my face.

O, my dear Lord, don't be offended at seeing me still sensible of my misfortunes. Your goodness, I hope, will make me lose the remembrance of them.

Her breath, the motion of her lips, while she spoke, I felt on my cheek, and some of her tears which fell on my face, extinguished my anger, and gave me the sweetest sensation I have enjoyed, during the three weeks I have been with her. I embraced and soothed her; she strove to smile while we were at supper, and during the conversation of the evening; but, sometimes, with all the charms of virgin modesty, turned away her eyes when my looks appeared too ardent.

Attractive creature, how couldst thou cease to be so? How comest thou to let me perceive thy inclination for Seymour?

The following days she strove to appear gay. I had brought her a lute, and she had the complaisance to sing a pretty Italian air of her own composing; in which she besought Venus to make her a present of her girdle, that she might retain the object of her tenderness. The thoughts were happy and well expressed, the music well adapted, and her voice so pathetic, that I heard her with the sweetest transport. But this pleasing dream vanished, when I observed that, during the most tender passages, which she sang the best, she did not cast her eyes on me; but declining her head, cast them on the floor, and uttered sighs, which certainly had not me for their object. When she had done, I asked her if this was the first time of her singing that air? No, said she, blushing. This gave birth to several other questions on the time when she began to think favourably of me, and her opinion of Seymour. But curse the frankness of her answers! her confessions broke all the tender bonds that bound me to her. A thousand trifling incidents, and even the pains she took to appear tender and happy, convinced me that I was not the object of her love. A pretty good opinion of my wit, some esteem for my liberality, the pleasure of settling in England, and a cold acknowledgment of the services I had performed for her in delivering her from her relations, and from the prince, were all she felt for me. She had even the imprudence one day, when I asked her what qualities she should like best in me, to paint Seymour feature after feature. In short, she has incessantly entreated me to hasten my departure, and set out on our journey to Florence, which is a certain proof that her mind is more bent on the gratification of her ambition, than on my happiness. She poisons my sweetest pleasures, by repeating every day this request, to which she has the art of giving all imaginable turns, and has even assured me, that she shall not love me till we arrive in that city. I have said that she poisoned my felicity; but in doing this, she has hardened my heart, which was before so weak, as sometimes to reproach me for our false marriage, and to plead her cause against myself.

In the third week of my being with her the evil grew worse. I had given her some English pamphlets, in which pleasure was painted in the most lascivious and flaming colours, in hopes that some sparks might kindle her imagination; but she had no sooner cast her eyes upon them, than her virtue obliged her to condemn them to the flames. The loss of these pamphlets, and the ill success of my design, put me into an ill humour, which she bore with calmness and resignation.

Two days after I went to her *toilette* just at the time when she was combing her fine locks. Her dishabille was white lawn over a pink lutestring, which sitting close to her fine shape, she appeared ravishingly beautiful. I took her locks, and wrapped them round her waist. She brought to my mind the Eve of Milton; my imagination was inflamed, and sending her chambermaid out of the room, I desired her instantly to undress, and give me the pleasure of admiring in her the copy of Nature's first masterpiece.*
A vivid blush overspread her face, and I received a flat refusal. I insisted; she persisted in refusing me, and, for a long time, defended herself, till my impatience being inflamed, I tore her clothes from her back, and, against her will, accomplished my purpose. Thou canst not imagine how ill she took this liberty, which, in our circumstances, was of so little consequence. My lord, cried she, you tear my heart; you destroy my tenderness for you. Never can I forgive this want of delicacy! O my God, how have I been blinded! – Thus she exclaimed, while she violently pushed me from her, and the tears streamed down her cheeks. I coolly answered, that she would have shown more complaisance to the desires of Lord Seymour. I am sure, said she, in the lofty tone of a tragedy Queen, my Lord Seymour would have thought me worthy of a more noble and delicate love.

Didst thou ever see such a fantastical caprice?[53] After dinner I desired her to explain the reason of it, and at the same time extolled her concealed beauties; when she answered, that she should always reject with indignation such praises as she could not obtain without the violation of modesty.†

---

* Such want of tact, Lord Derby! Surely you could have chosen your moment more carefully? – E.

† Indeed this answer can hardly be said to resolve the riddle. Lord Derby surely spares her these efforts. – So why is she so indignant? Why does she accuse him of tearing her heart, when all he tears is her dishabille? – Presumably because she does not love him, or because he had neglected to prepare her for such a scene by taking her through the appropriate stages, or because she was withal in a frame of mind too removed from his to oblige him in a whim consisting more of wantonness than affection. – E.

Canst thou believe that I can live happily with such a perverse wronghead? This mixture of wit and folly has entered into her whole character, and has given me a kind of languor and disgust. Sophia is no longer her whom I loved; I am therefore no longer obliged to continue what I seemed to be. – She herself has pointed out the way by which I may escape from her chains. Besides, the death of my brother has raised my ideas. Soon, perhaps, it will be necessary for me to return to England, and Seymour may then try his fortune with my widow; for I think she soon will be so; and if that should happen, she will have nobody to blame but herself. Since she thinks herself my wife, is it not her duty to comply with my will in everything? And has she not violated that duty? And what is worse, does she not love another? It is therefore just and reasonable, that as I am deceived by her ambition and conduct, I should be revenged on her ambition for the affront. It gives me great satisfaction, however, when I think that I have been the chosen instrument for punishing the baseness of her uncle, the treachery of the prince, and the folly of the rest of his agents. As to Sophia, she was to blame to elope with me; it is necessary that she should be sensible of this, and I shall have the merit of bringing her to repentance. For all these exploits I have had the necesssary degrees of abilities and address, which I have not ill employed. I have succeeded; and let the others improve by the chastisements they have received.

Know, moreover, that I am become Seymour's confidant. He had sat in a solitary village lamenting the loss of the fair maiden's virtue; while I, laughing at him, kept myself on my guard, and afterwards made him search for her on the side opposite to that I had made her take. He was desirous of knowing from me, who could be the husband she mentioned in her letters. He had sent couriers to Florence, but I found a way to put a stop to his enquiries, by means of the last letter. Sophia had written to me at D. for I tore off that part which might have betrayed me, and threw the other piece among Secretary John's papers. His absence had appeared very suspicious, and by my advice, his chamber was ransacked, when this paper being found, raised a strong suspicion of his being the deliverer of the delicate Sophia; a discovery which proved that she had very mean ideas and inclinations, and this for a long time served as a text for all the ladies of quality to preach to their daughters against marrying beneath their rank. Seymour's love, I suppose, is now turned into contempt, and he has put a stop to his couriers. – As for me, I expect one from England, and then thou wilt know, whether I shall come to thee or not.

LETTER XXVII

Rosina to her sister Emilia

O sister, how can I mention the horrible misfortune that has befallen my dear lady. – That monster Lord Derby! – Surely God will punish him; he will, he will! The villain has abandoned her, and set out alone for England! His was a false marriage: a domestic as wicked as his master, in the disguise of a clergyman, performed the ceremony. My hand trembles while I write it: that we might have no doubt of the excess of our misfortune, the abominable wretch himself brought the letter in which my lord took his leave. In that letter he says, my lady did not love him, and that Seymour has always had her heart: that this has extinguished his love, and prevented his being ever the same. What a wretch! Oh it was I, I myself, who took his part, who persuaded her to consent to this odious marriage! O that I had but addressed myself to Lord Seymour! Ah! we both were blind! – I durst not now see my lady. My heart is broke – She eats nothing. She is all day on her knees before a chair, on which she rests her head, and remains immovable, except sometimes she lifts up her hands towards heaven, crying, in a dying voice, O my God! my God!

She has shed few tears, and only some yesterday. The first two days I was afraid that we should both lose our senses, and it is a miracle that we did not.

It is two days since I wrote the above, and I again take up my pen. During fifteen days we had heard no mention of my lord; his servant left us, and five days after came this fatal letter, which renders us so unhappy. The hardened monster delivered it to her himself. Having run it over, she became pale and motionless; at length, without uttering a word, she hastily tore the letter, and another paper; threw them on the floor, and pointing to the scattered pieces with one hand, cried to the man, Away! away! in a voice of the most violent distress. At the same time she sunk on her knees, joined her hands, and for above two hours remained silent, and to appearance half dead. It is impossible to describe what I suffered. That God only knows. I kneeled down by her, held her in my arms, and entreated her so long, and with so many tears, to be pacified, that she told me stammering, and in a weak, broken voice, that Derby had abandoned her, that her marriage was a deceit, and that she had nothing to wish for but death. – She has no thoughts of revenge; it is with you, my dear sister, that she will conceal herself from every eye. You will receive her. My brother, I am sure, will consent to it, and assist her with his advice. We don't know what is become of my lord: his letter of exchange for six hundred carolines has been torn in pieces. All my mistress's money amounts only to three hundred, of which she gives fifty to the poor orphans her pupils, and as many to the poor of the village. Her jewels, and a trunk filled with clothes, are all we shall take with us. We are so altered by our grief, that you would not know us. My mistress no longer speaks to anybody. The brother of the two orphan girls will accompany us half way. We are coming, my dear sister, to seek consolation from you. She would even write to you, yet her hands, her dear beneficent hands, can scarce move. When I think of all the good she has done, and see her at present so unhappy, I am ready to complain. – But God will surely protect her, and out of these dreadful evils produce good.

LETTER XXVII

Lady Sophia to Emilia

O my dear Emilia, if from this abyss of misery into which I am plunged, my voice reaches you, stretch forth a generous hand to the friend of your youth, that she may pour into your bosom her grief, and her life. Oh how severe, how extreme is the punishment of my flight! O Providence! – But I will not arraign the dispensations of heaven. I have, for the first time in my life, conceived the idea of a kind of revenge. I have been permitted to make use of deceit; ought I not then to consider my having fallen into the power of the wicked and deceitful, as a just punishment of my fault? Why have I believed appearances? But, O God! Where is the heart like that thou hast given me; where is the heart that could entertain the thought, that good, that generous actions should proceed from bad principles?

Thou self-love art the cause of all my misery! Thou hast persuaded me to believe that Derby would learn from me, to feel the charms of virtue! – He says, that he has only deceived my hand; but that I have deceived his heart. Cruel, cruel man, such is the advantage thou takest of the probity of my heart, which sincerely endeavoured to show thee the most cordial affection, the most solid esteem! Ah! Thou does not believe that there is any such thing as virtue; else thou wouldst have fought for it, and have found it in my soul.

It is true, my Emilia, that there have passed some moments in which I have wished to owe my deliverance to Lord Seymour; but I tore that wish from my heart, which was filled with gratitude and esteem for the man whom I had chosen for my husband – a fatal name, how have I been able to write it! but my faculty of thinking, and my sensations are lost, as well as my fortune, my reputation, my happiness. I am bowed down to the dust: prostrate on the earth, I entreat of heaven only to prolong my life, till I have the consolation of convincing you of the innocence of my heart, and of seeing you shed over me a tear of compassion. Then, O Providence, put an end to a life unstained with guilt; but so wretched, that was it not for the hope of its speedy conclusion, it would be insupportable.

LETTER XXVIII

Derby to his friend

I am bound for England; but I will first pay you a visit. Mention not a word of my last love; I will no longer think about it: it is enough that the disagreeable remembrance too often recurs to my mind against my will. My half lady has left the village, where her adventures have been as romantic as her character. She marched off in a medley of pride and resentment; tore my bill of exchange into a thousand pieces, and left behind her all the presents she had received from me. On account of this last exploit, I had some thoughts of following her; but if she could have forgiven the injury she had suffered from me, I should have despised her. It is impossible, after what has passed, that she should love me; and as I can be no longer happy with her, to what purpose should I continue the farce any longer? She must always, however, respect my veracity, and admire my knowledge of the most secret emotions of the soul. I left her quite uncertain what I should do with her; but her repeated desires to be conducted to Florence, and her threatening to repair thither without me, induced me at length to write bluntly to her as follows:

'I plainly see that you only made use of my love to escape from your uncle, and gratify your ambition. You have never been sensible of my tenderness; and have little concern about my happiness, since you set no value on any part of my character, and have no esteem for me, except when I model myself according to your fancies, and appear to adopt your whims. It is impossible for me to resemble the picture you have drawn before me, of the qualities you should love in a husband, because I am not Seymour: for he alone possesses that tenderness which I was desirous of meriting from you. Your confusion at my mentioning his name; the care with which you have avoided speaking of him; even the blandishments you have used to remove my suspicions, are proofs of your inclination for him. You are the first woman who has made me resolve on marriage; yet in forming this resolution of a union with you, I had the prudence to obtain a certainty beforehand of your disposition with respect to me, and the means I chose to employ for this purpose was, to disguise one of my men in a clergyman's habit. My love and my honour were no less bound by this pretended marriage, than if it had been formed by the Primate of England, or the Pope himself. But as an union of minds, which is an essential article, is wanting, I believe it will be best for us to separate without noise, and without witnesses, in the same manner as we met; for I am not so mean-spirited as to be satisfied with the possession of your charms, without having a share in your heart; nor will be such a dupe as to conduct you to England, only to oblige Lord Seymour. You have no reason to complain, since I have snatched you from the pursuits of the prince, and the tyranny of your uncle. I have only deceived your hand; but you, in assuring me of a love which you did not feel, have deceived my heart. I therefore give you a full discharge.'

I sent away one of my servants with this letter, and posted to my opera girl at Berlin, as to an infallible remedy against every species of uneasiness, and she has accordingly restored me to no small part of my former gaiety.

My brother could not have died at a more convenient time than he has done. Cash began to run very low, and this silly romance has been a little expensive, though I should not have grudged what it has cost me, had she but loved me, and renounced her plaguy fanaticism. – I have been so weak as to repent of my letter, and to send two days ago to hear news of her; but she was gone, and was much in the right of it; for we neither could, nor ought to have seen each other. Her letters and picture I have torn in pieces, as she has done my letter of exchange: but my residence at D. where everybody lets their tongue run about her, and where everything reminds me of her, is insupportable. Prepare for me an amusing connection worthy of an English heir, that I may take advantage of the state of freedom I have now recovered: for my father will throw the bridle over my neck as soon as I am with him. He will give me what wife he pleases, and it is certain that the devil a bit of love shall I have for her. The little I had in my heart has been devoured by this German falcon – the place is void – I feel it empty. I sometimes imagine that the ghost of my wife of six weeks, is still wandering in the places where she formerly dwelt; but I strive to drive away the imaginary phantom. Reason and circumstances justify the plan I have formed, and if I recall her to mind, either at D. or anywhere else, where I have been accustomed to see her, it is only the effect of habit.

But with all this I swear, that no moralist[54] shall ever again become my mistress. Ambition and pleasure have alone votaries disposed to undertake and execute everything for their service; they shall therefore, for the future, be my only deities: the first, because I shall obtain, by her means, all the respect and power necessary to assemble and justify every pleasing enjoyment, till the moment when my life shall be terminated by a drunken bout at an election of a Member of Parliament, or till the day when I shall break my neck in hunting. Admire how I have improved the ordinary qualities of a nobleman; I have, by my artifices, seduced a fine girl, and torn from her whatever was capable of rendering her happy. In doing this I have foolishly squandered away my fortune, and now I shall assume the character of a patriot, at horse-races and elections, and leave time to determine, whether after so much fermentation, anything good remains at the bottom of the vessel.

The History of
Lady Sophia Sternheim

Volume II

The

History

of

Lady Sophia Sternheim

Rosina to her friend

Here, my friend, I am obliged to take up again my pen, in order to place before your eyes, in one view, the memoirs of my dear mistress, by connecting the facts which followed the unhappy revolution in her fortune.

My sister's house was the only asylum we could choose. I did not dare to propose to my lady, either to have recourse to justice, in order to be revenged on Derby, or to assert her rights, and, in such circumstances, she could not bear the thought of returning to her own seat. Her anguish of mind was so violent, that she hoped it would soon put a period to her life; and I was afraid that would be the case, if we did not speedily quit the fatal house which was the scene of Derby's baseness, and her distress. While we were preparing for our departure, I opened the door of Derby's chamber, when my lady casting an eye into it, I thought she would have been instantly stifled with her grief: but shutting herself up in my room, she continued there, till I had finished packing up our effects. All my lord's presents, which were very fine, as well as numerous, we left with the mistress of the house, and took only the little we had brought with us in our flight. The hostess, who was paid for a month, beforehand by way of advance, was desirous of keeping us still; but we set out on the fifth day after we had received the fatal letter, accompanied with her good wishes, which she mingled with imprecations against the villainous lord.

While we were on the road, my lady sat by my side, as pale as death, with her eyes cast down, and buried in a profound silence; no complaint, no tears assuaged the grief of her oppressed heart. Two days together we travelled through a beautiful and well-cultivated country, without any object fixing her attention; only sometimes she embraced me with a violent and convulsive motion, and for an instant reposed her head on my bosom. My anguish perpetually encreased, and I was unable to stifle my sighs and groans. At length looking at me with a tender air, she pressed me to her heart, and with a celestial voice, said, O my Rosina, your affliction shows me my wretchedness in its full extent! Before you used to smile on seeing me; but now the sight of me pierces your heart. O give me not cause to think that I have rendered you unhappy! Be composed, and you shall find that I am so.

I was charmed at hearing her speak so long together, and at seeing some tears fall from her languid extinguished eyes, and answered, I should soon be composed, could I but see you less dejected, and observe one spark of that pleasing satisfaction which the view of a fine country used to afford you.

She now continued for some minutes silent, lifted up her eyes, gazed on the heavens, cast a glance on the country around us, and then answered with tears of the tenderest friendship: Indeed, my dear Rosina, I live as if my misfortunes had snatched from the earth all the gladdening gifts with which it is embellished; and yet the cause of my grief lies neither in the creatures, nor their beneficent creator. O why did I stray from the path prescribed for me! –

She then entered into a repetition of the most important circumstances of her life. I endeavoured to calm her mind, by reminding her of the motives of her various actions, and in particular, those which induced her to contract a private marriage, and fly from her uncle's house. In short, I so far prevailed in cheering her mind, that the view of a plentiful harvest, and the autumnal labours carried on in the villages through which we passed, excited in her some emotions of joy. But the sight of the damsels, especially those who appeared to be of her own age, renewed all her sadness. On looking at them she joined her hands, and prayed, that God would preserve every pure and innocent soul, from the torment which preyed on her heart.

In this situation we arrived at Vaels,[55] where we found a sweet consolation in the tender reception and virtuous friendship of my brother-in-law and sister. They endeavoured to restore the peace of my lady's mind, but a little after her arrival she fell sick, and during twelve days, we were in pain for her life. She then drew up a concise account of her misfortunes, and made her will. But, contrary to our fears and her wishes, she recovered. When her health was restored, she applied herself to the education of a young child, who had been entrusted to my sister Emilia's care. This employment, and her conversation with my brother and sister, so visibly calmed her mind, that they ventured to ask her, what was her plan of life for the future. She answered, that she had no other than that of finishing her days on her estate; but till three years were expired, during which she had abandoned her revenues to the Count Löbau, she was resolved to live in ignorance of all the world. Nothing could shake her resolution. She changed her name, and in allusion to her unhappy fate, took that of Madame

Leidens[56] resolving to pass for an officer's widow. She sold the fine diamonds which surrounded her father and mother's pictures, and also disposed of her other jewels, resolving to live on the interest of the sum they produced; but in this change of fortune she did not give up the pleasure of doing good, and resolved to teach needlework to some poor girls in the neighbourhood.

This thought, which she put in execution, was, as you will soon see, the origin of the rest of the events of her life. One of her young scholars was god-daughter to Madam Hills, a very rich lady, at some distance; and waiting on her godmother, showed her some of her work. The lady made enquiries after the person who taught her, and desired my brother to send Madam Leidens to her, in order to found a charity-school in her house. This my dear lady at first declined, lest it should make her too public; but my brother-in-law earnestly representing to her, that it would be losing an opportunity of doing much good, she could not resist so powerful a motive; and this, with the fear of being the cause of some inconvenience in Emilia's family, (though she paid for her board,) at length determined her to comply.

She dressed herself with the utmost plainness, in a striped linen gown, with a white handkerchief and apron; for always something of the English manner was uppermost in her mind. She concealed under a large hood her fine hair, and a part of the features of her face, in order to disguise herself; but her lovely eyes, the smile of goodness which shone through an impression of secret sorrow, her enchanting shape and graceful walk, attracted every eye. Her departure gave us pain, Madam Hills's usual residence being eighteen miles[57] from our house; but her letters in some measure compensated for her loss, and you will doubtless[58] find in reading them a part of the satisfaction they gave us.

LETTER XXX

Lady Sophia, under the name of Madam Leidens, to Emilia

Ten days have I been separated from my tender friend, and it was impossible for me to write sooner: my soul was too much agitated, and my sensations too strong to be restrained by the slow progress of my pen; but the serenity of some fine days, and the prospect of extensive and smiling pastures, have in some measure restored the calm of my mind. I can now, without anxiety, without dejection, view the elevation from which I am fallen. My eyes have overflowed with the fondest tears on viewing my younger years: a trembling has seized me on thinking of the day in which I went to D. and I have rapidly passed over, and closed mine eyes on the scenes which followed. Only on the sweet period of my arrival at your house I thought with pleasure. Deprived of wealth, I doubly felt the value of the asylum I had chosen. A tender sympathy and compassion were painted on the countenance of my Emilia, respect and friendship were lighted up in that of her husband: I saw that they believed me innocent, and pitied my sufferings: I could look on them as witnesses of the purity of my heart. Oh, what satisfaction did I find in this idea! The tears I shed the first night I was with you, were those of gratitude; and I blessed God for the consolation he made me find in the faithful friendship of my Emilia. The morning of the following day was painful; for I then repeated the particulars of my unhappy story: but the reflections and exhortations of your husband calmed my mind; and more still my casting my eyes on your house, the humble abode in which resides, with you, all the virtues of our sex, and with your spouse all the merit and wisdom of his. We passed the whole day together: I saw you contented with a very moderate income; employed in discharging a circle of duties, and animated with a maternal tenderness for your husband's five children. I admired his conduct with respect to his family and his parishioners, and this, my Emilia, began to restore peace to my soul. This happy couple, said I to myself, were always faithful to the laws of prudence and virtue; yet fortune never smiled on them. They submit to the severity of their lot with the most noble resignation, and yet I groan under my destiny! I whom presumption and imprudence have led astray, and who, in spite of the most sincere love of virtue, have exposed myself to calamities and contempt. Much indeed have I lost, and much have I suffered: but ought I, on this account, to forget the happiness of my first years – to look with an eye of indifference on the opportunities of doing good which still present themselves, and give myself up to be governed only by the feelings of my self-love? I am still sensible of the value of the blessings I have lost; but the illness I have suffered, and the reflections which have followed it, have brought me to see that I am still in possession of the real blessings of life. My heart is pure and innocent: the knowledge I have acquired is still my own: the faculties of my soul are unimpaired; its good inclinations remain, and I have still the power of doing good.

My education has taught me that *virtue and abilities* can alone give us real happiness, and that nothing but *doing good* can afford true felicity to a noble soul: this my fate has proved to me by my own experience.

I belonged to the class of the rich and gay; I find myself now in that of the middle rank, even bordering on the station where penury and humiliation join their hands: but however I may be reduced, according to the idea commonly affixed to happiness, I find that I may do much real good in my new situation. The wealthy Madam Hills enjoys with me the complacencies of friendship and of science, and my young scholars have the advantage of being educated in such a manner as to give them the gladdening prospect of rendering their future days happy.

Madam Hills has put me in possession of a very pretty room, with two windows which afford a view of the country, and from thence I repair to a hall at particular hours, to give lessons to thirteen girls, whom she finds in food and all other necessaries, besides books and everything requisite for the works in hand. She hears my instructions with pleasure, and every now and then nods her head in token of approbation. Sometimes she sheds a tear, or squeezes my hand, at which a ray of joy breaks in upon my heart: so sweet is the pleasure of being beloved for one's own sake! I must now communicate to you a thought which I shall want your spouse's assistance to help me to put it in execution.

Madam Hills has some pride, but it is of a noble and beneficent kind. She is desirous of employing her vast fortune in a perpetual foundation; but it must be such a one as is quite new, that will do her honour, and draw down blessings on her: for this purpose she has desired me to think of a plan. – Now might not the little school, of which I am at the head, be improved into a receptacle named a *Seminary for Domestics*, in which poor girls designed for service might receive instructions suitable to their station and abilities? I would make the trial with my thirteen scholars, whom I would divide into classes according to their various capacities, tempers and inclinations. For example, those who have the best hearts, and the gentlest minds should be educated for nursery maids; those who have most wit and address should be destined for chambermaids; those who have most sense and activity, for housekeepers; and, in short, the last class should be formed of strong girls fitted for labour, and be employed in work that demands less abilities.

Such an establishment would require a convenient house, with a garden adjoining to it; a sensible clergyman to instruct them in the knowledge and love of the duties of their station; with a poor elderly widow, or old maid, distinguished by her honesty and integrity, and capable of superintending the several branches of instruction.

These ideas divert me from contemplating on my misfortunes, and my soul experiences a sweet consolation in thinking that I am become the instrument of benefits which will extend to futurity. In the mean while, I turn upon myself, and cannot help believing that self-love is of the nature of the polypus; though you sever her branches or arms, and even divide her trunk, yet she finds means to reproduce herself and extend new branches. You know how I was humbled and dejected. Re-examine what I have written, and observe what happy supports my faltering self-complacency has found, and how I have gradually risen to form insensibly a very grand project. – Oh, if the love of my fellow-creatures had not struck its root so deeply in my heart as to be incorporated with my very self-love, what would have become of me!

LETTER XXXI

Madam Leidens to Emilia

So, my dear friend, you are better pleased with my last letter than with all I have written since my departure from D. but give me leave to complain that my Emilia injures me in her animadversions on the change in my ideas and expressions. I myself am sensible of this difference, but think it a natural effect of the grand revolution I have experienced. At D. I enjoyed the respect of others; I seemed born for happiness; I was satisfied with myself, and my mind, diverted with the objects that offered themselves to my view, described, praised and blamed them according as they suited or clashed with my ideas. But since that time how has the scene changed! serene repose and the very appearance of felicity abandoned me; sorrow and tears became my portion: was it then possible for me to indulge the flights of imagination, when all the powers of my mind were employed in enabling me *to submit with patience*, a virtue which leaves the soul but little activity? Your husband knew me well; he perceived that it was necessary to draw me, in a manner, out of myself, and convince me that it was still in my power to do good: this idea alone was able to bring me again into active life.

I thank you, my dear friends, for the approbation and praises you bestow on the plan I have laid before you: it seems to me as if a charitable hand had raised my dejected soul, assisted its steps, and drawn it out of the thorny road into which it had been driven by error, to conduct it into a smooth path: it there indeed, meets not with the superb dwellings of the rich and great; but the eye contemplates the pure charms of unadulterated nature.

I had need, my dear friends, of such a consolation. – There is a noble pride which arises from the consciousness of being free from deserved reproach; but, alas! I have lost this support. I accuse myself of inconsideration, to which I owe a part of my misfortunes. I incessantly repeat this charge, and *submission* and *patience* are the fruits of this confession. Had I no cause for self-reproach, in my private marriage and my flight, I should have found in the exercise of constancy and magnanimity, that support on which the innocent leans, when the wickedness of others, or an unforeseen accident interrupts his happiness. The innocent can boldly look in the face of the person who has injured him, or turn away his eyes with a cold disdain: he looks not around for the pity of friends, but for witnesses of his noble conduct: his soul bears up against misfortunes, collects its vigour, and finds new resources to enable him to mount the ascent which leads to honour and felicity. While I, remembering my imprudence, have sought the veil of obscurity before I have suffered myself to be led into a new path. Yet the hope of success in an useful enterprise, has sown the new trod way with flowers as presages of blessings in store, that will communicate happiness to many: peace and sweet contentment now find access to my soul, and virtue, I hope, will be my faithful guide. My heart swells with joy when I think of the influence I am going to have on the happiness of many of my fellow-creatures: I renounce my favourite habits and wishes, and gladly consecrate my life and my abilities to the welfare of others.

But every step I take in this new path makes me applaud the wisdom of my education, which has placed every object in its true point of view. How happy is it for me, that this truth has been so strongly imprinted on my mind: *That the moral difference between mankind is that alone which God regards.* How much should I have suffered in my present situation, had I been governed by the usual prejudices of persons of my birth! With what prudence have my parents directed that self-love which was born with me! Had I, for instance, fixed my heart on dress, jewels, and outward splendor, I should now look with grief and the most humbling mortification on the simple habit I now wear, though its neatness and decency are sufficient to satisfy my female vanity. And what can I wish for more, since, under an appearance so modest and humble, I attract love and esteem, sensations for which I am solely obliged to the moral qualities of my mind.

I rise early, and at my window admire how Nature faithfully fulfils the eternal laws prescribed to her, of dispensing blessings, and of contributing, at all times and seasons, to the happiness of every creature. Winter approaches, the flowers have disappeared, and the sun having hid his resplendent rays, the earth no longer retains its cheerful aspect: but these despoiled fields still awake in my sensible heart the idea of pleasure; for there grew the plenteous harvest, and hence I lift my grateful eye to heaven. The kitchen garden and orchard are stripped of their rich produce; but the thoughts of the plenty they have yielded mingles a sweet sensation of joy with the shivering which the north wind begins to occasion. The trees have shed their leaves, the verdure of the meadows fades, gloomy clouds pour down rain, which softening the earth, renders it unfit for pleasing walks. At this the foolish murmur; but the man of reflection rejoices in this revolution. The dried leaves (says he) and autumnal showers nourish the earth, and prepare it for renewed fertility and fresh vegetation: a reflection which gives him a joyful sensation of the great Creator's care, and leads his thoughts to the succeeding spring. Yes, the earth, amidst the loss of her exterior beauties, amidst even the discontent of her children, whom she nourishes and recreates, labours in her bosom for their future welfare.[59] – I now stop, and looking into myself, say, The smiling prospect of my fortune is also obscured, and my exterior lustre is fallen like the faded leaf. Perhaps it is the lot of the human race to have also its seasons: if so, I will, during the gloomy days of my winter, nourish my soul with the fruits which my education and experience have heaped up for me; and, as the crop is plentiful, and the uncultivated soil of the poor produces little, I will give them a part of what I possess. In fact, my Emilia, I have found a new opportunity of being of some use. I am going to devote some days to a good work, and I flatter myself that my next letter will give you an account of my success.

Adieu!

LETTER XXXII

Madam Hills to the Rev. Mr Br.

Reverend Sir,

Don't be frightened at receiving a letter from me, instead of one from Madam Leidens. She is not ill: no indeed; but the dear creature has left me, and is to stay away a fortnight. She lodges in a strange house, where she works very hard; and what makes my heart ache, she is very ill-fed. But hear how things are come about: such an angel sure never before entered into a rich person's house, nor into a poor person's neither! I cannot tell how to express my thoughts, and as to writing, I understand nothing about it. But pray observe, your spouse knows very well, that since Mr G. has lost his employment, he, with his wife and children, are become very poor. Well, I have frequently assisted them, but I could not maintain them; so everybody says that the husband is proud, and the wife careless, and that all the favours done to them are thrown away. This vexed me, and I one day spoke of it to Miss Lehne, whom I relieved at the same time. Madam Leidens was also present, and asked Miss Lehne about them, on which she related their whole history; for she ought to know it, since she has always been with them from her infancy. The next day Madam Leidens went to pay Mrs G. a visit, and returned home exceedingly moved. While we were at supper she related to me so many affecting circumstances about them, that she made me shed tears, and filled me with such compassion, that I immediately said, I would take care of the father, mother, and the whole family. But this she opposed. The next morning she brought me the enclosed paper, which I send you; but I must have it back, for it must be included in my will, as well as something in praise of Madam Leidens, wrote by my own hand, with something for her, which at present I shall not mention. Well then, she went to her girls, and left me this paper. I never in my life saw anything more ingeniously contrived to catch two fishes with one hook, that is, to provide for these people, and to render them prudent. I was astonished, and shed tears twice, for I was obliged to read it over twice, that I might perfectly comprehend it. I wrote under it, 'I consent to everything, and we will begin tomorrow.' – But besides telling her this by word of mouth, I wrote down on a paper which I affixed to my will, that she should not call me her benefactress: for what do I give her? – A little food, and a little chamber. – But stay, I'll soon contrive something; she shall not leave my house, as she supposes. If I do but live to see my *Seminary for Domestics,* as she calls it, finished, I will have her name and mine cut on the same stone: I will call her my adopted daughter; and then what wondering will there be, that she did not pocket my money, in order to get another smart husband. People will then bless us both; and this I shall be charmed with, for she deserves it. She must likewise stand godmother for the poor infants, that we may have children of her name, and these, as well as my own godchildren, shall have the preference in being admitted into the seminary.

My spectacles begin to grow dim, and I can write no more this morning; and as the time seems long, and I am impatient to see Madam Leidens, I will go directly to Mr G.'s. – Well, I have been there, and I am sorry that I went; because these people oppressed me with their thanks, and might, perhaps, think that I came on purpose to receive them: but they were mistaken, since I only came to see my daughter – my daughter, I say, for I declare that, when she returns, she shall call me her mother.

I bade my maid open the door a little, and, to be sure, the company within the room gave it a fine appearance. As to the furniture there was nothing fine, it consisting only of a few rush-bottomed chairs and two tables. In one corner was the father and his eldest son, who was writing by his side. About the middle of the room was another table, at which Mrs G. was knitting. Miss Lehne sat between the two little girls, instructing them in sewing; and Madam Leidens had before her a nosegay of Italian flowers, from which she drew patterns for the seats of chairs to be embroidered and sold, and was talking with great affability to the youngest son and the eldest of his sisters, who were attentively looking at the progress of her work. I could not refrain from tears on seeing it; on beholding the children's fondness for her, and hearing them eagerly return me thanks as I entered the room. The rough husband reddened as he thanked me, while the wife acquitted herself with a childish laugh. But no matter, I will continue to assist them according to Madam Leidens' regulations, and at length Miss Lehne shall be my first under-governess. I brought some cakes and some good fruit, and you cannot imagine the joy this gave the children; but Madam Leidens appeared not quite pleased, she being afraid lest the coarse food they would be obliged to eat the next day should not appear so agreeable, after their having fed on these dainties: for she was not for rewarding them by gratifying their appetites. She herself ate only a piece of household bread with an apple. When I asked her the reason, she directed her discourse to the girls, and said, Our orchard can produce the same apples, but these cakes can be had from nobody but this lady. This I had for my pains; but I was not sorry; for she was in the right, and would not have them think their being obliged to eat common bread, a misfortune. – She has now been eight days with these people: the next week she will return to me, and shall then write to you. I recommend myself and my dear child to your prayers. Oh, I shall never forget that you have introduced this dear person to me! I have never been so satisfied with what I possess, as since I have had her with me.

A scheme for relieving Mr G.'s family, and Miss Lehne

My dear benefactress desires me to give her my thoughts in writing, on the subject of relieving Mr G. and his family.[60] – I would treat these people, who are, through their own fault, become unhappy, as a physician treats a patient who, in the gaiety of his heart, has ruined his health: he administers all necessary remedies, but at the same time prescribes a diet, which he proves to be necessary, by representing to him the danger he has run, and that with which he is still threatened: thus, by a long and constant regimen, the patient recovers fresh strength, and at length becomes able to live without his physician. Medicines too violent given at the beginning, would only serve to increase the disorder, while they seemed to remove it, and would be attended with prejudicial consequences. The considerable presents given formerly to Mr G. and his family have produced a like effect; it is necessary therefore to assist them with prudence, and to attack the evil at its source.

Madam Hills's bounty will furnish them with apparel, linen, and the like: but, with respect to these, it is proper that they should at first be provided only with such as are indispensably necessary; these should be given them ready-made: but afterwards they should have the linen cloth in the piece, that the mother and daughters may be employed in making it up with their own hands. This work being finished, they should be supplied with flax and wool, which they should spin for future clothes.

As for Mr G. I would reap advantage from his talents and his pride, and engage him to recover his reputation by devoting his time and care to the instruction of his children. Their education is a benefit for which he is accountable, and since his situation renders it impossible for him to pay masters, how commendable will it be in him thus to supply his want of fortune. I would therefore have him apply himself, with a zeal animated by paternal love, to teach his children writing and arithmetic, and to watch over the progress of his sons in Latin in a neighbouring free-school; and it is to be hoped that a man so faithful in the discharge of his paternal duties, will not be long overlooked in the disposal of the public employments. It may here be objected, that the indolence of Mrs G. will throw every thing into confusion: but this evil I hope to prevent by Miss Lehne's abilities.

She has been Mrs G.'s companion and friend from her youth, and has been much obliged to her parents, and I believe she would be glad of returning those favours to the daughter, if she herself was not in necessitous circumstances: but as she possesses a treasure in her abilities and address, these may render her of great use to her friend, if she will but have an eye on the use made of the benefits granted to Mr G. and superintend the instruction of his daughters. Miss Lehne is also under obligations to Madam Hill, and the true manner of expressing her gratitude is to concur with her in a good work, which, if it be attended with success, will procure her the esteem of people of probity, and the satisfaction of having contributed to the happiness of her friends and the welfare of their three innocent children.

Should Madam Hill be pleased to approve of these thoughts, I myself will communicate them to Mr G. and his family, and also to Miss Lehne. I will also, if she permits me, go and spend a fortnight at Mr G.'s, in order to convince them that this new plan of life has nothing severe or disagreeable. For this purpose I shall endeavour, by treating the husband with respect, and by affecting discourse, to make him fond of living in his family. Besides, I will by turns discharge the office of the mother, and that of Miss Lehne. I will endeavour to inculcate good principles into the minds of the children, and to study their tempers and abilities, that they may be assisted in following the bent of their genius. But with respect to food, dress, and furniture, it is necessary that they should have nothing to spare, in order that the sense of their wants may lead them to wise reflections, and convince them that nothing but industry, moderation, and good conduct, can make them regain that station, from which they have been plunged by dissipation and negligence. I will take particular care not to make them any reproaches; but by mentioning some circumstances of my own life, I will prove the inconstancy of fortune, and will tell the children, that, of all the blessings I have possessed, I have nothing left but my education, which obtained me the friendship of Madam Hills, and the opportunity of being of service to them. In correcting their ideas, I will show them that a noble pride ought to lead us to make a good use both of prosperity and adversity; for I cannot be contented with seeing their bodies clothed and fed, without correcting their minds and passions.

LETTER XXXIII

Madam Leidens to Emilia

I am now returned to Madam Hills, and was just going to give you an account of the good work I mentioned in my last letter, when that lady informed me that she had written a letter to you, in which she mentioned every circumstance. O, my dear Emilia, how admirable would be the moral part of our globe, did all the rich, after Madam Hills's example, rejoice at being furnished with an opportunity of making a good use of their wealth! I must now give you the reasons which made me choose Miss Lehne to fill the employment with which she is entrusted. You know that I came to be acquainted with this poor family by her speaking of them, before me, to Madam Hills. I observed in her half compassionate, half severe tone, a secret jealousy of the favours bestowed on these people, and the desire of engrossing them all to herself. At the same time she talked of what she would do, were she in Mrs G.'s place. It gave me pain to see such guilty sentiments succeed the friendship of youth, which was said to have been then warm and active, and I had the courage to form a plan for rendering this half-perverted being of service to her former friend. I took no notice to Miss Lehne of what I had observed with respect to her, and only desired her to introduce me to Mrs G. The distress in which we found her friend, and the affection with which she behaved to Miss Lehne, moved her. I took advantage of this disposition, and taking her aside, gave her an account of my scheme; and painting the part she was to act in the most pleasing colours, represented that if she acquitted herself well, she would draw upon herself the favour of heaven, and the respect of all good people. I endeavoured to convince her, that she would even do much more good than Madam Hills, who, with all her diffusive liberalities, only enjoyed the pleasure of distributing, from time to time, a part of her superfluities; while her patience, her assiduous and daily efforts, would show a heart richly fraught with the most generous and excellent virtues. I prevailed the more easily, as I added, that this would be a means of pleasing Madam Hills, who was fond of the scheme. My plan was therefore approved, and for the first fortnight I presided at its execution.

The first day, after having distributed Madam Hills's presents, I mentioned to Mr and Mrs G. the manner in which I viewed their situation, with the plan of life, which I believed would be agreeable to them, and desired them to inform me of their objections, and particular views.

Before they had time to answer me, I thought it necessary to give a picture of some parts of my own history. I particularly dwelt on the wealth and respect I had enjoyed. I mentioned the wishes and inclinations I then indulged, with the impossibility of my now gratifying them; and concluded my account with encouraging exhortations. The method I took to excite their confidence, disposed them to follow my advice. The best things that a person of wealth and prosperity could have said, would have made little impression on them; but the thought of my being poor and dependent, like themselves, rendered their minds docile and flexible. I asked them, what they would have done were they in my place? They answered, that they were delighted with my principles, and should be charmed at being able to think like me. I then expatiated upon what I would do in their situation, and they all heartily consented to all I had proposed. Oh, thought I, if in doing good, people always consulted the circumstances and inclinations of those on whom they pretend to confer favours, – if, instead of shocking that self-love which is natural to us all, they knew how to take advantage of it, with as much address as the flatterer employs to gain his ends, the empire of morality would long ago have extended its bounds, and the number of its subjects have greatly increased.

But to return. On the second day I personated Mrs G. and in that character reminded Miss Lehne of their ancient friendship; assured her, in Mrs G.'s name, that I saw her with joy in the post she was going to fill, from my being persuaded that she would make the best use of the authority with which I entrusted her. In short, I particularly explained everything I expected from her, I having before agreed with Mrs G. on what Miss Lehne was to perform; I recommended the girls to her care, and added (under the character of Mrs G.) that in everything we would act in concert. The two following days I took the place of Miss Lehne, and then I successively played off the three girls. While we were at work I endeavoured, by an improving conversation, to pour into their hearts instruction and peace, either by having recourse to the great truths of religion, or by fixing their views on the beauties of nature. Madam Hills furnished us with some books which I had pointed out to her, and the two sons read some passages by turns, and I added remarks suitable to their years. As the two eldest girls are very sensible and ingenious, I teach them embroidery, and, to excite their diligence, have showed them the advantage they will receive by excelling in it. A part of the gain you obtain for your works, said I, may be employed in purchasing new materials, and the rest in procuring for you various things which you want: I promised them also to teach that work to nobody but themselves. This idea of selling and buying renders the mother and her daughters very assiduous, and they work all day with great alacrity.

Miss Lehne assures me, that everything continues upon the best footing imaginable; and she herself is extremely delighted with the praises that are given to her conduct.

I could not leave the house without shedding tears. I intend to return thither twice a week, and each time to spend two hours in my visit. The fortnight I passed in that house glided away in innocence and peace: every minute was employed in the exercise of an active virtue, in doing good and in giving instruction. Pray to God, most dear Emilia, that these grains of good feed, scattered by a feeble hand, may produce a rich harvest for this family! Never, no never, did the produce of my estate, which put it in my power to relieve the unhappy, procure me such satisfaction as arises from this reflection, – that, without the help of gold, and only by exerting my own abilities and principles, and by consecrating to it some days of my life, I have done this family all the good they were capable of receiving.

LETTER XXXIV

Madam Leidens to Emilia

Consult, my dear, your husband's metaphysical skill, whence arose the contradiction to be found between my ideas, and the sensations which always subsist in my heart, when I complied with Madam Hills's entreaties to persuade the amiable widow C. to determine in favour of one of her admirers. Whence could I resolve to plead the cause of a man, and to paint the charms of love, when that passion had caused all my troubles? Was it not more natural that I should approve of the amiable widow's coldness? I cannot believe that it was caused by the spirit of contradiction; or that it can be possible, that in one of the folds of this heart, torn by love, there can be found any impression of that lovely form under which I used to consider it during the sunshine of my early youth. Have my long afflictions brought my juvenile reason to that degree of maturity necessary to enable me to canvass and decide on the concerns of others, without intermingling any sentiments of my own? Assist me with your opinion; for I am at a loss what judgment I ought to form of myself. The following is an abridgment of my conversation with the amiable widow.

It is known that four men of merit seek to obtain your hand; and may I take the liberty, madam, to ask, why you are so long in making your choice?

I can choose none of them. I would enjoy that liberty which I have obtained by many disagreeable circumstances.

I don't blame your love of liberty; but the best use you could make of it, would be voluntarily to make some worthy person happy.

Oh! the happiness you mention exists only in the warm imagination of a lover, and will soon vanish.

This may be true, where love only enters the soul by the eyes; but it cannot be applied to the woman who is beloved for her virtues and amiable endowments.*[61]

But everybody has particular ideas of happiness; and my second choice may again fall on one whose ideas of it may not agree with mine, and we may both have reason to complain.

This is an artful excuse, but it is not quite just. An interval of ten years between your first choice and the second, has made you acquire sufficient experience to know how to judge of the difference of persons and circumstances, and enables you particularly to avoid whatever was disagreeable in your first union.

You take advantage of everything. But tell me, dear Madam Leidens, which of them you would choose, were you in my place?

He who would render me the most happy.

And, in your eyes, this would be –

The exalted genius and good nature of an amiable man of learning assures you, that the least spark of your merit would not be overlooked, and that, by his conversation, the noblest part of yourself, already so excellent, may be much improved. With what happiness would his sensible heart be filled, from the abilities, the extensive knowledge, and sublime affections, of the lovely partner of his soul! And how sweet would it be, to a mind like yours, to add to the felicity of such a man, to have a share in his reputation, and in the warm regard of his friends?

O, Madam Leidens, with what address you present the fair side of things! But ought I not to foresee, that the same sensibility, which you so pleasingly describe, will make him discover my defects; and then to which side will the balance incline?

Your natural sweetness and complaisance would make those slight defects so light as to disappear.

What a dangerous woman! You conceal the chain by covering it with flowers.

You wrong me! I show you flowers because love strews them at your feet, and it is in your power to gather them.

But you say nothing of the thorns which lie concealed under them.

I can't answer for this; for I am afraid of offending your judgment.

Pray don't fear; but go on, and show me the beautiful colours of the other ribbons you intend as favours for me.

Let us see: perhaps the birth and personal qualities of a noble Prussian warrior, are more proper than the placid hand of the Muses, to tame that amiable vivacity which gives you uncommon charms. This would be a glorious union. I see an illustrious name, an elevated rank, a generous mind; you are beloved with a true affection, founded on your character; you will

---

* The rather precious tone of this dialogue – so unlike the simplicity we have come to expect from our Sternheim – suggests that she was not entirely at ease during her discussion with the widow C. – E.

have a prospect of inhabiting a fine house, and of acquiring new friends. In short, does not his sacrificing prejudices so common among the ancient nobility, merit that of your irresolution and mistrust?

With what art, thou enchantress, dost thou blend thy colours!

Why, my dear Mrs C. do you call me enchantress? Do you feel a strong attraction in the splendid union I have in view for you?

Yes; but, thank heaven, you fright me, by endeavouring to dazzle me.

Charming distrust! Oh, why cannot I place it in the soul of every sensible woman, who, attracted by the brilliant colours of an artificial fire, gives herself up to the pleasing illusion, till she suddenly falls into the gloom of misery.

O, Madam Leidens, how you soften me by this language! You awake in my maternal heart a soft solicitude for my daughter.

I could not forbear embracing her for this tender emotion of a soul in which true goodness resides. Allow me, said I, in this moment consecrated to sensibility, to fix your attention on a kind of felicity less brilliant, but more sweet, which you may enjoy in Mr T's delightful country seat. By uniting yourself to him, you will at once fulfil three essential duties: you will crown the wishes of a man of merit, who loves you, not for your personal charms, which he has never seen, but from the portrait that has been given him of your mind; you will crown the wishes of a man, who assures you that your daughter shall become his, and that he will leave her heiress to his great estate: thus you will secure the fortune of that beloved daughter: in short, you will fill your father's heart with joy, by forming an union which he highly approves, the happiness of which will recompence, in the decline of life, all the cares he has felt for his children. Weigh well the force of these considerations, O you whose benevolent and generous heart would contribute to the happiness of all around you! – I shall say nothing, madam, of your fourth candidate, though I have heard much of his person, his wit, his abilities, and his virtues. I have laid before you the motives which would determine me, were I in your place, and leave you to proceed as you think proper. I am very sensible that we have all a different manner of viewing objects, and that our sensations are influenced by the point of view in which we observe them; but there is one side on which we all should keep an attentive eye; that is, the happiness of our fellow creatures, which ought to be as dear to us as our own, and which we are not to prevent from trivial motives.

You plunge me (said she, shedding some tears) into the greatest embarrassment; but my sad experience renders me averse to every thought of marriage, and I heartily wish all these gentlemen wives more worthy of them. I do justice to their merit: but I have been so severely galled by my first yoke, that even a silken tie appears disagreeable to me.

I have now fully complied with your friend's desire; and, as you have taken your resolution, I have nothing farther to say, except wishing that you may be always happy.

She here embraced me; and at my return I earnestly entreated Madam Hills to trouble her friend no more on that subject: but having retired into my room, I no sooner began to recollect myself, than I was astonished at the part I had just acted, and at the zeal I had shown in this affair.

Help me, my dear Emilia, to unravel what passed in my soul; for I can give no account of it.

LETTER XXXV

Lord Seymour to Dr T.

My dearest Friend,

Assist me with your advice, and prevent my sinking under that distress into which I am again fallen, and from which I shall probably never be freed. You know that I had stifled my passion for the lovely Sophia Sternheim, from my belief of her having married John, which had alienated from her every spark of my esteem. I even began to experience the charms of a tranquil affection for Miss C. when an unexpected order from court obliged my uncle to go to W. Our parting cost the amiable Miss C. some tears, and I was as dull as she. Dissatisfied with the letters in which the ambition of my family, and my uncle's regard for me, kept me bound, I sat gloomy and silent by his side, vexed that nothing could remove the steady composure of his mind, and showed but little gratitude for the patience with which he bore my ill humour. But imagine, if possible, from the account I am going to give you, the revolution which soon happened in my mind. – On the evening of the second day of our journey our postillion lost his way, and the weather being very tempestuous, we resolved to pass the night in a village at a distance from the road. Our coach drove up to an house of entertainment, and we were just going to alight, when the hostels cried out, 'Oh, you are Englishmen! If you are, you may go farther; we have no room for you here! You may pass the night in the forest; for no Englishman shall ever more enter my doors!' While she uttered these last words she pulled her son by his arm, who appeared a civil young man, and endeavouring to soften her resentment, prevented her shutting the door. The singularity of this scene roused my attention. Our men instantly began to give them ill language; but my uncle commanded silence, and turning to me, said, Something is the matter: some very serious affair must have happened here, sufficient to stifle the usual greediness of gain among such sort of people. He then called the woman with great mildness, and desired her to be so good as to tell him the reason of her refusing to admit us into her house.

It is because the English have no conscience, said she. They make no scruple of rendering the best people in the world miserable, and I am resolved that none of them shall ever more darken my doors; so that you, with your fair speeches, may troop off! You all of you know how to give smooth words!

She then turned her back on us, and said to her son (who was doubtless urging the profit they should gain by us) No, though they would fill my room full of gold, it should not make me break the vow I made, for the sake of that dear lady!

My heart now burned with impatience; but my uncle calmly beckoning to the young man, asked him the reason of his mother's aversion to us, and of her refusing to let us enter her house.

About half a year ago, answered he, an English lord sent here his wife, a beautiful and sweet-tempered lady; he afterwards came himself, and then went away again. While he was absent she was always melancholy; yet she gave my cousins new clothes, taught them to work, and to make many pretty things, and did a deal of good to the poor. Oh, she was as mild as a young lamb! My father himself, who was harsh and cruel, grew better tempered from the time she entered the house, and we all loved her. But one day, when the cursed lord had been some days absent, one of his men came on horseback, and said that he brought a letter to the lady. We asked him if his master would soon come. No, (said he, in an insolent manner) he does not come again, and here is money to pay for her board a month longer. – My mother, suspecting no good, slipped into a chamber by the side of that where the lady was, in order to know what was in the letter, and saw her on her knees, all in tears. Her chambermaid also wept. Her marriage, she told her, was a base counterfeit; that the messenger who had brought the letter had performed the ceremony in a clergyman's habit; and that the letter informed her, that she might go where she pleased. She accordingly set out a few days after, but so ill, and in such low spirits, that she must certainly have died on the road: and for this reason my mother will suffer no Englishman to set his foot in her house.

My uncle, looking at me with concern, said, Charles, what says your heart to this story?

O my lord, it is my Sophia! cried I; but the rascal shall be punished – I will pursue him – It is Derby – None but Derby could be guilty of such horrid villainy!

Friend (said my uncle to the hostess's son) tell your mother that she has reason to hate this abandoned Englishman, who shall be punished with the utmost severity: but see and procure us admittance. At this he desired us to step out of the coach, and said that he would go and endeavour to appease her.

He then ran into the house, and soon after the woman herself came to us, saying, If you promise to bring this abominable villain to punishment, come in, and I will tell you all. You are a gentleman in years, and may chastise the cruel baseness of a young man. I hope you will make an example of him, and prevent his being guilty of any other crimes.

Slow and silent my uncle and I followed her up stairs. Here, said she, here stood the dear angel when her lord paid her the first visit. Well, he seemed to be very fond of her, and she held out her pretty hand so graciously to him, that I was quite rejoiced at their union: but she talked so slow and so little, and he so loud; besides, he stared at her in such a queer manner, and soon after made such a calling among his people, as easily raised a suspicion of something. My husband could also bluster and make a noise, though when we were first married he was as mild as anything: but every man has his way. Yet, after all, how could anyone think that this lord would deceive so pious, so beautiful, and so virtuous a lady?

We were then in the closet which belonged to her maid. She then showed us the outer room of the lady's apartment, and called a girl to tell us where she sat when she was instructing her young scholars. The landlady then taking down a drawing from the wall, said, Here is my little garden, my bees, and the meadow where my cows are feeding: it was she who drew all this. In giving this piece to my lord, she kissed it, and shedding tears, said, O my dear, dear lady, God for ever bless you! You are now certainly in heaven.

The first glance I cast on this design convinced me that it was drawn by Sophia. The exactness of the outline, and the delicacy of the shades, convinced me that it was hers. I felt my heart oppressed, and was obliged to sit down. My eyes overflowed with tears; for who could forbear lamenting the unhappy fate of the most noble of women? I was also affected by the sincere, though rude affection of our hostess. She was pleased with my tenderness, and said, clapping me on the shoulder, Well done! This grief is commendable! Pray to God to give a good heart, that you may not deceive anybody; for you are an Englishman, and a handsome man too, and may have some young innocent in your eye! The son, the maid, and all the people of the house now joining us, related many particulars in relation to the young lady, and many instances of her goodness. They at length showed us her bed-chamber, and our hostess continued, After she received the letter she never set her foot in this room, but lay with her maid. There is the chest of drawers where she shut up all the trinkets in gold and diamonds which he brought her, Oh, what fine things did he give her! But I had orders to give them to him again; for she would keep none of them. Two days after she was gone, came another letter, and the man said we should soon have him here again; but I delivered to him the packet of jewels, and drove him out of the house.

My uncle took exact informations of everything that had passed: I did not hear half: I was out of myself; and the woman not being able to tell me where the lady was gone, all the rest signified but little to me. I had heard enough to make me ready to die with compassion, and the adorable image of suffering virtue again seized on my whole soul. I entered the maid's closet, and contemplated the spot where Sophia fell on her knees, and felt the inexpressible grief of finding herself deceived and abandoned. Derby's bed-chamber inspired me with no less horror than it did her. I again entered the maid's room, and threw myself on the bed where my Sophia had passed nights of anguish. Here, said I, here rested the lovely creature, in whose arms I should have found the most solid felicity: here her tortured heart groaned at the treachery of the unworthy monster! Yet did this idea mingle a pleasing sensation with that despair with which was overwhelmed. O Sophia, I wept for thy fate, thy loss, and not less for my behaviour towards thee! Yes, I found a pleasure, a mournful pleasure, in thinking that my tears followed the traces of thine, and would be confounded with them. I arose, and kneeled on the same spot where the cruel idea of her injury had made her faint on the floor: there she had reproached herself for her blind credulity; there – I swore by her memory to revenge her.

O, my friend! why did not the wise maxims I have learnt from you strengthen my reason? Why did they not weaken my sensibility? – How miserable was I! how worthy of pity! I cursed the hours in which she had been Derby's, when her beauty, her ravishing charms were in the power of that villain! She loved him – she met him with open arms! – Oh! how was it possible that a soul so tender, so pure, could unite itself to the most insensible, to the most abandoned of mortals?

I bought of our landlady's son the little pillow of the maid's bed: upon it Sophia's head had lain, agitated with grief like mine; we both had wetted it with our tears. Her misfortunes link her to me. Separated from her, doubtless for ever, it was necessary that in this cottage I should again experience the charms and the torment of that sympathy, which she alone has made me feel.

In the morning my uncle found me feverish: his surgeon opened a vein, and an hour after we proceeded on our journey. But before our departure I stole from the hostess the drawing she had shown us, and gave some guineas to the young pupils of my Sophia.

That coldness which policy is more or less accustomed to communicate to the soul, and which passes slightly over any private disaster, allowed my uncle to use a multitude of arguments to calm my sorrow and my rage. I heard him in silence; but the night recompensed me for this constraint, and I passed it indulging my grief. My mind is at present more calm: my powers are revived by the hope of revenging on Derby, her whom I adore, even though he enjoyed the highest post in the kingdom. Observe him when you go to London: see if he does not discover deep traces of inquietude and remorse. Oh, may he ever feel their torments!

I take all imaginable pains to get information of the fate of Sophia, but hitherto they are as ineffectual as are all the efforts made to tear her image from my heart. – The torments I suffer for her are become the only satisfaction I can relish.

LETTER XXXVI

Count R. to Lord Seymour

My Lord,
You transmit me an account of my dear unhappy niece: but, good God, how afflictive is that account! The most noble-minded, the most accomplished, the best of young women, fallen a prey to an infernal villain! When you mentioned your uncle's secretary, I thought that a man of his rank could never obtain the hand of Sophia. Her seduction must have been the work of a skilful hypocrite, who knew how to cover himself with the appearance of virtue. I implored the assistance of Lord G. to bring the villain to justice, though he should be protected by the whole nation. Nothing but the unfortunate circumstance of my wife's ill state of health, and the illness of my only son, should detain me here; but being unable to leave them, all that I can do in favour of my beloved niece, is to demand of the court that her estates be, by order of the prince, put under sequestration, that, according to her intention, the revenues may be referred for Count Löbau's children: but neither their father nor mother ought to enjoy them; they were the first who tore the heart of the gentle Sophia, and were the only cause of that anguish which precipitated her into ruin.

Oh that I could soon repair to D. and that we had but some insight into the place where she is to be found! But happen what will, whether we find her or no, the wretch who did not know how to value such a jewel, who has seduced, who has abandoned her, shall suffer for his crimes.

I really pity you, my lord, for the torments you endure from a passion which has rendered you so unhappy. – But how could a man, who ought to have known the sex, fail of doing justice to this admirable girl, and for a moment suspect her virtue? Pardon me, my lord! It is cruel to add to your grief; but it proceeds from my warm affection for her, which carries my resentment too far, and makes me blame, with the same indignation, what has passed, and mention what might have been done to prevent it.

Spare neither enquiries nor expense to discover the reatreat of this dear girl. Oh, I tremble lest you should only hear of her death!

Woe to the Lord Derby, nay woe to yourself, if you refuse to join with me in revenging her! But on the contrary, all the proofs that you shall give of your tenderness to her, even though they should be slow, will make you find in the uncle of the best of girls, the most tender friend, and the most devoted servant. I will share with you in the whole expense; for our inquietudes, our interests are the same. – Here I keep our misfortunes secret, to preserve the tender heart of the countess from the 'deepest affliction.

LETTER XXXVII

Madam Leidens to Emilia

Lady C. the amiable widow, has a mind equally delicate and sensible. She lately observed that I had concluded my representations and my visit sooner than she expected. Some days after she came with a tender inquietude to ask me the reason of it. I myself had perceived that my silence and unexpected departure might appear strange; but not being willing to offer violence to her sensations, and being afraid of suffering myself to be drawn away by my own, I thought the only part I had to take was to make an abrupt retreat. On my return to my chamber, I clearly perceived that my displeasure against the lovely widow arose from her not being actuated by so warm a desire of communicating happiness as I should have been, were I in her place. It gives me inconceivable pleasure, that the husband of my Emilia has put this construction on my zealous solicitations, from his knowing my propensity to beneficence, though he accuses me of mingling enthusiasm with this virtue. Oh! may the excess of a lawful passion be the only fault of my remaining life!

I frankly answered the amiable widow, that I had been surprised to see a soul like hers, of such tender and delicate feelings, so cold to the interests of others. – I perfectly conceive, returned she, that your principles must lead you to dislike my irresolution. You do not know that it was a sentiment of benevolence that determined my first choice; and that I have too well experienced, that one may make another happy without being happy oneself, to venture again on so uncertain a step.

A particular air of tenderness gave fresh charms to her lovely features, which, with the sweetness of her voice, was irresistibly moving, and recalled to my mind the remembrance of my own hopes, in which I had been so cruelly deceived. The pangs which I have suffered have increased my compassion: warmly affected by whatever alarms this sensation, I give it to others with as much readiness as I formerly shared in the happiness of those around me.

Forgive me, said I; I acknowledge myself guilty, with respect to you, of a too common instance of injustice, that of desiring that others would always conduct themselves by the maxims we have adopted. Why have I hitherto delayed to put myself in your place? Indeed, the manner in which you have viewed my proposals has something terrifying in it; and as I now no longer look upon you to be in the wrong, I shall here dismiss the subject.

I am glad that you appear satisfied with me. It is no less certain that you have caused me great uneasiness, and that you have made me not quite satisfied with myself.

I here hastily asked her How? and Why? From the thought, she replied, that so many men worthy of my esteem are rendered unhappy by my refusal. But may not I expiate my fault by some act of beneficence? Have you no employment to give me in your seminary!

I frankly answered, No. However, added I, smiling and taking her by the hand, I would take advantage of your remorse. I have just thought, that as you forego making a husband happy, you may assemble the daughters or relations of your friends, and improve them by your conversation and your lessons: in short, by inspiring them with your manner of thinking, you may fill this place with amiable women, and while Madam Hills is forming good servants, you may employ yourself in preparing good mistresses for them. She relished this proposal, and desired that I would immediately furnish her with a plan to assist her in the execution of it. This I thought fit to decline, from my finding it too difficult to form one that would at once suit her views and inclinations. You, madam, said I, have prudence, experience, learning, a knowledge of the customs of the place, and a heart full of affability and kindness; with such guides you will, without difficulty, discover whatever is suitable to such a design.

Indeed that I very much doubt: only point out to me a book in which I may find directions how to proceed.

By following the method prescribed in a book, you would soon tire both yourself and your young friends. Among these you will find many who have been brought up in a very different manner, a number of circumstances having concurred to prevent their parents giving them a regular education; and girls of fifteen years of age, like your daughter's companions, will not submit to it. Besides, you are not to keep a school; I would only have you, in such conversation as may happen to arise, seize the opportunity of instructing these young people. Suppose, for instance, one of them, while they are with you, comes to complain that it snows, and is out of humour about the difficulty she will find in returning home: seize this opportunity to ask, if they would not be glad to know whence this phenomenon proceeds. Explain this clearly, and in a few words mention the benefits that proceed from it, according to the wise designs of the Creator; and then, with the gayest air, make them sensible how unreasonable it would be to murmur against that snow, which, however inconvenient it may be at present, will afford them the diversion of seeing a sledge race. This will lead your young hearers to talk of the pleasures of winter, and the dresses of that season.

Take particular care not to interrupt them by a too serious air, or any sign of discontent: show them, on the contrary, that you are very glad that they communicate their different ideas to you: join in their conversation, either in giving your opinion with respect to the good taste of their winter dresses, or in making a description of an entertainment which you will order when a proper occasion offers. Assume an air of gaiety in laying before them these smiling images: agree with your young audience, that, at their age, they have a right to enjoy all the sweets of life; but add, that virtue and prudence ought always to be the inseparable companions of pleasure.

During this first trial, it will be easy for you to found, to a certain degree, the understandings and dispositions of these young maidens; and I should be greatly deceived, if they were not very desirous of returning to your house to hear more of your lectures.

I am of your opinion; but allow me to mention one doubt. – You lead these young people to the knowledge of the nature and use of snow, and to form an idea of the benevolent views of the Creator; but would not the sledge race obliterate the remembrance of all the rest, and consequently of all your instructions.

I don't think it would; for we seldom forget what is connected with agreeable ideas. Hence true wisdom is indulgent; it smiles, condescends to the human weakness, and covers the rugged path of virtue with flowers. Virtue does not stand in need of appearing with a grave aspect, in order to attract our homage. Dignity and decorum are inseparable from her, even when she presents herself in the garb of festivity and joy; and then alone she inspires respect and love. In conducting youth we should not use menacing gestures, but gracious actions. As long as we dwell on this earth, our souls must communicate with each other by the senses, and if these are affected in a disagreeable manner, the contrast found between the formal constraint of lessons, and the natural inclination to pleasure, will produce fatal consequences with respect to our progress in moral improvement. It is not without a gracious design, that the Creator has rendered us susceptible of the sweet impressions of joy; nor that he has multiplied the sources from whence these sweet impressions spring. Paint therefore virtue under attractive forms; mingle with the idea that of innocent recreations, and then see if youth and gaiety will fly from you, to seek a recompense from false and dangerous pleasures for those virtue refuses. Even *divine morality,* in showing us the path of wisdom and virtue, fixes our regards on celestial and immortal joys.

While I thus spoke, Mrs C.'s fine eyes were fixed on me with a look of surprise and pleasure. I begged her pardon for having talked so long; but she assured me that she heard me with great satisfaction, and desired to know why I had not undertaken the education of young ladies, instead of stooping to teach girls designed for service.

I answered, that in comparing the several advantages attached to each rank, those of the inferior class of the human race had appeared so limited, so insufficient, that I was glad to add something to it, in this little corner of my country. The great and wealthy, independently of the advantages which arise from fortune and respect, find all the means of instruction, both in books and in the conversation of persons of learning and good sense; while the inferior class, though of such use to the community, have a most scanty measure of knowledge and improvement.

You talk of knowledge; ought I to make my young pupils learned women?

By no means; for among a thousand women, there is scarce one to be found to whom learning, properly so called, would suit. No, my dear Lady C. keep them close to the exercise of every domestic virtue. At the same time give them some knowledge of the air they breathe; of the earth on which they dwell; of the plants and animals by which they are clothed and sustained. Give them likewise a sketch of history, that they may not be reduced to silence, in the company of men, when they discourse on that subject, and that they may draw moral consequences from it. Give them only a definition of the sciences; for instance, what is understood by the words philosophy and the mathematics: but with respect to the idea affixed to the term a *noble soul*, as well as to all those expressive of the virtues that result from benevolence, make them conceive clear ideas of them in their fullest extent, either by definitions, or more particularly by examples of persons distinguished by the practice of this or that virtue.

Ought I to allow them to read Novels?

Yes, since it would be very difficult to prevent their doing it: but take all possible care to choose such in which the principal persons are guided by the best principles; those in which are represented such true situations as are to be found in real life. If we were to prohibit the reading of all novels, we ought also to forbid the mention, before young people, of those love intrigues which frequently pass in the town where they live, and under their eyes; it would here be necessary that the fathers, the brothers, the husbands, should not be allowed to mention before them the scenes of gallantry of which they have been witness. Without this prohibition, the view of a novel reduced to action in real life, on the one hand, and the prohibition of reading those pieces on the other, would produce a dangerous contrast. I must also add, that an excellent man, well acquainted with human nature, wished that the youth of both sexes might be led to gratify their curiosity by reading accounts of voyages and travels: for the natural history of various countries, and a description of the manners of the inhabitants, would become the source of a thousand subjects of useful knowledge. I would wish also to be able to collect moral pictures of the virtues of each state, and particularly those which fall to the share of women. The French are in this respect more happy than we: the merit of the sex obtains from that nation public and durable monuments.

Does it not thence follow, that our talents and our virtues are more meritorious than theirs, since we endeavour to acquire them without being animated by the hope of reward?

That is true; but it is only so with respect to the few minds who do not
suffer themselves to be deterred by any of the difficulties they meet with,
and not in relation to those who have need of encouragement to enable
them to overcome them. I would therefore have a model of conduct
proposed to each different class, taken out of the class itself. When a woman
has distinguished herself by her zeal in the cause of virtue, and by the
improvement of her mind has rendered herself respectable, and worthy of
being chosen as an example to others, she might have a distinguished seat in
public assemblies, or the particular form of some part of her dress might be
substituted instead of a reward; as was practised among the ancients, who
were so well acquainted with the human heart. But it is not for us to form
such an institution: it is sufficient for us to do all the good in our power. I
am today in the class of those who are poor and reduced to dependence; I
therefore think myself obliged to lead them, either by my example or
instructions, to all the degrees of light and happiness of which they are
capable. I shall, at the same time, take care not to inspire them with the
ideas and inclinations which belong to the shining state from which I have
descended, from the certainty that such a mixture would be only a source of
error and regret. You, madam, are a widow, and possess one of the first
ranks in this place: a happy temper, and an agreeable share of wit, render
your acquaintance sought after by all of your rank. You have a daughter to
educate, and it would be highly praiseworthy in you, to afford a share of the
instructions you give her, to the young ladies whose mothers are diverted by
other concerns from that important care. Teach their daughters to think
and to regulate their conduct in such a manner as to become valuable
women; and this will be a good way of repairing the injury you do to society
by your vow of celibacy. – This conclusion made her smile, as did also my
excuses for having taken the liberty to trace out a plan for her; and at our
parting I received from her all possible marks of her friendship and
satisfaction.

LETTER XXXVIII

Madam Leidens to Emilia*

I am obliged, my dear Emilia, in spite of myself, to accompany Madam Hills to the baths. It is true, I have lost my health, and am sensible that I have need of the relief which I am assured the waters will afford me. A secret uneasiness consumes my strength, and my application to labour, excited by my zeal, has lately contributed to that weakness for which you were pleased to express such a sympathetic concern, when I had last the satisfaction of being at your house. Yesterday your husband got the better of my aversion, by his promising to spend the first week with us; and by that time he imagines that my dislike to the company of the great will subside. He likewise affirms, that my heart has this winter so exhausted the faculties of my mind, that nothing but a clear air, and the charms of society, can restore my health. I am so meagre and pale; my eyes, which once attracted others, are so seldom lifted up, and my dress is so plain, that I have nothing to apprehend from the solicitations of men. So, my dear friend, adieu for two months. We shall set out tomorrow morning, with your husband, a maid, and one servant.

LETTER XXXIX

Madam Leidens to Emilia

The Spa

Tell me, my friend, how came your husband to obtain such an influence over my mind? It was he who in bringing me to Madam Hills, made me again engage in active life: it was he who drew me hither in spite of myself;

---

* Some months had passed between this and the preceding letter.[62]

and it is he, who, on the fourth day of my being here brought me acquainted with Lady Summers, and has formed so close a connection between that lady and me, that I am to accompany her to England. He has let you know that we arrived happily here, and that the report of Madam Hills's wealth procured us greater deference and respect than we desired. On the very first evening when he heard that Lady Summers was at the Spa, he paid her a visit, and the next day showed her to me on the walks. She is a graceful figure, notwithstanding her being extremely infirm; humanity is painted on her countenance; her large eyes are filled with sensibility, and a graceful dignity accompanies all her actions. She curtsied to Madam Hills and me, and viewed us with much attention, without speaking to us, but called Mr Br. from us. The day following she took him from us to dine with her, adding only on addressing herself to me, I hope this evening you will come and sup with me: but before I could answer her, she was got at a distance. But I should not have been able to speak to her without stammering; for you cannot imagine, Emilia, the painful sensation I felt from the genuine English accent which struck my ears. The fright I felt from it was as sudden as a flash of lightning, and with it crowded upon my soul the remembrance of the most painful scenes. Happy was it for me that my lady quitted us, for had she stayed, my embarrassment would have been too visible.

In the evening Madam Hills, Mr Br. and I supped with her. My lady was extremely obliging, but she kept a most inquisitive eye on every part of my behaviour. She commended Madam Hills for founding her seminary, and added, that at her return to England, she would follow her example. Mr Br. on interpreting this to Madam Hills filled her with a sensible satisfaction, and one might see her generous heart smile through her tears on hearing it; but suddenly taking me by the hand, she desired Mr Br. to inform the lady, that she had spent only some superfluous money in this good work, while the honour of the design was due to me.

I blushed extremely, which my lady perceiving, said, stroking my cheek, It is well done, my girl, true virtue should be always modest.

My attention to entertain Madam Hills, and to translate into German most of the things said in English, also obtained her ladyship's approbation. She will certainly, said she, see happy days, since she endeavours to give happiness to those of an advanced age. This reference to my future life, which is all wrapt up in obscurity, touched me to the quick, and it was impossible for me to avoid letting fall some tears. My lady, whom nothing escaped, leaned towards me with a look full of tenderness, saying, Amiable and sweet creature, I know a hand that will wipe away thy tears.

I bowed and cast my eyes on Mr Br. who with a look of satisfaction was going to speak, when the lady said, Not a word more today on this subject. Tomorrow will clear up everything.

Since this tomorrow six days have passed, during which my irresolute heart has fluctuated between the proposals that have been made me and the difficulties I have foreseen. At length I have determined to pass this year at

my lady's country seat, and to return with her the next season for drinking
the waters. Nothing should have made me content to go to London. Heaven
preserve me from meeting any of the English whom I already know! But
none of those will ever come to search the retreat of an old woman; I can,
therefore, without fear satisfy the desire I have long entertained of seeing
that country, and enquiring after the family of the Watsons. Mr Br. has
represented to Madam Hills, that she ought not to oppose my going, since
my presence will be of use to Lady Summers in superintending a charitable
foundation in England in imitation of hers.

O Emilia! my Lady Summers is a perfect angel, who for a long course of
years has proceeded from place to place, pouring the consolations of
friendship, a healing balm, into hearts filled with sensibility. Hence my soul,
by being united to hers, resumes a new being, and she alone can comfort me
in my absence, for a time, from the dearest of my friends.

LETTER XL

Madam Leidens to Emilia

Summer Hall

My first letter from hence should inform you of my being happily arrived in
England with my dear lady, and I hope my Rosina, Mr Br. and the
benevolent Madam Hills have as happily returned home. I am very sorry
that Rosina could not get the better of her dread of the sea, for I should
have been glad of her having accompanied us into the smiling abode in
which I now reside.

You, my Emilia, have certainly read some descriptions of the English
country seats: Imagine to yourself one of the finest in the Gothic taste, and
call it Summer Hall; but place on the side of the park a large village, and
represent to yourself my lady leaning on my arm, walking through the
streets, talking to the children or the laborious poor, visiting the sick, or
assisting others who are in distress. Thus is her ladyship employed in the
afternoon and the evening. In the morning I read to her and take upon me
the management of the family. The visits she receives from her few
neighbours, especially from the minister of the parish, who is an excellent
man, so fill up the remainder of the day as to leave me little time for my
own particular reading. Among the books my lady has selected, some turn
on the national spirit, others on the due sense of our approaching dissolution. In short, her library is composed of political tracts and the best English

sermons. I add to it the natural history of the country, being desirous of extending my progress in my favourite science, and I entertain myself on this subject in my walks with the clergyman's family, whose wife and daughters are very sensible women. I enjoy my health, and taste a sweet satisfaction; but it more resembles a calm repose than pleasure, because my ideas and sensations have no longer their former vivacity. Perhaps I may be infected by the breath of that sweet melancholy which is infused into the best minds in this island, and spreads like a light cloud over the most lively characters. I begin again to suffer my voice and lute to be heard, and I prize them both when after having sung and joined my hand in an adagio, I receive my lady's embraces. But judge, Emilia, of the strength of my inclination for England, when notwithstanding the torturing remembrance of one of its natives, I can find pleasure in breathing the air of a park, and regard this land as my country. I have adopted the dress of the English; I speak their language, and would also assume their manners: but my lady says, that in spite of all my endeavours, I cannot get rid of an amiable foreign air which accompanies all my actions. The confidence of those of her people whom I have gained, their attention to her, and their eagerness to serve her, which she condescends to attribute to my influence over them, is what of all my services most affects her, and this excites in her heart a tender gratitude. Seldom have I slept in this house without experiencing a sensation of pure joy, after having received the blessing of my dear lady, and the affectionate wishes of her people that I may enjoy a good repose. In the morning I go down into the park, where the shepherd wondering to see me at the rising of the sun, cries, Good morrow, good miss. This expression at the instant when I see the Creator's bounty spread out before me in rich luxuriance, seems to me a testimony that I also freely fulfil the law of beneficence, and with my eyes overflowing with gratitude, I bless the author of my being for having left this power in my heart. You know that the least of the beauties of nature claim my attention. Moss and the flowers of the field can attract my notice, and most objects awaken my sensations. The branches shooting from the root of a tree that has been blown down by the wind, have made me say, Am not I like a young tree torn up by a tempest? In the midst of its bloom it loses its top and its branches: long its sad remains lie extended withering on the ground, till at length new branches shoot from the root and grow under the care of nature, rising till its branches extend around a salutary shade. I have lost my reputation, my fortune, the place I filled in society: long was my soul buried in grief, but the good principles of my education, which my fate could not extinguish, have acquired new force, and enabled me to produce some acts of beneficence. Thus this tree has become my emblem; the young branches shade only the rising moss; I at first sought for objects only in the inferior class of the human race; but now the scene is changed, and I devote myself entirely to my dear Lady Summers, who reposes on me all the cares of life; I assist in smoothing the thorny path so difficult at sixty years of age, and conducting her between her fleeting pleasures and approaching infirmities.

LETTER XLI

Madam Leidens to Emilia

Summer Hall

Do we not see, my dear Emilia, that the rich feel a kind of want which they
in vain endeavour to supply, by assembling every kind of enjoyment? This is
owing to their not having learnt that the mind and the heart have a void
which all the gold of the Indies, all the jewels and all the luxuries of France,
are unable to fill. The inventions of art cannot supply, in a sensible heart, the
place of an absent friend, nor the charms of an instructive conversation with
those we love. As for me, I at present find myself rich: most of the blessings
of life are at my disposal: I am sensible of the value of the favours I have
received from Providence; but my heart wants to pour forth its effusions
into the bosom of my Emilia. I have here, however, the happiness to be
beloved: my principles, which I modestly express when an occasion offers,
procure me esteem. A sense of the beauties of Shakespeare, Thomson,
Addison and Pope, furnish my mind for conversing with our minister, and a
very philosophical nobleman in our neighbourhood. Emma, the clergyman's
eldest daughter, is mild, sensible, and possessed of an excellent mind; but I
find, in the midst of her embraces, that she cannot supply the place of my
first friend. Don't call me ungrateful to her, though I know myself possessed
of her friendship as well as yours. I write to you those sensations over which
I must here draw a veil. My Emma's conversation turns on the subjects
canvassed in my English abode; and I cannot help meditating on the length
of the way my poor letters have to travel, and sensibly feeling what a pause
this frightful distance gives to the favourite custom of my heart, in opening
itself to you. I may, my dearest Emilia, be destined to pass through the
whole train of moral sensations, in order that I may more readily and
accurately observe their many degrees and vicissitudes, prosperous and
adverse, however, in this part of my destiny I shall willingly acquiesce, while
I retain the same sympathy for my neighbours' sorrows and joys, and, as
much as I am able, lighten the burden of their affliction.

The kind Lady Summers has thought fit to consult her own honour and
my supposed pride, by representing me to her friends as a person of noble
birth, who losing her parents, made a very disadvantageous match, and was
soon after deprived of her husband,. The fineness of my linen, my laces, my
bracelets, and my behaviour, have contributed more to confirm her in the

truth of this account, than my way of thinking could have done. But it is a beautiful proof of the lady's virtue, that she gives credit to mine; and her friendship for me will not permit anyone to doubt the purity of my manners. The air my lady breathes, says the clergyman, is so moral that the vicious cannot approach it. The Lord Rich, the philosophical nobleman I have just mentioned, has a seat at a mile's distance, built in the most noble taste. The finest ornaments within it consist of natural curiosities, a collection of mathematical instruments, and a numerous library, in which are twenty volumes in folio, which contain most of the plants of our globe, dried and arranged by his lordship himself. The desire of seeing his fine garden, which is partly cultivated by himself, and his park which joins to ours, alone induced us to pay him our first visit: but the plain simple manner in which he showed us all his treasures, the fruit of his long travels into the East, with the vast extent of his knowledge, and acquaintance with the fine arts, give such charms to his conversation, that my lady has resolved frequently to repeat her visits; it being extremely agreeable, she observes, at the evening of life, to please our eyes, by viewing the wonders of the creation. My Lord Rich, who has lived here in the country a kind of solitary life, with no other companion but the clergyman, is much pleased with our acquaintance, and is disposed to cultivate it. He enjoys a perfect tranquility and repose which is visible in his whole behaviour; so that one might imagine that his mind partook of the nature of the vegetable world, whose operations are incessant without being perceived: it also appears to me, that he now observes the moral part of the creation with the same assiduity as he formerly studied the works of nature. My Emma and Lady Summers will be gainers by this, but I must own it makes me afraid. The other day, asking his opinion of one of my thoughts, he answered, To discourse freely with you on your refined sentiments, would be a noble pleasure; but the hand of complaisance only holds them out to us, from the mist which over-clouds your mind. This threw me into some perplexity, and I asked him, if he thought my mind clouded? He, giving me a kind and tender look, answered, Not as you are pleased to take it; but do not those tears, which I see rising in your eyes, show that I am in the right, else why do the emotions of your soul condense the mist I mentioned into rain? – Dear madam, I will mention it no more; but do not you ever ask what judgment my heart forms of yours.

You see, my Emilia, how much I want you. To you I would lay open all my sentiments; my heart would then be comforted, and no longer appear as through a cloud. I recovered myself so far as to answer, that I desired he would impute these clouds to circumstances, and not to my natural temper. I am convinced of it, said he, and you make yourself very easy; it required all penetration to perceive them; they would escape the observation of others. Our conversation was here interrupted by our being joined by Miss Emma; after which Lord Rich avoided observing me with such attention.

LETTER XLII

Madam Leidens to Emilia

Tell me, my Emilia, why are the best of men subject to prejudices? Why does a man of merit consider as a breach of decency, the love with which his perfections inspire a worthy woman, and cannot pardon her endeavours to gain the esteem, and to please the object beloved?*[63]

These questions took their rise from Lord Rich, whose mind appears to be divested of all prejudices, and to be only guided by wisdom and virtue; yet he seems to view with dislike Miss Emma's tender affection for him, though he always speaks of her in terms of esteem, and cannot refuse her the just praises due to her wit and discernment, and to the goodness of her heart. As an effect of the same caprice which prevents his returning the passion he has inspired, he begins to show me a particular respect that has all the appearance of love, and gives me no little uneasiness; though, except my esteem for him on account of his virtue and extensive knowledge, I am quite indifferent. Many sentiments do I suppress only to avoid his praise, and to prevent my pouring a drop of oil into a fire which I wish exting-uished for, being resolved not to return his love, it would be an instance of criminal vanity in me to endeavour to feed it.

This afternoon we are to pay him a visit, in order to be present at a new experiment in agriculture, (the sowing a piece of land by means of a machine,) and my lady is too fond of seeing the works of husbandry to lose this opportunity. Every day, says she brings me nearer to an union of this frame with my mother earth, and this, I think makes me love it the better.

We paid this visit yesterday, which my dear Emilia, would have been spent happily, if an accidental circumstance had not happened against my lord and me. I was seated by the side of the clergyman, while the Lord Rich talked to us of tillage, the difference of soils, and consequently the different means required for cultivating them with success. His language was noble simple, and intelligible. He gave us an account of the various inventions to which such or such a nation had recourse to correct the badness of the soil, and how far their labours were attended with success. When he had done speaking, I could not help saying to the clergyman, in a low voice, that it

---

* The answer to this question is simple enough: it is impossible to allow a noble-minded, virtuous young woman a separate morality of her own. – E.

were to be wished that moralists had studied man, the force and nature of his new-born inclinations and passions, in order to indicate the different means of rendering each, in his own manner, better and more useful.

They have long, said he, been employed about this, but they have hitherto found among mankind many ungrateful soils that refuse all culture, and the best seed is thrown away upon them. I continued, with a sentimental air, to draw some parallels between the moral and physical world.[64] The minister heard me with great composure; but Lord Rich, who was placed behind us, suddenly started up, and taking me by the arm over my chair, O madam! said he, what have you to do in the great world, with a heart like yours? You have certainly not been happy! – Doubtless my answer pleased him for in an enthusiastic transport he cried, Noble soul! happy is the country that gave thee birth! It was sweet Humanity, it was Virtue herself, that took pleasure in forming thee.

An emotion which sprung from my heart made me apply my lips to the portraits of my parents, which I always wear in my bracelets, and these were instantly moistened with some tears. I arose, walked to the window, and Lord Rich followed me thither. I observed that he partook of my sadness, when some minutes after I cast my eyes on him, his were fixed on my bracelets. Are those, madam, (said he, in a soft voice,) the portraits of your parents? Are they still living? Oh! no, my lord; if they were, I should not have been here, and my eyes would shed no tears but those of joy. – Was it a storm then which drove you to England? – No, my lord, it was friendship brought me hither; my own free choice. – I thank you, returned he, for your half confidence, since it lets me know that you are disengaged. It is on this assurance that the most noble passion a man can feel founds its hopes. – That can't be, my lord, said I; she who is thus free, is for ever excluded the hopes of what is called happiness. – My lady, who was walking up to us, heard these last words, and putting her hand upon my mouth, cried, you must not say that. Why will you confound the past with the future? Go, my dear, Providence will take care of you; but do not expect that all your unjust and unreasonable expectations will be answered. – This reproach exciting my sensibility, made me blush: I kissed the hand that would have imposed silence on me, and asked, in the most tender voice, Most dear lady, when have you found me unjust and unreasonable in my expectations? I blame your settled grief, said she, for what is past; a useless grief, as there is no returning from the grave, O my dear, my well-beloved Lady Summers, cried I, why, ah why – This exclamation proceeded from my being so affected by her goodness that I could not help inwardly lamenting my being reduced to the necessity of imposing on her by a false account; but she attributed it to another cause, and interrupting me, said, No more of your complaints; but, my dear girl, employ your sensibility on agreeable subjects, and depend on my maternal tenderness as long as you can receive, and I bestow it. I pressed her hand to my breast, and looked at her with all the affection of filial love: her heart understood mine, and she rewarded me with a tender embrace.

Lord Rich viewed us with emotion; and at that instant I saw Emma's fine eyes fixed on him with all the languor of love. I said to his lordship, in Italian, that it was there he would find generous unmixed sensations, and such only as would secure the happiness of a man of noble sentiments. No, madam, said he in the same language, that sensibility is not adapted to render a solitary happy. – What did he mean? – I was at a loss to guess. – Shaking my head, with a look but half pleased, O my lord, said I, of what kind then are your sentiments? Of the most durable, he returned; for they are produced by virtue. To this I made no answer, but, dropping a curtsy, turned towards Emma, who giving me her arm, walked with me towards Summer Hall, but during all the way was buried in pensive silence; and today I hear that she is disposed to leave us.

LETTER XLIII[65]

Madam Leidens to Emilia

Lord Rich persecutes me with his love, his admiration, and his proposals, which give me pain, from my being certain that it is in my power to render him happy. Oh! could I have foreseen that the conformity of our tastes would have inspired him with the thought that a sympathetic love might be kindled between us, I would have carefully concealed the power which the beauties of nature have over my mind, and have denied myself every kind of private conversation with him: but I was the more easy in this respect, from my not being ignorant that he had brought from the isle of Scios a very accomplished Grecian beauty. For a long time I attributed his eagerness to converse with me, and the desire he expressed to know my opinion, to the pleasure he found in conversing on his favourite subjects. With the most fixed attention I sometimes listened to the history of a foreign country, and the wonders of distant regions; sometimes to the description of a plant, a stone, or some Grecian ruin. Thus I made him taste the satisfaction of communicating his knowledge, and of obtaining the praises which the useful employment of his life and wealth deserved. I set a high value on this nobleman's conversation, and on the improvement I received from it. His resolution, after travelling ten years in the most distant countries, to employ the rest of his days in the improvement of the agriculture of his native land, claims also my approbation and esteem; but his love is a superfluity which perplexes and disturbs me. He has made many enquiries of Lady Summers about me, and whether that lady's answers have or have not increased his flame, they seem to have rendered him more pressing; and a single word I dropped to her ladyship, engaged him to dispose of his fair Greek, and to send her to London, with the husband he has given her. I cannot express how much this pretended sacrifice weighs with me. His secretary, he says, has for a long time loved this girl, and was beloved by her, and both have begged him on their knees to favour their union: but he feels the void which this separation has left in his heart. At the break of day he is seen in our park, which deprives me of the morning air; for I shun it, in order to avoid meeting him. Never, no never, will I, for the future, have recourse to artifice to draw myself from any perplexity.

Lady Summers having one day bantered me on Lord Rich's growing passion, I amused myself with contradicting her in the same strain, and maintained, that in him it only proceeded from self-love, and from the manifest pleasure I showed in hearing him talk: but she seriously answered, His lordship loves in you the laudable desire of acquiring knowledge, and when he enlightens you with his literary rays, ought your raillery to be his recompense? This reproach affected me; for though I cannot bear the least appearance of injustice, I now felt that I had been guilty of it. However, her ladyship continued, in a very kind manner, to remind me of the convincing proofs his lordship had given of his tender esteem and settled affection for me. I agreed that his sentiments merited a return on my part; but, observing that at every declaration of my friendship for him she shook her head, and required something more, I assured her that, to me, it appeared impossible that my lord could require more, as I supposed he enjoyed, in his beautiful Greek, all that he could expect from love. Her ladyship then broke off the conversation, without letting me perceive that she imagined she had now discovered the only obstacle to my lord's wishes. He, for some days, did not say a single word of his passion, yet appeared more gay than usual, especially when he told us of the marriage and departure of his Assy. I was struck with this news, and feared that he would offer me the entire possession of that heart which, by Assy's engagement, was reverted to the right owner. He still said nothing to me; but her ladyship spoke for him. How is it, said I, how is it, my dear lady, that you want to part with your adopted daughter? Do you cease to love her? − No, my dear child, answered she, taking hold of my hand, you are infinitely dear to me, and I shall certainly feel the absence of her who takes such tender care of my declining age: but I have sufficiently provided for the autumn of my life, and need not to strip your spring of its fairest flowers. You are young, beautiful, and a stranger, and what would become of you, should I die!

Should I survive that misfortune, I will return to my Emilia.

My dear girl, consider things well! A woman of your birth and figure ought to be under the care of her near relations, or under the protection of a worthy husband. You have a sincere esteem for his lordship, and indeed he deserves it; you know that his happiness is in your hands; you prize his friendship; you are delighted with his acquaintance: in short, you are your own mistress, and the most noble motives concur to make you agree to this union. Procure then, – for the mother you have found, the satisfaction of seeing united in your person and that of his lordship, the most beautiful models of virtue that can be held up to either sex.

How pressing was my lady! I reclined my head on her hand, which I kissed and bathed with my tears. Her voice penetrated through my soul, and seemed to be the echo of the voice of my own tender mother. Such virtues, such motives were the bonds of the union she formed: but alas! how different was my former choice from hers! but here can my lord's merit be compared to that of my father, and my happiness be equal to that she enjoyed? but the circumstances, the fatal circumstances of my story! – O Emilia, write to me – delay not to write to me – communicate to me your thoughts! – Yet I can love no more – no more can I dispose of myself. Even the tender esteem I feel for Lord Rich rises against that thought. A perfidious hand has humbled me in the dust. Humanity might have raised me, and I was entitled to her assistance; but my thoughtlessness has ravished from me every other blessing; and I will not usurp a happiness to which I am a stranger – a happiness of which I am unworthy.

LETTER XLIV

Madam Leidens to Emilia

O my dear friend! an unforeseen misfortune is rushing upon me, which I doubt whether all my constancy will be able to support. What adds to my pain is my seeing myself forced to have recourse to dissimulation, an expedient, which of all others, I most dread and detest. But in the circumstance wherein I am placed, a candid account of all I have suffered can be of no use to me, and may be prejudicial to others; I am therefore determined to confine within my own heart, the torment which preys upon it. Nay more, I will employ for the amusement of him who caused it, all the imagination I have left, and which was formerly so inventive. Read, my Emilia, and pity the misfortunes which pursue the friend of your youth. But first I ought to give you an account of my conversations with Lord Rich.

A few days ago I was obliged to hear the history of his heart, which he concluded with a description of his love for me. This love, said he, is the passion of a man of forty-five years of age; reason gave it birth, and my knowledge of mankind, with all the lights I have obtained by experience, have conspired to strengthen it.

My lord, said I, you deceive yourself, reason never pleads in favour of
love against friendship; my heart offers you the highest degree of that; but
cease –

Not a word more, madam, till you have heard me. My reason has made
me your friend, and a man of equal merit could have inspired me with an
equal degree of esteem. – Here he enumerated the virtues and improvements of which he imagined me to be possessed. I answered, that he drew
an agreeable picture of an object to which I was a stranger. He continued his
elogium, and concluded with saying, that both my heart and mind were in
such unison with his thoughts and sentiments, that on our being united
there must result the most perfect harmony.

The image of his felicity was touched with such affecting strokes, that I
plainly perceived his lordship was acquainted with all the springs of my soul,
and knew what would lead me to render a worthy person happy. With all
possible delicacy he delineated the felicity of our union. O my Emilia, it was
the faithful copy of the wishes and hopes I had formerly nourished! Deeply
affected, I could not restrain my tears. He rose from the green bank on
which we were seated, seized both my hands, and pressing them to his
breast, examined me with an attentive and tender air. Then cried, O
madam, what an expression of grief is spread over all your features! Either
death has snatched from you a person whom you adored, or there is in your
situation an hidden source of the most bitter grief. Oh give it vent: pour it,
pour it into the bosom of the most tender, the most faithful friend.

I let my head sink upon his hands, by which he still held mine. The ideas
of my misfortunes, the merit of this generous man, the heavy chain of my
marriage, though only supposititious, the thought of the happiness which he
lost by placing it upon me, at once rushed upon me, and overwhelmed my
soul. I could not speak, but my sighs forced themselves a passage.

He was for a moment silent, then with an agitation which made his hands
tremble, he said in the most dejected and mild voice: Oh the agony of your
grief gives light to a most alarming day – Your husband is not dead – an
accident merely the effect of the laws of nature might deject, but could not
thus overwhelm a soul like yours. But this man is unworthy of you, and the
idea of his chain wounds your heart. – Am I in the right? Oh tell – tell me if
I am mistaken. His discourse made me tremble, and I found it still more
difficult to speak than before. He was so good as to say: Enough for today.
Compose yourself; let me only gain your confidence. – I lifted up my eyes,
and from an involuntary emotion squeezed his hand. – O my Lord Rich! was
all that I was able to say. Excellent heart! he cried, Who is the unhappy
wretch that could not distinguish thy worth, and that could make thee
suffer?

My dear lord, you shall know all, all without reserve. You deserve my
confidence.

Scarce had I spoke these words when one of Lady Summers's servants
came to let me know that she would speak with me on some important

letters she had received from London. I strove to compose myself, and
hasted to my lady, who immediately told me, that her only niece had just
married Lord N. and that this would procure her, within a fortnight, a visit
from her brother and the new married couple. We must, added she, strive
some pretty rural entertainment, in order to give pleasure to these young
folks, while they are at their old aunt's. She then, rising, put into my hand
the letter the young couple had written to her, and left the room to dismiss
the messenger. O Emilia, how did I tremble on seeing by the hand that the
letter was written by Lord Derby, who is now the Lady Alton's lawful
husband! With trembling steps I proceeded towards my chamber, in order
to conceal my confusion from Lady Summers. I could not shed a tear, but
was ready to be stifled with grief. How sensible was I now of my imprudence in coming to England! I saw myself reduced to the necessity of
quitting my tranquil my blest asylum. It is impossible, said I, for me to stay
at Summer Hall. Ah! I cannot envy the villain his happiness; but why must I
again become his victim? I approached the window in order to recover my
breath, and lift up my eyes towards heaven. O God, O my God, cried I, the
supreme Ruler of all, support me under my misfortunes! What must I –
What ought I to do?

It was by a kind of miracle that I was enabled to recollect my spirits – I
resolved to conceal all, to assist my lady in her preparations for their
reception, and at length to feign a sickness that should oblige me to keep my
bed, and to dispense with my seeing strangers. This is the only part I can
take in this extremity. I stifled my grief, and went to Lady Summers, whom
I heard speaking from the window to the messenger, whom she dismissed
with a handsome gratuity. She then, addressing herself to me, expatiated on
the opulence and influence of the family of Lord N. who, by his brother's
decease, was become the sole heir of that house. Now, said she, my brother
will surely be satisfied, his only fault is ambition, and most heartily do I
share in his joy.

Friendship and gratitude were, at this instant, my supports; without
which could I, amidst the disorder of my soul have had the strength to keep
my seat, or the power to feign a smile! The part I took in my benefactress's
joy served to fortify me. During the first hour my heart experienced the
most dreadful torment it had ever felt; but it would have been cruel to have
filled the soul of my dear lady with anguish, by revealing my secret to her.
She loves me, she is just and virtuous, a sensation of horror would fill her
with aversion to this wicked man now her nephew, and the beloved
husband of her niece. Perhaps too, he may be filled with remorse; perhaps
he has resolved to become an honest man, and certainly he himself would be
in the greatest perplexity, could he know that I am here. – He has never
known me; never has he suspected that it would be one day in my power to
hurt him. But I will not make use of this power. Let him enjoy the happiness
which fortune has granted him. I will not disturb him and it shall not be in
vain that Virtue offers to my heart the delicate trial, by which she

distinguishes her true disciples: the opportunity of doing good to my enemy. O Providence, cried I, let me acquire this proof of a true greatness of soul! After this devout exclamation, I burst into a violent but sweet flood of tears, which watered the bed on which I was laid. This act of beneficence, my vow in favour of my most cruel enemy, was rewarded with the most unsullied joy: my heart felt the full value of virtue; it was elevated, it was expanded. My hands then joined from an emotion of the most pure gratitude, though but a few hours before they had been clasped in a fit of despair. I slept peaceably; my awaking was sweet; and with tranquillity I drew up the plan of their entertainment to be given by my lady. – Yet observe, my Emilia, how easily evil insinuates itself into what is good; for some moments I resolved to execute, in little, the rural festival of Count F., with a view of giving some confusion to Lord Derby: but I rejected this thought, considering it as a species of disguised revenge, which glided into my imagination after I had banished it from my heart.

*   *   *   *   *

I really believe, Emilia, that Lord Rich penetrates into almost all my thoughts. He did not return hither till the fourth day after our conversation. Her ladyship told him, at dinner, the reason of his finding us so busy, and after it was over conducted him into the rooms already prepared. His lordship seemed to view everything attentively, praised the whole, but in few words, and followed all my motions with an uneasy and curious eye. – Lady Summers left us alone during some minutes and he approached the table where I was sorting and tying up Italian flowers. He took one of my hands, and looking upon me with the most tender concern, said, You are not well, my friend, your hands tremble while they are employed: a kind of precipitation in your motions pierces, in spite of yourself, through a feigned gaiety: your smiles do not proceed from the heart. What is the meaning of all this? My lord, answered I, your penetration frightens me. – Then I am right, said he. Ask me no more questions, my lord: my soul has suffered the most violent conflict; but at present, I would sacrifice everything that concerns myself to the pleasure of the Lady Summers.

I am only apprehensive that you will sacrifice yourself too.

Fear nothing! I am born to suffer, and I must fulfil my lot. It seemed to me that I uttered these words with great composure and with a smile; yet his lordship was struck with them, and said, Do you know, madam, that a language like this is expressive of the deepest despair, and that it involves me in the most torturing inquietude! – Speak – I entreat you to speak to Lady Summers, cried he: you will find in her a maternal heart. I know it, my worthy lord; but at present that cannot be. Banish your inquietude on my account. This agitation which you now see, is the last effort of a storm that will soon be followed by a calm. O God, cried he, when will cease the anguish in which I am involved by the thoughts of your sufferings! – I began to be afraid of my being too much softened; but my lady luckily came in, and Lord Rich left us in a seeming uneasiness and displeasure, which we both observed, and her ladyship said, How can you, who have a good heart, take a pleasure in thus tormenting your neighbour. Oh! would I might hope that one of those flowers was to be worn by you, on your accompanying Lord Rich to the altar. – My brother will stand father, and as for the mother, she is always at hand.

Dearest lady, answered I, with the most lively emotion, my resistance becomes every day more painful: but hitherto it has been impossible for me to come to a resolution. Kindly suffer me to be as I am a few days longer. A torrent of tears which I could not restrain, made her ladyship also weep, and promise to suspend her solicitations.

LETTER XLV

From Lord Derby, now become Lord N.
to his friend at Paris

You know that I am married to the rich and high-spirited Lady Alton, and that she is not a little proud of her having chained me by the laws of Hymen. She bridled her head with the most silly air, when I, to know her thoroughly asked her with great complaisance, in what I could oblige her. At first I meant only to amuse myself, for a while, in completing my register of female fools; but it so falls out, that I have by this means rendered myself an essential service. After all that wretched bustle was over, during which the new-married pair seem to show themselves in a mutual triumph, I asked my lady if she should not like to spend a few days in the country, and she instantly proposed a visit to her aunt Summers, a tiresome old woman, but she is rich, and her estate will be worth having. We accordingly wrote, and sent John with a letter to inform her of our intended visit. This old lady received him as kindly as possible, and while she was answering our epistle, John walked about the anti-chamber with the house-steward. My lady, immediately after he came asked for Madam Leidens, and within a quarter of an hour nimbly stepped in a young person in an English dress, who, with her eyes half cast down, proceeded through the anti-chamber, and went to my lady. John, quite thunderstruck, perceived it to be no other than Sophia Sternheim; yet instantly recovering himself, he asked who that lady was? The steward told him, that she came from Germany with his mistress, who loves her extremely; that she is an angel in wisdom and goodness, and that she and Lord Rich, whose estate borders upon my lady's, are to make a match of it. – My poor devil now trembled for fear of being called before Lady Summers, and pretended a mighty hurry to be gone. The old lady appeared, but was happily alone. John got himself dismissed as soon as possible, then mounted and set spurs to his horse.

Judge yourself how much I must be surprised on receiving this news. Never did any of my pranks give me such uneasiness, as that I now felt for the tricks I had played this enthusiast. How the devil came she to venture to show her face in England! Yet it is always so. The most fearful creature becomes courageous in the arms of a man, and I have certainly communicated to her some share of my impudence: yet had I met with her at Lady Summers's, I might have stood in need of it myself, and have obliged her to return it. Upon my honour, it is very lucky that I have kept John in my service, for the cunning dog was beforehand with me, and discovered the only step I had to take; that is, to carry off Sophia as soon as possible, and convey her over the hills, and a great way off from Summer Hall. I applauded the thought, and assigned for the retreat of this fair lady, that which Nancy possessed for some years, on the Hopton estate, in the midst of the mountains of Scotland. Her father, though a barrister learned in the law, was never able to find her; and how then should they be ever able to unkennel a stranger? I agree with you, that it is a cursed fate for one of the finest girls in the world, to be taken so far from home, to eat oat-bread in Scotland, in the hut of a wretch labouring in a lead mine. But how the deuce came she to throw herself in my way in England? Does she not deserve to be punished for this rashness? She does, and is already arrived at the place of her destination, where I have ordered that she shall be well fed. John has had the management of the whole affair: having learned from the steward that my heroine frequently conversed with Lord Rich, the parson, and his wife and daughter, in the garden and park, he caused her to be informed that Miss Emma desired she would be so kind as to walk with her, which she complying with, he carried her off: and he says that it was with very great difficulty that he took her alive into Scotland. All the way she would take nothing but some water, and, except an exclamation in which she uttered the name of Derby, she continued wholly silent and motionless in the carriage, which, with her dejection and paleness, rendered her the image of death. Had you been here, weak as you are, I would have put her under your care, and could you have brought her to be tractable, her conquest would have been worth more than all you purchased at Paris; for she is one of the finest flowers of all those that have withered in the glowing bosom of your friend.

No sooner was I informed that she had been missed at Summer Hall for two days, than I went thither with my wife and her father. We found the old lady keeping her bed, all in tears, for her beloved daughter, the comfort of her old age. All the people of the house and of the place, the minister's family, and especially the Lord Rich, an old bachelor who affects the philosopher, join in mourning for the loss of Madam Leidens. Lady Summers implored my assistance; and I, in appearance, left no stone unturned in order to find her. This gave me an opportunity of learning by what accident Sophia appeared in England. Everybody are lavish in the praises they bestow on her charms, her talents and her heart, Rich in particular, the wise Rich, has chosen me for his confidant, and it is an excellent stroke that I have persuaded him to believe, that it is *he* who has made Madam Leidens fly, by his having the art to make her promise to relate her adventures to him. He presumes they must be very singular, as everything in the conduct of that young lady, he says, shows that she has received a most excellent education, that she is possessed of every virtue, and the most exquisite sensibility; and he makes no scruple of believing that some villain has taken advantage of the goodness of her heart, and placed in it the foundation of that distress with which she is incessantly struggling. Now was it not a cursed affair to have all these things laid before me, and yet to be obliged to affect an air of ignorance? He showed me a picture of her that is a very exact likeness, in which she is represented leaning on a table, where there are a heap of butterflies, which were to serve for I don't know what use in an entertainment provided for us, and of which she herself had given the plan. But this thought did not appear to be one of the happiest, for she does not in the least understand butterfly hunting; for if she did, she would have found, means to tie my wings. But her picture made a stronger impression on me than all they had told me of her. Upon my life, I can't think of her without pity. I would fain know what she has done to dame Fortune, to be thus, in the flower of her age, snatched from her friends, stripped of everything, and cast into the most miserable corner of the earth; and what business had the fickle goddess to choose me to be the rascal entrusted with her decree? Oh, I swear that, if ever I bring up a girl, she shall know all the snares with which the villainy of our sex surrounds the innocence of hers! – But what is poor Sophia the better for all this? – Give us your company here, and we will go to see her in the spring: as for this winter, it is necessary that she should pass it in her exile, though, upon my honour, I can't help pitying her.

I find myself obliged, my friend, to resume my pen, in order to fill up a void! which I here find in the papers I communicate to you. When my dear mistress, in conformity to Lord Derby's barbarous plot, was called into the garden to converse with Miss Emma, she had just finished her letter to Emilia. Her first care was to put it in her pocket, not being willing that those who might enter her chamber should discover anything to the disadvantage of Derby, and being pressed to make haste, she snatched up some loose sheets with it.[66] Sophia took the way to the park, and after having walked some minutes, returned to the side of the garden facing the village, when perceiving nobody, she thought it best to return by the way she came; but suddenly a woman appeared in the park, and made signs to her. My mistress advanced towards her, while the woman coming to meet her, seized her hand. At the same instant appeared two men in masks, who rushing from behind the trees, came up to the unhappy Sophia, threw over her head a round and thick hood, which covered her face, and with the utmost violence dragged her way. Her resistance and her cries were in vain, they forced her into a light carriage, which instantly set off, and travelled all night. In the midst of a wild forest they offered her some food; but she would only take a glass of water, and they again proceeded forward. Terrified, dejected beyond expression, she was forcibly held in the carriage by an unknown man dressed in woman's clothes, who sat by her side. Once she slipped down on her knees to implore his pity; but she received no answer, and at length found herself removed into a miner's hut in the mountains of Scotland, where they laid her on a wretched bed.

This was all that she has since been able to relate, so much was her mind disordered. Her journal, which I am going to lay before you, proves that excess of affliction may distract the most worthy heart; but it proves at the same time, that no sooner was my poor lady able to recover her spirits, than the excellent principles of her education displayed all their efficacy.

You can better imagine than I describe the concern the news of her disappearance gave to Lady Summers, and the sighs and tears it cost Emilia and me. They redoubled, on our hearing that all the methods used to discover any traces of her were in vain. Amidst the cruel uncertainty we were in with respect to the fate of the dearest and best of friends, the following winter was the longest and the most melancholy we had ever known.

THE

JOURNAL

OF

MADAM LEIDENS

IN THE

HIGHLANDS OF SCOTLAND[67]

Emilia! name dear and precious! once thou wast the consolation and support of my life; but now only servest to increase my pain. The plaintive voice, the letters of thy friend can no longer reach thee. All, all is taken from me, and the anguish of those I love is a new burden which weighs down my heart. Worthy Lady Summers! – Dear Emilia! Why should you be involved in the anguish of my misfortunes? – O God, how severely do I suffer for the only false step I have made in the road of duty! – Could my private marriage offend thee? – Poor thoughts – none will read yet – Why then do I write? These sheets forever unknown, like her who fills them, will perish with me. Nobody but my persecutor will learn that I have ceased to live and he will be filled with joy, at seeing the witness of his cruelty removed from the earth. O Providence! thou seest my submission – thou seest that I ask no indulgence – thou wilt make me feel the horrors of a slow death. Thou wilt have it; and I ask thee only to save the hearts of my friends from the grief which preys upon them.

At the beginning of the third month of my exile
Another month is now elapsed. I recovered the powers of thought, but it is only to realise the full extent of my wretchedness. Happy days, where are you at whose first dawning my hands were lifted up towards heaven, while my mind overflowed with sensations of gratitude and joy, and I blessed the author of my renewed life! Now, at my awaking, the sensation of the continuance of my existence here, shows itself by my tears and expressions of despairs! O my Creator! is it possible that thou receivest more pleasure from the bitter tears of distress, than from the sweet tears of filial gratitude?

*   *   *   *   *

Destitute of all hope, without seeing the least glimpse of succour, I struggle with myself; I reproach as a crime the excess of my grief, and follow the inclination which prompts me to take up my pen.

At this instant the hope of more happy hours, rises in my soul. – But formerly the same flattering voice made itself still more loudly heard, and has it not deceived me? – Did I then abuse my happiness? Has my heart been captivated by the splendour which surrounded me? Or proud of the soul I had received from nature, was that pride my crime? – Poor, poor creature, with whom dost thou presume to dispute! Frail heap of dust, thou risest against the power who tries and upholds thee! Wouldst thou, by mingling thy impatience and murmurs, still more embitter the cup of calamity? Pardon, pardon me, O my God! Assist me rather to acknowledge the benefits which, in this state of exile, thou hast not refused to my feeling heart.

*   *   *   *   *

Come, thou remembrance of my Emilia, thou image always engraven on my heart, supply the want of her presence! come and bear witness that Sophia, this instant, renews the vows she has made to virtue: bear witness that she re-enters the path of duty; that she condemns the excess of her sensibility; that she at length gratefully opens her eyes to the succours of a liberal Providence that has never forsaken her! – It is now near three months since a deceitful invitation made me find in the park of Summer Hall, instead of the dear and sensible Emma, a barbarian who carried me from thence, and made me travel day and night till I reached the desert where I am placed. Derby! none but thee could have been capable of this base cruelty! At the very time when I was labouring for thy amusement, thou thoughtest of nothing but forging for me a new chain of misfortunes! – Honour and generosity are names to which thou art a stranger! Thou didst not think that they would oblige me to keep silence, and to fly thy looks. Thou makest a sport of tormenting a heart with whose sensibility thou art well acquainted! Whence, O Providence! whence hast thou permitted all the designs of this perverse man to be attended with success, while all the useful plans I have formed are buried with me in these dreary mountains?

*   *   *   *   *

How does self-love render my virtue wavering and uncertain! Two days ago I formed the most noble resolutions: I was determined to walk with patience in the thorny path which opens before me; but suddenly self-love recalled to my remembrance what I would have forgotten, and instead of fixing my thoughts on the present and the future, I stopped at what was past and irrevocable. – I cried, Yes lessons of virtue, of knowledge, of experience, to me are lost! My cruel enemy will then have the power not only to strip me of my fortune, and the respect I enjoyed, as a robber seizes a garment, but also to disturb my soul in the practice of virtue.

*   *   *   *   *

Ye blissful hours, ye happiest moments of my life, when I recovered the possession of my whole heart, when was revived the sweet conviction that even here the paternal hand of my Creator provides for my true interest! It is he who put a period to the errors to which my mind abandoned itself during the first weeks of my exile: it is he who inspires my ignorant hosts with humanity and compassion. The good principles imbibed in infancy insensibly prevail in lightening the weight of my affliction. The serenity of the sky which covers this desert, though I cannot view it without sighing, diffuses through my heart peace and hope, like those I enjoyed at Sternheim, Vaels, and Summer Hall. The height of these mountains proclaims to me the omnipotence of Him who formed them: the whole earth is filled with manifestations of his goodness, of his wisdom, and I am everywhere equally surrounded by the works of his hands. Here, it is his pleasure to confound my vanity: he has determined that the last hours of my state of trial, and of my life, shall pass without any other witness, but his eye, and the gratulations of my conscience! Perhaps my death approaches; ought I not then to distinguish the remainder of my days with the virtues that are still in my power? O thought of death, how salutary, how comfortable, when accompanied by the lively hope of a blissful immortality! How dost thou awaken in the soul the sense of duty, and give activity to the desire of doing good! It is thou who hast enabled me to surmount affliction! It is thou who hast inspired the desire of finishing my course with the most holy dispositions, and of still looking for some opportunity of being useful!

*   *   *   *   *

Yes, I can and I will do good. Patience, the virtue of suffering beings, be thou my faithful companion, that, supported by thee, I may see, with tranquillity, the will of Heaven accomplished! It is not till after careful researches, that we are able to collect the salutary plants proper to heal the disorders of the body: not less attentive should we be in the diseases of the mind, to discover all the means of relief, which, like the other remedies, are often found within our reach; but we are accustomed to look for them at a distance, and to neglect those that are near at hand. This has been my case: my wishes and complaints have carried me far from the objects around me, and till lately I did not reflect on an advantage I had in my possession, by my having brought some sheets of paper from Summer Hall, which have been of such use to me in disentangling and rectifying my ideas. Was it not the protection of Heaven which preserved me from outrage during a painful journey, and has permitted me to preserve all that could be of use to me in a more tranquil situation?

*   *   *   *   *

O Emilia, sacred friendship, dear remembrance! thy image rises smiling above the ruins of all on which I used to place my happiness! Thou hast cost me tears, floods of tears – but now these sheets are consecrated to thee! From my early youth I have poured my most secret thoughts into thy tender and faithful bosom. – It is possible that these writings may be preserved: they may reach thy hands, and thus wilt thou see that my heart has never been able to forget the virtue and tenderness of thine. Perhaps, when I shall be no more, thou wilt bedew with thy tears this pledge of the friendship of thy once unhappy Sophia. Thou canst not weep over her tomb, for Derby's villainy has induced him to bury his victim in a desert: but since the thought of death and eternity is now come to absorb both my wishes and my complaints, I will take advantage of the calm they inspire, and describe some circumstances of the precipitate fall which hurries me to the grave. Hitherto it has been impossible for me to attempt it; for I could not think of it without horror.

*   *   *   *   *

I had scarce any remains of life when I arrived at this cottage, and during three weeks my mind was in a situation impossible to be described. What I have been during the second and third month, is evident by the pieces I wrote when I found myself less agitated. But judge, Emilia, of the disorder of my soul which was so great as to be unfit for prayer. I did not even call death to my relief; but stunned by my misfortune, I should have seen the murderer ready to threaten my head without turning to avoid the blow. I was whole days on my knees, not from submission, not to implore the divine compassion; but rather from the sensations of pride, which induced me to think that I had not deserved so cruel a fate. But, O Emilia! that thought aggravated my calamity, obstructed the virtues I was yet able to perform, though the performance of them could alone pour the balm of consolation into the wounds of the soul. This I experienced here for the first time, from a poor girl, in the fifth year of her age, who had been ordered to stay with me; I felt myself affected on seeing her feeble hands endeavour to raise my dejected head. I did not understand her discourse; but I was moved by the sound of her voice, and the language of her countenance was that of nature, tenderness and innocence. I clasped her in my arms, and shed a flood of tears; these were tears of consolation, and the first of this kind I had ever shed. The gratitude excited in my heart by the affection of this little creature, was mingled with the idea that God had given a poor infant power to make me enjoy the sweets which flow from pitying others. From this day

I compute *the cure of my soul*. The loss of my strength and the pain I felt from my being obliged to live on oaten bread, made me think that my death was near: the remainder of my life was passing away far from those I love, but I resolved to offer to my Creator a heart filled with resignation and love, and that thought restored all the springs of virtue in my soul. I kept my little benefactress in my own small room, made her share my bed, and received from her the first lessons of the strange language spoken here. I afterwards took this child with me into my host's room. This man has long worked in a lead mine, but being disabled by illness, employs himself with his wife and children in cultivating a small plot of ground granted him by Lord Hopton, near an old ruinous castle. They there sow hemp and oats, the former for apparel and the latter for bread. Poor as they are they are good-tempered , and all their wealth consists in the few guineas they have received for keeping me. They rejoiced at seeing me more composed, and at my coming to sit with them; they were desirous of teaching me some of their language, and in about a fortnight I was able to ask them short questions, and to answer such as they asked me. These people have received strict orders not to take me beyond a certain distance from their house; but on one of the last days of autumn my guide took me something farther. Oh what a poor appearance does nature make in this part of the country! we plainly see that its bowels are of lead. I could not behold without tears the barren and ill cultivated field which produces our oaten bread, nor the cloudy sky over my head. Recollection drew from me deep sighs; but a look I cast on my pale conductor made me say to myself, Have not I, during my youth, enjoyed in plenty all the blessings of life, while this man and his family have hitherto only known penury and want, yet they are the work of my Creator. None of the nerves, none of the muscles necessary for the enjoyment of the blessings of nature is wanting in their bodies: so far there is an entire resemblance between us: but in their souls how many faculties sleep and remain in torpid inaction! How deeply concealed, how incomprehensible is the reason of this distribution, which rendering the corporeal faculties common to all, leaves millions of creatures in arrears with respect to the unfolding of the qualities of the mind! How have I rejoiced, and I do so still, that in cultivating my mind, and the dispositions of my heart, I have been taught what I owe to God, and to mankind, my brethren! Sacred duties! real blessings! those alone, which being collected upon earth, we can take with us. Oh may impatience never make me abandon you!

I endeavoured by behaving with the greatest affability to reward my keepers for the goodness of their hearts, and eagerly applied myself to learn their language. Surprised at the harshness with which they sometimes seemed to treat the little girl, I discovered by my questions that she was not their child; but judge of my confusion when I heard that she was Lord Derby's, that her mother had died with them, and that her barbarous father allowed them nothing for her support. On receiving this information, I was obliged again to have recourse to solitude, and again I felt the whole extent of my misfortune. O the poor mother! she was beautiful, like this infant, young also and of a sweet temper – Near her grave will be dug mine! O Emilia, Emilia, how shall I support this trial! The amiable Lydia came to me. I had thrown myself on the bed, and she seized one of my hands which hung out of it, while my face was turned towards the wall. I had heard her coming, and this, with the sound of her voice, set me a trembling, and by an involuntary motion I snatched my hand from between hers. The poor child, all in tears, went sobbing to the foot of my bed. I then felt the injustice I was guilty of, in making the unhappy innocent suffer; I resolved to conquer this aversion, and to give proofs of my affection to the daughter of my murderer. What a pure joy arose in my heart, when rising, I called the little Lydia, took her in my arms, and in her bosom vowed to be kind to her! I will not break this vow: it cost me too much before I made it.

*   *   *   *   *

O Derby! thou completest the severity of my fate! This day a messenger arrived with a large packet, and he who sent it had the safeness to make a jest of the affair. He wrote, that as my time at court appeared long, because I could not work there in embroidery, I might be in the same case in the Highlands of Scotland, and on that account he thought some work for the winter would not be unacceptable, and he would take care to send for it in the spring – I will begin this work – Yes, I am resolved upon it. He will receive the pieces after my death: he will see the last effects of the barbarity with which he has treated me, and may remember how happy I was, when for the first time he saw my hands employed at my needle, and into what an abyss of misery he has thrown me, and then left me to perish.

*   *   *   *   *

Never, no never, for the future, will I yield to the murmurs of self-love. How false and capricious are the judgments it dictates! I complained of what is now my entertainment. Yes, my labour brightens the dark days of winter; my keepers examine it with an ignorant astonishment, and I take pleasure in teaching it to their daughter, who, having worked the first leaf, looks about her with an air of pride and satisfaction. Poverty is the mother of invention, and this I have found by experience. Lord Hopton, the owner of the mine, has a house a few miles distance, where he from time to time spends a few days. When he was last there, he had a sister with him, for whom he has a great affection, and who, being a widow, seldom leaves him. Upon her I found hopes and schemes, which the continuance of my life prompts me to form. I advise my keepers to place their daughter Mary in that lady's service, and promise to instruct her in everything necessary for her to know, in order to be admitted. I am already teaching her to speak and write English. – She comes on very well in embroidery, and necessity having obliged me to make two caps of the lace of my neck-handkerchief, I have taught her to do it. As to other things, I give her my instructions while we are at work. This girl is uncommonly sensible and ingenious. It is through her means that I hope to become free; for I flatter myself that it will be in her power to make me known to Lady Douglas. Oh, may I not be deprived of this hope!

*   *   *   *   *

I now also employ myself about my little Lydy, who begins to be pleased with the use of the needle. My keepers, from their love to me, keep up something of cleanliness in their dwelling, and my oat-cakes begin to agree with me. The wants of nature, my Emilia, are easily satisfied: I rise contented from the most frugal table, and my keepers hear me talk with surprise of other countries. I have still the dear pictures of my father and mother; I have shown them to these good people, while I was relating my education and former kind of life, as far as they could comprehend it, or as it would be of use to them. I have seen them shed tears on my relating the happiness I have enjoyed, and the patient resignation which has now taken possession of my heart. Seldom do I speak of you, Emilia; for I have not yet strength sufficient to support the idea of our separation, and that of the pain you feel on my account. Could I, by my sufferings, remove those which you and my dear lady feel for me, I believe I should at length be able to say that my sufferings are at an end. But Providence knew what would render me most worthy of pity: it knew that, comforted by my innocence, and fortified by my principles, I might bear up against my own calamities; and being destined to be unhappy, I can be only so from the grief of my friends, and this wound is incurable, since it would be criminal to wish it cured. – How happy did my friends render me, when my wealth enabled me to watch their desires in order to gratify them, and to penetrate into their troubles in order to remove them. Two years ago I filled a place in a brilliant circle, where everything seemed to promise me a happy futurity; where I saw myself beloved; where I was able to choose or reject. – O my heart! why hast thou so long armed thyself against the recollection of one thought? – I have not even dared to pronounce the name of Seymour: now I ask myself, what he would think of my present state? and I weep at being forgotten! Oh that he was for ever banished from my memory! – His heart never knew mine, and now it is too late! My paper, Emilia – ah! my paper is almost filled: I dare not write much more; the winter is long, and I would employ what remains of it, in talking to you of my hopes, which are still uncertain. O, my dear friend, how happy would some sheets of paper make me, and yet I cannot procure them! I must spare some canvass, and write to you with my needle.

IN THE MONTH OF APRIL

O Time, thou most beneficent of beings, for how many advantages am I obliged to thee! Thou, by degrees, hast scattered the gloomy impressions of sorrow which over-clouded my soul, and hast insensibly placed the objects of grief in the obscurity of a distant prospect, while at the same time thou sheddest a cheerful serenity on all around me. Experience, whom thou leadest by the hand, has brought me to have recourse to the exercise of wisdom and patience, and every step I advance in this tranquil path smooths the asperity of my way. O Time! my friends, I hope, will also feel thy salutary influence, that tranquillity may be restored to their hearts; that, encircled by the favours of Heaven, they may taste the sweets of life, without any remembrance of me intervening to embitter them! Hail, love of my Creator, thou sense of his goodness, what sweet consolations do ye afford! The same goodness, which shelters a weak worm under some grains of sand, I experience amidst these barren mountains, where I enjoy my returning reason, where the beams of knowledge again irradiate my faculties, and where I feel virtues awaking in me which slumbered in the bosom of ease and prosperity. Here, where the natural world seems to grudge its produce, and unwillingly to share its gifts among its dejected inhabitants, I distribute in the cottage of my keepers, moral riches, virtue and knowledge, and with them feel all their value. Stripped of everything that bears the name of fortune, splendour, power; delivered into the hands of these strangers, I become their benefactress, by exciting in them the love of God, by enlightening their minds, by interesting their hearts, from the picture I give them, in our hours of recreation, of the other parts of the universe, and of the people who inhabit them. By my pains, my tenderness, and my instructions, I spread sweetness over the days of a young orphan, doubly unhappy. Thus deprived of what is called earthly happiness, I enjoy the noblest gifts of Heaven, serenity of soul, and the pleasure of doing good. – Sweet fruits of true Humanity, pure joy, solid advantages, ye will follow me into the celestial regions, and the happiness of having known you will be the first subject of my immortal songs.

AT THE END OF JUNE

Emilia, did you never put yourself in the situation of a man exposed in a light bark to the fury of a stormy sea? Trembling, he looks here and there to discover some subject of hope: but long tossed by the waves, he is seized with despair; when suddenly he perceives an island which he believes he can reach, and joining his hands, he cries, O my God, I see land! – I, my friend, I have felt what is here described, and *see land.* Lord Hopton is returned into our mountains, and his sister, the Lady Douglas, is pleased with the daughter of my keepers. Mary, accompanied by her brother, took some of her embroidery, and went to offer her service to that lady. She, surprised at Mary's answers and her work, immediately asked, who had taught her? on which the girl's grateful heart made her tell all she knew of me, and all that I had done for her; at which the lady was so moved that she melted into tears, promised to keep her from that time, ordered provisions to be set before the two young people, and let the brother return alone, giving him two guineas for his parents. She also promised to come and see us before her departure. I have desired her to procure me paper, pens and ink, for I would seize this opportunity of writing to Lady Summers; but I will send my letter open to Lady Douglas, in order to convince her of my veracity. I should be really guilty of a criminal negligence, was I not to employ every honest means of recovering my liberty. I design also to solicit the Lord Hopton in favour of my keepers. These honest people are unable to express their joy at seeing their daughter so well provided for, and caress and bless me by turns. My orphan will not stay here: accustomed to the kindness with which I treat her, my departure would render her worthy of pity, and her remembrance would embitter all my moments, if, on finding myself again in a happy situation, I knew that she was here a prey to want.

*   *   *   *   *

O, my dear friend! the comparison I made in my last leaf, of a bark driven in a tempestuous sea, was a presage of what was to happen to me. I was destined to feel the keenest agonies of soul, and then to die in the moment of hope. The inconceivable wickedness of my persecutor drags me to the grave, as the foaming waves draw to the bottom of the deep the fragile bark and the unhappy mariner. This power has been left him, and every means of succour have been taken from me. Soon a solitary tomb will put an end to my complaints, and the secret reasons of my suffering so many trials will be unveiled to my disembodied soul.

I am calm, I am filled with satisfaction; my last day will be the happiest of those I have passed these two years. To you, tender Emilia, whom I have loved to the end of my race, will be delivered, by Lady Summers, all my writings; and the idea that my torments will be lost in an eternity of happiness, will afford consolation to your sensible soul. As you were a witness of my happy life, if I have strength enough, you shall also be informed of the last scene of my misfortunes.

While I was filled with hope, and elated with confidence, Derby's infernal

agent arrived here. The villain proposed, on the part of his master, that I
should go and meet his lordship at London, because, as he did not love his
wife, and had for some time been ill, my company would be extremely
agreeable to him at Windsor, where he principally resided. He himself
wrote to me, that if I would consent with a good grace to come to him, and
was disposed to love him, he would think of dissolving his marriage with
Lady Alton, and confirming ours, as my merit and the law required; but if,
on the contrary, from the continuance of my former fantastical principles, I
refused to consent to his proposals, it would be necessary for me to submit
to his orders with respect to my fate. – This was what I was obliged to hear,
for I would not read the letter; but in the midst of so many insults, the most
cruel circumstance was my seeing before me the wretch who had performed
our false marriage. Afflicted, and irritated in the highest degree, I rejected
his offers with indignation, and the barbarian resolved to revenge his master.
After I had twice refused in the most express terms, the wretch, in a violent
rage, seized me by the arm, dragged me out of the house, drew me to the
old tower, which is at a little distance, and pushing open a door, threw me
on the fallen ruins, crying, with a thundering voice, Perish then, that my
master and I may at last get rid of you!

My resistance, my fright, the fear of being carried to London in spite of
myself, had weakened me, and almost deprived me of my senses. I fell
prostrate on the rubbish and mire with which this building is filled; my left
hand and half my face were so wounded by the stones, that much blood
streamed from my nose and mouth. I fainted, and know not how long I
continued in that state. On recovering my senses, I found myself deprived of
all strength, and filled with pain; while the moist and unhealthy air I
breathed so oppressed my breast, that I thought the last moment of my life
was approaching. It was now dark, and I could see no object; but with one
hand I felt that the earth descended with such a declivity, that I apprehended if I made the least motion I should fall into a vault, where I could
not think of dying without horror. Thus, languishing on the verge of the
grave, I passed the whole night in these ruins. The clouds poured down rain;
I was soaked, and stiffened with cold. – But what I then felt is impossible to
be described: oppressed by the weight of my misfortunes, I only wished for
death, which appeared to approach too slowly. I then seemed to be inwardly
convulsed, and my senses failed me.

This is all that I can recollect. On recovering the use of my senses, I
found myself in my bed, around which were my poor and timid keepers,
who gave vent to their sighs, and Lydia sobbing bedewed my hand with her
tears. I felt that I was extremely ill, and lifting up my hands towards Heaven,
I desired these people to fetch Lord Hopton's chaplain, to assist me in my
last moments. My landlord's son set out, and his parents told me, that they
had not dared to come to my assistance before the departure of Sir John (for
so they called him). – How deplorable an effect of poverty, which seldom
allows those who are depressed by it to oppose the designs of the vicious

rich! The villain had been stopped by the rain; yet they said, that before he set out on his return, he went to the tower, where having listened for some time, he shook his head with an air of concern, and at last went away without shutting the door, or saying a word more to them. The fear with which he had inspired them, had held them in suspense during an hour after he was gone, before they ventured to go with lights in search of me: they then removed me, and thought I was dead.

The chaplain arrived, and Lady Douglas came with him; both of them attentively examined me with eyes of pity. I held out my hand to the countess who kindly gave me hers. Noble lady said I, God will reward your humanity. I observed that she fixed her eyes on my bracelets – It is the picture of my mother, said I: she was the grand-daughter of Sir David Watson – and here, lifiting up my other hand, here is my father, a worthy gentleman of Germany. For a long time they have both reached the realms of glory, and soon, soon, I hope, I shall be reunited to them. Her ladyship wept, and bid the clergyman feel my pulse: he did so, and assured her that I was very ill. The countess, looking about her with a tender inquietude, asked, If I could not be removed? Not without the danger of her life, returned the chaplain. I am very sorry, said the amiable lady, squeezing my hand, and retired, to leave the minister at liberty to talk with me. I told him, in a few words, that I came of a noble family: that, abused by a false marriage, I found myself exiled from my native country, and that Lady Summers, who had honoured me with her protection, would give him an account of my conduct while I was with her. I also delivered to him the papers I had written to you, adding, without his asking it, an account of my principles. I then solicited him to enter into a correspondence with your worthy husband. Her ladyship now knocked at the door, and entered with Mary, the daughter of my keeper, who brought a box filled with medicines and cordials, and they made me take something. Little Lydia came also, and threw herself on her knees by the bedside. The tender Lady Douglas cast an eye of compassion on the child and me: at last she bid me adieu, left Mary to attend me, and the clergyman promised to see me again the next morning. Yet he did not appear the whole day; but there twice came a person to enquire after my health. This morning, finding myself better than I was yesterday, I began to write, and have continued it by intervals. At present it is six in the evening, and I visibly grow worse; of this my uneven writing and trembling pen will convince you. Who knows whether this night will not be the last of my life? I bless God that I am mortal; I also offer up my thanks to him, that my heart can still speak to yours. I am entirely resigned, and touch upon the moment in which worldly happiness and misfortunes are equally indifferent.[68]

AT NINE O'CLOCK IN THE EVENING

For the last time, my Emilia, I have extended my weak arms towards the country you inhabit. May God bless my friend! may he reward her virtues and the friendship she had for me! – You will receive a paper, which your husband himself will deliver to Count R. my uncle. It includes the disposal of my fortune, an exact account of which is in the hands of your brother-in-law.[69]

All that I have inherited from the family of P. ought to return to the children of the Countess of Löbau. What I have received from my beloved father, must be divided into two equal parts, one of which shall be employed in the education of poor children. Out of what remains shall be deducted a thousand crowns for my present keeper and his family, and as much for the unhappy Lydia. The remainder I leave to your children and to my friend Rosina: but at the foot of my parents' tomb I would have a stone erected with this inscription:

IN MEMORY OF THEIR DAUGHTER

SOPHIA VON STERNHEIM,

WHO WAS NOT UNWORTHY OF THEM

I would be buried here, under that tree at the foot of which I have so often, during the last spring, thrown myself on my knees, to beg of God to give me patience. Here, where my mind has been tormented, my body ought to be dissolved. It is also a maternal earth that shall cover me, till the moment when, in a glorious form, I shall rise, and be united to the sacred assembly of the virtuous, and shall there see again my Emilia. In the mean while, my friend, save my memory from the assaults of calumny, from the shame which follows the appearance of vice: say, that though unhappy, I have faithfully preserved my virtue; that, plunged in the deepest abyss of grief, I, with filial confidence, and full of love for my fellow creatures, commit my soul into the hands of my Creator: say, that with my dying breath I tenderly blessed my friends, and that I sincerely forgave those who had injured me. Plant, O my dear Emilia! plant a cypress in your garden, and let it be entwined by a solitary rose-tree. Consecrate that spot to my remembrance. Go thither sometimes: perhaps I may be permitted to hover about you, to perceive the tears you will shed on seeing the young bush despoiled of its roses. Me you have also seen flower and fade; only the last breath of my life will be exhaled far from you. – This, my Emilia, is a happiness: you would suffer too much on seeing me now – Adieu, O the most tender of friends! May the tears you shall shed for me be peaceful tears, like those which from these dim eyes now flow for you!

LETTER XLVI

Lord Seymour to Dr T.

Good God! must an indisposition then prevent your coming to see me only for two days! This almost oversets my reason and renders me frantic. My brother Rich, whom you knew in the house of my mother's first husband, notwithstanding all his stoicism, is struck with the same blow. Within two days we shall set out for the Highlands of Scotland, and that – oh heartbreaking thought! to search for the grave of the murdered Sophia Sternheim, and to remove her body to Dumfries, where it is to be interred with great pomp. O eternal Providence! how hast thou permitted the most lovely gift ever bestowed on this earth, to become the prey of the most odious villain! My servants are preparing for my departure: I can do nothing. I wring my hands, and abandoned to my grief, have a hundred times struck my forehead and my breast. Derby, that abandoned monster, has the impudence to say, that it is on my account, and from his jealousy, that he has deceived, tormented, and barbarously murdered the most noble, the most amiable of women. He now weeps for it – the monster weeps![70] The excess of his grief has brought him to the brink of the grave. He trembles at the approach of death, and his situation shelters him from my just revenge.

Hear, my friend, hear the severest sufferings virtue has ever felt; the most dreadful crimes a wicked man has ever committed. – You know that four months ago I returned sick to England with my Lord G. and that I repaired immediately to my mother at Seymour House in hopes that I should there recover my health. I enquired after Derby, now Lord N. I was told that he was ill at his country house at Windsor, and on that account I thought proper to delay the execution of my design till his and my recovery. Soon after I received this information, he sent to me, desiring to see me; but as I was not well, I refused to go.

Some days after I went to see Lord Rich, who received me with tenderness, though his mind was not less clouded than my own. The difference of fifteen years between our ages putting an obstacle to our brotherly confidence, his mournful silence did not encourage me to pour my troubles into his bosom. During a fortnight we only talked of our travels, and that by fits and starts; till, on the arrival of a messenger from Lord N.

we instantly opened our hearts to each other. This messenger brought me a letter, in which his master earnestly entreated me to come to him, with Lord Rich, on an affair relating to the Lady Sophia Sternheim; adding, that I might tell my brother, that was the name of the lady whom he had known at Summer Hall, and who had been taken from thence. I started as from a frightful dream. I cried aloud to the servant, that I would come, and hastily advancing towards my brother, asked him what he knew of the young lady whom he saw at Summer Hall? — He, in turn, asked me, with an eager emotion, if I knew her, and what I could have heard concerning her? I showed him the letter, and gave him a concise account of everything relating to my dearly beloved Sophia. He, in as few words, and with as much disorder, informed me how he had seen her, and how much he loved her; extolled the nobleness of her sentiments; spoke of the secret melancholy which hung upon her mind, especially after she had heard the news of Derby's marriage with Lady Alton; and, in fine, showed me her picture.

We now both hasted to be gone, and soon reached Windsor; Rich, thoughtful but calm; I, full of inquietude and projects. A violent shuddering and a flaming indignation seized me on entering Derby's house. My hatred for him was risen to such a height, that I paid no attention to the ill state of his health, and the weakness which obliged him to keep his bed. Gloomy and silent, I darted at him looks of declared emnity. He opened his heavy eyes, and giving me a supplicating look, held out to me his burning and shrivelled hand, crying, Seymour, I know you — I know that you hate me — but you don't know that the violent conflicts which pass in my heart are caused by you. I answered, pushing away his hand, I know no other reason but the difference of our principles. Seymour, replied Derby, you would not behave thus were I in health. The pride with which you boast of your principles is no less culpable than the abuse I have made of my talents.

My brother interrupted him, saying, that this was not the business which brought us thither; but to obtain some tidings of the lady who had been carried away.

Yes, my lord, said he, you shall hear all; there is more humanity in your cool blood, than in Seymour's impetuous sensibility. He may have told you what passed at D. at the time when we became acquainted, with the Lady Sophia. We both loved her to distraction; but I first perceived her regard for him, and left no stone unturned in order to make her stifle it. By my disguises and my artifices I availed myself of the Prince's assiduities and of Seymour's weak indecision, and by means of a pretended marriage, prevailed on the lady to throw herself for protection into my arms. Yet my pleasures were of short duration: the sentimental gravity of her disposition agreed but little with the levity of mine, and her secret passion for Seymour seemed to discover itself, whenever my thoughts clashed with her's. Jealousy prompted me to seek revenge; while the death of my brother, by increasing my fortune, seemed to second my scheme, and I abandoned Sophia. Yet a few days after I repented of this, and sent to the village where

I imagined she still continued; but I found she was gone. For a long time I was ignorant of her retreat, and of her fate; till at length I was informed of her being with my wife's aunt. As she could not be left there without danger to myself, I determined to have her carried off. From that time I sighed at my own severity; but it was the only part I had to take. – Displeased with Lady Alton, my heart became again fixed on my Sophia: She is mine, said I to myself, and to escape the miserable life she leads, in the barren mountain where she is placed, she will doubtless consent to return to my arms. In this opinion I was flattered, by my hearing of the kindness she showed to a daughter I had by Nancy Hatton; for I attributed her goodness to the child, to a kind of inclination for the father. Filled with a thousand agreeable projects, I sent away my confidant; but Sophia rejected my offers with indignation and contempt. –

Here Derby's sighs and violent emotions interrupted his discourse. He cast his eyes sometimes on me, sometimes on Lord Rich, till carried away by my rage and impatience, I, stamping, cried aloud, Finish your story! – Seymour, Rich, said he, with a melancholy and trembling voice, Oh, unhappy that I am, that I did not go myself, to implore her forgiveness on my knees! John, that monster, would force her to follow him – He was well convinced how dear her presence would be to me – he shut her up in the ruins of an old building – she remained there twelve hours, extended on the ground, and – there – Oh! how shall I speak it? – there died of grief.

Died there! cried I – and thou, monster! devil! art yet alive! – After this murder thou still liv'st!

Lord Rich says, that I had the air and voice of one deprived of his reason, and instantly taking me in his arms, he drew me out of the chamber. Long did he strive in vain to calm my rage, before he could prevail on me to promise to hear the wretch with silence. Derby, said he, is prey to the most bitter remorse – to the dreadful anguish of reflecting on a life stained by irreparable crimes. Would you lift your hand against an object of the Divine justice? O brother! believe that our pain is sweet, when compared with what he feels. – The misfortunes of Sophia, caused by his crimes, wound his awakened conscience, and plant daggers in his heart. Nature and Virtue combine to revenge her sufferings; but leave me, I entreat you, to ask him, what he would have of us. Endeavour to conquer yourself! Be generous, Seymour, and let the guilty Derby, while he is unhappy, be the object of thy compassion! – I promised everything, but resolved to be present at their discourse.

The miserable wretch wept on our returning into the room: he entreated us to go into Scotland, to cause the body of that angel to be dug up, and removed to Dumfries in a brazen coffin. He has also appropriated two thousand guineas for the erection of a monument that should express the virtues and misfortunes of Sophia, as well as the repentance of him who had injured her. He made us promise to send an account of the whole to the court of D. and delivered to us letters relating to Sophia, written by himself to his friend Lord B. In short, he made us promise to hasten our departure, that, before he died, he might have the consolation of knowing, that public honours were paid to the remains of the most noble of women. – Lord Rich, in a few words, made him a pathetic exhortation, and I was brought to moderate my grief and restrain my resentment. Tomorrow we set out for Dumfries. – What a journey! what a dreadful journey!

LETTER XLVII

Lord Rich, in the Highlands of Scotland to Dr T.

Dear Doctor,
I believe you scarce remember me, but our souls nearly resemble each other, and Seymour is my brother. It is of him, and the object of his grief, that I am now going to write. We have been here ever since yesterday evening. Never was there a more melancholy journey, and our anguish increased as we drew near to its end. I question whether there be, on the whole surface of the earth, a spot more wild and frightful than that which encompasses this wretched cottage, destined for the melancholy prison of the lovely Sophia; and everything has concurred to promote the barbarous design of torment-ing the most sensible of human souls. When I call to mind the noble emotions of her heart, and her filial gratitude to the Creator on viewing the beauties of nature, I feel how deeply she must have been affected with the sight of this dismal uncultivated waste – with this mud wall cottage, her unworthy abode for so long a time – and that straw bed, on which it seems this inimitable woman drew her last breath, and ended her exemplary life. O doctor! were these objects before you, your eyes would become, like ours, fountains of tears, especially if you had seen at the foot of a lonely tree, the hillock of sand which covers the inanimate remains of the loveliest of women. – Poor Lord Seymour sunk upon it, and wished there to breathe out his soul with his tears, that he might, at least, have the same grave with his beloved Sophia. I was obliged to call for the assistance of our men to drag him from thence. When in the house, he was for throwing himself on the bed where she died; but I caused him to be removed, and led into the room where these people told me she used most frequently to sit. There he sat immovable, leaning on his elbow, for two hours, without seeing or hearing anything that passed. The miner and his family do not seem to me to be the most honest people: I am afraid they had a hand in her imprisonment: their looks show that they are full of fear, and several times

they have left the cottage to converse together in private: their answers to my questions are short and confused, and their uneasiness visibly appeared, when I told them, that tomorrow morning the lady's corpse is to be taken out of the grave. I myself tremble at this, and am filled with the apprehension of finding, upon that dear form, the marks of a violent death. O heavens! should that be the case, what will become of my brother? I take no notice of myself, I endeavour to conceal the excess of my grief, that I may not increase his: but certainly never did the dread of a tempest, from the fear of being buried in the waves, nor the torment of a burning thirst in the scorching sands of Africa, give me such pain as the idea of the sufferings of this visible angel.

My brother, exhausted by the agitations he has suffered, has fallen asleep, with only our men's clothes spread on the floor for his bed: his blood is still in a ferment, and he sighs and groans; yet the surgeon we brought with us does not apprehend his life to be in danger. It is impossible for me to obtain rest; for the thoughts of tomorrow keep me perpetually on the rack, and I endeavour to collect all my spirits, that they may enable me to support Seymour; and yet I am but a feeble reed, and tremble lest I should sink with him, at the view of those lovely features disfigured by death. 'Tis true, I did not love her, like Seymour, with the violent ardour of a juvenile passion: my affection rather arose from the sympathy which a man of probity feels for everyone that bears the marks of rectitude, wisdom and humanity. Never did I see a person in whom were united such moral ideas and affections; nobody ever placed more dignity in great things, nor treated those that are small with a more amiable sweetness. Her conversation would have constituted the happiness of an entire society of men of learning and virtue. – Yet it is here, it is amidst these rocks, and among men as insensible as they, and in the midst of the most cruel torments, that she has resigned up her lovely soul. O Providence! thou seest the questions which agitate my mind; but to thee also is known the reverence for thy incomprehensible decrees, which restrains me from uttering them.

*   *   *   *   *

Dear doctor, thou friend of humanity, share with us in our joy! – The angel Sophia still lives! the protection of Heaven has preserved her! Seymour sheds tears of joy, and repeatedly embraces the poor inhabitants of this cottage, whom we now no longer suspect, and whom we now esteem with all the ardour of friendship. It is not above an hour ago, when pale, trembling, and in a mournful silence, we walked towards the garden, where yesterday they told us was her grave. The miner and his son followed us with an irresolute air, and a visible reluctance. When we were come to the heap of sand, I ordered our men to remove it. My brother threw his arms about my neck, hiding his face; and this motion from Seymour, at the very instant of my seeing the spade throw up the earth, pierced my very soul. I lifted up my eyes towards Heaven, and prayed that our hearts might be strengthened; when suddenly the husband, the wife, and their son, fell on their knees before us, and with loud cries begged that we would grant them our protection. Seized with an extraordinary fear, I expected nothing less than the discovery of an assassination.

What do you mean? cried I. – Speak! – Why do you ask our protection? We have deceived Lord N. said they. The lady is not dead: she is gone – Where is she, my friends – where is she? – Don't deceive us!

No, my good lord. She is with Lord Hopton's sister. My lady would take her with her, and bid us tell my Lord N. that the young gentlewoman was dead; and we loved her so well that we let her go: but if my lord should come to know it, he will be revenged on us.

Seymour, overpowered with joy, was at first ready to sink; but recovering himself, he cast forth a shout, embraced the poor man, and cried, O my friend, you shall come with me! I will protect you, I will reward you! Where is Lord Hopton! How was all this brought about? My dear brother Rich, we must instantly be gone. – I, being no less impatient than he to see again my dear Sophia, said, Give orders to prepare for our departure, while I talk to these people. I soon calmed their fears, by telling them that Lord N. was exasperated at the violence his servant had committed, and would be charmed at hearing of their affection for the lady, and reward their kindness to her. I joined to this discourse a handful of guineas, and asked them many questions on the manner in which Sophia lived with them.

O doctor, how did the simple and concise account given by these people shed a lustre over my incomparable friend! Yesterday I murmured at her unhappy fate, and today I am ready to thank Providence for the example she has set to the rest of mankind, in her trials, wherein her heroic soul obtained the victory. Ah! all the virtues of Sophia are engraven on my heart in indelible characters – We are going to set out. At the foot of the mountain I shall send one of our men to Derby, to carry to him the joyful news: it will come at a time in which we always regret our having neglected the good we might have done, or deplore our having committed the crime we might have avoided; and what comfort will he experience, if he be still alive, on seeing the sum of the evils he has caused, so much diminished!

LETTER XLVIII

Madam Leidens to Emilia

Tweedale, seat of Lord Douglas-March

I write on my knees, to express my humble gratitude to God for the sweet sensations that overflow my heart. I yet enjoy life, and with it liberty and friendship! O my dear, my tender Emilia! through what troubles, what anguish, am I arrived at this happy period, in which I can at last calm your alarms, and those of my dear Lady Summers. Tomorrow the Countess of Douglas will send a courier to her ladyship. He is to continue his journey to Harwich, and is to carry a packet to your husband, that your uneasiness may not be prolonged for a moment. The extract of my journal, which I was obliged to write with a pencil, will show you how much I have suffered. How thorny was the path through which I have walked; but how agreeable is this opening, to which the hand of the Source of all goodness, has graciously conducted me! Is it not a sign, Emilia, that during the days of my trial I have not rendered myself unworthy of the care of Providence, as one of the most noble souls has been sent to my succour?

On my concluding my last sheet, I thought I had reached the period of my life, and that I should no more see the light of the sun: I also persuaded myself that I was abandoned by the Countess of Douglas; but at about eleven o'clock came the chaplain, accompanied by a surgeon. The next morning was brought a litter, and the lady herself came and offered me, in the most obliging manner, her house, her good offices, and her friendship. The excess of my joy was near proving fatal to me; while I pressed her ladyship's hand to my breast, I fainted away. When I came to myself, they all exhorted me to be still and composed. Soon after my dear deliverer told me, that she had prevailed on my keeper to dig a pit in the garden, in the manner of a grave, and to send word to Lord N. that I was dead. These people agreed to everything, and her ladyship resolved that I should be carried to Lord Hopton's. After dinner I found myself strong enough to leave my bed, and Mary dressed me in her ladyship's presence. Having five guineas about me, I gave it to my keepers; and at the moment when I was going to speak to my lady in behalf of my little orphan, Lydia came into the chamber, and falling on her knees, with many sobs and groans, begged me to take her with me, at the same time lifting up her hands to me in agony. Deeply moved, I cast my moistened eyes on her, and on the countess. The latter, after a moment's reflection, held out her hand to the child, and in a tender voice said, Yes, my little dear, you shall go with us. God bless you, my worthy lady, cried I, for your goodness! I was going to ask your permission to save this innocent victim. I grant it freely, very freely, replied she; I am affected by your tender solicitude for this innocent child. I thanked her with an effusion of joy, and affectionately embraced my poor keepers, whose faces were bathed in tears; then took a last view of this desolate spot, and being laid on the litter provided for me, set out with the countess.

My Lord Hopton received me with civility; but casting his eyes on me, he seemed to examine whether I was most worthy of the addresses of a lover, or the compassion due to a woman of virtue. A glance of his eyes towards me, after he had viewed little Lydia, made me blush: he perceived it, and smiled. I apprehended that he took me to be that child's mother, and perceived how much that opinion must diminish the favourable sentiments he seemed to have entertained of me. Lady Douglas conducted me into a handsome chamber, and desired me to take some rest. Mary being present, asked where little Lydia should be. Here, answered the countess; for doubtless you, madam, prefer having her near you; and it gives me great pleasure, that, in the midst of your calamities, you have so faithfully adhered to the dictates of nature. Dear lady, said I, interrupting her, you – Don't make yourself uneasy, my dear, said she briskly, but with much sweetness. Lie down. I will return soon; but I'll not have you mention a word of any disagreeable circumstance that is past.

She was going away while she spoke thus; and I threw myself on the bed, with the melancholy reflection that I was to purchase the first hours of the liberty I enjoyed, by the mortification of being exposed to injurious suspicions. Unwilling that Lady Douglas should have time to feed them, I desired Mary to bring me pen, ink and paper, and the next morning I wrote to clear up to the countess everything relating to little Lydia, and to inform her of the motives which had induced me to take that child under my care. I entreated her also to furnish me with an opportunity of sending the Lady Summers news in relation to myself, she having not heard from me, as the arrival of the cruel wretch sent by Derby had prevented my finishing the letter I had begun to write to her; and I added, that the testimony of that lady would confirm the truth of all I advanced with respect to myself, and also convince my deliverer that she would have no reason to regret the favours she had bestowed on me.

She had no sooner read over the letter than she came to me, and, after begging I would excuse her mistake, endeavoured to apologise for it. How, said she, could it be thought that a stranger had such tenderness and concern for the child of her enemy? I have praised that affection which I supposed to be maternal; but how do you increase my friendship and admiration, by this generous love for the issue of your odious persecutor! – For two hours together she talked to me on various subjects, and the turn of her conversation confirmed me in my opinion of the tenderness and delicacy of her soul. This dear lady distinguishes herself by a quality seldom found among the great: she interests herself in the distresses of the soul, and, with a goodness equally noble and judicious, offers to the unhappy consolation and relief. I have often observed, while I lived among the illustrious favourites of fortune, that their pity was excited by certain disgraces, certain exterior evils, as sickness and poverty; but I have seldom found them feel for the pain of the mind, even though they themselves are the authors of it. Seldom have I found them obtain the habit of valuing objects according to their real worth. They dazzle others by their apparent lustre, and are dazzled in their turn. Wit assumes the place of judgement; the endearing name of friendship is prostituted on frigid compliments, and pomp and parade are accounted happiness. – O, my dear Emilia, should I ever again obtain a place in that brilliant circle, I will avoid with extreme care whatever would have been disagreeable to me in my state of humiliation. The countess herself will take care of little Lydia. You have done enough for that child, said she, and for the future no room must be given to attribute to the consequence of weakness, what must have arisen from the highest virtue: besides, it is particularly necessary that Derby should not have the least shadow of reason to imagine, that your compassion for the orphan arises from your inclination for the father. I was sensibly affected with the delicacy of this proceeding, and heartily thanked her ladyship for not only sheltering me from the false judgement of others, but also for saving me from the praises which might perhaps, have been given me for what she called my generosity. I prevailed on the countess to read my letters to Lady Summers, though she at first refused it, in order to show her confidence in me. As to my journal, it being written in German, it would have required some time to make an entire translation of it, and being impatient to convey it to you. I have only translated for her what appeared to me most essential, sliding lightly over such passages as I apprehended might draw praises on me; because I cannot help thinking that the pleasure of hearing myself praised, diminishes, in some measure, my inward satisfaction. I long to hear from Lady Summers, that I may go to her, and then set out to throw myself into the arms of my Emilia. My enthusiastic fondness for England is extinguished: this is not, as I imagined, the country of my soul – I wish to retire to my own estate, to live there, and only employ myself in doing good. Neither my mind nor my heart are now proper for society, and I can only be of service to some of the unhappy, by teaching them how to support misfortunes. Indeed, one of the first wishes I have formed, since a more smiling prospect has opened before me, is that in cultivating a young heart, I shall never forget to sow the principles of my education: happy seeds, whose fruits have ripened, and have been of such value to me in my severest sufferings; which have silenced my murmurs, and have given me the strength to exercise those virtues which still remain for the unfortunate!

Yesterday we arrived at Tweedale. I cannot express the delightful sensations which the beauties of nature make me again experience: they are grand and varied, according to the different points of view from this mansion; where, from a steep mountain, we see the smiling banks of the Tweed, which form a range of gently rising hills covered with numerous flocks. The blessing of sight seems in me to have acquired fresh force, while in the midst of the lead mines it appeared to be dimmed. May I not flatter myself that the powers of my soul will also revive with the sensation of the beneficent wonders of the creation, and the sweet hope of grasping in my arms the friend of my heart?

LETTER XLIX

Lord Rich to Dr T.

Tweedale

If it be just that the stronger should not only bear his own burthen, but also aid the weak to support his, I have today fulfilled that duty. I sigh under the pressure of sensations which accumulate in my heart, and prevent Seymour's sinking under his passion. The letters I shall write to you, dear doctor, will support my firmness. My brother is at this instant actually at the feet of the object of all my wishes; while I am at a distance, though Sophia's eyes seemed to bid me stay with her: but Seymour held her hand, his heart felt the sweet pressure, which she returned, perhaps, without knowing it. I likewise felt the same pressure, and retired to hide my emotions.

We arrived here two days ago. Six horses entering the courtyard all at once on full speed, surprised the servant, who ran up to us. My brother, throwing himself from his horse, called out, the Countess of Douglas, and the lady found among the mines, are they here? On their answering, They are, Come, come along, said he, seizing my arm. – Whose name must I carry in? asked a servant. Lord Rich, Lord Seymour, said my brother hastily, running after the valet. Scarce had he time to knock at the door, before we were in the room.

The countess sat facing the door; but Lady Sophia, who was reading to her, had her back towards us. Seymour's abruptness, the noise of the domestics, and their repeated questions, filled the countess with surprise, and obliged my charming friend to turn her head. Heavens! cried she, with the most lively emotion, dropping her book on the floor. Seymour, saying, Excellent people! she is still alive! – she is still alive! was instantly at her feet, and extending his arms, said, O my divine, my adorable Sophia! – The dear lady, half beside herself, cast her eyes alternately on Seymour and me; but an instant after turning aside her head, let it sink on her trembling arm, which was placed on the table.

The Countess of Douglas looked around her with astonishment, and I found myself obliged to speak; but my first care was excited by Sophia. Worthy lady, said I, support the angel whom you have near you! I am Lord Rich, this is Lord Seymour. The countess hastily stepped up to my lovely friend, who perceiving her, threw her arms about her, and during some minutes hid her lovely face in her deliverer's bosom. Seymour, impatient at her hiding her face from him, cried, in a mournful voice, O uncle, why did you force me to conceal my passion from her! Now all the torments, all the tenderness of my heart, will not be able to move her. – O Sophia! Sophia! what will become of me, if, amidst the joy of finding you again, I meet with your hatred? Grant me, grant me one kind look! – With an enchanting air, and that true dignity which accompanies virtue, Sophia lift up her head, and blushing, held out her hand to my brother, saying, in a low voice, Rise, Lord Seymour! I assure you, I have not the least hatred against you; and sighing, added, How had I ever a right to hate you? – He kissed her hand in a transport of joy. I cast down my eyes; but she rose, and drew near to me with an air of gratitude, and taking me by the hand, said, My worthy lord, this is friendship indeed! Pray, how did you find me? Did Lady Summers tell you where I was? How does my ever honoured mother? – I kissed the hand she had given me, and answered, Lady Summers is well, and will be happy when she sees again her dearly beloved daughter; but it is not she, it is justice and repentance that have brought my brother and me here. – Is Lord Seymour then your brother? said she, with a still deeper blush. – Yes, we are sons of the same mother, one of the most excellent women that ever lived. A smile full of expression was her answer; then turning to the countess, My dear deliverer, said she, see here two irreproachable witnesses to the truth of all I have related of my birth and my life; and I bless God for my being come at the happy time, when your heart may say, My goodness to her has not been lost. – No, interrupted Seymour; none ever merited the homage of the whole earth so much as this adorable woman. What gratitude do I owe you, for having generously delivered her! With eyes filled with tears, he then pressed the countess's hand to his bosom.

I endeavoured to recover myself, that I might be able to mention the cause of our journey. During some minutes we were all silent, till, taking Lady Sophia's hand, I said, Can you hear your persecutor mentioned, without injuring your health or your repose? He draws near to the close of life, and his greatest anguish arises from the remembrance of your virtues, and the cruelty with which he has treated you. Reduced to despair at the news of your death, he sent for us, and made us both promise to repair immediately to the desolate spot where he had placed you; to cause your body to be disinterred, and then removed to Dumfries, where it was to receive such funeral honours as should at the same time eternise your virtues and his remorse. – I shall not mention how painful such an office was to us. After having sought for you in vain, to find you dead, my poor brother and (I cannot help adding) your poor friend Rich! – Lord Derby, said she, while a tear rolled down her cheek – Lord Derby has been barbarous, very barbarous to me. May God forgive him! As for me, I have forgiven him from the bottom of my heart – but – to see him would be impossible – the sight of him would give me immediate death. On pronouncing these last words, she hung down her head, and lowered her voice.

Seymour felt the affecting disorder of her pure soul, and walking up to a window, endeavoured to compose himself. Lady Sophia then left the room. We followed her with our admiring eyes. Though she was only dressed in a Scotch linen, she appeared enchanting, from the beautiful proportion of her stature, and the nobleness of her behaviour and walk: and though she was still pale and meagre, the beauty and dignity of her soul appeared, as usual, on all her features. We gave the countess an account of everything relating to Lady Sophia, and she, in her turn, communicated all she knew since Mary, the miner's daughter, entered into her service. I at first thought, said the countess, that this young stranger had been extremely well educated, but that an unhappy moment had turned her out of the track appointed for her. She inspired me with a tender pity, particularly by the care she took of a child, which I thought was her own; from that time I resolved to bring her hither, when my brother and I should leave the Highlands: but the ill treatment she suffered, which was near depriving her of her life, made me hasten the execution of this design. How do I at present rejoice, that I have followed the emotions of my heart!

The countess now left us to go in search of Sophia, and we were left alone. I was buried in thought. Seymour, with his eyes swimming in tears, coming up, embraced me, crying Rich! – my dear brother! I am unhappy in the midst of happiness, and feel that I shall always be so. I see all your love, and all your merit. She is displeased with me; she has cause to be so – infinite cause. It is just that she should show more confidence, more friendship for you, than for me. I am sensible of it; but it is with the extremest grief. My health has already suffered greatly by this passion: today I have seen her again; I am satisfied, and willing to die for her, – I here pressed him to my bosom with an emotion that had something strange in it, and I believe I answered him with some coldness, Yes, Seymour, you are unhappy in the midst of happiness; yet there is one who has more reason to complain. – Why must your rivals be always more clear-sighted than you? Derby is in the right; you are the person she prefers. Her reserve is a proof of everything he said to us. Be worthy of her, and don't envy her friendship and confidence. – O Rich, O my brother, said he, is it, can it be possible? Does not your passion blind you as much as mine does me? – Oh! I must either obtain her, or die! – But who will speak in my favour? I dare not utter a word, and you – I will speak for you, said I, but it shall not be today; her sensibility, and her weak state of health, require precautions. Seymour, in an ecstasy of joy, hugged me in his arms. O thou most dear, thou most noble of brothers, cried he; ask my life, ask all that I have, I cannot give thee too much! Wilt thou – wilt thou indeed, speak for me? God for ever bless my faithful, my generous friend! – Dear Seymour, I returned, I only desire that you may be happy, and worthy of your happiness. O! you do not know, like me, the extent of that happiness; but great as it is, I do not envy you – I wish that you may obtain it!

The ladies coming in again, the conversation turned on the fine situation of the house. Our friend mentioned the impressions which the smiling beauties of nature had made, on her leaving her barren waste; and then of some circumstances of her being carried off, and of the first days of her exile. In the evening she delivered to me some papers she wrote there. I know enough of German to understand them, and Seymour and I read them together. O doctor, what a soul is hers! How happy would she make me! yet I stifle my wishes – I renounce them for ever. Seymour must live: his mind cannot support the loss of his hopes; but the reason, and the experience of my riper years, will support me. It is necessary that Seymour's happiness should be complete, in order that he may enjoy it; while, on the other hand, I shall bring myself to have a lively enjoyment of the happiness that will fall to my share. Send us, as soon as possible, the letters my brother wrote to you, on the subject of Lady Sophia: it is necessary that they should intercede for him.

LETTER L

Lady Sophia to Emilia

What, O my Emilia, are the designs of Providence with respect to me? I have been preserved amidst such calamities as have overwhelmed my reason, and threatened my life. I am not preserved in order to be devoted to fresh misfortunes, but that I may undergo every kind of trial. I alone, my Emilia, must now decide my fate, and yield to the solicitations of eloquent friendship. Lord Derby is no more. The annexed sheets, which contain my journal at Tweedale, will inform you of the arrival of the Lords Rich and Seymour, and the poor reparation Derby intended me, by heaping honours on my lifeless form. God grant that his eternal existence be more happy than he made mine here, while it was under his disposal. Lord Seymour solicits me to give him my heart. He has loved me, O my Emilia, he has loved me with the most pure and tender passion, ever since he first saw me: but the pride of his uncle, his dependence on that nobleman, and his own excessive delicacy with respect to honour, engaged him to observe the strictest silence till I had triumphed over the snares which the Prince laid against my virtue. You know how fatal that silence has been to me; but you were ignorant, as well as I, of what it made Lord Seymour suffer. I send you the letters he then wrote to a friend, and those of Derby to one of his companions; in return, my dear Emilia, I desire you to transmit to me all those I have written to you. In reading those of Derby, you will be shocked at the ill use he has made of his wit, and at seeing his infamous profanation of virtue and love. Should not I myself have been capable of baseness if I had suspected his artifices? Ah how different is Seymour's heart from his! O my Emilia, how glad should I now be of your advice! Lady Douglas, the only person I can consult, is on the side of love. Lord Rich, the noble, the excellent Rich, entreats me to become his sister. The amiable Seymour is at my feet: all the scruples dictated by my delicacy, are strongly assaulted; and O thou friend of my heart, thou to whom I have always opened its most secret recesses, I cannot, I will not conceal from thee, that a secret voice speaks to me in favour of Seymour; and is he not the man my heart had chosen? He knows it, and ought I now to deprive him of his hopes? If I should, Lord Rich, I fear, would endeavour to fill his place.

Seymour has, ever since his arrival, been lavishing on me the marks of the most ardent and most tender love. His brother has had long conversations with him; but to appearance they were cold and tranquil, and often he had his eyes long fixed on me: I thought that I could read his looks, and resolved not to enter into any engagement. Seymour's letters arrived, and two days after they had been delivered to me, Lord Rich came to bring me back my journal, to which was added the last letter I wrote to you from Summer Hall. On his entering my room, he appeared to be greatly moved, and had a very expressive countenance; after kissing my journal, he pressed it to his bosom and begged pardon for having taken a copy of it, which he however delivered to me, as well as the original: but added, Allow me to ask your leave to keep this faithful transcript of your sentiments; allow me, my adorable friend, to possess this copy of your soul, and make my brother Seymour happy in the possession of yourself. His letters must have convinced you of the rectitude of his heart, and the gift of your hand will render him the happiest and the best of men. After some moments silence, laying his hand on his breast, he fixed his eyes on me, and with a most tender and respectful look, said, You know the sentiments with which you have inspired me, and which will for ever subsist in my heart. You know the ardent wishes I formed, and which I have always nourished. Well, these I have stifled. Never doubtless could I have brought myself to conquer my dearest hopes, had I not in the midst of the illusions of love said to myself, Seymour is worthy of her; he merits her esteem, her pity – Here fixing on me a tender and attentive look he stopped.

O Lord Rich! said I to him, with a sigh – It is in your power, resumed he, interrupting me in the gentle voice of friendship, to render unhappy a young man of merit, by rejecting his love: but with a heart so noble and so tender, rather choose to exert your power in making a whole family happy! You alone can preserve my mother from the mortification of seeing her two sons vow an everlasting celibacy: and if you become my sister, and love your brother, you will render him happy. Consider likewise, that by this means your virtues will be enabled to exert themselves in an extensive sphere.

Oh! my lord, said I with emotion, how urgent you are! But do not you see difficulties? I here covered my face with my hands. He threw his arms about me, and kissing my forehead, cried, Most dear Sophia, I understand you: I know your difficulties, and the delicacy from which they arise renders you still more adorable; but do not destroy Seymour's hopes; suffer me, I entreat you, suffer me to give him your permission to hope. This worthy man looked at me with his eyes swimming in tears, and a tear from mine fell on his hand. He viewed it with a strong emotion, his lips gathered it up, and his looks were for some time fixed on the floor. I took the writings he had returned to me, and presenting him the original, said, Receive, excellent man, what you have termed the copy of my soul, and keep it as a pledge of the most pure and tender friendship – Sister, said he, interrupting me – No wiles, Lord Rich! cried I, there is no need of art to engage me to become what you earnestly desire I should be – In an ecstasy he now blessed me, covered my hands with kisses, and hastily ran to the door of the room. On which I cried, Say nothing yet, I earnestly entreat you. Extremely affected by his behaviour, I indulged the soft impression, and resolved to obtain the name of Lady Seymour; and after pouring out my soul in prayer for the divine direction, I was confirmed in this resolution.

P.S. Seymour knows all, and my pen cannot express his joy. My dear countess embraces me with a maternal fondness, and Lord Rich with the affection of the most tender brother. Lord Seymour keeps me in his sight, as if he was afraid that somebody would make me change my resolution. His valet de chambre is just sent to his mother, who in good sense and merit is said to be a second Lady Summers. Bear a part, my friend, in my joy. How sweet are the emotions of my heart! What felicity arises from a resolution approved by prudence and virtue! How do I rejoice at the thought of the journey I am going to take to visit the tomb of my parents! Tears of gratitude shall bedew their ashes, because they imprinted on my soul the love of virtue and beneficence; because they taught me to form just ideas of happiness and misfortunes. – I shall again embrace my Emilia! I shall again see my tenants! How delightful the thought!

My dear Lord Seymour makes his brother his model, and consults him in everything – and what tender gratitude do I owe to that brother for his care and attention to enhance my felicity, by endeavouring to give more sweetness and quality to the too hasty temper of Seymour, who like a fine river, says Lord Rich, is sometimes impetuous in its course; but always rolls over sand mingled with the purest gold.

LETTER LI

Lord Rich to Dr T.

I am now come from the altar where my brother has just tied the indissoluble knot, and where I have vowed to remain for ever free. I have given him that hand which I had so long wished to possess, and which I resigned to him, purely because I felt myself more able than he to support its loss. It was her soul, her manner of thinking, and her sentiments that I loved. The writings she has presented me, those writings in which she gives such a candid portrait of herself, prove that she granted me all that was in her power, a distinguished esteem, an unreserved confidence, and ardent wishes for my happiness. The inexplicable power of a first love which perhaps had seized on her heart without her consent, must for ever have prevailed. – I am sensible of the value of her soul, her friendship is more tender than the endearments of love in other women. The autumn of life, which is my season, leaves me the tranquil enjoyment of the pure charms of friendship. I shall live with this happy pair; their second son will bear my name, and to him I shall be a second father! I shall every day converse with my sister; I shall enjoy the beauties of her mind; I shall add to her felicity; and my mother blesses me for having contributed to the marriage of her dear Seymour! Thus is my happiness founded on the happiness of those I most love. Soon, my friend, shall I have the pleasure of seeing and conversing with them.

LETTER LII

Lady Seymour to Emilia from Seymour House

The first hour in which I find myself at liberty here, amidst my new family, should be employed in thanksgivings to the divine Providence, which has terminated all my troubles and afflictions in the greatest felicity this earth can afford; but the next hour ought to be consecrated to that faithful friend who has shared all my woes, who has alleviated them by her tenderness, and whose example and advice, have revived the fortitude and virtue of my heart O Emilia! I am happy, perfectly happy. Henceforth I may devote all the days of my life to the discharge of the most sweet and sacred duties. My tenderness for my dear husband constitutes his felicity; my filial love for his mother, is regarded by that excellent woman as the reward of her virtues; my fraternal affection for my dear Lord Rich, fills his noble and sensible heart with true content.

Lord Seymour has very large possessions and sets me no other bounds in doing good but those of his vast fortune. O my dear Emilia! what an advantage is it to me that my sensibility has been tried by misfortunes, since by this means I am become much more capable of relishing every delicious and every agreeable sensation. You know that in the midst of all my distress I blessed God, that he enabled me to alleviate them, by leaving me the use of my reason, and the power of performing benevolent actions. At present I feel more strongly than ever, how greatly prosperity and happiness increase our duties; mine have in some respects changed their nature or their object; in my heart gratitude succeeds patience and humble submission: My powers and abilities, which supported me under all my distresses, and were the source of some pleasures, will be consecrated to the happiness of all around me, to the discovery of their secret calamities, and to invent the means of curing or relieving them. I cannot repeat it too often, since experience has taught it me, even on the brink of the grave, that goodness of heart, piety, resignation, and the other endowments of the mind, can alone render us happy on earth. They sustained me when I hung over the gulf of despair; and on them are founded the happiness I at present enjoy. I will lean upon them while I can do good in tranquillity and peace, and will implore the Divine bounty that in conjunction with my noble and generous spouse, I may continually exhibit a model of the manner in which wealth and interest ought to be employed.

You see, my dear Emilia, that all my scruples have necessarily subsided, as I saw the tranquillity of so many worthy hearts depend on my decision.

My lord intends to build a school and an hospital, like those of Sternheim he has ordered the plan of them to be drawn; and these edifices are to be erected during our travels in Germany. Next week we set out for Summer Hall; we shall there wait for Count R.'s answer to a letter we have sent him, and then, Rich and Seymour say that we are to visit all the sacred places to which I have been conducted by my misfortunes. They will then see my Emilia, and will be convinced that the first inclination of my heart was placed upon the most worthy person of my sex. Tomorrow my Lord G. and Sir Thomas Watson, my grandmother's nephew, will be at Seymour House. As to my other relations, and the numerous gentry in the neighbourhood, I shall not contract any acquaintance with them, till my return from Germany.

LETTER LIII*

Lord Rich to Dr T.

I am returned to Seymour House; for I am unable to support the void I find within, while I am at a distance from my brother's family. My sister links me to her by a thousand engaging ties. I have seen that admirable lady at Summer Hall, at Vaels with her Emilia, in her seminary, at the court of D. at Sternheim, among her tenants, and at the tomb of her parents. – In all these different circumstances, in all the various situations of her life, she appears a benevolent genius, come down to show her sex a pattern of the virtues which more particularly belong to them, and are their greatest ornament. At our return to Seymour House, she became a mother, and what a mother, dear doctor, must Lady Seymour be! I must have been more than man, not to renew, a thousand times, the wish that she was my wife, and the mother of *my* children! Ah, how justly is the sacrifice of our own happiness placed among the highest virtues! How painful it is to the most generous heart! – We ought not therefore to wonder at its being so uncommon. Yet far am I from having repented of my having sacrificed myself for my brother. No, never did I feel the torment of a mean envy: but keenly have I suffered by the silence under which I thought it necessary to conceal my sentiments; for I could not trust them to any of the profane, for fear they should judge falsely of a passion which is the most respectable, and I have feared also to place my sister's noble and pure friendship in a dubious light. Hence I insensibly fell into a deep melancholy. I quitted for some months Seymour House, and repaired to my own country seat. The calm of that retreat; where formerly I enjoyed an agreeable repose after my long travels, did not then afford me all the tranquillity I expected. I endeavoured to overcome myself; but accustomed to the sweet conversation of the most sensible persons, nothing could supply their place, and their letters were not themselves. At length they wrote me word that little Rich was born, and I immediately flew to Seymour House.[72] In a happy moment Lady Seymour gave me that child in my arms, and with all the charms of a voice and countenance full of sensibility, I heard her say, There is your young Rich: God grant that, as he bears your name, he may likewise be possessed of a mind and heart like yours! A sensation at once gloomy and delicious seized on my soul: there it remains and I shall not attempt to describe it to anyone. The

---

* This letter is dated about two years after the former.[71]

dear infant has all its mother's features, and this resemblance gives me real happiness. If my life be continued, this child shall have no other instructor, no other guide in his travels – All his expences shall be set down to my account, and his domestics shall be doubly rewarded. My chamber joins to his, and I am going to build a lodge at the end of the garden, where we will live together, as soon as he has completed his second year: in the mean time I employ myself in forming the people who are to be about him. This infant becomes the support of my reason, and to him I shall owe my repose. What a value does every care, and all the caresses he receives from his mother, impart to him! He and his brother grow up under the eyes of their tender parents, and all their actions are models of wisdom and goodness. A blessing rests on all the places where Seymour resides, and joy accompanies his steps and those of his spouse. With one hand they relieve distressed merit, and give succour to others of the unfortunate: with the other they spread embellishments over the whole lordship, in which they show the most elegant taste. In the country, says Lady Seymour, art should never appear to triumph over nature[73]: let us rather follow her traces, and endeavour to improve rather than to disguise them. Nothing can be more agreeable than our evenings, and our repasts: in these moderation reigns, and they are animated by cheerfulness. We often mingle in the country dances of our tenants, and increase their joy by sharing it, Lady Seymour's company is sought for by persons of merit, while vice and folly, struck with dread, carefully avoid it. Our house is the rendezvous of all those in our neighbourhood who are distinguished by their abilities and virtues, and it is one of the beauties in my sister's character, that she delights in finding out and rendering conspicuous the merit of others, especially of persons of her own sex. My brother is the best of husbands, and some hundreds of tenants bless him as their most worthy landlord. Happiness beams in his looks, when he sees his son clinging to the bosom of his charming wife, and sucking in her virtues with her milk. Every day sees some abatement of that impetuous ardour which predominated in him, and he has learned the difficult art of enjoying his happiness without parade or ostentation. The uniform plainness and simplicity in our dress permits the families of the smallest fortunes to visit us. Lady Seymour from time to time asks for some of their young daughters, and keeps them for a while, in order to inspire them, by her example and engaging lessons, with a love of virtue and useful knowledge. In short, the enthusiasm of beneficence actuates her whole being: not contented with thinking well, she is incessantly putting the good she meditates into practice. Never perhaps were more fervent thanks offered to Heaven than those of Lady Seymour, for being endued with the gift of a feeling heart, and blessed with the power of diffusing happiness to all around her. – What praises, what rewards do those deserve, who thus furnish such illustrious proofs, that all which morality requires is possible to be fulfilled; that the practice of our duties, so far from disturbing our pleasures, ennobles and secures the enjoyment of them, and becomes itself our most real and substantial happiness, in all the stages and situations of life!

NOTES

[1] *To D.F.G.R.V.*******: To D[ie] F[rau] G[eheime] R[ätin] V[on La Roche] = Madame Privy Councillor von La Roche. The wives of court officials were customarily addressed by their husbands' titles. Georg Michael Frank La Roche (1720–1788) was appointed to a senior ministerial post at the court of the Elector of Trier in April 1771, but was not actually ennobled until 1776.

[2] Philipp Eramus Reich (1717–1787). Leading Leipzig bookseller and an influential figure in the development of an organized book-trade in Germany; publisher of *Sophia Sternheim* and the works of Wieland, his most prestigious author.

[3] Christoph Martin Wieland (1733–1813), whose footnotes to La Roche's text are indicated by a bold asterisk and initialled E.

[4] Perhaps the least felicitous of the words chosen by Collyer to negotiate the German 'Untertan', a word meaning both the 'subject' of a king or territorial prince, and the tenant, bondman or retainer of a feudal landlord. In later passages he opts for more neutral words such as 'tenant', 'dependant', or 'subordinate'.

Collyer's somewhat embarrassed resort to a word that would have struck even eighteenth-century English readers as quaintly medieval underlines the difference between contemporary English rural socio-economic relations, and the conditions in many German states, where feudal relations persisted well into the nineteenth century. For a succinct account of eighteenth-century German rural society see W.H. Bruford, *Germany in the Eighteenth Century, The Social Background of the Literary Revival*, (Cambridge, University Press, 1965) pp. 45–129.

[5] Writing-desk, an eighteenth-century variant of 'escritoire' (from French *écritoire*).

[6] cf. Mr B's thoughts on unequal marriages in Samuel Richardson's *Pamela, or Virtue Rewarded*, 6th edn (4 vols, London, 1746), II, 283–284.

[7] cf. Pamela's letters to her parents on the subject of Mr. B's marital 'injunctions' in *Pamela* II, *passim*.

[8] i.e. the management of the whole household, including the control of expenditure.

[9] cf. the sentiments of Richardson's virtuous protagonists on a master's duties and responsibilities towards his dependants in *Pamela*, II, 62. IV, 283–284; *Clarissa, or The History of a Young Lady*, 3rd edn (8 vols, London, 1751) VIII, 212–213, and *The History of Sir Charles Grandison* (7 vols, London, 1754), VI, 41–42. ˋ

[10] Collyer here omits a passage in which Sternheim criticizes the orthodox clergy: 'I am convinced of the utility and benevolence of the great truths of our religion; but the small effect produced upon the majority of our congregations by those who preach them causes me rather to doubt the manner of instruction, than to subscribe to the widespread notion that the heart of man is naturally inclined to evil. How often have I come away from a sermon by a celebrated divine in order to meditate upon its usefulness to myself and its possible advantages for the common man. How much of it must have struck the latter as mere empty talk! That part of it which was

devoted to the praise of learning or to the exhaustive, if scarcely comprehensible, examination of various speculative propositions contributed but little to the *improvement* of the majority of those present, though they could hardly be blamed for a lack of goodwill.

For if I, who have been familiar with abstract ideas since my early years, found it difficult to discern the practical application of these refined discourses, what could the artisan and his children be expected to make of them? Let me say at once that I do not share the arrogant opinion voiced by certain persons of rank and fortune that one should seek neither to broaden the common man's understanding nor to acquaint him with enlightened religious ideas.'

[11] Sternheim's concluding thoughts are omitted: 'A minister concerned to promote piety only in those members of his flock who are approaching the end of their days on earth would certainly not win my approval; nor would there be a place in my parish for any minister who sought to reform souls merely by citing the Divine Law and threatening eternal chastisement. The pastor who emphasises regular attendance at church at the expense of the actions of everyday life is, in my estimation, no true philanthropist and a poor spiritual counsellor.'

[12] The portrait of the Sternheims' domestic life in the following pages is derived from Rousseau's descriptions of Julie's life with Wolmar in *Julie ou La Nouvelle Héloise* (2 vols, Paris, 1782), II, *passim*.

[13] The colonel's wife dies after bearing him a still-born son – Collyer abbreviates La Roche's already perfunctory announcement.

[14] The Count and Countess of Löbau have some of the features of Clarissa Harlowe's brother James and sister Arabella. See *Clarissa*, I, 81.

[15] Here La Roche continues: 'My father sought to rid her of this antipathy, saying that she did her aunt an injustice by it; and he was in general concerned to recommence her education and to encourage her musical talents. Often, he would remind us of the truth and aptness of the saying that the virtues were all attached to each other like the links of a chain, so that modesty too was to be regarded as an aspect of virtue. And, indeed, what might have become of Lady Sophia Sternheim had her awareness of her merits matched the degree of their perfection?' – Collyer's excision relieves the reader of the difficulty of reconciling the minister's active defence of the Countess of Lobäu with the dying colonel's emphatic condemnation of her morals, and his express purpose of preserving Sophia from her influence by appointing him her guardian.

[16] Collyer here adopts a sentence added by Mme de la Fite, whose French translation of *Sophia Sternheim* was published in 1774.

[17] The court at D. is modelled on the summer court of Duke Karl Eugen of Württemberg (1737–93) at Ludwigsburg. One of the more ambitious of *ancien régime* – Germany's many miniature Versailles, it was famous for its lavish festivities and ostentation.

[18] Dress-maker.

[19] A gown of waved or watered silk tafetta.

[20] This passage is La Roche's tribute to Count Friedrich von Stadion (1691–1768), her husband's former employer and benefactor. At the end of his political career in 1762 Stadion retired to his estate at Warthausen, near Biberach in Swabia. G.M. La Roche followed him there and continued as his secretary and administrator until his

death. Sophie von La Roche later described these Warthausen years as the 'happiest' of her life.

[21] Her friend Emilia's husband.

[22] An unmarried gentlewoman seeking admission to a Lutheran convent or 'Damenstift' would be required to prove a pedigree of at least sixteen armourial quarterings. La Roche's model for Sophia's admired canoness is Friedrich von Stadion's sister, the Countess Maximiliane von Stadion, canoness and later (from 1775) abbess of the Imperial Convent (*Reichsstift*) at Buchau.

[23] Latin, a unique phenomenon or prodigy; literally, 'a rare bird'. The phrase is added by Collyer.

[24] A reference to *Pamela*, IV, 84; c.f. also Joseph Addison's satire on the unrealistic conventions of Italian opera in *The Spectator*, No. 5, March 6, 1711.

[25] A three-cornered scarf or shawl worn round the neck or shoulders, the ends hanging loosely from the shoulders in front.

[26] cf. Lovelace's correspondence with Belford in *Clarissa*. Somewhat unnecessarily, Collyer underlines La Roche's indebtedness to Richardson for the figure of Derby by changing his name to 'Loveill'.

[27] Greek, song of triumph or victory.

[28] In Greek mythology, Argos Panoptes ('the all-seeing'): a giant with a hundred eyes appointed by Hera to watch the cow into which Io had been transformed. He was eventually outwitted and slain by Hermes, messenger of the gods and patron of thieves, whereupon Hera transferred his eyes to the tail of the peacock.

[29] Ecclesiastes 1, 9; though here borrowed from Richardson's Lovelace. See *Clarissa*, II, 57.

[30] cf. Lovelace's bribery of Joseph Leman, the Harlowes' servant, in *Clarissa* I, 200. III, 1, 2.

[31] i.e., I am as sharp-witted or as quick on the uptake as the next man.

[32] In La Roche's text Derby's letter is followed by a letter from Sophia to Emilia which Collyer omits in its entirety. It is included as an appendix to this edition (pp. 212–216).

[33] cf. *Clarissa*, III, 3, 4: 'I knew that the whole stupid family were in a combination to do my business for me. I told thee that they were all working for me, like so many nederground moles; and still more blind than the moles are said to be, unknowing that they did so. I myself, the director of their principal motions: which falling in with the malice of their little hearts, they took to be all their own.'

[34] Collyer reduces this to an indeterminate 'twenty pieces' – possibly suspecting La Roche of ignorance of English monetary values. In an age in which half this sum would cover the annual stipend of a schoolmaster or member of the lower clergy it is indeed an extravagant reward. However, in view of Derby's close affinity with Richardson's similarly infatuated and free-spending Lovelace, and of his complaint, in a later letter to his friend in Paris (see Letter XXVIII, p. 127), that the wooing of Sophia has left him severely out of pocket, La Roche's inflation seems intended.

[35] The caroline (German *Karolin*) was a gold coin originally minted in Bavaria by the Elector Karl Albrecht (ruled 1726–1745) and subsequently used in the neighbouring south German states. It was worth slightly less than a guinea.

[36] Collyer allows him no more than 'a farther reward'.

[37] In the Greek myth, the nymph Daphne is rescued from Apollo by Earth who turns her into a laurel tree.

[38] T's German title is *Rat*, indicating that he is – or was – a middle-ranking court official or administrator.

[39] Or faro: a card-game, in which the players bet on the order in which certain cards will appear when dealt singly by the banker from the top of the deck.

[40] A gambling game at cards played by two people with a deck reduced to thirty-two cards by the exclusion of the two to the six. The rules combine features of poker and sixty-six.

[41] Here La Roche continues: 'The rural peace and stillness, the noble simplicity of my secluded Sternheim would be as refreshing to my heart and spirits as the sight of an open field to courtiers whose eyes have grown weary from gazing at the force and artificial beauties of an ornamental garden. How happy they are, in such rare moments, to exchange the hard marble corridors of their customary abode for the yielding moss of the earth, and to look upon the boundless mixture of woods, fields, meadows and brooks, where Nature lays out her bounty in charming disorder! On these occasions I have observed in some of them the overwhelming effects of a first pure experience of nature. Even their gestures and their manner of walking lacked the forced stiffness and constraint of their perambulations through our so-called pleasure gardens. Just moments later, however, I saw how the force of habit, reanimated by a single thought, destroyed their soft contentment. Judge for yourself, my Emilia, how wearied my moral eye has become at the daily prospect of unnatural and affected ideas, sensations, pleasures and virtues.'

[42] La Roche continues: 'It is to resemble the English masked balls at Vauxhall Gardens.'

[43] A period of licensed disorder and misrule, celebrated on December 17th–19th; extended to seven days in the imperial period.

[44] Sweetheart: originally the name given by Cervantes' Don Quixote to the peasant girl Alonza Lorenzo whom he makes the lady of his heart in imitation of the courtly tradition. The allusion does not appear in the German text.

[45] Seven nights, i.e. a week, from today.

[46] A masquerade costume consisting of hood, loose cloak and a half mask covering the upper part of the face.

[47] Lady's maid. Abigail was a common middle class christian name in the seventeenth century. The 'waiting gentlewoman' in Beaumont and Fletcher's *The Scornful Lady* is called Abigail and the name was later used by Swift and Fielding in their novels. It was probably popularised by 'Abigail Hill', the original name of Mrs Masham, waiting woman to Queen Anne.

[48] cf. *Clarissa*, III, 3: 'Securely mine! – mine forever!'

[49] cf. *Clarissa*, V, 7: 'Her good angel is gone on a journey, is truanting at last.'

[50] Sophia's sham-marriage resembles the ceremony planned, though not performed, in *Pamela*. Pamela is warned to expect 'a parson ... or rather a man in a parson's habit; but who is indeed a sly, artful fellow, a broken attorney, whom he [i.e., Mr. B.] has hired to personate a minister.' *Pamela*, I, 271.

[51] In La Roche's text Derby's letter is followed by a passage by Rosina, the narrator, which concludes Part I of the work: 'In Lord Derby's wicked letters, my friend, you

behold the despicable intrigues used to bring this most excellent of young ladies to the brink of the most appalling misery. You will imagine my own distress when she fell ill upon her return from the ball and was plunged from one condition of the most alarming nervous agitation into the next. She no longer received letters and we believed that they had been intercepted by the prince or the Count Löbau. The refusal of her request to be allowed to return to her estates and the prince's visit only served to further Lord Derby's design. To my undying shame, this inhuman creature also succeeded in numbing my wits, so that I assisted him in all that could help him remove my Lady from her uncle's power. His letters show the full degree of his cunning and resourcefulness. Yet he was withal a fine-looking man, and my Lady was looking forward to satisfying her desire to visit England – Oh, you will read much more that will astonish you, and I will hasten to satisfy your curiosity.'

[52] The prince and Sophia dance the *Wirbeltanz* (from *wirbeln*, to whirl or spin), a slow waltz similar to the Austrian *Ländler*. The word *Walzer*, from *walzen* (to turn or roll) did not become current until the end of the eighteenth century.

[53] Following La Fite, Collyer here shortens and blurs the argument of a passage which prompts one of the most criticized of Wieland's editorial interventions. The full text reads: 'Didst thou ever behold a stranger set of bells on the fool's cap of virtue? A woman loath to have her greatest personal charms seen and admired! How wilful and obtuse her distinction between my eyes and my feelings! Later that afternoon I asked her to explain herself and, after a long and thoughtful silence, all she could say was that she would offer similar resistance to the exposure of the finest moral qualities of her soul – although she freely admitted that she was pleased to hear others praise her intelligence and the beauty of her figure. Nevertheless, she would sooner dispense with this pleasure than stand accused of seeking to induce it by her own efforts.'

[54] 'or metaphysician' – omitted by Collyer.

[55] A small town near Aachen.

[56] *Leidens* = sorrows or sufferings; restored from Collyer's 'Mrs Suffering' which seems to have been suggested by La Fite's 'Mme Souffrances'.

[57] La Roche: 'three hours'.

[58] La Roche: '. . . doubtless prefer them to my scribble'. Collyer's alteration stems from La Fite.

[59] La Roche continues: 'Why, I then ask myself, why is the moral world so wanting in the fidelity to a prescribed course that is the abiding feature of the natural world? The acorn never produced less than an oak-tree and the vine forever yields grapes. So whence the magnanimous father's small-minded son, or the ignorant and wretched successors of great artists and men of learning? Why is the child of virtuous parents so often a villain? I reflect upon this inequality and chance reveals to me the many obstacles in the moral world (and indeed often in the natural world) that are apt to cause excellent vines to produce sour and useless grapes for lack of good weather, or the best of parents to give birth to thoroughly bad children.'

[60] cf. *Pamela*, III, 338. IV, 52.

[61] Again following La Fite, Collyer here edits out the places in La Roche that give rise to Wieland's (omitted) footnote. The fuller text reads: 'This may be the case, my dear Lady C., where love only enters a young man's soul by his eyes and blazes

brightly by the side of a fresh young thing, whose immature character prevents her
from offering his fire a more durable nourishment. But you, who are loved for your
soul and your noble heart, cannot fail to render a man's love inextinguishable.

By which I take you to mean that my merits are endowed with the properties of
Persian naphtha ... But who among my suitors has a heart that could withstand an
equally constant flame?

All of them, for love and happiness are the inconsumable substance of which our
hearts are made.'

[62] This footnote is added by Collyer, following La Fite.

[63] Sophia's original phrasing is rather more direct and better explains the sharpness
of Wieland's editorial retort: 'Why should a noble-minded, virtuous young woman
be prevented from being the first to declare her love for a man of merit? Why
should she be condemned for trying to please him or for endeavouring by all means
to gain his esteem?

[64] This sentence is a summary rendering of a passage in which Sophia compares the
process of civilization and moral improvement to the gradual reclamation and
cultivation of barren land.

[65] The beginning of this letter is omitted by Collyer: 'Let me tell you, my Emilia,
that once deprived of its powers of beneficence affluence destroys the proper use of
wealth. It enters the souls of the frivolous and dismantles the restraints we impose
on our desires, weakens the pleasures of enjoyment, and plunges the contented
heart with its modest ambitions into an disagreeable state of confusion. – I know
that my friend will hardly guess the cause of an outburst which must strike her as
quite out of keeping with the mood of my last letter. But knowing how peculiarly
sensitive I am to everything around me, you will not be surprised to hear that the
sentiments of my Lord Rich are the real cause of my irritable reflections on
affluence. He persecutes me ...' etc.

[66] Sophia, like Pamela, is well supplied with writing-paper before her abduction: cf.
Pamela I, 125-126, 136-137.

[67] cf. Pamela's journal during her imprisonment at Mr B's house in Lincolnshire.

[68] Sophia's last journal entries and will are modelled on Clarissa's dispositions in her
final letters. See *Clarissa*, VII, 234-236; VIII, 98f.

[69] The steward of the Sternheim estates who married Emilia's elder sister (see
p. 33).

[70] cf. Lovelace's remorse after Clarissa's rape and death. *Clarissa*, VIII, 126-131.

[71] Footnote added by Collyer, following La Fite.

[72] For Rich's description of Sophia's married life La Roche again draws on the
Wolmars' life at Clarens in *Julie ou La Nouvelle Héloïse*: cf. note 12 above.

[73] cf. *Pamela*, IV, 37-38: 'I have heard Mr B. observe with regard to Gentlemen who
build fine Houses, and make fine Gardens, and open fine Prospects, that Art should
never take the place of, but be subservient to Nature.'

APPENDIX

Joseph Collyer's translation of *Die Geschichte des Fräuleins von Sternheim* omits the letter from Sophia to Emilia which is given below. La Roche places it after Letter XII ('Lord Derby to the Lord B. in Paris'). See p. 73 above.

Lady Sophia to Emilia

I am just returned from the most agreeable visit I have ever made with my aunt. We spent ten days at the estate of Count T***, where we met the widowed Countess of Sch*, who is now living there. Two other ladies from the neighbourhood were also of the company and, to my indescribable pleasure, Mr **,[1] whose excellent works are so congenial to my tastes and sentiments. The gentle, free and relaxed tone of this gentleman's society masks a wealth of perspicacity and learning, and his imperturbable good humour in the face of conversations and distractions unworthy of the distinctions of his genius and attainments aroused in me an admiration for the affability of his character akin to that professed by others for his intellectual accomplishments. It was my constant hope that he would be encouraged to communicate to us his thoughts concerning the most useful aspects of the fine arts, and particularly of our German literature, as I was sure that this could but enhance our taste and understanding. But alas, Emila, how bitterly disappointed was this hope! For no one entertained the slightest thought of seeking his improvement in the company of this wisest, kindest and most refined of men. His patience and complaisance were abused by a thousand trivial and small-minded concerns, and his failure to go into raptures over the latest French periodicals and his restrained enthusiasm for works which others would have praised to the skies were often pointedly resented.

Oh, how I treasured every moment I spent with this worthiest of men! In a manner both charming and perfectly tuned to the particular character of my sensibility and desire for instruction, he answered my questions, gave me

---

[1] A portrait of Wieland, which he coyly acknowledges in the second 'explanatory' footnote below p. 213.

the titles of many excellent books, and taught me how I might best profit from reading them. With exquisite candour, he told me that, although mental ability and intellectual curiosity were mine in almost equal measure, I was not a born *thinker*. On the other hand, however, I could bless my good fortune for having been richly compensated for this by Nature herself, who had endowed me with the kind of disposition most apt to fulfil the true purpose of our existence, which consisted in actions rather than abstract speculations.* And in the light of my prompt and discerning sensitivity, both to the manner in which people abused their time, and to the moral deficiencies of their lives, he believed that I should strive to complement my observations with the noble actions of which I was so capable.†

I was never happier, my Emilia, then when I received this testimony to the noble and virtuous character of my temperament from this most precise observer of the innermost recesses of the heart. With the most solicitous kindness, he reproved my reticence and timidness in judging works of the intellect, and credited me with a soundness of sentiment, which gave me as much right as another to express my thoughts. But he cautioned me against adopting a masculine tone in my speech and writing. He was of opinion that the habit of bestowing special praise upon a woman possessed of masculine qualities of mind and character was the sign of a wrongly educated taste. He declares that we women have as good a title as men to all the virtues and to all the knowledge that promotes them, enlightens the understanding, or contributes to the improvement of morals and sentiments; but that the differences between the sexes must always be observed in the manner in which the virtues are practised. Nature herself has assigned us our roles: in the passion of love, for example, she has made the man vehement and passionate, where the woman is tender; where the man arms himself with anger against insult, woman's protection is her moving tears; the man of commerce or learning is endowed with strength and profundity of mind, where the woman is pliant and graceful; in times of adversity the man is found resolute and courageous, the woman patient and resigned; in domestic life it falls to the former to provide the means of sustenance, the latter to see that they are apportioned prudently, etc. In this way, and provided that each party remains within its appointed sphere of activity, both will progress towards the ultimate goal of their existence along the same path, albeit from different directions, without disturbing the moral order by an

---

* It should be borne in mind, however, that once the speculations of men of science and learning prove to be of benefit to human society they are by that very fact entitled to the name of good actions. – E.

† In reply to our inquiry, Mr** (with whom we have the honour to be acquainted) informs us that what he actually meant here was as follows: He had observed in Lady Sternheim a certain tendency to try to apply general principles to moral questions, to make subtle distinctions and to seek to give to her thoughts a kind of systematic form, and had discovered that it was precisely this that she failed to achieve. In his opinion, her particular strength lay in the refinement of her sentiments, her powers of observation, and her wonderful capacity to activate all the powers of her soul in unison; all of which gave her a kindness of heart that was ready to be exercised at any moment. – E.

enforced mixing of roles. – He sought to reconcile me to myself and to the fate of which I complained, and advised me to look always on the positive aspect of things, and by this means to soften my unfavourable impressions, upon which I should dwell no more than was necessary in order to quicken my response to the charm and value of the good and the beautiful.

O Emilia, some of my mind's most glorious days have been spent in the company of this man! Something within me tells me that they will never return, and that I shall never have the good fortune to live simply and contentedly, and in harmony with my desires and inclinations. Do not chide me again for my melting dejection. Perhaps it is the departure of Mr ** that leaves this house so horribly empty for me. He comes here but seldom. He visits this house as the pilgrim visits a ruin that was once the abode of a saint, seeking to pay his respects to the shade of the great man who once lived here; whose mighty spirit and wisdom he admired, and who was his friend and benefactor.

On the day after his departure a minor French author arrived. He was drawn hither by lack of success in his native Paris and by the strange infirmity that causes our aristocracy always to prize French above German letters. The ladies made an elaborate to-do of the company of a man who had come to us straight from Paris and the society of goodness knows how many a *Mme Marquise*. He launched into veritable treatises on the fashions, manners and amusements of the elegant Parisian world; counselled the ladies in all their domestic pursuits and, in the extravagant phrases and expressions peculiar to his native language, assured the courteous widow of his astonishment at the refinements of her mind, the grace of her person and the quite *un-German* qualities of her soul.

I was at first amused to view the original of the image I had acquired from books of these hirelings of the great and rich of France; but I own that by the fourth day of his visit I was heartily weary of his endless stories of furniture, clothes, parties and assemblies, for they seemed merely to clothe the same matter in different words. However, the scene changed upon the return of Mr ** who was at pains to show this French menial his proper place.

You would surely have shared my irritation, my Emilia, had you witnessed the pomp and display with which our aristocracy, with its slavish adulation of France, surrounded the presentation of the Parisian to Mr **, or had you beheld the preening complacency with which the Frenchman heard himself praised as the author of popular little books.

But how brightly the modesty of our sage fellow-countryman shone forth! With the humanity which the genuine philosopher is ever prepared to show towards the fools by whom he is surrounded, he concealed his poor impression of this tedious *bel esprit* and, with true condescension, even remembered that he had read one of his little works.

Mr ** asked his opinion of the great men of France whose works he had himself read and valued highly. Like the rest of us, however, the *bel esprit* knew only their names, and, at every mention of a man of learning and achievement, he would contrive to let fall the name of a man of wealth or of an owner of one of the great houses.

Notwithstanding the abuses to which his obligingness and sociability were subjected, no one permitted Mr T** to leave the company as long as the Parisian was holding forth. And this but increased my annoyance, for this swarm of enviously buzzing wasps merely hindered me from gathering a little honey for myself. At length I asked the Frenchman to tell us something of the profit to the ladies of France from the company of their men of learning.

From his answer I gathered that the distinguished men of France taught their ladies: the refinements of language and expression; to obtain some idea of all the various sciences, in order occasionally to blend with their conversation words which would gain them a reputation for extensive learning; and to be familiar with at least the titles of all the great works of literature and science so as to be able to deliver themselves of something resembling an opinion.

I learned in addition that ladies were in the habit of accompanying gentlemen of learning to public lectures on natural history, from which they were able, without great exertion, to extract many very useful ideas; that they also visited the studios of the great artists who had placed their genius in the service of pleasure and splendour, and that all these activities and accomplishments contributed greatly to rendering their conversation pleasant and varied.

It pained me to realize that if it were capable of propagating itself in this dignified and useful manner, the self-regard of the French must be credited with excellent good sense. For the desire to know the names of the blossoms on the trees is soon succeeded by the wish to study the growth and ripeness of the fruit.

How far advanced is this nation, for nothing spreads more rapidly through society than the tastes of women.

For years our noblemen have returned from Paris only to fill the minds of their sisters and female relatives with countless pernicious tales of fashion. Why do their narratives contain no descriptions of these sensible pursuits, when they would have made up for all the others? I suppose that, being concerned merely to gather trivial and morally damaging objects for *themselves*, they could scarce be expected to seek out things which would be useful and improving for *us*.

I also tried to assess the profit accruing to the genius of the man of learning from the questions of those eager to conquer their ignorance. For the inquiries of the novice must often lead him to observe and reflect upon those aspects of objects which he at first may have disregarded as insignificant, or which, being confined to the sensible realm, may have been more perceptible to a woman than to a man. It is certain, that when we begin to instruct others in a branch of learning, or in one of the arts, our concepts become clearer, better defined and more comprehensive. Indeed the pupil's inverted grasp of a subject, even his most artless questions, can give rise to important and useful discoveries. Did not the Florentine gardener's observations on the variation of the water-levels in his fountains according to the character of the weather lead to the invention of the barometer? – But I see that I am straying too far from the subject of our amiable German gentleman, whose refined genius, with its inexhaustible treasure of knowledge, was intent upon a careful study of the various human specimens of which the company was composed. At least this is what he told me later, after I had praised his cheerful readiness to participate in so many empty discussions: such occasions, he said, provided him with an opportunity of collecting *moral nuances for his portraits of mankind*.

In him I learned to recognize the soul of true friendship when he spoke of a worthy man who had been brought up by the former owner of this house. He told me that this gentleman's accomplishments could be cited as the living proof of the myriad capacities of our intellect. For he combined the political genius of the most able statesman with all the erudition of the philosopher, the natural historian and the man of letters; he had the most exquisite artistic tastes; possessed a thorough understanding of all the elements of agriculture and oeconomy; spoke and wrote several languages and played the piano like a master. To all these intellectual achievements were joined the noble heart and great character of a true friend of humanity —

Judge from this portrait, Emilia, whether Mr** was right to regard the friendship of such a man as the greatest blessing of his life! You will doubtless share my joy at his decision to take this friend's eldest son with him to his new place of abode. Separated by half the length of Germany from the friends closest to his heart, it is his intention to heap all his fond regards for the parents onto the head of this boy and to lead him along the path of virtuous manhood, so that, though far from his friends, the bonds linking his heart to theirs will remain strong and firm. O Emilia, what is fortune, what are the honours of princes compared to Mr**'s generosity to the son of his fortunate friends? How my heart venerates him! How I pray that Providence will preserve him! And how blessed must be his evening hours after days so nobly spent!

My letter grows long, but I know that my Emilia, with her delight in descriptions of practical virtue, will thank me for it. Mr** departed in the evening, and I was glad that we left two mornings later. For the sight of the places in the house and garden where I had seen him plunged me into a state of inner melancholy which has not been lessened by our return to the court. But, following his advice, I shall seek out the pleasanter aspects of my fate and try to dwell only upon these in my future letters.

I must now prepare myself for a festivity which Count F. is to give at his country seat. Although I have little liking for these endless amusements, there is to be dancing on this occasion, and of all diversions, this, as you know, is my favourite.